PEAC

W9-DET-453

81

Crowning Deception

By the same author

The Cruel Trade

Crowning Deception

Clifford Peacock

ROBERT HALE · LONDON

© Clifford Peacock 2013
First published in Great Britain 2013

ISBN 978-0-7198-1053-4

Robert Hale Limited
Clerkenwell House
Clerkenwell Green
London EC1R 0HT

www.halebooks.com

The right of Clifford Peacock to be identified as author of this
work has been asserted by him in accordance with the
Copyright, Designs and Patents Act 1988

2 4 6 8 10 9 7 5 3 1

Typeset in 10 /13pt Sabon
Printed in the UK by the Berforts Group

Have you heard of Madame Lupescu
Who came to Romania's rescue?
'Tis a wonderful thing
To be under a king
But is it democracy
I esk you?

London music hall ditty, 1920

Prologue

It was a fairy-tale beginning. Ioin Tampeneau, a young lieutenant on field manoeuvres with his regiment in northern Romania, saw Magda Lupescu picking spring flowers in a wood. The daughter of a wretchedly poor peasant, she was seventeen and beautiful, with glorious copper-coloured hair. They fell in love and two weeks later, despite strong opposition from Ioin's aristocratic family, were married in the tiny village church.

On their return to Bucharest the dashing hussar and his lovely young bride quickly became the toast of the capital's high society and an invitation to a grand ball at the palace soon arrived. Magda was presented to the priapic Prince Carol, heir to the Romanian throne who, in an elegant salon adjoining the ballroom, swiftly and delightfully seduced her. The following day Ioin was ordered to a remote fort on the distant Russian frontier. Unloved and already forgotten, he died of cholera within the month.

Although married to Princess Helen of Greece, Carol moved the newly widowed Magda into a sumptuous apartment in the palace. The ensuing scandal forced the prince to abdicate his succession and accept banishment. For the next five years he and Magda lived at the centre of the *beau monde* of Paris at the height of its decadence. On the death of his father, Carol returned to Bucharest where his abdication was rescinded and, to popular acclaim, he was crowned king. He promptly reinstalled Magda in the palace. With her sparkling French wit and *chic,* she quickly out-queened poor Queen Helen.

Carol dismissed the weak government that had so recently welcomed his return and made himself dictator. The country lapsed into chaos and financial ruin. As the Second World War began, the Germans marched into Romania and seized the Ploetsi oil fields. His Majesty fled to Paris. In Bucharest Magda prepared to rejoin him.

Chapter One

Magda Lupescu joined the long queue at the second-class ticket window. It was here, in the harsh light of the concourse of Bucharest's main railway station, that her disguise would be tested for the first time. She had cut short her famous red hair; with shoulders hunched and an old cloche hat pulled well down, to a casual observer she was merely an urban peasant, an ageing domestic bowed low after a lifetime of washing the clothes of her betters and scrubbing their floors. Her forged travel document showed she was suffering the additional burden of a family bereavement, a convenient explanation for her journey at this time of national crisis.

The queue shuffled forward with agonizing slowness. An elderly Jewish man two places ahead of her reached the ticket window where the booking clerk immediately began yelling abuse at him. The smartly dressed woman immediately in front of Magda stepped forward and pushed the old man aside. As he shuffled away, the clerk smiled at the woman and they chatted amicably as he issued her ticket.

Magda moved up to the window. 'A single to Paris, please, sir,' she whispered nervously, pushing her travel permit and money through the gap below the glass. Ignoring the permit, the clerk snatched up the crumpled notes, punched a ticket and threw it down with the change. She was fumbling to pick up the coins when a voice behind her said, 'Madame Lupescu?'

She turned. A policeman stood with his eyes fixed on her. 'Come with me, please,' he said. 'A few questions only. It won't take long.'

'I'll miss my train,' she said anxiously.

'The next train for Paris does not leave for two hours.'

His strong fingers gripped the crook of her elbow as he steered her through the crowded concourse. They walked up a wide cast-iron staircase leading to a bridge spanning the main platforms. On one side were railings and a view of the station below, on the other a line of closed doors. The officer unlocked one and stepped aside to let her enter. It was not, as she had expected, a working police office: the walls were bare, the floor uncarpeted. The furniture comprised a rickety table and two bentwood chairs; a smoke-grimed window overlooked the main railway tracks running west to Hungary.

'Take a seat, Magda,' the policeman said, ominously confirming he knew precisely who she was. She heard the door close and the sinister sound of the key grating in the lock. She sat clutching her bag as the officer's footsteps came up behind her. He snatched off her hat before walking round the table and sitting down opposite. He smiled across at her.

'Please return my hat,' Magda begged. 'I'm embarrassed to be seen with my hair so short.'

He shook his head. 'I shall keep it as a memento. And your hair is most attractive. You look like a French mademoiselle!'

She looked steadily at him. He was good-looking in a common sort of way, well built and no more than twenty years old. His eyes continued to meet hers; it was futile to continue the pretence. She sat up, squared her shoulders and adopted a haughty attitude.

'Is this a formal interrogation?' she asked crossly. 'What do you want?'

'I would like to know why you are travelling alone. You are the king's mistress. He fled to Paris two days ago. Why did you not accompany him?'

'There is no mystery. His Majesty wanted me to go with him but I would have been an embarrassment. He is popular, I am merely his mistress and public opinion strongly favours Queen Helen. The people blame me for winter floods and bad harvests. Some swear I am a witch! I would have been jeered at, or much worse, had I been recognized leaving the country with the king. And His Majesty would have been highly embarrassed.'

'You must have a travel permit. I assume it is false?'

'It is genuine, although it carries an assumed name.'

Smiling at the ambiguity, he continued to stare at her.

'Why are you detaining me?' she demanded. 'I cut my hair short and wore these old clothes simply to travel to Paris incognito. I was unaware these are now criminal offences.'

'Allow me to congratulate you on the excellence of your disguise. I seem to be the only one in Bucharest to have seen through it.'

'Have you told anyone who I am?' she asked.

'No. And I have locked the door in case we are interrupted.'

'Why have you brought me here, to this awful room? If it's money you want there are a few French francs in my purse. Take them and let me go.'

'Have you anything else?'

9

'Anything else? What do you mean?'

'Valuables you have taken from the palace, perhaps?'

She stared at him. Surely the crowns hadn't been missed already!

'Look in my bag,' she said, outwardly calm. 'You'll find nothing else.'

He gave her a sly licentious look, an expression she had often seen on men's faces since her fourteenth birthday. 'Then I must search you,' he said.

'Search me?' She opened her eyes wide in apparent innocence. 'What on earth for?'

The directness of her reply unnerved him. His former self-assurance, bolstered by a cheap uniform and an excess of testosterone, collapsed. His face reddened and he could no longer meet her eye.

She said gently, 'You know I'm Magda, but I don't know who you are.'

He pulled a small wallet out of the breast pocket of his tunic and held it up. There was a blurred photo of him staring stiffly at the camera. 'Here is my warrant. I am Untzofficier Heinrich Bremen.'

'Good!' she said, smiling at him. 'Now we're properly introduced!'

For a moment a little of his earlier confidence returned. 'I feel I know you well already!' he said brightly. 'I have seen you often. Once last year you were in the back of a large car, sitting beside the king....' He sat gazing longingly at her as his bottom lip quivered and his voice dropped to a whisper. 'You were the most beautiful woman I had ever seen. I was on traffic duty, and although it was strictly against orders, I waved to you. I thought my heart would burst when you smiled back. Do you remember?'

'I'm sorry, Heinrich, I don't. But I would have noticed how handsome you were and wished we could meet. Now at last we have!'

'Since that moment not a day has passed without me thinking of you.' He gabbled the words at her. 'At night in bed you fill my thoughts. Sometimes I even pretend we're married! That's how I recognized you in the queue. You're never out of my mind.'

He was hers for the taking. 'I know you must return to duty soon, my darling,' she said softly. 'Your colleagues will be wondering where you are. But first we must arrange how to meet again. Turn your chair round. I'll come and sit on your knee and we'll have a cuddle!'

She slipped off her coat and, giving a girlish giggle, walked round the table holding the front of her dress high to show her taut suspenders. She sat astride his legs, facing him with her creamy thighs spread wide. Holding his head with both hands, she kissed him firmly on the mouth then, smiling coyly, sat back and undid the top buttons of her plain black dress. Pulling open the neck, she slipped off her brassiere straps and pushed down the cups to bare her full firm breasts. Heinrich gazed in wonder before reaching out to lock his arms around her and begin suck-ling. Moments later Magda felt an urgent movement in his crotch and eased herself free of him.

'No more, my darling,' she murmured. 'Not here. Next time we'll make love in a big wide bed with a mirror on the ceiling. And red roses every-where!'

Heinrich sat mute and uncomprehending as she quickly tugged the brassiere back into place and buttoned up her dress. She slipped on her coat and hat then picked up her bag. He got unsteadily to his feet, went to the door and unlocked it. They walked together in silence down the stair-case to the concourse where she paused, tilted her face towards him and allowed his lips to brush her cheek.

'Don't forget to write, darling,' she whispered then walked away.

He called despairingly after her but she did not look back. He could have arrested her; important questions relating to the king remained unan-swered. But he had let her go having been amply rewarded. He was a moment in her history and would soon be forgotten. Like poor Ioin.

Magda made her way to the main departure platform where a uniformed official sat at a table alongside the Paris express. Beside him lounged a young German soldier cradling a machine gun. The official snatched the travel permit from her hand.

'Name?' he grunted, reading the details.

'Marie Vouzier.'

'Age?'

'Forty-one.'

'Where were you born?'

'Liege, Belgium.'

'Why are you travelling to Paris?'

'I am returning home to Beauvais,' Magda replied. 'I have been attending my brother's funeral. Here is my sister's letter telling me he had died.'

'That is of no interest. Why do you not have a return visa?'

'A return visa? It's there, on my permit!' she exclaimed in alarm.

The foreign minister who arranged the forgery of her papers had assured her all necessary details were included. As a mark of her gratitude Magda took him to bed for the afternoon. Afterwards over tea in the orangery he thanked her effusively for granting him the fulfilment of one of his greatest ambitions. A wave of panic now swept through her. Perhaps he had told his aide to include an error in the permit in order to keep her available to him.

'A visa to enter Romania, yes,' the official snapped, 'but not to leave.'

'I am sorry, sir,' she said apologetically. 'I thought the same visa served for both journeys.' Lying came easily to her.

'The rules have changed. Your permit is not in order. Are you a Jew?'

'No! ' she snapped.

'You claim to be a widow. Was your husband a Jew?'

'No! I don't like the look of them.'

'Was he circumcised?'

'Of course not.'

'Did you see it often, Madame?' The German soldier smiled at her. He was tall and handsome so she smiled back.

'Not often enough,' she replied, shaking her head.

The two men laughed. 'Belgian men are no good in bed,' the official declared; clearly he regarded himself a man of the world.

'You should've married a German,' the soldier told her. 'My grandfather was seventy-five last week and still keeps three mistresses satisfied.'

'I wish I could meet him,' Magda said playfully.

'Let her pass, Franz,' the soldier said, still smiling at her. 'She'll keep our old soldiers happy.'

'The young ones too, give her half a chance.' The official smirked as he stamped the permit and handed it back to her.

'I'll be on leave in Paris in a couple of weeks, Madame,' the soldier called as she walked away. 'Try to keep your knees together for me.'

Glancing back, Magda gave him a saucy wave as she boarded the train.

The compartment soon became crowded. To avoid conversation Magda merely nodded in response to the gossipy comments from the woman crushed up against her. Closing her eyes, her thoughts turned to Grigor. It had still been dark as she watched him drive out of the deserted courtyard earlier that morning. Strapped in the car's luggage compartment was the leather trunk containing the three crowns they had stolen only an hour previously. Carol had left them behind, confident of being recalled by Hitler as soon as the German occupation was secure.

Grigor was the king's private secretary and, for the last five years, had been Magda's secret lover. When she told him Carol was proposing to travel alone to Paris, abandoning the jewels and leaving her to join him later, Grigor had immediately seen the golden opportunity the arrangement presented to them. He swiftly convinced her that Carol's hope of restoration to the throne was an impossible dream. Why should Hitler recall him? Romania had no need of a king now that he, the Führer, ruled! The jewels the king was leaving behind were worth at least one million

American dollars even in these troubled times. Why should they not steal them before the Germans arrived in force and took them for themselves? The palace held no secrets from her. She had been the royal mistress for over twenty years and knew the combination of the lock to the hidden safe in which the crowns were kept.

Grigor assured her he could whisk them out of the country within hours by driving to Constanta and taking the daily ferry along the Black Sea coast to Istanbul. Turkey had remained neutral in the war and he would find a remote village in the hills where he could sit in the sun, reading and enjoying the local wine, with the jewels safely hidden. When peace came he would take them to Amsterdam where an old friend, Reuben Eshkol, would buy them and ask no questions. With a million dollars in the bank they could live together in luxury for the rest of their lives, independent of the ageing Carol.

But how would they meet again? Magda had asked. It would be impossible to keep in touch and when the war ended Europe may be in chaos. But clever Grigor had planned that too! Whoever won the war, it would not be long before the great liners were ploughing the Atlantic once more. They would each buy a ticket to New York. How marvellous if they happened to travel on the same ship! But if not, they would simply wait for each other on the steps of the Statue of Liberty, on the first day of every month following the declaration of peace.

'I shall be there from the very first month,' Grigor had assured her. 'And I will wait for as long as it takes. You will only need to come once.'

Lying in the dark in each other's arms, it had all sounded so simple.

Magda had always hated the king's bedroom with its heavy dark red drapes and gloomy carved wooden panels. She much preferred her own apartment on the top floor with its wide views across the city. But the crowns were kept in the royal bedchamber so this visit was unavoidable. The palace was deserted. Reprisals against the household were inevitable and most of its members had already fled. But the sudden departure of the king was not yet widely known so looters had yet to swoop although their arrival would not be long delayed.

It was too dangerous to turn on the lights so Grigor held the powerful torch as they hurried up the grand staircase. In the gloom of the royal bedroom the thick carpet muffled their footsteps. Magda pressed the hidden button below Carol's full-length portrait and the painting swung aside on hidden hinges to reveal the safe. It took her only seconds to twist the knob to and fro in the correct sequence to open the door and turn on the soft light in the display case where the royal jewels lay on purple velvet cushions. Alone on the upper shelf was the magnificent crown of His Majesty, made in Paris a century earlier by a renowned Russian jeweller. Traditional in design, its headband was studded with diamonds and emeralds; large rubies adorned the four buttresses arching upwards to meet at the gold cross forming the pinnacle. On a lower shelf, similar in design but smaller and a little less ostentatious, was the crown of Prince Michael. Magda felt a sense of awe as she reached out to lift them from the cabinet and pass them to Grigor. He had pulled out the red leather trunk in which the jewels were transported when the family moved every year to the summer palace in the Carpathians. Each piece fitted snugly into its own padded compartment.

The third item of royal jewellery, the piece Magda loved most of all, was Queen Helen's fabulous diamond tiara. It was a simple circlet of nine bands of perfectly matched white diamonds set in platinum. She held it in both hands, gazing longingly before handing it to Grigor. Closing the safe, she spun the knob to destroy the setting and pushed the portrait back into position. Grigor shut the lid of the trunk and buckled the two broad straps across the top. Hoisting it onto his shoulder, they hurried out of the apartment.

Everything else has gone equally well, Magda thought. *I'm safely on board the Paris express and tomorrow afternoon I'll be with Carol. Grigor will be nearly to Constanta by now, in good time to catch the ferry to Turkey. Dearest Grigor! I shall miss him so. And his wonderful lovemaking. He promised me this stupid war will be over next year and he'll bring the million dollars from Amsterdam. And we'll be together for the remainder of our lives....*

Sleep came to her as the train at last began to move.

Chapter Two

Hating and fearing the car in equal measure, the royal chauffeurs had long ago christened it 'the Beast'. A primitive twelve-litre engine, stagecoach suspension and a total lack of refinement made it difficult to start, laborious to manoeuvre and arduous to stop. Despite its mechanical limitations the car's impressive outward appearance was ideally suited to Grigor's escape plan. To prevent anyone else taking it from the basement garage below the palace, he had earlier removed the coil and leads, replacing them at the last moment before his departure.

Happily, in the two hours since leaving Bucharest, the car had behaved impeccably. It was a contrast between reputation and behaviour that reminded Grigor of an ageing aunt whose visits had been dreaded by his parents yet, as a young boy, he had found the old lady both gentle and generous. It was thanks to the Beast's faultless performance his escape was unfolding exactly as planned. The Cernavodo Bridge across the Danube was only twenty-five kilometres ahead; beyond lay a clear run to Constanta and the daily ferry which would take him along the Black Sea coast to Istanbul and freedom.

No one could quite recall when or how Grigor had become a member of the Romanian royal household. Officially designated as a private secretary to His Majesty, he dined well at the top table in the servants' hall where he had a reputation for wit and good sense. Rumours regarding his past were rife. It was said he had been a famous motor-racing driver who prematurely retired after witnessing a terrible accident in which a close friend had died. He was reputed to be one of the few survivors of the 1937 Hindenburg airship disaster. A butler claimed to have seen positive proof that he was the illegitimate son of one of the older unmarried princesses and occupied a high position in the line of succession to the throne. He was presumed to be homosexual since he never bothered any of the maids although many strove eagerly for his attention.

In truth, Grigor took great delight in launching such tales himself. A few words here, a knowledgeable comment passed at an appropriate moment there, and a new story spread like a forest fire. Cultured and urbane, with the demeanour of a senior diplomat, his linguistic talent in the five principal European languages was often called upon to smooth out differences arising in the multinational crowd thronging the court. He was invariably courteous, particularly to those with power and influence. Dark and tall, with an athletic physique, he was a man to respect. And the perfect lover for Magda.

Following his coronation Carol had, like his father King Ferdinand before him, reigned but not ruled. It was not a situation he enjoyed, yearning as he did for power and international acclaim of his political skill and achievements. As a bold first step soon after his coronation, he dismissed the government that had recently welcomed his return and made himself a virtual dictator. It was not long before the enormity of the task facing him became all too apparent. He became burdened with great matters of state with which he was unable to cope. Although spectacularly endowed, and with an awesome libido, the unaccustomed stress rapidly diminished his renowned sexual powers and he was no longer able to meet Magda's constant physical demands. As a result she became increasingly restless and began searching elsewhere for physical satisfaction. It was not long before the handsome, highly intelligent and somewhat mysterious Grigor, ever-present at court, was called upon to demonstrate his prowess as a lover. It was a position in which he proved highly satisfactory and Magda initially retained him in that capacity. A loving and passionate relationship quickly developed which was to have consequences far beyond anything either of them could have imagined.

Sodden fields lining the main road to the east gave way to pleasant woods dappled by morning sunshine. A long bend came into view and Grigor hauled on the steering wheel. The Beast, with usual reluctance, began rounding the sweeping curve. It was sheer misfortune that a German soldier happened to be sauntering along the middle of the road towards them at that moment; he threw himself to the side as the massive car bore down on him. Grigor pulled hard on the tall brass brake lever and the Beast slewed broadside, coming to rest with the front wheels perched on the grass verge. The soldier, short and cocky, came strutting up to the open side window of the car. His face seemed to be held together by acne; he was trying to grow a Hitler-style moustache.

'Do you speak German?' he bawled. 'Why do you not keep your eyes on the road? You rounded that corner at one hundred kilometres per hour!'

'I speak a little German, sir,' Grigor replied haltingly. It was a language he spoke perfectly, and the Beast was incapable of travelling more than sixty kilometres an hour. He saw no reason to inform this buffoon of either fact. 'I am sorry if my car startled you,' he added.

'Startled me?' the soldier snarled. 'It almost killed me, you Romanian oaf. Where are you going?'

'I am under orders to deliver this car to the docks at Constanta, sir. It is to be taken to a museum in Berlin.'

'I am cancelling your orders,' the soldier snapped. 'My general's car has broken down. It is a stupid French car, the oil pump has seized. I was walking to seek assistance when you almost killed me. You have not heard the last of that. I am commandeering your vehicle in the name of the Führer. You will drive myself and the general to our destination.'

Hands on hips, he swaggered round the Beast, eyeing her carefully before settling into the front passenger seat. He peered at the polished oak dashboard and richly embroidered seats. 'This is a German motor car,' he said grudgingly.

'Yes, sir,' Grigor replied in a chastened tone. 'It is a special model, built by the Daimler-Benz company in Stuttgart in 1925. The engine has twelve one-litre cylinders.'

'I know all that, you idiot,' the soldier sneered. 'You can't tell me anything about motor cars. Drive on. We must get back to the general. He will be getting impatient.'

The general's car, a large Citroën with a rigid Swastika pennant bolted on each front mudguard, stood at the roadside five kilometres further on, facing Budapest.

'Turn the car around,' the soldier snarled.

'It has a very large turning circle, sir,' Grigor said, continuing to speak with humility. 'Whilst you are informing the general of the situation, may I have your permission to drive on to the next junction? There will be sufficient room to turn there and I shall be back in a few minutes.'

'Do you think I am stupid?' the soldier shouted. 'Once out of my sight, you will speed away, never to be seen again! You will wait here.'

He got out of the car, straightened his crumpled uniform and, with arms swinging to shoulder height, marched over to the Citroën. He was back within a minute, his face scarlet; Grigor guessed he had been severely reprimanded by the general for his lengthy absence.

'Damned French!' he was muttering to himself. 'They can't make decent motor cars. They should stick to making dresses and running brothels. Oil pumps never seize on German vehicles!' He suddenly noticed the Beast was still facing Constanta. 'Why have you not turned the car around?' he shouted.

'As I explained, sir, it requires a great deal of room to do so.'

The soldier spat contemptuously. 'Nonsense! German cars are the most manoeuvrable in the world. You Romanians are too ignorant to understand. I shall turn the car around myself!'

Grigor got out of the driver's seat, leaving the engine running. The soldier slid behind the wheel. Leering out of the open window he said, 'Watch me. This is how to turn a Daimler-Benz.' He put the car into gear and let out the clutch, whereupon the Beast promptly stalled.

'It's your fault!' the soldier yelled at Grigor. 'You have upset this car. It should only be driven by a German. Now I have to show you how to start the engine!'

'Take care, sir,' Grigor warned. 'The handle has a tendency to kick back.'

The soldier ignored him. He got out, strutted to the front and swung the starting handle. The engine immediately burst into life.

'You see?' he sneered. 'A Daimler-Benz always recognizes its true master!' Still chortling, he got back into the driver's seat, put the car into gear and let out the clutch. The engine stalled a second time. 'You are a damned stupid foreigner and unfit to drive this car!' he shouted.

He stamped to the front and swung the handle again. The Beast's huge bonnet hid the tragedy that followed. Grigor caught a glimpse of the soldier cartwheeling in the air like a rag doll thrown out of its pram by a bad-tempered child. A terrible scream followed.

'What is going on here?'

Grigor, bent over the unconscious soldier, spun round in surprise. An elderly general, tall and thin, in a grey uniform with red stripes and polished knee-length boots, was staring at him. His cadaverous face was scarred by duelling slashes; the luger in his gloved hand was levelled at Grigor's chest.

He straightened, clicked his heels and bowed. Speaking German with an educated Berliner accent, he said, 'Good morning, Herr General. I regret your driver has met with a serious accident. He insisted on driving my car but stalled the engine. The mishap occurred as he was trying to restart it.'

'This is your motor car?' the general asked, raising his eyebrows and gazing at the Beast. 'It is a very fine German model, I think.'

'Yes, Herr General. It was built in Stuttgart in 1925 by the Daimler-Benz company. Your driver was greatly taken by it. Sadly, no, it does not belong to me. It was found in the garages of the royal palace in Bucharest and formerly owned by the recently deposed King Carol. I am under orders to deliver it without delay to the docks at Constanta where it is to be loaded on a ship and taken to Germany.' For the general's benefit, he added a further embellishment. 'The car is to have pride of place in a new museum to be opened by the Führer himself.'

'*Ach so,*' murmured the general. Still gripping the luger, he walked slowly round the Beast, admiring her from every angle. He gave a casual glance at his driver, who lay unconscious in the road.

'It is dangerous to start this car when the engine is hot, sir,' Grigor explained. 'Despite my warning, your driver attempted to do so. The handle kicked back and injured him.'

'He is Austrian,' the general said contemptuously. 'He knows nothing about German cars. Or French ones, now I think of it. If he did, we would not have broken down in the first place. Drag him onto the grass and start your car. You will convey me to my destination.'

'With the greatest respect, Herr General, my orders are to deliver the car to Constanta docks as soon as possible. The ship taking her to Hamburg sails at noon. I regret I am unable to interrupt my journey.'

The general stared coldly at him. 'Germany rules Romania now. Had this vehicle belonged to you, I would have requisitioned it for my personal use. But, as my Führer has expressed a prior interest, I am merely ordering you to take me to Ulmeni aerodrome. I have an important meeting there and am already late. When you have done that you may resume your journey to Constanta. Your delay is of no importance. The Führer will raise no objection to an order by one of his generals taking precedence over a delay in the delivery of a museum piece.'

An icy hand closed round Grigor's heart. Before entering a military airfield, the Beast's luggage compartment was certain to be searched and the trunk containing the crowns would be found.

'With the greatest respect, Herr General,' he repeated, trying not to appear over-anxious, 'the car has only sufficient petrol to reach Constanta. It would be impossible for me to divert to Ulmeni.'

'That is enough to take me there. On arrival I will give orders for you to be supplied with more fuel. Do as I say. Without further argument.'

To emphasize the point he waggled the luger from side to side. Grigor knew he could easily snatch the gun and shoot the elderly general dead on the spot. But his body would soon be found and troops mobilized to hunt down the assassin. He would be caught and with luck instantly killed. If not, a gruesome demise at the hands of the Gestapo was inevitable. Filled with trepidation, he walked to the front of the car, gripped the starting handle and gave it a quick upwards jerk. Intense relief flooded through him as the engine began purring.

'Ha!' the general snorted triumphantly. 'A German car always starts first time! Let us get on our way.'

'It will be difficult to turn round here, Herr General,' Grigor explained. 'This is a very large car. Have I your permission to drive to the next junction to carry out the necessary manoeuvre?'

'Yes, of course!' the general said, slipping the luger back into its holster. 'It would be impossible to do otherwise in the width of this road. Bring my briefcase from the Citroën.'

Four kilometres further on there was a minor crossroad where Grigor achieved the 180 degree turn after three reversals. He drove back to the Citroën where the soldier lay motionless on the verge.

'See if he is dead,' the general ordered coldly from the rear seat.

Grigor got out, crossed the road and checked the man's pulse; it was faint and erratic. His head lay in a pool of blood and his right arm was twisted and extended at an unnatural angle, palm uppermost. Grigor returned to the Beast. 'He remains unconscious, General,' he reported. 'He struck his head on the road and may have fractured his skull. Also, his arm appears to be broken due to the starting handle kicking back.'

'Those Austrian boys are stupid, but tough,' the general said. 'When he comes round he will realize I have left him to guard the Citroën. When we reach Ulmeni I will send men to collect them both. Drive on.'

The road unwound steadily in front of the Beast's bonnet. As each kilometre passed Grigor became more alarmed. By now he had hoped to be nearing Constanta. Magda would be imagining him already there. All hope of catching that day's ferry to Istanbul had gone and his whole escape plan lay in ruins.

A signpost indicating a turning to Ulmeni eventually came into view. Grigor slowed the Beast to a snail's pace and made a wide sweep into the minor road. His earlier worries were quickly justified when, after a few hundred metres, the lane was closed by a checkpoint. An armed guard stepped out and held up his hand. Fortunately the man caught sight of the general in the rear seat and snapped to attention. He saluted then waved to his colleague to raise the barrier. Grigor gave him a solemn nod as he drove through.

Thick hedges and tall grasses brushed the windows on both sides for ten kilometres before the car burst out of the confines of the lane into a vast open area. In the distance were the hangars and control tower of the

Luftwaffe aerodrome. Constant streams of transport planes were taking off and landing on the two long runways. A concrete road bordered the airfield and Grigor steered the Beast onto it. After only a short distance a large open staff car, driven at high speed by a flaxen-haired officer gesticulating wildly whilst apparently standing at the wheel, overtook them then pulled up dangerously close. Grigor narrowly avoided a collision by swerving violently and heaving on the tall brake lever. A lieutenant in an immaculate Luftwaffe uniform with pilot's wings walked back to the Beast in measured steps. Grigor pulled down the side window and the officer thrust his blond head through the opening, staring at him with cold blue eyes.

'What do you think you're doing?' he snarled. 'This is a live taxiway which aircraft use continuously. You will cause a terrible accident!'

He suddenly noticed the general sitting bolt upright in the rear seat and, stepping back, extended his arm in a military salute.

'Heil Hitler!' he barked. 'My apologies, Herr General. I saw your vehicle being driven in a prohibited place and gave immediate pursuit.'

The general pulled down his window. 'Heil Hitler,' he said politely and quietly. 'That's quite all right, Lieutenant. You were in order to stop my driver. He is a civilian and unaware of the regulations. Perhaps you will be good enough to return to your car and lead us by an approved route to the headquarters building.'

'*Jawohl*, Herr General!'

Grigor drove the Beast behind the staff car to a paved area in front of an administration block. The lieutenant jumped out, ran back and opened the rear door. The general emerged and looked around.

'Thank you, Lieutenant,' he said. 'The driver of my official car sustained an injury whilst tampering with this Daimler-Benz. He is lying at the side of the road, twenty kilometres from Bucharest. Send a team to retrieve my vehicle and arrest the driver. He is to be charged with damaging the personal property of the Führer and sent immediately to a labour battalion on the eastern front.'

'*Jawohl*, Herr General.'

'This gentleman is on an important mission which he has interrupted on my behalf. Take him to lunch and see that his car is supplied with fuel and whatever else he needs to continue his journey to Constanta.'

'*Jawohl*, Herr General.'

'Now, take me to General Grossmann at once. He is expecting me and I am already late.'

*

'This is a very beautiful motor car,' the lieutenant commented when he returned from conducting the general to the commanding officer. 'A Daimler-Benz,' he added knowingly.

'Yes, Lieutenant,' Grigor agreed. 'You are most observant. It is a unique model, built in 1925, and still in its original condition. It was formerly the property of the recently deposed King Carol. I am driving it to Constanta from where it is to be taken by sea to Germany and delivered to the Führer in Berlin.'

'The Führer! You are privileged to drive a car in which he will soon be travelling. Turn left here for the officers' mess.'

'Thank you, Lieutenant.'

Grigor parked the Beast in front of the mess and walked up the entrance steps with his host. They sat in comfortable armchairs by a window looking out over the aerodrome. The lieutenant ordered aperitifs from the mess waiter.

'So, you are taking the car to Constanta?' he said. 'That's an enormous responsibility. There'll be hell to pay if you have an accident. You could find yourself in a concentration camp!'

'An accident is, of course, a constant concern,' Grigor replied evenly. 'But I see from your insignia that you are a pilot, Lieutenant. You yourself must be continually under great stress.'

Although seated, the lieutenant somehow managed to swagger. 'I'm totally without fear,' he said, without a trace of embarrassment. 'And the Junkers 52s we fly here are so slow. We call them Aunties. You can see why.' He nodded at a J52 lumbering noisily past the window, heading for the runway. 'Piloting one is less complicated than driving a tramcar in Berlin. Or so I'm told.'

'I'm amazed you can be so modest. And how often do you fly?'

'Every day. I'd be in the air at this very moment but my engines are being serviced this morning. I shall be making a major check flight this afternoon.'

'Really!' Grigor exclaimed. The germ of an idea sprang to mind.

'I don't mind telling you, I'm wasted in a transport squadron,' the lieutenant went on. 'Day after day, all I do is take dumb paratroopers up for practice jumps. My proper place is in the thick of the action!'

Grigor nodded, the idea began to crystallize. 'Your enthusiasm should be properly rewarded,' he murmured sympathetically.

Encouraged by this comment, the lieutenant became expansive. 'With my abilities,' he said confidently, 'I should be in a fighter squadron flying a Messerschmitt 109 over London and shooting down Tommies in their

Spitfires. Or, if that's not possible, I'd like to be the pilot of a Stuka dive-bomber. They've got trumpets under their wings that scream when they dive. Did you know that? They call them the Sirens of Jericho! They frighten the wits out of the enemy, civilians as well as soldiers.' He made a diving motion with his right hand, palm down, and made a cat-like howl. 'I must get my hands on a 109, or a Stuka, soon! If I don't, England will be invaded and the war will be over. There'll be no hope then of me winning an Iron Cross with Oak Leaves and Diamonds.'

'I'm full of admiration, Lieutenant.'

'Thank you. Few men have what it takes to be a first-class pilot. I am one of them but it's not fully recognized.'

'That is wrong. You should receive the acknowledgement you deserve.'

'I have applied for transfer numerous times. But I am irreplaceable in this squadron. My commanding officer has frequently told me how anxious he is to receive orders for me to be sent elsewhere. He has strongly endorsed each of my requests for a move but so far they have all been turned down.'

'That must be disappointing for you,' Grigor murmured; the commanding officer's desire to be rid of him was understandable.

'Yes. It is most aggravating to see lesser persons than oneself sent into action, or receiving promotion,' the lieutenant went blithely on. 'However, I live in hope. Now, let's have lunch. You'll be keen to get on your way. Is there anything else you need, apart from petrol? The general seemed especially anxious that I look after you.'

Grigor looked around the room as if checking no one was listening. 'I suspect the general recognized my true identity,' he said quietly.

The lieutenant raised his blond eyebrows and stared at him. 'You're not just a civilian then?' he asked.

Grigor shook his head. 'No. Don't mention it to anyone, but I'm a senior Gestapo officer.'

'Gestapo! Then I'd better watch my step!' The lieutenant laughed uneasily; everyone lived in fear of the secret police.

'We don't all wear black hats and pull out fingernails,' Grigor said coldly, sounding offended. 'That's left to the lower forms of life.'

'Of course! I apologize for my remark. How may I address you?'

'I never disclose my rank. Please refer to me only as "Rupert".' The soubriquet came to mind as he spoke.

'Very well, Rupert. Ever since we met I've had a feeling there was something different about you.'

Grigor smiled and leaned forward in a friendly way. 'Lieutenant sounds rather formal. What shall I call you?'

'Günter. I am Günter von Schmelzburg.'

'As a matter of fact, Günter,' Grigor said, 'we in the Gestapo are constantly on the lookout for suitable officers to join us. On an *ad hoc* basis, you understand. They carry on with their usual duties whilst at the same time serving our cause. There is a shortage of men who know how to keep their eyes and ears open and their mouths shut. Would you be interested in joining us? It could be advantageous for someone like yourself who has, shall we say, certain professional ambitions?'

'I would be delighted to serve in any way possible!' Günter declared, with barely suppressed excitement.

'Very well. Enquiries will have to be made into your background, of course, but from what you have told me I anticipate no problems. You are tall, good-looking, blond, blue-eyed and er –' Grigor nodded in the direction of Günter's crotch '– intact down there, are you?'

'What? Where? Oh, yes! Absolutely!' Günter replied, grasping the subtle reference to circumcision, a Jewish practice shunned by the Master Race except in cases of dire medical necessity.

'Well, then, you are precisely the sort of man we need in our organization. Young, fearless and popular with his comrades.'

Günter shifted uneasily in his seat. 'A few pilots in the squadron have taken a dislike to me for some reason,' he admitted. 'I've no idea why.'

'I am sure it's pure jealousy on their parts,' Grigor assured him. 'Lacking your skill and courage in the air, their only weapons will be sarcasm and innuendo. There are ways of dealing with such people, believe me!'

Günter's eyes blazed with joy; his desire to taste the sweetness of revenge was obvious.

'But they'll not trouble you for long,' Grigor went on. 'I assume you'll have no objection to a transfer at short notice to an operational Messerschmitt squadron in northern France?'

'Not in the least,' Günter said, gazing at Grigor in admiration. 'I look forward to it with more eagerness than I can put into words!'

'Very well. Now, you mentioned lunch?'

'I'll be honoured to present you to my brother officers, Rupert.'

'Thank you. But remember, not a word to anyone about this discussion.'

'I shall be as silent as the grave,' Günter promised.

Chapter Three

The row of cottages in the centre of the screen silently dissolved into clouds of dust and tumbling rubble. The flickering black and white film ended abruptly. Peter Farquhar stopped the projector and turned the room lights back on.

'That's what a few ounces of PBF in the right place can do,' Professor Brasher, Dean of Engineering at Leeds University, remarked. 'Complete and total demolition. We've blown up a dozen similar structures, now we need to try it out on something much bigger. We hope you can help us and, in the process, we'll help you beat the Germans.'

He knocked the charred contents of his pipe into a glass ashtray and stared earnestly across at the visitor from the War Office. He was sitting with arms folded and lips pursed, his bowler hat set squarely on the table in front of him. Short and plump, he had said little since his arrival from London that morning yet conveyed the impression of having fully absorbed all he had heard and been shown about PBF, the new explosive under development in the department.

'If you don't need me any more....' Farquhar said, anxious to return to a crucial experiment in the lab. He stood up.

'Just one thing, before you go,' the little man said quietly. 'There's a railway bridge we'd like knocked down. Quite urgently, in fact.'

'Lead young Farquhar to it!' exclaimed the professor.

'Gladly. There's only one snag. It's in the middle of occupied France.'

'Ah!' said the professor. Looking sideways at Farquhar he asked jokingly, '*Parlez-vous Français* at all, Peter?'

Events moved quickly. The following day an army motorcycle despatch rider roared into the university quad and handed a startled porter a sealed official envelope addressed to Farquhar. Marked 'URGENT', it contained a rail warrant to London and a card with an address in Streatham. On the back was a scrawled note telling him to report there at ten the following morning.

'It'll be a secret War Ministry lab,' the professor said knowledgeably. 'Their boffins will want to grill you about PBF.' Farquhar detected a note of envy in his voice and wondered if he, as Dean, thought he ought to have been invited to such an important meeting rather than a lowly research assistant. 'Tell them whatever they want to know. Make it plain I am very keen for this department to become more involved in the war effort.'

In order to reach Streatham by ten, Farquhar had to catch a midnight express. The train was packed and much delayed due to a heavy Luftwaffe bombing raid on Sheffield. The journey to London took over seven hours. A pretty WAAF boarded at Rugby and stood in front of him, hopping uncomfortably from one foot to the other, smiling sweetly at him each time their eyes met. He eventually succumbed and gallantly surrendered his seat to her. An RAF officer with pilot's wings above his breast pocket immediately pushed past him and took up position in front of the WAAF, pressing his knees firmly against hers. They tilted their heads towards each other and whispered as lovers do. She did not spare Farquhar another glance as he stood for the remainder of the tedious journey to Euston.

His mother had packed a bottle of milk and two bacon sandwiches for his breakfast which he ate sitting on a bench in the station before taking a train to Streatham. It did not take him long to realize the professor's assumption had been wide of the mark. The address on the card was not that of a secret government laboratory; it was a run-down antique shop in a narrow lane off the High Street. After walking past the premises twice to make sure he was not mistaken, Farquhar entered. He showed the card to the elderly man behind the counter who said nothing but led him up a flight of dark narrow stairs to the first floor. Off the landing was a dingy room, empty apart from some shabby chairs and a battered table. Through the window all that could be seen was the blank rear wall of the house opposite. The man drew the grimy curtains and growled, 'Wait.' He left, locking the door behind him.

Farquhar sat with his feet up on the table for half an hour. *What in hell am I doing here? It's over ten hours since I left home. I had a rotten journey and as soon as I arrived that old fogey locked me up without explanation. Who do these buggers think I am?*

He was on the point of hammering on the door and demanding to be released when steps pounded on the stairs. He stood as the door burst open and an officer wearing a Black Watch uniform strode in.

'I'm Colonel Fraser!' he snapped. He ripped the curtains apart, sat down and motioned to Farquhar to do the same. He pulled a wad of folded papers from inside his uniform jacket.

'Sign at the bottom, old man,' he grunted, thrusting the typewritten pages across the table. 'No need to read them through, it's just the Official Secrets Act. Merely a formality. Thanks. It tells you to keep your mouth shut regarding anything we discuss.' He glanced at Farquhar's signature and pocketed the pages. 'Now, you know what this is all about?'

It was a statement rather than a question. Farquhar shook his head. 'No, Colonel. I was told there's a railway bridge in occupied France that needs to be demolished. That's all.'

'That's the bones of it,' the colonel said briskly. 'Not much more to say, really. As you must have heard on the wireless, things aren't going too well in France for us just at the moment. Before the situation gets any worse it's been decided we'll fall back to the Channel coast, towards Dunkirk, in good order, mind you, to re-group. The Krauts will try to keep us pinned down with our backs to the sea. Their trains will be using the bridge in question to bring fuel and ammunition up to the front. Your job is to wreck it, slow the bastards down for a few days. That's all we want, a breathing space before we kick their arses back over the Rhine. Any questions?'

Farquhar stared across the table in disbelief. 'You expect me to demolish the bridge, Colonel? Surely there are men, saboteurs I suppose they're called, specially trained for that sort of thing?'

The colonel shook his head. 'You're the only man available. Everybody else is committed. I see no difficulty. You know all about explosives.'

'Only their chemistry, Colonel.' Farquhar struggled to adjust to the startling news. 'The biggest structure I've knocked down to date was a row of derelict cottages in Scotland. That's a lot different to blowing up a railway bridge carrying ammunition trains. We're looking for something to demolish methodically with different sizes of PBF charges. We need accurate scientific measurements of their effect on steel and reinforced concrete structures.'

'Haven't you been told? Your new stuff's been classified top secret. We can't risk the Krauts getting hold of it. You'll be using standard issue dynamite on this job.'

'I thought I was here to talk about our research into PBF!'

The colonel shook his head. 'No. You're here because you know how to handle explosives.'

'I'm a chemical engineer. What you need is a demolition expert.'

'Where's your sense of loyalty, of honour, man?' the colonel demanded sharply. 'Do you want us to win this bloody war or not?'

'Of course I do.'

'Prove it then!' the colonel snorted. 'Every man has to do a lot more than his duty these days. Kids of eighteen who can't even drive a motor car are piloting bombers over Germany! And although you're in a reserved occupation you could still get a gong out of this. A George Cross on your record'll prove you weren't a damned conshie, even if you weren't in uniform.'

'I'm not interested in medals, Colonel. And the explosives research I'm already doing is for the war effort. I could be responsible for the deaths of thousands of people. I can't sleep at night worrying about it.'

'Yes, yes,' the colonel snapped irritably. 'But that's neither here nor there. Think of the bridge as another of your damned experiments!'

'There's no similarity at all, Colonel. The tests we've done so far were carried out under controlled conditions in broad daylight on a Scottish grouse moor, miles from anywhere. The bridge you're talking about must be vital to the Germans so they'll have it closely guarded round the clock. The job will have to be done silently, and at night. That's not something I can do.'

'There are local resistance wallahs in the area. They know the set-up and will take care of you. One of them even speaks a bit of English.'

'What's the bridge made of?' Farquhar demanded. 'Steel? Reinforced concrete? What's the span? Is it arched? Suspended? Cantilevered? This information is vital in calculating the correct charge size.'

'There's no time for theoretical bullshit. It's not going to be a textbook job. We just want the fucking thing blown to buggery as soon as possible.'

'Find someone else to do it, then. I'm a scientist, I don't work like that.'

At this the colonel stiffened and leaned forward in a threatening manner. 'Now you listen here, laddie,' he snarled, jabbing a finger hard on the table. 'From now on you'll do whatever I damned well tell you! There's a war on and you've just signed the Official Secrets Act. If you refuse to accept my orders I can have you clapped in jail. Or shot. Just like that.'

He snapped his fingers in front of Farquhar's face then pulled out a small diary and consulted it. 'Let me see now. Today is Tuesday, there's a full moon next Monday night. That's when we'll drop you.'

'Drop me?'

'In France. There's just time for you to do a quick parachute course.'

'Parachute course?'

'The bridge was a hundred miles inside occupied territory this morning and the Krauts will have pushed on by next Monday. Dropping you in is the only way. You can't expect to pass undetected through enemy lines and travel two hundred miles carrying a suitcase full of bloody explosives.'

'What you are asking me to do is quite impossible.'

It was as if he'd not spoken; the colonel just carried on talking. 'The Krauts won't be expecting it so you'll have the advantage of surprise. You can plant your stuff and get clear before the buggers know what's hit them!'

'I won't go, Colonel. I refuse. You'll have to lock me up, or shoot me. What about my mother? She's a widow and so nervous about the bombing I didn't dare tell her I was coming to London today. She thinks I'm at a meeting in Newcastle. And you're talking about sending me on a parachute course and jumping into enemy-occupied territory, loaded with dynamite, next Monday night. She'll die of shock if she ever hears that!'

The colonel shrugged. 'When you get home, tell her the university's sending you to the States for a couple of weeks. Before you take off for France I'll give you a dozen American postcards date-stamped New York. Scribble something about having a wonderful time. I'll see she gets one through the post every few days.'

'What about my research at the university?'

'Your professor is being briefed this morning. He'll have signed the Act just like you and been told to keep his mouth shut. Your absence will have been explained to him. Once the job's done you can go back to playing with your test tubes as if nothing has happened.'

On the train back to Leeds that evening, Farquhar tried to push aside the dangers he seemed likely to face. *My dad volunteered for the army in the First World War*, he mused. *He told me he was lucky to be wounded. I never really understood what he meant until now. Perhaps I'll be just as lucky and break a leg learning to parachute. Then that bloody Scotsman will have to find someone else to send to France.*

'That's nice for you, dear,' his mother said that night at supper when he told her he was going to America the following day for a few weeks. 'Daddy would have been so proud. Would you like more stew?'

She said nothing about the short notice, nor did she ask how he was to cross the Atlantic, or what he'd be doing when he got there. But later, sitting by the fire, she suddenly put down her knitting and asked, 'Will you be going anywhere near Hollywood, dear?'

'I don't think so, Mother.'

'It would be lovely if you could meet Greer Garson! She's on at the Odeon next week. I've asked Mrs Fox to come with me if she's well enough.'

Next morning she packed a case for him and made sure he had a good breakfast before leaving on an early train.

*

Number One Parachute Training School was on the outskirts of Manchester. An RAF driver was waiting at the station with a car and drove him to Ringway. A taciturn corporal in the duty office checked his name off a list and took him to the stores where he was issued with a battledress, a camouflaged jump suit, a pair of heavy boots and a para-trooper's helmet. After pointing out the dining hall, and grunting that supper was at six, the corporal led the way to a Nissen hut on the edge of the airfield. It was bitterly cold; an empty stove stood in the middle of the concrete floor. Fifteen iron beds, each with a straw mattress and two blan-kets but no sheets or pillows, stood along each side.

'You're on your own, so take your pick,' the corporal growled. 'The last lot left yesterday. The next proper course doesn't start for another week but as you're just a civvy the old man's arranged a three-day special for you. Don't get boozed up in the NAAFI tonight, you'll need a clear head for tomorrow. Be at number nine hangar, eight hours sharp.'

Next morning, feeling ridiculous in the baggy overall, helmet and clumsy boots, Farquhar was waiting at the hangar when Sergeant Tombs arrived. A grizzled RAF veteran with 900 jumps to his credit, he had a long mournful face and a tired grey moustache. He walked with a limp and held his head at an unusual angle, legacies of mishaps that had befallen him whilst performing daring deeds at air shows before the war. Having introduced himself, he wasted no time in starting the first lesson.

'Most important thing to learn is 'ow to fall from the sky without killing yourself,' he announced. 'Played rugger at your college, did you, sir?'

Farquhar nodded. It was the first time anyone had called him 'sir' and he found it highly embarrassing.

'Good,' Sergeant Tombs said. 'Young gentlemen usually 'ave these days. So you know all about falling down without 'urting yourself too badly. Right. It's not much different when you drop from an airyplane, except you've got more time. All you have to do is keep your knees together and bend them just before you land. And when you reach the ground, roll like this.'

Tombs suddenly threw himself forward onto a coir mat on the hangar floor, landed on his shoulders and, silently executing a perfect roll, was back on his feet in a couple of seconds.

'There, it's that easy. I'm a bloody old cripple yet I can still do it so a fit young bugger like you will have no trouble. Put this harness on and climb that ladder.' He pointed to a tower built of metal scaffolding poles that reached up into the lofty roof of the hangar. 'At the top you'll find a cable. Clip it onto the ring on your harness.'

Farquhar clambered up an apparently endless number of rungs to reach a small wooden platform. A wire passed over a pulley above his head and down to a drum on the hangar floor. He clipped the free end onto the large ring on the strapping across his chest. Gripping the handrail with both hands, he peered down. A head-reeling distance below the tiny figure of Sergeant Tombs was holding a megaphone.

'Remember what I told you, sir,' the metallic voice boomed among the steel roof trusses. 'Knees bent, close together, relax and roll. Ready? Go!'

Farquhar felt a sudden rush of adrenalin. This was without doubt the most exciting thing he had ever done in his life. His mother, excessively protective, had refused to buy him a motorbike to travel to and from the university. He took a deep breath and stepped off into space. The hangar floor began to rise towards him at a terrifying rate until his descent was suddenly slowed by the sergeant applying a brake to the drum from which the cable was rapidly unwinding. Farquhar thudded onto the mat and lay winded; his return to earth had taken less than five seconds.

'That'll never do, sir,' Tombs said, helping him to his feet. 'Bend your knees more next time. If you don't, an' you land with them rigid, your legs'll be knocked clean up through your stomach into your chest an' you'll look 'orrible. We've got coffins in the stores only four feet long for lads what don't land proper. An' roll like I showed you. Get back up the tower an' try again.'

Farquhar made a further eight descents from the tower before Tombs grudgingly admitted he had grasped the principles of landing without serious injury. 'We've got a busy session after lunch, sir. Be back at two, sharp.'

The afternoon was even more bruising than the morning. It was spent practising jumps from the back of an RAF lorry driven at a steady twenty miles an hour along a grass runway. Tombs could only describe the technique since his old injuries prevented him from giving a practical demonstration.

'The trick is to curl into a ball, nice and easy, pulling up your legs and keeping your head in. Roll when you land, just like this mornin'. There's nothin' to it. Remember to tuck your head in though. Last week one lad forgot and snapped his neck clean in two.'

Tombs stood beside him at the open back of the lorry. When it reached a steady speed, he slapped Farquhar hard on the shoulder and yelled, 'GO!'

There was no time to curl up as the sergeant had described. Contact with the ground seemed instantaneous and was a painful, bone-jarring experience. Lying motionless on the grass, Farquhar tweaked various muscles to check for broken bones. *This is getting serious. It wasn't too bad this morning when I knew the sergeant would slow me down with the brake. But jumping off the back of a speeding lorry is sheer lunacy. I could cripple myself for life....*

The lorry pulled up fifty yards away; he dragged himself to his feet and limped back to it. Tombs held out a hand and hauled him on board.

'You wasn't tucked in enough, sir, and far too tense. Not too limp, not too stiff. Nice and pliable, just how the ladies like it. We'll try it again, over and over, 'til you get it right. The older ones often say that, you'll find.'

Most of day two was spent in a wicker basket slung below a barrage balloon being slowly hand-winched upwards by two bored airmen. At the designated height of 800 feet, the only sound was the wind sighing through the rigging suspending the basket from the balloon. The early-morning air was sharp and clear and Farquhar, with a bulky parachute strapped to his back, stood gazing at the stunning views across the Pennines. As the sergeant had instructed, he checked the static line was securely clipped to the ring in the basket then sat with his legs dangling through the circular hole in the floor. Between his knees, far below, Tombs was a mere speck.

'GO!' The order reaching him through the megaphone was barely audible. Farquhar wriggled forward until his backside slipped off the edge and he dropped through the hole. He seemed to fall a very long way before there was a welcome crack above his head and after a mighty wrench on his harness he was floating serenely above the intersecting runways of Ringway.

The sergeant's sudden shout through the megaphone came as a complete surprise. 'Bend them bloody knees, for Gawd's sake!'

Suddenly the earth was very close. Farquhar struggled to get ready to roll ... he thudded heavily on the grass ... the world went black ...

'Bloody day-dreaming you was, sir,' Tombs said mournfully through the mist. 'Admirin' the view. I could see that when you was still a hundred feet up. Get back in the basket and we'll try again. This time....'

On the morning of the third and final day of the course, Farquhar sat huddled in the stripped-out fuselage of an obsolete twin-engined Whitley bomber. It trundled down the main runway and reluctantly lifted into the air, climbing slowly and noisily. It was very cold; Tombs had thoughtfully brought a thermos of hot coffee. 'Mind your 'ead as you exit, sir. The 'atch is a bit on the small side,' he shouted in Farquhar's ear.

The Whitley flew east over the Peak District for a while before turning back and descending as it approached Ringway. Farquhar sat on the rim of the opening in the floor, looking down at the foothills of the Pennines unrolling like an endless three-dimensional map of toy-sized buildings and trees, fields and roads. Above his head two red lights came on. Tombs checked the static line was properly hooked to the overhead rail and stuck up his thumb. Farquhar watched one light turn to green, then the other. Tombs' fingers squeezed hard on his shoulder as he shouted, '*GO!*'

The bulky parachute made it awkward to squeeze through the narrow opening. Farquhar was still struggling when his lower body emerged into the slipstream. As he was dragged from the aircraft, his face smashed against the edge of the hatch. Blinded and half-stunned, he felt blood flowing in a warm stream into his mouth as the roar of the twin engines diminished to the west. He was conscious of a jerk as the static line pulled out the chute and the main canopy filled. He gulped a mouthful of salty blood and shook his head to clear his thoughts as he sank to earth. Instinctively, he tucked up his knees as the ground raced towards him. As he rolled over on the short grass, the silken folds of the canopy wrapped round him like a shroud.

A tough-looking RAF sergeant with parachute wings and a Red Cross armband on his sleeve sauntered up and stood looking down at him. 'That was a lousy fucking landing,' he said laconically. 'And you've got yourself a nice Whitley kiss there. Don't worry, I'll fix it!'

Bending down, he gripped Farquhar's broken nose firmly between his finger and thumb, twisted it back into position and continued squeezing until the bleeding stopped. The Whitley landed and lumbered over. Sergeant Tombs dismissed his injury lightly. 'You forgot what I told you about watching out for the 'atch, sir,' he said sorrowfully. 'But never mind, it's an 'onourable wound as they say. Take 'alf an hour's rest and we'll go up again.'

By mid-afternoon Farquhar had completed his fifth and final drop from the Whitley. As he was able to walk unaided, the RAF considered him a fully trained parachutist. He returned his kit to the stores and was relieved to change back into his familiar blazer, grey flannels, shirt and college tie. The storeman presented him with a maroon beret and a pair of cloth parachute insignia. As he finished knotting his tie, Sergeant Tombs walked in and handed him an official brown envelope.

'This 'as just come for you, sir. It looks like you're going to war.'

*

Farquhar walked back to the Nissen hut in which he had spent the previous three nights. He lay down on the iron bed. The RAF sergeant had given him three Aspirins to ease the pain in his face but they had had little effect. In the mirror in the washroom he saw both eyes were blacked; his swollen nose was throbbing and continued to leak blood. *I've been far too complacent, obeying the colonel's orders as if I was one of his bloody foot-sloggers. I'm supposed to be exempt from call-up because of the work I'm doing on explosives in the lab. But I can't pack up and go home now. What would Mother do if she saw me looking like this? Have a heart attack probably.*

The brown envelope contained a rail warrant from Manchester to London, and a typed order to report in two days' time to an address in Edgware Road. After a sleep, he felt better and went to the NAAFI where he had fish and chips and a sticky cream cake to celebrate his survival so far.

Chapter Four

The train was agonizingly slow, stopping at every station however small. It was repeatedly shunted into sidings alongside the main track where it stood for long periods whilst more important traffic thundered past. As time dragged on, Magda's thoughts drifted to happier journeys she had made with Carol along this same route. His elegant private sleeping car had been kept at Bucharest station, ready to couple up at short notice to the famed Orient Express that before the war had run between Istanbul and Paris. Elaborate meals and the finest wines were consumed in the company of the cream of European society. Royalty, expensive *filles de joie,* con men, Hollywood celebrities and international spies had delighted in the train's opulent comfort; every journey was an unforgettable experience. Carol was not the only crowned head who loved the Express. King Boris III of Bulgaria was an ardent railway enthusiast and often mounted the footplate to drive the engine himself. *Surely those days cannot be gone forever*, Magda thought. *Whoever wins this stupid war, there will always be men with the money and power to demand their return.*

Earlier that morning she had stood in the shadows of the kitchen doorway and watched Grigor drove out of the courtyard. As the noise of the Beast's exhaust faded into silence, she whispered to herself, '*Goodbye, my dearest, until we meet again. Take care. You are so precious to me.*' Mischievously she added, '*And so are the jewels. Remember, you're only my bagman!*'

Smiling, she went back into the palace to begin preparations for her own departure. The big iron stove in the kitchen was cold. It had not been tended since the servants fled the previous evening so hot coffee was out of the question. In the larder she found an unopened jar of Beluga caviar and a box of superb savoury biscuits. Supplies of both were included in a delivery of groceries sent weekly in a large hamper from Harvey Nichols in London. From a rack in the butler's pantry she took a bottle of her favourite burgundy. She carried these finds on a silver tray to the long dining table in the echoing servants' hall. The morning sun slanted through the windows set high in the wall, brightening the austerity of her surroundings. It was strangely exciting, breakfasting alone in the silent palace before the start of her journey.

After an unusual but most enjoyable meal she left the tray on the table and walked upstairs to her apartment. There she undressed, throwing her clothes onto the tangle of satin sheets and heaped pillows on which she and Grigor had made such wonderful love little more than an hour before. It had been even more sensual and satisfying than usual. *Harder, darling, harder! Please! Faster! Don't stop!* she had gasped. Both had known this would be the last occasion for a long time, if not forever, they would make love.

She ran a bath. The menials responsible for stoking the boilers in the basement had also fled so the water was barely tepid. After drying herself she sat naked in front of her wide dressing table mirror. The poised elegant woman looking back at her was unquestionably beautiful. Her lovely oval face implied a Eurasian heritage. She had a flawless skin and a superb figure with full firm breasts, unravaged by childbearing. Her crowning glory had always been her glorious red hair. Small wonder that Carol, first as a handsome prince and then king, had found her irresistible. As had Grigor. *Forever and always,* he had repeatedly sworn in his love to her. *So long as I live....*

Magda had been born in Lithuania. Her parents were both from Transylvania, a country of great beauty renowned for mystery and magic. Magda was certain she possessed an inherited ancestral power, an infallible sense of the lingering presence of those who had once been in the place where she stood at that particular moment.

Despite her acknowledged beauty, a shrewd observer may have detected traces of coarseness about Magda. Her eyes were a trifle too bold, the mouth at times over-inviting; close friends secretly agreed her figure was verging on the voluptuous. She had acquired a veneer of sophistication during the five years spent in Parisian high society but the crudity of her farmyard upbringing still lingered. Her language was frequently coarse and she enjoyed lewd conversation. It was not unknown for her to fart and belch loudly during state banquets. Yet Carol, blind to these social defects, had continued to adore her. In this he was not alone. The previous year a Spanish nobleman visiting the court had become completely smitten by her, as had many before him. In a lyrical after-dinner speech, emboldened by rich food and excellent wines, he had made a clumsy attempt to compare her to an exotic fruit. A papal *nuncio,* who knew Magda well and was much less enthused, was one of many high-ranking guests that evening. He turned to his friend His Excellency the Italian ambassador, who was slightly deaf, and in a loud aside to him commented if this were so she was ripe to the point of rottenness. Many, including the servants in attendance at table, overheard the remark and found it highly amusing. When Grigor reported the comment to Magda, she too had giggled.

After a final glance at her reflection, she picked up a pair of scissors and began snipping off her glorious but all too recognisable copper-coloured hair.

The train arrived at the Romania-Hungary border the following morning. As it jerked to a halt, a strident voice from the platform loudspeakers warned passengers to have their tickets and travel documents ready for inspection.

All Jews were brusquely ordered off the train and told to assemble with their luggage at the western end of the platform. Having thought she was safe from arrest, this sudden instruction filled Magda with fear. She felt physically sick and close to vomiting. Her father had been Jewish.

To escape the savage pogroms of the 1920s, he and his wife and young family had managed to escape from Lithuania and travel south to Romania. In the course of the long and terrible journey, some by cart but much of it on foot, he had taken advantage of an opportunity to convert to Roman Catholicism. To complete the transformation her father had shaved off his beard, cut his long hair and changed his name from Wolff to its Romanian equivalent, Lupescu. His wife, Magda's mother, had steadfastly refused to do the same and retained her Jewish name and faith. She insisted on declaring to anyone who would listen that the natural beauty of baby Magda's wonderful red hair was proof of a Semitic ancestry. It was dangerous talk and there was much unspoken relief when she later died in childbirth. Undoubtedly a tragedy, it nevertheless saved the entire family from certain arrest and deportation.

Magda's hands were shaking as she took the travel permit and ticket from her bag and for the first time began looking with interest at her fellow travellers. Directly opposite a mother was holding an infant in her arms whilst struggling to feed two other small children with pieces of dark bread from a tin. Magda gave the woman a sympathetic smile and leaned forward, extending her arms to relieve her of the baby. The mother gave a weary smile of gratitude and handed it to her. Magda cradled the mite to her breast, looking down and cooing at the tiny pinched face. She was unused to children and, never having borne one herself, did not particularly care for them. During her first year in Paris with Carol, she had miscarried. Whilst convalescing the doctor had warned it was unlikely she would ever become pregnant again. The prospect had not upset her unduly and she suspected Carol was pleased there would not be an unwanted bastard to complicate the already tottering Romanian succession. The prognosis proved correct, to no one's disappointment.

A railway official barged noisily into the compartment. Magda avoided looking at him by keeping her head low, concentrating her full attention on the infant. She merely held out her arm, gripping the ticket and permit between finger and thumb. The man snatched them and hovered close by. She could smell the reek of garlic and stale tobacco on his wheezing breath and the stink of dribbled urine and stale sweat from his greasy uniform. There was a long wait before the papers were roughly shoved back into her hand.

It was a further two hours before the train resumed its journey. Magda caught a final glimpse of the Jewish families being herded into a grim, windowless stone warehouse in the station yard. She shuddered. Had the foreign minister not provided her with a permit, she may have been one of them, about to be sent to a place from where no letters were received and no one ever returned.

As the train slowed at a small country station, Magda again relieved the woman of the baby as she began collecting her things ready to leave. Waiting on the platform were a well-dressed elderly couple. The two children ran to them and were closely hugged; the mother was laughing and held out the baby for the grandfather to kiss. It was a happy family reunion and the woman turned and waved her thanks to Magda as they made their way to the exit.

It was afternoon when the train ground to a halt in Budapest main station. The engine was taken off and the carriages shunted into a siding, indicating the wait would be lengthy. The train stood cold and silent; no official appeared to offer an explanation for the delay, or give a likely time of departure. Evening came and the soup stall on the platform closed without warning. After a short discussion, the two men in the compartment went to seek food in town, leaving their belongings behind. Ten minutes later the engine reappeared out of the darkness and was connected to the leading carriage. With a short blast on the whistle, the train crept out of the siding onto the main line and resumed its journey. The only occupants of the compartment were now Magda and an old woman trying without success to comfort her small granddaughter. The child sat sobbing quietly; her father had been one of those who had gone to buy food. The old woman and the child were left without money or travel papers, whilst the father had lost his few pitiful possessions; they lay abandoned on the overhead rack. There was nothing Magda could do to help and it was impossible to avoid watching their distress. Wordlessly, she turned her back on them and stretched out full length on the slatted wooden seat on her side of the compartment. Resting her head on her bag, she fell into a dreamless sleep.

When she awoke she was alone in the compartment. What had become of the grandmother and the child? she wondered. Examination of papers at the Hungarian-Austrian border must have been perfunctory since she had slept through it. With both countries now firmly under German control, restrictions had probably been eased. Magda hoped a railway official had taken pity on them and was arranging a reunion with the missing father. If they were Jewish they would have already joined the ranks of the disappeared.

It was mid-morning when the train arrived at Vienna's Neustadt station. The platforms were crowded with soldiers laden with kitbags, rifles and equipment; military announcements interspersed with strident marching songs blasted out of the loudspeakers. Leaning out of the carriage window, Magda bought a bacon roll and coffee from a man with a barrow on the platform. The train rapidly filled with troops; none of them spared her a glance as they sprawled on the hard seats, smoking and swearing at the vagueness of their orders as soldiers have done throughout history.

The train crawled on. The German-Franco border was crossed at Salzburg and finally, three days after leaving Bucharest, drew into Gare de l'Est in Paris. Magda walked out of the station into the afternoon sunshine. She took a taxi, telling the driver to take her to an address in Quai Voltaire, a short leafy avenue in a quiet suburb. She pushed past the manservant who opened the door and rushed into the hall where Carol stood holding out his arms. She ran to him and wordlessly hugged him tight.

'My darling, safe at last!' he murmured, pushing back her hat, kissing her brow and stroking her close-shorn head. 'You've been so long, I feared you'd been arrested. Your disguise is marvellous! No one could have recognized you. We'll send for a wig-maker. She'll give you something that will do until your hair grows again, as lovely as ever!'

Magda said nothing. She held the king close, wondering if Grigor had by now found his idyllic retreat in the Turkish hills. She was merely the royal mistress and could not inherit from Carol. Grigor was her only life-line to independence.

Later, Carol sat on a chair beside the bath, listening intently to her account of how she had slipped away from the palace. Lying back in the deliciously warm foamy water, she described the misery of her journey. She made no mention of Heinrich, her memory of him was already dim, but made much of the smelly ticket official at the Romanian/Hungarian border.

'I'll send a telegram ordering him to be shot,' Carol snapped angrily, quite forgetting he was no longer in a position to do such a thing.

Magda took his hand and kissed it. 'It's all in the past, my darling. We are together and nothing else matters.'

'You've not mentioned Grigor,' Carol suddenly asked. 'What became of him?'

'Grigor?' she exclaimed, taking care to hide the momentary alarm his question had caused her. 'Oh! That stuck-up secretary of yours! He fled, darling, like the other cowards. Too scared to stay without your protec-tion. He told one of my maids he was planning to settle on an island in the Aegean until the war ends. He had the impudence to beg her to go with him but wisely she refused. I never liked him. He was much too oily and ingratiating for my liking. I suspect he had Jewish ancestors.' She hoped Carol would notice her uncertainty proved she had not seen Grigor without trousers. 'I'd swear he had a criminal past,' she added. 'Robbery, perhaps, or blackmail. Even murder! Nothing would surprise me about him.'

'I enjoyed his company,' Carol admitted. 'He was always pleasant to talk to, and had some interesting stories to tell.'

'I think he was a liar too,' Magda said, adding further to her lover's sins.

But Carol was not easily diverted. 'I received reports that you were on friendly terms with him. Did the two of you ever sleep together?'

'Me? Sleep with a commoner like Grigor?' Magda clapped her hands and laughed gaily. 'Darling, what a ridiculous idea! I was the mistress of the most handsome man, the greatest lover and the noblest king in all of Europe! What need did I have to look elsewhere? Whoever told you that was lying!'

'Even so,' Carol persisted, 'you were seen whispering together.'

Magda shook her head. 'He was an awful gossip, darling! Just like an old washerwoman. He used to bring me sordid bits of tittle-tattle from the kitchen. You know how I always loved keeping up to date with the scandal. Who was sleeping with whom, how many maids that horny old butler had got pregnant lately, which of the footmen preferred men to women. That sort of thing. The servants are always first to know. But there was nothing going on between Grigor and me! Honestly, darling, there wasn't! Would I lie to you?'

Chapter Five

Günter was anxious to hear more about his transfer to a Messerschmitt squadron but the mess rapidly filled with pilots seeking lunch and their presence prevented further discussion. Günter introduced Grigor to them as 'Rupert'. They had all seen the Beast parked at the entrance and when they learned he was the driver he became the centre of attention at the long dining table. He spoke with authority, answering their questions with ease and charm. As the wine flowed the chat became more animated.

'You must know Bucharest well, Rupert,' one pilot remarked. 'Did you ever meet The Runaway King?'

'Often,' Grigor said, grinning wickedly as laughter rippled round the table. 'His luggage has permanent return labels to Paris.' Carol's first exile in Paris was common knowledge and his latest departure would be head-lines in the morning newspapers.

'What about that red-haired tart of his? With those lovely big titties?' another pilot called, raising a clenched fist and smacking his biceps.

'She'd been to the well too often for my taste,' Grigor replied, giving a broad wink. This created more mirth. He had no sense of disloyalty; it was the sort of repartee Magda herself enjoyed.

As lunch drew to a close, Günter stood and tapped a fork against his wine glass. His delight at being master of ceremonies was obvious.

'Gentlemen, our guest is on a highly important mission and we must detain him no longer.' He glanced haughtily around the room. 'I know it will go no further when I tell you, in the strictest confidence, that Rupert is a personal emissary of our beloved Führer.'

There were gasps of astonishment at this statement and every eye was suddenly on Grigor. He bent his head, studying the tablecloth, delighted that Günter was behaving exactly as he had hoped.

'As you know, he is driving the beautiful Daimler-Benz you have all seen outside,' Günter continued. 'It is a symbol of our Fatherland, and we wish him Godspeed. I am privy to certain other information, highly secret in nature I may add, which I am not at liberty to disclose at this time. A momentous event is on the horizon, I shall say no more. Now, let us stand and toast our visitor. We thank him for gracing our table, and wish him good luck wherever the path of duty takes him. Heil Hitler!'

The officers leapt to their feet with much scraping of chairs. 'Heil Hitler,' they shouted, holding their glasses aloft.

Grigor stood to respond, much at ease in the situation. 'Gentlemen, please be seated. I am greatly privileged to have met you all today. I take pleasure in thanking Lieutenant Günter von Schmelzburg for the warmth of his hospitality. We are all far from home, separated from our loved ones and the Fatherland. But we are here for a highly honourable purpose, to serve our glorious Führer. It is a noble duty we perform without question, or complaint, or thought of recompense. That is why we cannot lose this war. With such great ideals, our final victory is certain. A toast, gentlemen. To the Führer!'

'The Führer!' was the resounding reply as the pilots again leapt to their feet. To round off the proceedings, Günter led the singing, in English, of the British army's First World War favourite, 'It's A Long Way To Tipperary'.

Grigor and Günter stood by the door as the pilots filed past to return to duty. Grigor shook hands, wishing each of them good luck.

'What a marvellous day this has been, Rupert,' sighed Günter as the door swung shut behind the last officer. 'Quite wonderful, actually.'

'It has been good for me too, Günter,' Grigor replied, smiling. 'It's not often I meet a man with such potential as yourself.'

'I can't believe I am about to achieve my dream! A Messerschmitt pilot! And serving the Führer as a member of the Gestapo! It all seems too good to be true! I wish I had been able to announce my transfer over lunch. I would have loved to see their faces!'

'It is a pleasure in store, Günter. I am delighted for you although in my opinion it is nothing less than you deserve. Now, if you will show me the way to the fuel depot I shall fill up with petrol and be on my way.'

'Certainly, Rupert. There'll be no difficulty about that, I assure you.'

'Thank you, my friend,' Grigor replied. He lifted a hand in mock surprise.

'It has just occurred to me, I've not seen your aeroplane! I'd very much like to do so before I leave.'

'Of course! As I told you, I'm taking her up this afternoon for an engine test. She'll be out on the apron by the control tower, ready to go. We'll pass her on our way to the petrol depot.'

*

'To tell the truth, I'll be sorry to be parted from the old Junkers,' Günter remarked as they drove along the service road a few minutes later. 'She's reliable and rugged, yet very forgiving. But when I'm strapped in my Messerschmitt I'll soon forget about her! Turn left here.'

The J52 was a distinctive aircraft with three engines, one on the nose of the fuselage and one on each wing. Her top and sides were camouflaged in dark brown and green; the underside was pale grey to make her less visible from the ground. Black crosses adorned her wings and fuselage sides; her rudder carried a bold swastika on each side. Günter stood on the concrete apron, hands on hips, looking up at her.

'I put her into a vertical dive over Hamburg a few weeks ago. It terrified the crew, they were scared her wings would break off. I remained perfectly calm, of course. It will be even more exciting doing it in a Messerschmitt 109! I can't wait to get my hands on mine!'

'Patience, my friend!' Grigor said with a smile. 'You'll do so soon enough. Tell me, could you take this aircraft up alone and land at another aerodrome?'

'Of course! I shall be flying solo this afternoon on the engine test. I never allow anyone else to handle the controls. Regulations require me to carry a co-pilot on normal duties but I only give him boring jobs like checking the doors are properly closed, and helping with parachute drops.'

No wonder you're unpopular, Grigor thought. Aloud he asked, 'How far can she fly without refuelling?'

'That depends on the overall weight and wind strength. Today, for instance, empty but with full tanks including the long-distance reserve and little wind, about 1800 kilometres.'

It was all Grigor needed to know. Taking Günter by the arm, he led him under the port wing. 'You said an amazing thing in your speech in the mess.'

'I did? What was it?'

'You said a momentous event was on the horizon.'

'I meant my transfer to a Messerschmitt squadron. And joining the Gestapo, of course.'

'I realized that. Your change of squadron is straightforward. But it was uncanny that you should use the phrase "momentous event"! As a senior Gestapo officer I am involved, at this very moment, in something truly momentous. But I urgently need your assistance.'

'You have only to ask, Rupert, and I will do it.'

'Fly me to Turkey in your Junkers.'

'Turkey?' Günter gazed at Grigor in disbelief.

'Yes, Turkey. I'm on a highly secret mission.'

'Secret mission?'

'I wouldn't ask you to risk your life and a valuable aircraft for the sake of a mere joyride! It's vital I reach Turkey this evening.'

'Go on, Rupert!'

Grigor spoke quickly, injecting his voice with fevered urgency. 'My mission is vital to the entire war effort. The Führer has of course been kept fully informed. He personally agreed to the Daimler-Benz being used as part of my cover. I am also carrying equipment essential to the operation. It must travel with me.'

'Such a flight cannot be made immediately, Rupert. Turkey is a neutral country and special clearance will be needed.'

'Surely not!' Grigor exclaimed.

'Confirmation will have to be obtained from your headquarters.'

'Gestapo missions are never acknowledged,' Grigor replied shortly.

'Why did you not arrange for a plane to fly you direct to Turkey instead of travelling by car?'

'My movements must not arouse the suspicion of the Turks. The original plan was for me to drive to Constanta and leave the car at the docks. A fast motorboat would immediately take me to a rendezvous off the coast this evening. In delaying me, the general was unaware he was ruining everything.'

'You could have explained your urgent need to reach Constanta. He would have understood and allowed you to carry on with your mission.'

'I can never disclose my identity. But he guessed who I was. Remember his exact words: "This gentleman is on an important mission which he has interrupted on my behalf. Take him to lunch and see that his car is supplied with fuel and whatever else he needs to continue his journey to Constanta." He was letting me know you are fully at my disposal.'

'But I can't take off without clearance!'

'Listen to me carefully, Günter. You're making a test flight this afternoon to check the engines. Report to the control tower that you are ready to go. Do not mention Turkey, or that I shall be with you. All you require is clearance for a normal flight. This aeroplane has a range of 1800 kilometres. The area I need to reach is only 700 from here so you have ample fuel to get there and back. Make a normal take-off and head east until you are out of sight of the tower. Then turn south towards Istanbul. I shall tell you where to land. I'll disembark with my equipment and you can immediately take off again. You'll get back later than expected but knowing how conscientious you are it will be assumed you made an extended flight to ensure the engines have been properly serviced. Such a mission will make an excellent start to your Gestapo career.'

Günter stared at him. 'Do you honestly think so, Rupert? It all sounds too good to be true. I've been disappointed so many times in the past. I want to help but I'd have to break strict rules to do as you ask. What if something goes wrong? Will you confirm I acted on your orders?'

'Of course. I give you my solemn word. And remember, you have the full authority of the general. You'll be disobeying him if you don't do as I ask.'

Seconds ticked by before Günter finally nodded his agreement. 'Yes, Rupert. I'll fly you to Turkey. Because I am a German patriot. And you are a true friend.'

He held out his hand and Grigor shook it firmly. 'You'll never regret it,' he lied, wondering why he did not feel in the least ashamed.

Günter went to the control tower to get clearance; as soon as he was out of sight Grigor walked over to the Beast, which stood close to the Junker's open mid-fuselage door. Pulling the trunk out of the car's luggage compartment, he carried it to the aircraft. Climbing inside, he settled it in one of the metal bucket seats and fastened it in place with webbing straps. He brought his suitcase from the car and secured it in the adjoining seat. Walking up the sloping floor, he sat in the pilot's seat on the left side of the cockpit and looked at the array of dials and clusters of switches, levers and knobs. Grouped in the centre were the gauges relating to the performance of each of the three engines; below was a diagram of the fuel system, studded with the valves and switches necessary to operate it.

'I have clearance for the engine check flight, Rupert.'

Grigor spun round; he had not expected Günter back so soon. 'Excellent,' he replied. 'No problems, I trust?'

'Well, they were not busy but I was deliberately ignored for several minutes. Childish comments and insulting noises were made, I suspect for my benefit. I shall put every one of them on report when I get back. I have a reputation for discipline which I think the Gestapo will appreciate.'

'I am sure we will,' Grigor assured him.

'Is that your secret equipment strapped in the seats back there?'

'Yes. I'm sorry, but I can't show it to you, or discuss its purpose. My orders are explicit on that point. It concerns the Russians and our defence of the Ploetsi oil wells.'

'The communist swine! I suspected oil might be at the root of your

46

mission. It's no secret the wells are behind the Führer's interest in this wretched country. That's why the Luftwaffe are here.'

'You are most perceptive, Günter! I was correct in my assessment of you. My mission will prevent the Ruskies interfering in our future plans. But please, do not refer to the matter again. Now, I am keen to get going. I'll give you details as we proceed. First, take off, fly east and climb to two thousand metres.'

Grigor moved to the back of the cockpit out of sight of the control tower and watched Günter clicking switches and pulling levers, muttering to himself as he worked through the list of pre-flight checks. The three engines burst into life one after the other with a satisfying roar of power; a red light on the side of the control tower came on. Günter moved the centre throttle forward and the aircraft rolled up to the start of the runway. The final checks were completed and he waited until the red light was replaced by a green. He opened all three throttles and the cockpit began to vibrate. When the brakes were released the Junkers accelerated down the runway, reached flying speed and lifted into the air. The under-carriage was raised; it banked east and continued to climb.

The Junkers droned south as the afternoon sunlight slanted through broken cloud over the Black Sea. Grigor sat in the right-hand seat. *Landing at Istanbul airport is out of the question,* he decided. *The Turks would open the trunk and find the crowns. The guards will shoot us on the spot and share the loot. So, finding another place to land has to be my first job. Then, what about Günter? If I allow him to get back to Ulmeni he's sure to blab about me being a Gestapo agent and how he flew me to Turkey on a secret mission. The commanding officer will get to hear of it and enquiries will be made. The lies I told the general will come out and the real Gestapo will be desperate to get their hands on me. Thanks to Günter's big mouth, they'll know where I landed in Turkey and come looking for me. I can't let him get back to Ulmeni. I've got to kill him....*

Behind the co-pilot's seat was a navigator's table, and above it a shelf for charts. Grigor took down an air map of western Turkey. On the southern shore of the Sea of Marmora lay the town of Bandirma with a symbol on the outskirts indicating the location of a private landing strip, possibly used by a local flying club. A railway station was also marked on the main line running west along the coast to the Dardanelle Strait, the gateway to the Aegean. The town had everything he needed. Returning to the cockpit, he settled into his seat and held up the map. 'Günter,' he shouted above the engine noise, 'I want you to land at this airfield near Bandirma.'

Günter stared at the map. 'It's only a grass strip,' he shouted back. 'Before landing I'll have to check it's safe. I'll work out a course.' He stood up. 'We're on autopilot so she'll fly herself. Don't touch the controls.'

He moved behind to the navigator's table and Grigor resumed his study of the diagram of the plane's fuel system. Four tanks were shown, one for each of the three engines and a fourth holding a reserve supply. Unlike the other three, the reserve tank did not have a fuel gauge. Beside its symbol was a red handle with positions marked CLOSED and DUMP. It was an obvious safety precaution; if the plane was about to crash, spare fuel could be got rid of before hitting the ground, reducing the risk of fire. Grigor glanced over his shoulder; Günter was still bent over the navigation table, working out the new course. He reached forward and turned the pointer to DUMP; a minute later he changed it back to the CLOSED position. Although there was no gauge to show it, the tank was now empty. Günter would only discover that during his return flight to Ulmeni when he tried to transfer petrol from the reserve to the main tanks. His fuel-starved engines would soon splutter to a stop and the Junkers plummet into the uninhabited Bulgarian mountains. The wreckage and Günter's remains could lie there undiscovered for months, possibly years.

'We're approaching the Turkish border, Rupert,' Günter announced when he returned to the cockpit. 'We'll reach Bandirma in thirty-five minutes.' He slid back into his seat, then stiffened. 'Petrol!' he exclaimed. 'I can smell petrol!' He scanned the instrument panel anxiously. 'You've not touched any of the controls, have you?'

'No!' Grigor retorted, with apparent alarm. 'Of course not! I know nothing about aeroplanes! Do something, Günter, for God's sake! Remember the importance of my mission!'

'Relax,' Günter said, smiling at the sight of a terrified Gestapo officer. 'The centre engine must be running rich. The idiots who serviced her this morning have got the mixture wrong. I'll lean it.' He made a slight adjustment to a knob on the instrument panel. 'There! I can't smell anything now. It was just a whiff as I came back to the cockpit.'

'You've done superbly well, Günter. I'm amazed how cool you were. I was scared out of my wits! You won't tell anyone, will you?'

'Of course not. As a professional airman I have nerves of steel. And a careful pilot always expects the worst. But wait until we are safely on the ground before offering your congratulations. Things can go wrong at any time.'

*

To starboard the Sea of Marmora was a sheet of shimmering gold; to port rose a range of craggy mountains, their steep rock faces glowing fiery red in the light of the setting sun. There was no sign of Bandirma airfield which, according to the map, lay on the narrow strip of flat land between the mountains and the shore. Günter lowered the flaps and undercarriage and the plane sank lower. He stared intently ahead with the fingers of his right hand spread across the three throttle levers. The altimeter was showing less than 500 metres when he called out, 'I see it, Rupert! Directly in front!'

Peering through the windscreen, it was several seconds before Grigor was able to pick out the landing strip, marginally greener than the surrounding area. The single white dot of a building stood at one side. Günter took the plane in a wide sweep, peering down at the ground.

'It looks safe enough, I'll take the risk,' he shouted. 'A Junkers is built for rough landings.'

He lined up with the narrow runway, closed the throttles and pulled back the control column. Seconds later the Junkers touched down in a perfect three-point landing and taxied over to the white building, stopping with the three engines quietly ticking over. Grigor peered out of the side window, waiting for someone to appear but there was no sign of movement.

'You'd better prepare for take-off, Günter,' he said. 'It'll be dark soon.' He felt a sudden pang of remorse but it was too late to undo the damage. 'I'll take my equipment. Then you can leave.'

'What will you do, Rupert? I hate leaving you alone.'

'I'll be all right,' Grigor said. 'There's a powerful radio transmitter in my trunk. I'll send a coded message and someone will come to collect me.'

'Even so, after all you are going to do for me –'

'Günter, my friend, you've saved my mission. I wish I could tell you more about it but I'm sworn to secrecy.'

He unfastened the straps to free the trunk and suitcase then opened the door and jumped onto the grass. Günter handed the luggage down to him.

'Go now,' Grigor called. 'Goodbye! Forget that you brought me here!'

'What about your car? It'll still be on the apron at Ulmeni.'

'Someone from Headquarters will come for it. Have a good flight!'

Framed in the fuselage doorway, Günter looked like a little boy being hustled off to bed when he was longing to stay up with the visitors. But he managed to square his shoulders, click his heels and give a smart salute.

'Heil Hitler!' he shouted.

Grigor could not bring himself to copy the idiotic gesture so he merely flapped his hand quickly up and down as he had seen Hitler do in newsreels. Günter stepped back and closed the fuselage door. The engines revved; the Junkers turned onto the runway and vanished in the gathering gloom. It reappeared momentarily, a dark shape rising against the pale evening sky, before the drone of its engines faded into silence.

Chapter Six

For their second meeting, colonel Fraser was waiting in a modern office suite above a branch of Marks and Spencer. Glancing at Farquhar's battered face he grunted, 'Good. I see you've done the para course.' He led him across to a table on which lay four large aerial photos of a modern lattice girder bridge carrying a double railway track. The single span rested on concrete abutments on opposite sides of a broad river flowing through wooded countryside.

'It's a simple job,' the colonel assured him. 'Set your charges, hide in the trees and press the plunger. You'll have a grandstand view of the whole bloody lot collapsing into the river. All the better if there's a train load of Krauts on it at the time.'

'Where is it, exactly?' Farquhar asked, peering at the photos.

A large-scale map of an area of northern France was pinned to the wall. The colonel smacked the end of his swagger stick against it and moved the tip to a patch of bright green.

'The bridge crosses the river in these woods. Plenty of good cover. You'll be dropped here' – he smacked the map again – 'a few miles from the target, in open farmland. Jacques will be waiting for you. He speaks English, works on the railway and knows the bridge well. He'll look after you.'

'If all goes to plan, how do I get back?' Farquhar asked. This part of the mission, vital so far as he was concerned, had not yet been mentioned.

The colonel snorted. 'Nothing's been arranged but don't worry about it. Jacques has a radio. He'll listen every night for a message broadcast on the BBC. It'll give him details of how to send you home. Do whatever he says.'

'What if I'm captured? I've heard the Germans shoot spies.'

'So do we, if we catch them wearing civvies. But you'll be OK on that score. I've arranged for you to be in RAF uniform. If they nab you say your plane was dropping leaflets when it got hit. That sounds harmless enough. Tell them your face got bashed in when it crashed. Your broken nose will back up the alibi. Give them the impression the bang on your head made you lose your memory. Swear that all you can remember is wandering about the countryside and you're glad they found you. Ramble on, talking rubbish. They'll lock you up until the Red Cross repatriate you as a nutcase.'

Two nights later, under a brilliant full moon, an unarmed Hudson bomber lifted off the runway at Tempsford aerodrome in Bedfordshire. It was bitterly cold. Farquhar, huddled in thick flying overalls over an RAF uniform, sat on his parachute halfway down the fuselage. A satchel packed with dynamite, detonators, a reel of wire and a firing box with a plunger was attached to his belt by a long strap. He was surrounded on three sides by twenty bulky bundles of supplies to be dropped to the French resistance en route to his destination. The three RAF dispatchers responsible for this part of the operation, a sergeant and two airmen, lay wrapped in blankets at the rear of the plane, already sound asleep. This suited Farquhar; he had no wish for company. Disturbing thoughts tumbled through his mind like leaves in an autumn gale. *What am I doing here? I can't believe it's only ten days since that little man came to the lab and mentioned the bridge. Before long I'll be jumping in the dark into enemy-held territory. In less than two hours I could be in a Gestapo torture chamber....*

The dispatchers opening a door in the side of the fuselage wakened him. There was a howling icy blast accompanied by the deafening roar of the Hudson's twin engines. Farquhar peered out of a window and saw the colonel's promised full moon riding high in a black velvet sky. Two red lights blinked above the door. The aircraft banked sharply and one of the lights changed to green. There was a short delay before the sergeant yelled, 'Two greens. Let 'em go!' The airmen dragged frantically at the bundles destined for the French resistance, heaving one after another out into the inky blackness. In less than a minute they had gone and the trailing static lines were hauled in. The engine note changed and the plane began to descend. Thick cloud was streaming past the open door as the sergeant came down the fuselage.

'The pilot says five minutes to your target, sir,' he shouted in Farquhar's ear. 'Better get ready.' He offered his hand and hauled him to his feet. 'It'll be cold. And a tricky landing for you if this stuff reaches all the way down.'

Farquhar's stomach felt as if it had been packed with ice. He hooked his static line to the rail and the sergeant checked it. There was a welcome diversion when one of the airmen held up a wire cage in front of his face.

'Homing pigeons, sir,' he yelled above the engine noise. 'Little bloody heroes they are. I'll release them when you're clear. Their loft's back at Tempsford. They've got coded messages in tubes on their little legs saying we've delivered you safely. It's in case we don't get back ourselves.'

'Poor little bastards,' the sergeant yelled in his other ear. 'Fancy having to fly back to Blighty through this.' He gestured at the cloud now blotting out the world beyond the door. 'Bugger that for a game of soldiers!'

'Clipped on.'

'Two reds. Stand by.'

'Red and green! Get ready.'

'Two greens. Best of luck, sir!'

Visibility failed to improve as Farquhar sank earthwards. The cloud thinned a little in time for him to see the spread of a large tree rising below his feet. He dragged hard on his lines but the edge of the canopy snagged a branch and the next moment he was suspended, spinning and swinging wildly. The strap round his waist went slack indicating the satchel had reached the ground. He unclipped his harness, groped with his boots until he felt a thick lower branch. He scrambled along and dropped the final ten feet onto French soil.

There was total silence. He had no idea where he was, or what to do next. *The colonel said I'd be dropped in open farmland but I've landed in a bloody forest. How far am I from the target? And where's Jacques, the English-speaking resistance man supposed to be here to meet me?*

A bird chirped close by, heralding the dawn. It was time to get out of sight and think what to do next. He turned aside and in the darkness fell over a bicycle some fool had left lying in the undergrowth. He was struggling to disentangle himself when a large dog bounded up and began furiously licking his face. A blink of light through the trees was accompanied by a hoarse cry, '*Ici, Pierre! Ne tirer pas!*'

A man called Pierre begging me not to shoot, Farquhar decided, after trawling through his barely remembered grammar-school French.

'*Couché, Simba! Couché,*' the voice called, now much nearer.

Farquhar shoved the dog off and scrambled to his feet. Pierre, carrying a torch, emerged from the gloom. Heavily built, elderly, with a large red face and several days' growth of whiskers, he wore an ancient beret and rough working clothes.

'*Pardon, m'sieur. Simba, il est très gentil. Je suis Pierre, m'sieur. Bienvenue en France,*' he gasped. Following Simba's example, he kissed Farquhar wetly on both cheeks.

'*Où est Jacques?*' Farquhar demanded, stepping back from this equally unwelcome greeting. '*Jacques? Où est il?*'

Pierre shrugged and produced a guttural torrent bearing no relation to the few words of basic French Farquhar remembered. He dragged the parachute down from the tree, bundled it up and put it on his bicycle seat. They set off along a path through fields, Pierre pushing his bicycle with Simba loping joyfully at his side. Farquhar stumbled behind them carrying the satchel of explosives and looking anxiously about. *Surely there must be Germans nearby. This isn't called Occupied France for nothing!*

Yet Pierre strode on, making no attempt at concealment in what was rapidly becoming full daylight. After a mile they reached a collection of farm buildings grouped around three sides of a cobbled yard. From an open byre a gathering of mottled brown and white cows and calves stared out at them. Pierre leaned his cycle against a gate, tied Simba to a post and led Farquhar up to the house. A young woman in a shapeless grey dress opened the door. Pierre grunted a few words and pushed past her; Farquhar held out his hand but she turned from him. The kitchen was dark with a vast stone fireplace at one end, its grate piled high with blazing logs. The girl placed a loaf, a hunk of cheese and a jug of milk on a long wooden table and signalled to Farquhar to sit. He realized he was hungry; his last meal had been at Tempsford back in the safety of England. When he had finished eating, Pierre called sharply to the girl. With obvious reluctance, she came across and sat down opposite.

'My name is Elise,' she said in good English, looking down to avoid his eyes. 'Pierre is my father. By coming here you have put both our lives in great danger. I do not welcome you but it is my father's wish that we oppose the Germans. I shall do my duty by him; that is all. Expect nothing more from me.'

'I understand, Elise. You are very brave. I shall leave as soon as I can. If I am captured by the Germans, I shall not betray you or your father.'

She raised her head and for the first time looked directly at him. Her face was white and drawn, her eyes grey and sad. 'That is easy to say.' Her voice was bitter. 'Those people are barbarians. You cannot imagine what they will do to force those who have information to talk.'

Farquhar said nothing but her words chilled him. The true seriousness of his situation was suddenly, horrifically clear. This was not a game, a cheap thriller in which he had somehow become involved. It was a world where torture and an agonizing death were permanently close. Pierre noisily cleared his throat and muttered a couple of incomprehensible sentences.

'My father says to tell you Jacques, the man you expected, has gone away,' Elise went on quietly. 'He was here two nights ago and asked my father to meet you. Tonight he will take you to the bridge you have come

54

to destroy. From tomorrow I shall listen to the radio each evening for a BBC message concerning your return to England. When it comes you must leave.'

'Thank you, Elise. I am very grateful to you.'

Pierre took him across the yard to a byre and motioned to him to climb a rickety ladder to a space above the cow stalls. Farquhar was exhausted; he mumbled a reply to Pierre's *'Dormez bien, m'sieur'*, curled up on a pile of hay and fell sound asleep.

It was late afternoon when he woke and several seconds passed before he realized where he was. He crawled to the side of the loft and peered out through a gap in the planks. Pleasant rolling farmland lay in the soft evening sunshine and he thought how lovely it would be to take Simba for a stroll across the fields, watching him chase rabbits. The satchel of explosives, lying in the hay near where he had slept, brought him back to reality. He began to assemble the necklaces, chains of dynamite sticks linked by wires to their detonators, ready for connection to the electric firing cable. An hour later Elise brought a tray with soup, bread and a thick omelette. She placed it on the ground at the bottom of the ladder and looked up. On seeing him watching her she turned and left without a word.

It was almost dark when Pierre came for him. On leaving the farmyard, they crossed several fields before a path led to a steep wooded ravine filled by a roaring stream. It was eerie, hurrying through the menacing darkness with the deafening noise so close. Farquhar's fevered imagination was fed by the thought that at any moment an order to halt would ring out. He was in RAF uniform but the feeble cover story suggested by the colonel, that he was an airman shot down whilst dropping leaflets, would be destroyed the moment his satchel was opened and the dynamite discovered. *If I'm challenged, I'll run like hell. There won't be a hope of escape but with luck I'll be shot in the back and killed instantly.* The fear of being merely wounded and dragged off for interrogation made him light-headed. Elise's drawn face and her warning filled his thoughts. Despite his assurance to her, he knew he would be unable to withstand Gestapo torture; the mere threat of it would destroy his will to remain silent.

The stream swept round a bend to join a major river. Alongside it was a path, gleaming silver in the moonlight. Pierre marched on, keeping to the right in the shadow of a line of tall trees, with Farquhar following. After a mile the path entered a cutting; on the right was a steep wooded bank, the black swirling river lay on the left. In the darkness ahead a solid image began to form and solidified into a substantial stone bridge. The moon emerged from the dark cloud to reveal a pair of graceful arches spanning the river; a smaller arch carried the bridge over the path along which they were walking. Above the parapet a railway signal light glowed bright red. Farquhar walked into the opening. There was sufficient light for him to recognize the square-cut limestone block walls as part of the masonry of the original railway, built fifty or more years earlier. The photos in the colonel's office had shown a single span steel structure resting on concrete abutments. Pierre had brought him to the wrong bridge. '*Combien kilometres aux l'autre pont?*' he hissed.

'*L'autre pont?*' Pierre asked. '*Pas un autre, m'sieur! C'est le bon!*'

For once Farquhar understood his French. 'What do you mean, this is the right bridge?' he snarled in English. 'It's too bloody old!'

Instead of replying, Pierre held up his hand. From above came the sound of voices and the crunch of heavy boots.

'*Boche!*' Pierre whispered hoarsely, urgently jabbing a finger upwards.

Standing in the arch, Farquhar was unable to breathe. The two voices, unmistakably German, became clear. *This is my first contact with the enemy! The men have stopped directly above and are probably looking down on the path we have just come along. Jesus! What if they come down to check this arch?* He cowered back into the darkness.

One of the guards was doing most of the talking, '*Das frau*' was frequently repeated and Farquhar guessed he was telling a tale about a woman. The second man responded at intervals with amused grunts. After a couple of minutes they both guffawed loudly. The glowing butts of their cigarettes fell at the entrance to the arch and they moved away.

The tension had eased Farquhar's anger. *Pierre's not responsible for bringing me to the wrong bridge. He was wrongly briefed by Jacques. It's too late to start searching for the correct target; there wouldn't be time to get back to the farm before daybreak. The colonel didn't say what to do if anything went wrong but I've got more than enough dynamite to blast this lot to kingdom come. It's important enough for the Germans to patrol it. After all the effort involved in getting me here, he'll expect me to do something instead of just creeping back to the farm. Bugger it! I'll blow it and argue later.*

Signalling to Pierre to keep watch, he began unpacking the satchel.

Sufficient moonlight reached inside the opening for him to work without the use of a torch. Kneeling on the ground, he began to dig into the earth at the base of the pillar with a trowel. *Ideally a whole limestone block should be chiselled out and the necklaces placed inside the wall for better containment. But I've not got time to do that. The two guards might come back. I'll bury extra charges alongside the face. They'll smash it and collapse the pier.*

Six necklaces were in position when Pierre again whispered, '*Boche!*'

Farquhar looked up. Bathed in moonlight, a solitary dark figure in a steel helmet and heavy greatcoat, with a rifle slung over his shoulder, was trudging along the riverside path towards them. A bend had hidden him from view until that moment. Farquhar realized why the two guards had not come down to examine the arch; the underside was patrolled separately! By only one man, it seemed, now a mere twenty yards from them. The satchel and the unburied necklaces, the reel of wire and the firing box were spread out on the ground. When he reached the arch, the soldier could not fail to see them.

'What can we do?' Farquhar whispered hoarsely.

Pierre took his arm and led him deeper into the darkness of the arch. With their backs flattened against the wall, they watched as the guard, a bulky menacing shape, reached the entrance. He took a few paces forward then stopped and gave a surprised exclamation, peering down at the wires and charges spread out before him. His shadow lay over the discovery and he stepped to one side for a better view. Pierre moved silently behind him. The soldier was unaware of danger until the old man's arm suddenly wrapped around his neck. He struggled, gurgling horribly as the grip tightened. Pierre's shoulders jerked and there was a crack like the breaking of a dry stick. It was a French farmer's traditional method of killing a sheep; snapping its neck is easier and less messy than slitting its throat with a knife.

Pierre released the body and it slumped to the ground. The head lay at a strange angle, the lifeless eyes open and staring in the moonlight. It was the first time Farquhar had seen death. Until that moment his closest encounter had been attending the funeral of an elderly aunt. He had shrunk from his mother's suggestion that he accompany her to the chapel of rest to see the old lady lying in her coffin. Now he had witnessed a brutal, cold-blooded murder! A deed to which he was an accessory. *This is the end of the mission, that's for sure. We've both got to get the hell out of here. Leave the scene of the crime before the body's found.* Dazed and uncomprehending, he watched Pierre pick up the soldier's rifle by the muzzle and hurl it far out into the river. He dragged the body by the heels out of the archway and rolled it off the bank side into the water with barely a sound.

Straightening up, he wiped his hands on his trousers. '*Salaud! M'sieur,*' he muttered. '*Salaud! Maintenant, l'explosif! Finis vitement!*'

We can't! We've got to run! We're fucking bloody murderers!

The words screamed in Farquhar's brain but their translation was far beyond his limited vocabulary. He remained silent as Pierre stood expectantly, waiting for him to carry on laying the charges. He was trapped. Common sense insisted he must flee. But to where? *I'd never find my way back to the farm alone. Even if by some miracle I did, what would I tell Elise? That her father had killed a German soldier and I'd run away, leaving him on his own?*

Wearily he turned and knelt beside the half-finished excavation. His hands shook uncontrollably as he worked jerkily, like an automaton, unable to think rationally. More necklaces had to be buried against the outer face of the pier immediately above the river. Kneeling on the narrow strip of bank his mind was filled with an image of the dead soldier's hand slowly rising behind him to grip his ankle and drag him down into the dark icy depths....

The longest minutes of his life passed before he completed the job. He gathered the twelve electrical leads from the detonators then twisted and taped them to the firing cable. Pierre kept watch as he walked backwards along the path, unwinding the wire from the reel. Thirty yards from the bridge, they climbed a slope into the trees where he cut the cable, stripped off the insulation and connected the two wires to the firing box terminals. His final task would be to raise then press the plunger to create the necessary sparks at the detonators.

The red signal above the arch turned green, indicating the approach of a train. *This will please the colonel. Blowing up a train and the bridge. It may be carrying ammunition, or petrol, or troop reinforcements. Perhaps all three. Killing hundreds of German soldiers means nothing; it's different to the guard.*

The sound of a whistle and the dull rumble of the train reached him. *I'll press the plunger when the engine crosses the central pillar. The driver will see the track explode ahead of him and slam on the brakes but there'll not be enough time to stop the train. I hope he's not French but there's nothing I can do if he is. The momentum will carry the train and everybody on board to their doom. Just a few more seconds to wait....*

Pierre suddenly seized his wrist in an iron grip and shook his head.

'Non, m'sieur! Non! Mes amis et mes voisons!' he whispered hoarsely.

The aged engine, snorting steam and smoke, swept over the arch above the path. Farquhar caught sight of two women in hats peering from one of the windows of the dimly lit carriages. This was a local passenger train, the women were two of Pierre's 'amis et voisons', his friends and neighbours! *He's prevented me committing an atrocity! The dead guard had been in uniform and armed, a legitimate enemy. But these women are harmless peasants, probably coming home after a day at the market.* He seized the old man's hand and shook it with profound gratitude. He had no words, in any language, to explain the relief he felt. The noise of the train faded; the moon hung over the quiet countryside.

'*Maintenant?*' Farquhar whispered.

'*Maintenant, m'sieur.*'

He pressed the plunger. There was an immediate *Crump!* Above the parapet a blue flash lit the sky as the electrical signal connections were torn apart. Rail ballast and limestone fragments fell like hail on the path, the base of the pillar slid sideways. The bridge folded like cardboard at the centre of the second arch; giant spouts erupted as the debris collapsed into the river. The acrid smell of dust, ash and explosive filled the air. It would be a long time before the next train crossed here.

Farquhar knew he could not stay at the farm. An intensive search for whoever was responsible for destroying the bridge would certainly follow and be all the more vicious when the Germans discovered the guard was missing. Inevitably his disappearance would be connected to the explosion; if his body was found a post mortem would reveal his neck had been broken, proving he had been murdered. There would be nothing to connect his death directly with the sabotage but, as he had been on duty in the area, the connection would be made. The safe crossing of a local passenger train, minutes before the explosion, would be seen as implicating the local population and result in terrible reprisals. Elise was clearly relieved when Farquhar told her of his decision to move out. He asked if she knew of somewhere he could hide until the BBC message giving details for his return to England was received. Pierre protested volubly when Elise told him of this change of plan, insisting it was quite safe for him to remain at the farm. But Farquhar remained adamant, all the more when he saw fear return to Elise's face. She told him there was a ruined cottage deep in a wood six kilometres from the farm. It would, she assured him, be a safe hiding place. Pierre took him there before dawn.

The following days seemed endless. Nothing disturbed the silence apart from the occasional bark of a fox and the hooting of night owls. The ruin lay deep in the shadow of a copse of ancient gnarled oaks, their trunks buried in dank undergrowth. After Pierre left, Farquhar removed all traces of their tracks, leaving no evidence of anyone having been there for years. Elise had given him a jug of milk, a slab of cheese, two loaves and half a cooked leg of lamb. It was, she said, enough to last three days by which time, according to Pierre, the BBC message would have been received. Farquhar thought this unduly optimistic and prepared for a stay of five days and worked out a daily ration for that duration. By the second morning the milk had turned sour but luckily it rained every day and using the jug he was able to catch the trickle that ran through a hole in the remains of the thatched roof.

After four days, with no contact from the farm and food beginning to run low, he adjusted his estimate from five days to seven and reduced his already meagre ration accordingly. He considered venturing out into the woods to look for berries, or perhaps apples or pears; the cottage may once have had an orchard. But the idea was stillborn; last year's fruit would have rotted by now. He thought of making a sling out of rusting barbed wire, of which there was an abundant supply, to catch rabbits but dismissed the plan as he had no means of cooking. And hunting for food would create tracks disclosing his presence if the woods were searched. He abandoned the idea of living off the land.

After six days he was extremely hungry. He fought against thinking of his next meal, visualizing instead the hunt that must be in progress for those responsible for wrecking the bridge. *Has the soldier's body been found? Perhaps the Germans have somehow connected Pierre with the bridge and he's under arrest. They might be torturing the poor old bugger! Or the BBC message may not have been sent and Elise can't leave the farm in case she misses it. But surely there'd be a repeat transmission? Perhaps the Germans have invaded England and fighting is in progress along the south coast. How will Mother cope alone? She'll be frantic with worry, especially if the colonel's postcards she thinks I'm sending from America stop arriving....*

Each hour was longer than the previous sixty minutes. He developed an irrational urge to calculate the precise time remaining before he could eat his next frugal meal. Lacking any means of writing, the process involved lengthy exercises in mental arithmetic and scratching the intermediate totals on an area of crumbling plaster with a rusty nail. But each time the count was interrupted by thoughts of a favourite meal, causing him to lose track and start again from the beginning. It was a serious blow when he woke one morning to find his watch had stopped; he had forgotten to wind it the previous evening. Low clouds permanently obscured the sun so he could only guess the time. His planned eating schedule was reduced to chaos.

It was early on the ninth morning, with only a scrap of cheese rind and half a crust of mouldy bread remaining, that he heard Elise's voice. His first thought was that he had become delirious and it was not until he peered through a hole in the thatch and saw her standing by a bank of nettles holding a basket that he knew she was real. She was softly calling,

'Fokker, Fokker,' pronouncing his name as if he were a type of German aircraft. He clambered down, went to the doorway and waved to her.

'No message yet, Fokker,' she said as he pushed through the long wet grass towards her. 'I've brought more food. The Germans are searching, that is why I am late. They've been to the farm but it was just a routine check. My father is not a suspect. They gave him some cigarettes.'

'Thank you, Elise. You are very brave. Give your father my respects.'

She told him the correct time and quickly left.

It was a week before she came again; once more his food supplies were running low. This time it was late in the afternoon. She gave him more bread, milk and cheese and, most importantly, the news he had been waiting for.

'There was a message on the radio this morning. "*The six brown eggs will be delivered on Sunday.*" That means an aeroplane will pick you up tomorrow night. Father will come and take you to the place after dark.'

After she had gone and he had wolfed some food, tearing lumps off the loaf with his teeth and ramming chunks of cheese into his mouth between great gulps of cool fresh milk, he paced the derelict rooms. His heart was thumping with excitement. Picked up by a plane! It was marvellous news! He had feared being ordered to swim out to a darkened ship or submarine and unable to find it. Or getting lost, attempting to cross the Pyrenees on foot to reach Gibraltar. *But the good old colonel has come up trumps, sending a bloody aeroplane! It shows he approved of me blowing the wrong bridge. When we meet, I'll tell him the cock-up over the target wasn't Pierre's fault. That fool Jacques has to take full responsibility. But that's immaterial right now; I've done my bit. I could be back in the lab this time next week. Poor Elise, I can't blame her for being scared. I would have been, in her place. Despite everything she's looked after me so well. And old Pierre. After the war his neighbours must be told how he saved their lives by stopping me blowing up their train. Just in the nick of time. I'll bring Mother to meet him and Elise. And I'll be able to thank them properly for all they've done for me....*

Pierre came for him the following evening as the last of the daylight faded. They walked for an hour along paths, across fields, past silent farms. A narrow lane finally led to a meadow where a cluster of resistance men waited. After greeting them both warmly, they led the way to a clump of bushes at one end of the field. They lay in the wet grass in silence for over an hour before the distant purr of an aircraft engine was heard. In the dark sky above the trees there was the rapid, double on-off blink of landing lights. The Lysander swooped like a giant bat out of the darkness, touching down between two lines of hand torches. Pierre gave Farquhar bristly kisses on both cheeks before releasing him to hurry out to the aircraft. A pair of dark figures jumped down as he reached it, brushing past him without a word. The plane was already turning into the wind for take-off, its engine roaring loud enough to waken every German soldier for miles around. His foot groped for the step and he hauled himself upwards, found a bucket seat and slammed the door. The plane jerked forward, bumping and bouncing over the rough ground until the ride became smooth; through the side window Farquhar saw France tilt and fall away below.

He sat in the cold cramped seat in the rear of the cockpit, peering down at the choppy wave-tops of the Channel a few hundred feet below. Contact with the pilot was impossible as a steel bulkhead separated them. It was unfortunate that an anti-aircraft battery near Newhaven was carrying out a training exercise with live ammunition that morning. An unexpected low-flying aeroplane suddenly emerging out the coastal mist was a tempting target; shoot first and ask questions later was a standing order. Farquhar saw the first dark puff of smoke away to his right and looked at it with professional interest rather than fear. Even when there were two sharply audible bangs much closer and a pair of small black clouds appeared on his left he remained calm, failing to appreciate the danger. There was a word for the phenomena and he was still trying to think of it when there came a deafening explosion from the engine. The Lysander lurched violently; the cockpit canopy was whipped off and the pilot's head and shoulders appeared briefly above the bulkhead before his parachute dragged him clear.

Farquhar remained strapped in his seat as the plane dipped and began to scream in a near-vertical dive.

'Oh God!' he screamed aloud. 'Jesus Christ! This is it! Goodbye, Mother!'

He remembered the word he had been seeking. It was 'bracketed'.

Chapter Seven

Magda had lost all sense of time. One day was exactly the same as the next, as the previous ten, as the previous twenty. Carol had leased the house for two years with an option to renew. The German occupation authorities in Paris knew who he was but no action had been taken against him. The situation was unlikely to change although there was no guarantee this tolerant state of affairs would continue indefinitely.

In spite of the temporary security it afforded, Magda quickly developed a hatred of the house. The décor was not at all to her liking; the place had a fusty smell of age and neglect. The rooms were too small to hold the lavish dinner parties that had been a major part of her life in the palace in Bucharest. There was no accommodation for the servants so they all had to sleep out. As a result, once dinner had been cleared, or if during the night if she woke and felt like a snack or a drink, there was no one to answer when she rang the bell for attention to her needs. Breakfast was not available until the maids arrived in the morning to prepare it and bring the tray to her room.

Carol constantly urged her to be patient. The war could not last much longer even though Hitler's plans for the invasion of England appeared to have been shelved, at least for a time. The streets were decidedly unsafe. The movement of Parisians was subject to severe restrictions and there were spies everywhere. Factions with long memories had bitter cause to remember Magda in the years of exile before the war. A single phone call to German headquarters implying she had Jewish connections could result in arrest and the near certainty of her joining the thousands of those who had disappeared.

Her hair had grown back but to her horror traces of grey were visible. She sent for a wig-maker but the samples the stupid woman brought made her look ridiculous. In refusing to wear any of them Magda denied herself the opportunity of taking shopping trips, or meeting friends for coffee or lunch at a restaurant. Until her own glorious hair returned, perhaps with some judiciously added colouration, she was condemned to remaining indoors, out of sight.

Relief came from an unexpected source. Carol's secretary was an elegant German lady in her sixties whom Magda was convinced had been sent to spy on them. Her silver hair was so beautifully cut and styled that one morning Magda could not refrain from commenting on its appearance. The lady merely smiled and thanked her. A few days later Magda received a card with the address of a *coiffeuse* who before the war was renowned as the best in Paris. The authorities allowed her to continue serving the needs of the wealthiest Parisiennes and the wives of high-ranking German officers. The salon was in an unmarked suite on an upper floor of the Montmartre Hotel. Following her first appointment, Magda was delighted with the improvement and booked a series of weekly visits. Within a month her former confidence had returned; her appetite was restored and she began to enjoy life again despite the limitations of the house and the tiresome wartime restrictions.

On her fourth visit to the establishment she was delighted to find herself sitting next to her old friend Blanche. They had been close friends during the years of exile but lost contact after Magda returned to Bucharest with Carol and became the royal consort. Blanche was a tall, flamboyant blonde the same age as herself. Her husband, a highly successful businessman, had died soon after the war began, leaving her a large fortune. Her period of mourning was brief; within months she was enjoying life, as far as was possible in wartime, as one of the capital's most vivacious widows. Rumours spread that she was a collaborator, and the mistress of a German general, but no definite proof ever emerged. It was whispered she was active in the French resistance under the code name *La Chatte* but she was never taken in for questioning. She walked a narrow, dangerous line between friend and foe with no outward sign of allegiance to either. She made no secret of her distress at the loss of her beloved red Bugatti Atlantic sports car. The beastly Gestapo requisitioned it on the day of France's surrender and she never saw it again.

Blanche began visiting Magda at Quai Voltaire regularly and a bedroom was kept permanently ready for her. Carol enjoyed her lively company and Magda suspected that if anything happened to her, Blanche would happily step into her shoes as his consort. The conversations between the two women were mainly *à la recherché du temps perdu*. Both had outrageous senses of humour and it was not unusual for Carol to put his head round the door to enquire the cause of their peals of laughter. It became their habit, after dinner when the servants had gone home and

Carol was tucked up in bed, to retire to the library where they snuggled together on a wide sofa, holding hands and drinking fine old brandy in front of a flickering log fire.

Tentatively, they began exchanging their most secret secrets *sotto voce*, occasionally punctuated by giggles. Blanche enjoyed whispering details of her numerous love affairs and startling escapades, some involving two or more men at once. More sombrely, Magda told her of Carol's long-standing impotence and his lofty disregard of her physical needs. She described at great length the years of wonderful lovemaking she had enjoyed with Grigor, and how she missed his romantic attentions. Her cloistered existence now precluded the lascivious affairs she had once enjoyed and for which she longed. One of the footmen, who was tall and very handsome, clearly adored her and paid far more attention than his duties warranted. She confessed to Blanche that she was greatly tempted but as Carol never left the house, consummation was quite impossible.

It was in the course of an evening of frank discussion, with rain pattering against the windows, that they kissed as lovers for the first time. Blanche took the first step, lips apart and tongue gently probing. It came like an electric shock to Magda and long moments passed before she responded. Gradually, zips were pulled down, gowns fell open, articles dropped to the floor. Wrapped in each other's arms, they kissed with passion and expectation again and again....

For Magda, the experience was strangely new, far removed from the sexual games she had long played with men. Over breakfast next morning she said so to Blanche, who clapped her hands and cried, 'Vive la différence, chérie!' Their 'petit jeu', she assured her, was 'très chic, et très Parisienne!'

On each of her successive visits their little game was repeated, with increasing enjoyment, although Magda could not imagine ever repeating the experience with anyone but dearest Blanche.

Chapter Eight

The door of the white building beside the runway was locked but when Grigor pushed his shoulder against it the flimsy catch gave way. He dragged the trunk and suitcase inside and groped for a light switch but was unable to find it. The unmistakable smell of Turkish tobacco smoke hung in the air; in the gloom he could just make out a chair, a table and curiously, a leather sofa. A proper examination of the room, which must be some sort of aerodrome control office, would have to wait until daylight.

Magda had thoughtfully slipped a litre bottle of vodka into his suitcase; Grigor took a stiff drink from the neck before lying down on the sofa. The events of the day crowded into his mind, each clamouring for its moment of remembrance. His first thought was of Günter and he shifted uneasily on the sofa, acutely conscious of having sent him to his death. Despite earlier reservations he had become quite fond of him in a paternal way. He was handsome, full of energy and enthusiastic to a fault. On discovering the Junker's reserve petrol tank was empty he would blame the mutinous ground crew for deliberately not filling it. As the fuel ran out, and the three engines began to splutter in turn, there would be time for him to put on a parachute, open the side door and bail out. But Grigor could not imagine him taking that option; it was too easy for such a fervent patriot. Günter would prefer a Wagnerian death, plunging to earth at the controls of his doomed aeroplane, singing aloud, 'It's a long way to Tipperary....'

It was the perfect solution, Grigor thought. What's left of him is lying somewhere in the Bulgarian mountains and may not be found for years. With nothing to draw German attention to Turkey, I'm out of their grasp for good. I'm truly sorry about Günter, but this is war. A rotten stinking bloody war and he is a single casualty. Thousands more are going to die before it's over. I was faced with a simple choice. Let him live to tell the Gestapo where I am, or kill him and spend the rest of my life with Magda. The English call it Hobson's Choice, meaning no choice at all. Poor Günter....

Grigor had another drink, closed his eyes and fell asleep.

*

It was early morning when he woke. He got to his feet and cast a bleary eye at the leather sofa on which he had spent the night. It sagged badly and the cushions were worn and badly stained yet he had slept well enough on it. Light filtered through the grimy window; electric wires hung loose against the wall, the switch and ceiling light fitting had both been smashed. A door in one corner opened into a tiny room with a filthy toilet and washbasin; only a trickle of rusty water came from the tap. The window looked out over the landing strip to the far side of the field where two empty aircraft shelters stood, simple camouflaged roofs with open sides. In a drawer in the table he found a few stale biscuits and a half-eaten bar of chocolate. Clearly the tap water was unsafe to drink so he washed down a couple of biscuits and the remains of the chocolate with sips of neat vodka from the neck of the bottle. Then he sat on the chair, put his feet up on the table and assessed his situation.

It was not unfavourable. First, he had a travel document Magda had obtained for him from the Turkish ambassador to Romania. His Excellency, elderly and long besotted by her, had avidly accepted an invitation to an intimate supper in her apartment and did not leave until morning. That afternoon the letter, hand-written in Turkish on thick Embassy notepaper and bearing the personal signature of His Excellency, was delivered to the palace buried in a large bouquet of exquisite orchids.

Grigor's second advantage was his fluency in Arabic. It was his mother tongue and Turkish Muslims spoke a dialectic form.

Thirdly, he had an ample supply of money in a variety of convenient currencies in a compartment in the lid of his suitcase.

Finally Günter, the only person aware of his whereabouts, was by now almost certainly dead. Grigor pursed his lips. *Almost, but not certainly. Dead men could still tell tales. Where had the Junkers crashed? The area may be remote, but there was always a chance that a peasant searching for a lost goat may stumble on the wreckage. With no fuel on board, the plane may not have caught fire and the logbook could have survived. With Germanic efficiency Günter may have written it up early in the flight, possibly mentioning 'Rupert'! If the Gestapo recover it they'll send agents to capture me. The map in the Junkers showed there's a railway station at Bandirma. That's my next destination. But how can I get there?*

Grigor was a fastidious man; his habit of bathing and shaving daily had been a constant source of amusement at the palace. Even the king had not gone to such excessive lengths of personal hygiene. It was a routine Grigor refused to break even in these primitive surroundings. Taking a towel, mirror and razor from his suitcase, he went to the washroom and began to shave using the dribble of rusty water from the tap. He had almost finished when there came the unmistakable clink of harness followed by the gruff sound of a man's voice. Hurriedly drying his face, he slipped on a shirt and went to the window. Immediately outside an old man was laboriously climbing down from a high cart while a young boy stood holding the horse's bridle. Grigor opened the door with a flourish.

'*Assalam-o-Alaikum!*' he called cheerfully in Arabic.

An agonizing silence followed as the old man, concentrating on getting down from his cart, ignored the greeting until he was safely on the ground. He then turned, took off his cap and, twisting it nervously in his hands, made a clumsy bow. '*Alaikum-o-Assalam, effendi,*' he muttered nervously. He had an anxious look, as if he had been caught stealing.

'Who are you?' Grigor demanded authoritatively.

'I am Basha, *effendi*. I live in Bandirma,' the old man replied, continuing to speak in Arabic and waving his hand to the east.

'What are you doing on this aerodrome?'

'I have my papers, *effendi*, and those of my grandson Hussein. We are permitted by the government to enter this place.'

'Show me.'

The old man handed over a greasy wad of folded documents, incomprehensible to Grigor since they were written in Turkish. They bore scrawled signatures and the official crescent and star stamp in purple ink. Grigor thumbed quickly through the pages and handed them back.

'You have yet to tell me what are you doing here,' he snapped.

'We have come to cut grass, *effendi*,' the old man replied.

'Grass?' Grigor echoed. 'You are here to cut grass?'

'We come every week, *effendi*. For the flying machines.' He flapped his hands helplessly by way of explanation.

'What my grandfather means is the wheels of the aeroplanes get caught if the grass is not kept short,' the young boy called across from his position beside the horse's head.

Grigor realized why Günter had circled the plane and inspected the strip before landing. If the undercarriage had become entangled, the Junkers could have overturned and killed them both. He nodded. 'Grass cutting should be the responsibility of the Luftwaffe, not civilians. However, that is of minor concern at present. I am here to inspect the aerodrome and make a report. I am glad it is being properly looked after.'

He stepped forward and peered into the empty cart. 'How do you cut the grass? With a sickle? A scythe? I must include all details in my report.'

'No, *effendi*,' Basha replied. 'It would take more than a month using hand tools and it would still be too high. And the grass would have grown high again where we started. We use the government cutters. If *effendi* follows me I will show him.'

The old man led the way round the building where he pulled a tarpaulin sheet aside to reveal a large mower with shafts enabling it to be drawn by a horse. Beside it was an agricultural rake, also horse-drawn. Both machines were old and badly rusted.

'I will report they are in urgent need of replacement,' Grigor said briskly. 'How much does the government pay you to do this work?'

The old man shook his head sadly. 'Nothing, *effendi*. We are allowed to keep the grass we cut to feed to our cattle. We take it home in the cart at the end of the day. The closer we cut, the more grass we collect. But grass does not grow in winter so cutting is unnecessary. We get nothing and our cattle go hungry. If you can help us in any way we will be very grateful.'

Grigor nodded sympathetically; the old man could prove useful. 'It's a cold morning,' he said cheerfully. 'I have vodka. Come inside and have a sup.'

Basha gave a toothless grin and pressed his knuckles to his forehead. 'Thank you, *effendi*. I'll help Hussein harness the horse to the cutter and he can begin work.'

'When you came to the door, *effendi*, I thought you must be the new officer,' Basha said, handing the bottle back. They were sitting side by side on the sofa. He showed no curiosity as to how Grigor had got to the aerodrome.

'The new officer?' murmured Grigor, puzzled by the statement. 'Oh yes, I'm in charge for now. He will be here later.'

'You know him then, *effendi*?' Basha enquired politely, eyeing the bottle of vodka. Grigor passed it to him.

'Of course,' Grigor said cautiously. 'I appointed him.'

'Baksi, the last officer, was a rogue,' Basha said, wiping his mouth with the back of his hand. He kept hold of the bottle.

Grigor nodded, wondering what misdeeds Baksi could have committed on a remote grass aerodrome lacking electricity and aeroplanes. 'Have a last drink before you go back to work,' he said.

'Thank you, *effendi*. You are very kind.'

'Tell me, how often do aeroplanes come here?'

'Not often, *effendi*. Perhaps two or three times a month. They do not stay long, just an hour sometimes. But Baksi came every week. Each time with a different woman.' He gave a frightening leer and patted the leather cushion beside him. Grigor nodded again as the function of the sofa became apparent. 'He gave me a few lira to keep my mouth shut about the women,' Basha added, replacing the leer with a sly look. Having been paid for keeping Baksi's secret, it seemed he was now looking to benefit from divulging it.

'It was wrong of you to accept money from such a criminal,' Grigor said sharply, pouncing on the opportunity to put the old man at a disadvantage. 'You should have reported his neglect of duty, not profited from it.'

'I am sorry, *effendi*. It will not happen again.'

'It had better not. I shall overlook your mistake this time. But in future you will do exactly what I tell you. Do you understand?'

'Yes, *effendi*.' Basha was upset and sat with his head bowed. For a moment Grigor felt sorry for him but there were pressing matters to attend to.

'Where is my car?' he demanded.

'Your car, *effendi*?' Basha looked up, bewildered.

'Yes, my car. It should be here by now.'

'By now, *effendi*?'

'It was ordered to pick me up here half an hour ago.'

'Half an hour ago, *effendi*?'

'That's what I said. As it has not arrived you will take me to Bandirma in your cart.'

'In my cart, *effendi*?'

'Stop repeating everything I say! You will take me to Bandirma. Hitch the horse to the cart and take me there at once.'

Basha lurched to his feet and stumbled to the door. The vodka was having its effect on his movements. Grigor watched him hurrying across the field, waving his arms and calling to Hussein, a distant speck perched on the back of the horse-drawn mower.

There was a high wooden seat at the front of the cart. Basha sat on the left holding the reins with Hussein in the middle. On the right-hand end, in suit, shirt and tie, Grigor sat upright, looking about with as much dignity as he could muster in the circumstances. The trunk and his suitcase lay in the back of the cart, bouncing from side to side as the tall wooden wheels lurched along the rutted muddy track leading from the airstrip. The old man raised a hand in greeting as they passed two men hoeing a crop in a field. Grigor saw them stop work and stare. No doubt Basha in due course would have to explain the presence of the well-dressed stranger sitting beside him.

The mud track joined a concrete road leading into Bandirma. After a further mile the double tracks of a railway crossed the road on the outskirts of the town and they came to an area of sidings crowded with hissing steam locomotives, passenger coaches and a variety of railway vehicles. It was still early morning and the wide main street was quiet. Outside the station building Basha clicked his tongue and tugged at the rein to stop the horse.

'I'll leave my luggage in the cart with you,' Grigor said sharply. 'Guard it with your life while I enquire the time of the next train.'

'Where are you going, *effendi*?' Basha asked.

'Ankara,' Grigor lied.

There was a train to the west within the hour. Grigor returned to the cart with a porter wheeling a trolley. After Basha and Hussein had helped him load the luggage, he curtly dismissed them with orders to return to their grass cutting at the airfield. No doubt there would be a flurry of local gossip in the wake of his brief visit but hopefully it would soon die down. If official enquiries were ever made, the report of this morning's activities would be rambling and confused.

Grigor bought a first-class return to Canakkale on the Dardanelle Strait, the narrow stretch of water connecting the Sea of Marmora to the Aegean. He had no intention of coming back to Bandirma; buying a return was a device to mislead anyone seeking him. There was a refreshment room with tables on the station platform. With the trunk and suitcase on the trolley at his side, Grigor ate his first proper meal since lunch in the pilot's mess at Ulmeni the previous day.

The train, an express from Istanbul, was on time and the comfortable journey to Canakkale took only two hours. Grigor moved his luggage into the corridor before the train drew to a halt. He signalled to a porter who loaded them onto a barrow and wheeled them out to the front portico of the station. A line of gaudily painted taxis lay baking in the hot afternoon sun. Grigor asked one of the drivers to take him to a good-quality hotel. The Anatolia stood on a rise at the outskirts on the edge of town. At reception the manager was courteous and pleasant and barely glanced at Grigor's Turkish travel permit. He merely said, 'If you would be kind enough to complete a registration card, sir, I will have your luggage taken to your room.'

Grigor entered his name as Eban Albaba, occupation tourist, and place of birth Beirut. He was shown to a spacious room with a wide comfortable bed and a luxurious bathroom en suite. He had an excellent dinner served in his room. Afterwards, with a spectacular sunset over the Aegean, he sat out on the balcony with a bottle of whisky and a tub of ice. Relaxed and secure, he looked across to the distant ruins of the city of Troy, over land that had been walked upon by some of the greatest men in human history.

A waiter brought the morning papers as he breakfasted in his room. The sole item of news from Romania was the long-awaited arrival in Bucharest of a Nazi delegation for talks with General Antonescu. Much was made of the Germans' victorious sweep across Europe. In an editorial it was stated plans to invade England had reached an advanced stage. In North Africa the Italians had suffered another defeat at the hands of the British and there was a suggestion that Hitler would soon be obliged to send troops to save the remains of Mussolini's army.

At reception the manager greeted him affably. 'How can I serve you this morning, Mr Albaba?'

'Whilst I am in Canakkale I would very much like to visit the off-shore islands,' he replied. 'Do you have a list of ferry sailings?'

The manager shook his head and gave a sad smile. 'Until recently it would have been my pleasure to provide you with a full itinerary. But I regret to inform you those days are past. They will not return until the current unpleasantness is settled.'

'Indeed?'

'Yes, sir. You have come to Canakkale at a most unfortunate time. War between Italy and Greece is not far off. Mussolini's ships are patrolling the Aegean and his troops have already occupied some of the Greek islands. All ferry services have been suspended.'

'Why should these matters concern Turkey? It is a neutral country and not involved in any way.'

'We did not seek this war, Mr Albaba. It has been brought to our door. As well as the Italians, the Germans too have an armed presence off our coast. These are dangerous days.'

'Are there no private boats available for charter?'

'I regret not, sir. There are plenty of motorboats and yachts down in the harbour but hostilities have made fuel impossible to obtain. Their owners are reluctant to put to sea even under sail for fear of striking a mine, or having their vessels used for target practice by the Italians.'

'What about fishing boats? Surely there are plenty of those?'

Again the manager shook his head. 'Fuel restrictions apply to them also. Even if petrol became available our fishermen would not venture into the Aegean. They would remain in the Sea of Marmora.'

'I came with the express intention of visiting the outlying islands. I am dismayed at being informed this is no longer possible.'

'I am indeed sorry to be responsible for breaking the bad news to you, sir. I trust nevertheless you will enjoy your stay. There is much to see here on the mainland. It is only five miles by taxi to the ruins of ancient Troy. The battlefield of Gallipoli in the last conflict can be reached by sailing boat. You can also visit the Hellespont where legend tells us Hero watched her lover Leander drown as he swam to her. The English Lord Byron is reputed to have completed the swim without mishap in the year 1810.'

Grigor went back to his room and lay on the bed. There were 2000 islands scattered across the Aegean. With Turkey no longer a haven he had been confident of finding a remote off-shore idyll where he could sit in the sun and drink the local wine for a couple of years until this stupid war was over. But it seemed he was trapped in Turkey. *Is the manager over-pessimistic? Is he hoping I'll extend my stay? It may be worth taking a look round the harbour myself. There may be someone willing for a sum to take me out to one of the islands. Or perhaps I can steal a boat and sail it single-handed.*

He dragged the trunk into the wardrobe out of sight, locking the door and taking the risk of leaving it unguarded for an hour. A taxi took him to the harbour where he strolled along the curving breakwater on the north side. Twenty or more small yachts lay tied up and half a dozen larger craft were moored out in the bay. All were stripped down to standing rigging and in no condition to put to sea without considerable preparation. The south side of the harbour had been the commercial area of the docks but the warehouses lining the quay were locked and deserted. A cluster of fishing boats nestled against the dock, their decks cleared of equipment. Two tall cranes stood idle beside a rusting freighter. It was not until he had walked past this vessel that he saw the old steamer. Her name was *Milos*, port of registration Istanbul. Her design was antiquated, two holds separated by a central island with a wooden wheelhouse perched on top. A plume of black smoke curled from her old-fashioned funnel. A man leant on the rail watching two hands winching barrels from the quay and swinging them on board. Grigor walked over to the steamer's side.

'Are you sailing soon?' he called up to the man in Arabic.

He took the pipe from his mouth and pointed the stem at the smoking funnel. 'The chief's getting steam up. We'll be off as soon as we've finished loading.'

'Where are you going?'

'Heraklion in Crete, then Alexandria.'

'Will you take me?'

'You'll have to speak to the captain.'

An hour later, with the trunk and his suitcase safely on board, Grigor stood on the deck of the *Milos* as she headed out into the blue Aegean.

Chapter Nine

Farquhar woke in a hospital bed with an attractive nurse bending over him. 'You're a very lucky boy,' she told him. 'You were pulled from the wreckage just before your aeroplane caught fire.' She patted his thigh through the blanket and he immediately felt better.

The following day colonel Fraser came to see him. He sat by the bed and listened in silence to his report on the mission.

'We knew right away you'd blown the wrong target,' he said when Farquhar had finished. 'The target bridge was two miles further downstream. A recce plane flew over next morning and photographed them both.'

'I'm sorry, sir,' Farquhar muttered. 'I have to say –'

'However,' the colonel added, interrupting his intended explanation, 'you did what you thought best in the circumstances. You showed initiative and I like that. Damned lucky you weren't wearing a parachute by the way. The pilot was. Must have panicked. Bailed out far too low. Body unrecognizable.'

'How did I get away with it?' Farquhar asked.

'The undercarriage scraped a Down and turned over. The high wing saved you from decapitation. By chance a farmer was passing and dragged you clear just before the petrol tanks went up. Somebody up there's looking after you.' The colonel stared hard at him. 'You're OK,' he said finally. 'Bit of concussion, nothing serious. And your mother's fine. She's not expecting you back for a while. I sent an extra card saying you'd be staying on in the States for a while. I knew you wouldn't mind.'

Farquhar minded quite a lot but he shrugged and said, 'There's nothing I can do about it now, Colonel. So long as she's not worrying much, it's OK.'

'Write her a letter saying how much you're enjoying it over there. I'll see she gets it. And I'll give you a few more postcards for me to send at intervals until you see her again.'

'I'll have some explaining to do when that happens. When can I go back to work? What about the prof?'

The colonel shuffled his feet and began a searching inspection of the tip of his swagger stick.

'Ah, the worthy Professor Brasher. We decided to keep him in the dark to be honest. He struck me as an old gasbag so we didn't tell him you'd gone to France. He was told you're working on a special job for us. Didn't say where or when you'd be back. He'll keep your job in the lab open for you until this is all over.'

'Thank you, Colonel. He's inclined to gossip and I've had nightmares about him ringing up and spilling the beans to my mother.'

'Well, he's as much in the dark as she is. You're being discharged in a few days. We need to have another chat. I'll send a car for you.'

It was a week before he was released from hospital. As he was finishing breakfast, a very pretty ATS private came to the ward.

'I'm Colonel Fraser's driver, sir,' she announced. She handed him a suitcase. 'He said you're to wear these clothes. I'll wait in the car.'

Farquhar eyed her speculatively as she walked away. She had long legs and her well-fitting brown uniform skirt concealed what was obviously a most attractive bum. Thrusting lewd thoughts aside, he opened the suitcase. It contained underwear and shirts, a pair of new brown shoes, a tie and a smart Sam Browne belt. And the uniform of a captain in the Royal Norfolk Regiment.

'Delightful spot, this, Farquhar,' the colonel said genially, waving his wine glass at the scene. They were standing in a bay window of an impressive manor house set in rolling parkland in mid-Sussex. 'This is the England we're fighting for! Country houses like this. And the village down there, with its Saxon church and black and white cottages. And a genuine Tudor pub, full of real old Sussex characters! The uniform looks good on you.'

'Thank you, Colonel. I never took the RAF one off all the time I was in France. It was in tatters by the time the Lysander picked me up. But why the Norfolk Regiment uniform? Surely the Engineers would be more appropriate?'

The colonel shook his head vigorously. 'It's a question of security, old chap. We can't have you walking about in civvies; folk would think you were a conshie. And as a commissioned sapper they'd know right away you were into something technical. In the Norfolks, well, you're just another poor footslogger like me. It'll throw anyone watching you completely off the scent.'

'I see,' Farquhar said, although he didn't really.

*

'I'm a member of an outfit Churchill has set up to coordinate subversive activities,' the colonel announced rather pompously over lunch. 'His orders are to "Set Europe Ablaze!" Typical Winston bravado, of course! In future, anyone who goes over the Channel will be fully trained by experts. They'll be taught how to handle weapons, work radios, use codebooks, all that sort of stuff. You were just an amateur by comparison, if you don't mind me saying so. They'll be bilingual, and fluent of course. But there'll always be a demand for specialists to train them in the job, and that's why we're having this chat. I want you to join us. You've proved you're up to it by doing an operational drop and using your initiative to destroy a railway bridge. You may be sent into the field now and again, for special one-off jobs, nothing long term. There's a job in the offing at the moment actually, but I can't tell you anything about it yet. Your main function will be to teach new agents about explosives. How to handle and lay them where they'll do the most damage. That sort of thing. I don't need your answer now, take a few days' leave and think it over first.'

Later, as they strolled along the terrace after lunch, the colonel suddenly stopped and said, 'By Jove, Farquhar, I've just had a thought! There's an old pub up north where I used to stay for the odd weekend's fishing before the war. It's in a nice part of the country, quiet and out of the way. Just the place to relax for a few days and think about what I've said. I'll ring and book you a room. There's a train from Kings Cross this afternoon that'll get you there tonight. I'll issue you with a rail warrant and a few quid to enjoy yourself. Come and see me when you get back.'

The ATS driver who had brought him from hospital took him to Kings Cross station. On the journey, sitting in the back of the car, he gazed hungrily at the nape of her neck; the way the blonde hair curled below her cap roused him to a ridiculous degree. He opened the envelope the colonel had given him. It contained twelve one-pound notes and a return railway warrant to Wylam, a place he had never heard of.

'Do you fancy a few days in the country?' he asked the driver hopefully. 'A quiet little place, nice pub. Just you and me.'

'Whereabouts, sir?' she enquired, without turning round.

'Up north,' he said. 'Wylam.'

'That's in Northumberland,' she said. 'I've been there.'

Her tone was friendly and Farquhar felt a surge of optimism. He decided not to reveal his inadequate geographical knowledge.

'How about it then? I'll hang about while you arrange leave.'

'That would be very nice, sir,' she said and held up her left hand to show off a ring. 'But see, I'm engaged. I'd have to ask my fiancé. He flies a Spitfire and somehow I don't think he'll agree. Sorry.'

At Kings Cross he was told there was a train to Newcastle upon Tyne leaving in half an hour. He had to change there for Wylam.

It was dark and raining heavily when he finally arrived. The solitary porter on the darkened platform directed him to the village pub, the Black Bull, across a bridge over the river Tyne.

He pushed open the front door into an empty bar. He put down his suitcase, took off his drenched cap and greatcoat, laid them on a chair and banged on the brass bell screwed to the counter. The landlady emerged silently from a room behind the counter. She was elderly, tall and thin and dressed entirely in black.

'Good evening,' she said, peering over her spectacles at him.

'Good evening, I'm Captain Farquhar,' he announced. 'I believe a room has been booked for me.'

'Yes, pet,' she said, 'it has. I got the phone call from Vickers-Armstrong just this afternoon. Here about the tanks, are you?'

'Vickers-Armstrong? Tanks? No. Oh! I see. Yes, well, sort of.' Colonel Fraser had said nothing about needing a cover story. 'I'm here to, ah, carry out inspections.'

'We get lots of officers coming to see about the tanks,' she said evenly as she pushed the register in front of him. 'Just sign in, please. They test them up on the moors at Otterburn. But you'll know all about that, of course. I often hear them firing at night. Boom-boom-boom. It goes on for hours sometimes.'

'What time's dinner?' Farquhar asked.

'I'll start making it now. It'll be on the table in half an hour.'

He picked up his sodden coat, cap and suitcase. 'Is anyone else staying here?' he asked.

'Just one young lady. On her own, like you.'

He had a pint of beer and a whisky chaser in the bar before going into the tiny dining room. Only two of the six tables were laid, each set with a single place. He took the one farthest from the door, hoping to get a good look at his fellow guest when she arrived. *A young lady, on her own, the landlady said. I wonder if I'll have more luck with her than with that ATS driver this morning. What will she be like? Plain or fancy? Intelligent or dumb? Why is she staying alone in a place like this? Waiting for her husband, perhaps, or a lover? The landlady would know. I wish I'd asked her. Perhaps she lives here and works locally. A big, jolly Land Girl maybe?*

Unlikely, though. They usually stay on the farm, or in a hostel.... Dinner consisted of a single slice of tough cold roast beef and two veg followed by unsweetened rice pudding. He dallied over the meal hoping his fellow guest would join him but there was no sign of her and he wanted another drink. He got up and had almost reached the door when it suddenly opened and she walked in.

'Hello,' he said, smiling and standing to one side to let her pass. She smiled back at him; Farquhar experienced a frisson of excitement. She was attractive, tall and dark, about his age. He hesitated, wondering whether to start a conversation. But he decided it was better not to; it might give her the impression he was the pushy type. He contented himself, temporarily, with the thought that it was still early and they would, at the very least, be spending the night under the same roof.

The brown-varnished sign on the door said 'Lounge – Strictly Residents Only'. It was even smaller than the dining room, gloomy and cramped. The heavy blackout curtains were drawn, the only light came from a low-powered bulb in a leaning standard lamp propped up by the badly worn sofa. An oak sideboard, a battered leather armchair and a small occasional table took up the rest of the floor. Farquhar sat down in the armchair; the landlady brought in his coffee. 'I've got no biscuits left, pet,' she said apologetically, putting the tray on the little table in front of him. 'It's the rationing, you know.'

'That's quite all right,' Farquhar replied. There had been no wine at dinner either. 'Could you bring me a whisky?' he asked. 'A large one, if you can manage it.'

The landlady looked doubtful. 'I only allow a guest two spirits per night, and singles at that. You've already had your full ration, really. That chaser in the bar earlier was a double. But then, it's a cold night, and you're in here on your own. I suppose it'll be all right. Just this once.'

'Thank you, that's very kind.' He smiled up at her. 'The young lady who's having dinner. Does she take coffee? Will she be in here later?'

'I couldn't say, it's only her second night. She didn't bother last night. I'll find out for you, shall I?

'Yes, please do. And ask if she'd care to join me for a drink.'

The landlady was soon back with his whisky. 'The young lady says to thank you very much, sir,' she said cheerfully as she put the tumbler and a brimming jug of water on the table. 'She'll join you for coffee as soon as she's finished her pudding. And she'll take a small port, please. It's her lucky night as it turns out. I've got half a bottle of the Ruby left. Lord knows when they'll send me any more.'

'Thank you very much,' Farquhar said. He took a ten-shilling note from his wallet and held it out. 'Perhaps, as it's a cold night, you could bring another whisky, and another port, in about twenty minutes?'

She stood looking dubiously at the note. 'Well, I'm not sure. As I say, everything is short. But who knows if we'll still be here this time next week? Or even tomorrow morning! We could all be blown to bits tonight! They say the German bombers follow the railway lines and we're only five minutes from the station.' She took the proffered note and slipped it into her apron pocket. 'Twenty minutes, you said?'

She came back carrying a coffee tray with the girl following, a book tucked under her arm. Farquhar politely stood and she sat on the sofa opposite him. The landlady put down the tray, gave them both a brief smile and left the room. Farquhar sat back in the armchair and looked across at the girl. Her eyes were wide set; she had a pert nose and smiling mouth. The low glow from the standard lamp cast a shadow across the lower part of her face. She reminded him of a cat inspecting a visitor; safe and self-confident for the moment but poised for flight at the first sign of trouble. She put her book down and picked up the glass of port.

'Cheers,' she said, taking a sip. 'This is really very kind of you. It's such a nice surprise to have someone else to talk to apart from our landlady. She's very sweet but greatly taken up with the problems of rationing.'

'Yes, I'd noticed that,' Farquhar said, smiling pleasantly. 'And you've had more experience of her than me. She told me you spent last night here too.'

'Yes.' As she poured coffee from the pot into her cup Farquhar saw her hands clearly for the first time. Relief flooded through him; she was not wearing a ring.

'Are you staying for long?' he enquired innocently.

'I'll be here for a few days,' she replied. 'Or nights, rather. I work for the Ministry of Food. During the day I visit local farms trying to persuade them to sell their hens' eggs to the Ministry for less than half the price they can get for them on the black market.'

'I'm sure you're very successful,' Farquhar said with a smile. 'You'd not have any difficulty persuading me to do anything for you.'

She ignored the comment and Farquhar realized he had overstepped the mark in making such an inane remark. He hastened to recover the situation. 'Sorry. I suppose every man you meet says something stupid like that. Forgive me. I hear this is a nice part of the world.' That was what the colonel had said; being a townie Farquhar knew nothing about rural Northumberland and didn't particularly care. However it was better to sound cheerful. 'It was dark and raining heavily when I got here. I've not yet been able to see for myself,' he explained.

'It's lovely, even when it's raining,' the girl replied enthusiastically. 'There are plenty of birds and rabbits, squirrels and lots of butterflies. It's nice and green and rolling, rugged in places. You'll find it a big change from where you come from,' she added, smiling and nodding at his regimental shoulder flash.

Oh God, Farquhar thought, *she probably knows Norfolk like the back of her hand.*

'The Roman wall's not far from here,' she was saying, unaware of the panic she had induced in him. 'It's all most interesting.'

'I must try and see it while I'm here,' Farquhar said, desperately hoping she wouldn't mention Norfolk again.

'You shouldn't miss it,' she said. She picked up the book she had brought and waved it at him. 'I found this in my room. It's about Emperor Hadrian and his men building the Wall two thousand years ago.'

'I'd no idea there was so much to see!' He struggled to match her obvious enthusiasm. 'Sorry, I've not introduced myself. I'm Peter Farquhar. I had some leave due and no idea where to go. I just stuck a pin in a map and Wylam was the nearest place with a railway station. I just wanted to get away for a few days of peace and quiet.'

'You tell fibs, Captain Farquhar.' She smiled across at him and he gaped back at her.

'Pardon?' he asked, hoping his voice was steady. 'Tell fibs? I don't understand.'

'Yes, fibs,' she said, raising her chin and looking across at him in a cheeky way. 'You told our landlady you were here to inspect tanks.'

He laughed, greatly relieved. 'No, she assumed I was. I didn't bother to disillusion her, that's all.'

'I see. So you are, honestly and truly, here on leave?'

'Absolutely, I swear it,' he said with conviction. It was, after all, more or less the truth.

'All right then. I won't ask about your job in case it's hush-hush. Then you would have to tell me proper fibs.'

'I'm sorry to disappoint you but I don't do anything in the least exciting,' he said easily. 'I'm only a pen-pusher, organizing pay and rations in a training camp.'

'Well, if you say so. I'm Josie Shirran,' she said. 'Would you like to come farm visiting with me tomorrow? I'll show you the Roman wall on the way.'

When Farquhar walked into the dining room next morning Josie had just finished breakfast. She had been in his thoughts when he fell asleep and had come to mind the moment he woke.

'Good morning! The bacon is very nice,' she said brightly across the gap between the two tables as he sat down. 'Local, I imagine, like the fried eggs. I won't enquire how the landlady came by them.'

'No, you'd better keep in with her,' he replied. 'She's only got half a bottle of the Ruby left.'

Josie laughed and Farquhar knew it was going to be a wonderful day.

'What are your plans?' he asked as he drained his cup of coffee; it had been made with gritty powdered milk and without sugar. 'Am I still included on the disappearing egg hunt?'

She smiled. 'Yes and no. The offer still stands but we're not going egg hunting. I've decided to skip my visits today and take you up onto the Roman wall instead. We can walk along the top and pretend we're legionnaires on the look-out.'

'That sounds fine to me. Do you think Madam might manage a couple of sandwiches and a flask of tea for us?'

She nodded. 'I've already asked her. She said it's all right, so long as we don't mind thin ham with just a scrape of marge on one slice, and none on the other. And no sugar in the tea in the thermos.'

'Anyone would think there was a war on,' Farquhar said.

Josie stood up. 'I'm going to get my coat,' she said. 'Perhaps you'd better bring yours too. It can get chilly up on the moors. Meet me in the car park out at the back in five minutes.'

Farquhar got his greatcoat and walked down the narrow stairs from his room to the rear door. Stepping into the car park, he stopped short in amazement. Josie, dressed in khaki riding breeches and a brown leather jacket, was sitting astride a green camouflaged motorbike with its army number painted in white on the petrol tank.

'What did you expect, Captain?' she called mockingly. 'A Humber staff car flying a pennant? Sorry, one of those would never get me down the farm tracks around here. The army lets the Ministry of Food have their old bikes; that's how I got hold of this one. Our sandwiches and thermos are in the haversack on the step beside you. Put it on and get on the pillion behind me.'

She briskly kick-started the engine. Farquhar had never been on a motorbike in his life as his mother considered them highly dangerous. Still, it couldn't be more scary than parachuting and a month ago he'd not done that either. He took off his officer's cap, tucked it inside his jacket and slipped the straps of the haversack over his shoulders. He swung his leg over the rear saddle and put his arms round Josie's waist, gripping her more firmly than was necessary. She appeared not to notice as she twisted the throttle open. The bike swept round the car park in a wide circle, roared down the narrow passage at the side of the pub and out onto Wylam High Street.

There was little traffic on the long straight road heading west towards Carlisle; the noise of the bike's engine made conversation impossible but Farquhar didn't care. Josie's long brown hair was blowing back into his face and he couldn't have been happier. After twenty minutes the bike slowed and swung up a narrow lane. At the top Josie steered onto a patch of grass and nudged Farquhar with her elbow. He got off the pillion feeling slightly sore. The bike's lack of springing had made it a hard ride. Josie put it back into gear and rode it into a clump of bushes out of sight. The engine spluttered and died; the sudden silence was wonderful.

'This is where we start marching, Captain,' she said with a smile as she emerged from the bushes. 'The bike will be safe in there. I've taken the rotor arm out.'

Farquhar followed her through a small white gate a short distance down the lane. Immediately beyond lay the crumbling remains of Emperor Hadrian's wall. Six or more feet wide at the base it was built of blocks of squared stone and stood about five feet high. It stretched in a sweeping line across the moor into the misty distance where it disappeared to the west over a ridge.

'According to the book when the Romans built it two thousand years ago it was twenty feet or more high,' Josie announced. 'Most of the farmhouses I visit around here are built of stone pinched from it a couple of centuries ago. The folk around here used the wall like a quarry in those days. Some of the windowsills and door lintels were once Roman altars. Come on, we'll get on top. There's a thick layer of nice springy turf to walk on.'

After two hours of walking they stopped for their picnic. Above wide moors the pale blue sky was vast, speckled with high scudding clouds. Josie pointed to a dark line on the northern horizon. 'That's the Cheviot Hills,' she informed him. 'Beyond them is bonnie Scotland. And there, away to the south, you're looking at the hills of the Lake District.'

To the west the wall went on; just beyond where they were standing it plunged into a steep valley, climbing again on the far side. On the floor of the valley nestled the stone outlines of a small square fort that had once stood against the wall.

'That was a mile-castle,' Josie told him, nodding down at the ruins. 'There were ninety of them, one for every Roman mile between the Tyne and the Solway. Can you imagine what it was like for the poor old legionnaires, patrolling up here in all weathers? How they must have missed the Italian sunshine. And the wine, of course. According to the book, to warm themselves up they used to roll naked in beds of nettles.'

A couple of hours later they found a grassy bank sheltered from the wind by the wall. They sat side by side and Josie divided the sandwiches into equal piles. They took turns drinking tea from the screw top of the thermos, eating in silence and looking out over the rolling landscape from their high viewpoint. Farquhar watched Josie closely but to his disappointment she paid him little attention. Most of the time she seemed unaware of his presence. Instead she peered keenly about, shading her eyes against the sun, watching the birds wheeling overhead and a distant shepherd and his dog herding a flock of sheep. When she finally spoke her words came as a shock.

'Were you in France, with the BEF?' she asked.

Farquhar shook his head. 'No, I only got my call-up papers a few months ago. I'd been to university and could read and do sums, so they made me a captain.' He sensed his lie had suddenly opened a gap between them and he dared not look at her in case she saw the guilt in his eyes.

'My brother was there,' Josie said, 'in the infantry, like you. He was badly wounded at Dunkirk and cannot walk. A shell landed close to him and he has shrapnel in both lungs. The X-rays show one piece is too close to his heart ever to be taken out. I suppose it'll kill him, eventually.' She sat silent for a full minute, plucking at tufts of wiry grass. 'He went through all that,' she said quietly, 'suffering so much. And all I do to win the war is look for hens' eggs.'

Farquhar sat rigid, waiting for the questions that were already screaming in his head. 'What about you, Captain?' she's going to ask me. 'You're not really just a pen pusher, are you? Surely not. I bet you've done some really exciting things. Go on. Tell me about them'. But the minutes passed and she said nothing as he sat staring at the distant Cheviots.

'Come on,' Josie said after a while. 'We'd better start walking back. The bike has probably been pinched by now. I've just remembered I left the rotor arm lying on the seat.'

The landlady was hanging out washing in a corner of the car park when the bike turned in off the High Street. She greeted them with a wave. 'I've put you both at the same table for dinner tonight,' she called, giving them a shrewd smile. 'Seeing you've become friends, I thought it's only right!'

It was a pleasant, moonlit evening so after dinner – cold roast beef and veg followed by rice pudding, exactly the same as the night before – they declined the landlady's offer of coffee in the residents' lounge and went for a stroll instead. Farquhar felt more relaxed than he had been during their walk along the wall. Josie was not inquisitive and had seemed unconcerned at his lack of active service. Eventually he would tell her about

France and the plane crash. But not tonight. There were other, more pleasant things to talk about.

'I think it would be better if we walked hand in hand,' he said, grinning along at her. 'If the locals see us together like this they might think you've just picked me up on the corner.'

'Oh, Captain, you are forward,' Josie giggled. 'But I forgive you.' She took hold of his hand and gave it a squeeze.

Wylam's main street led downhill through the village, turning onto a bridge at the bottom. They stopped in the middle, leaning against the parapet and listening to the dark water surging below. It reminded Farquhar of the bridge in France, Pierre throttling the German guard. The memories were suddenly sharp and disturbing.

'I enjoyed this morning,' he said, pushing aside the bad memories.

'Me too,' Josie agreed. Her voice was soft and warm in the darkness. 'It was lovely. But something's been worrying me. You hardly spoke as we walked back to the bike. And you were almost totally silent at dinner. Have I said something to upset you? I'm sorry if I did.'

'No, not at all. I'm the one who should apologize. I couldn't stop thinking about your brother and all he has gone through.'

She shrugged. 'Not everyone can be a hero.'

Farquhar said nothing, just stood holding her hand. In the station at the far end of the bridge a locomotive hooted and clanked as it moved off into the darkness; a noisy army lorry with dimmed lights rumbled past behind them.

'A penny for them,' Josie said. 'A penny for those big manly thoughts that are going through your head at this very moment. Do they concern me, by any chance?'

He shook his head. 'No. Well, yes. Partly.'

'You're thinking of someone else?'

'No, there is no one except you.'

'What is it then?' she asked softly.

He paused, unsure of how to begin. *It's against all the rules. The colonel warned me to keep my mouth shut. Like the slogans on the posters say:* 'You Never Know Who's Listening.' 'Guard Your Tongue.' 'Careless Talk Costs Lives.' 'Trust No one.'

'Is not telling the whole truth as bad as lying?' he asked.

Josie sighed. 'You're married,' she said dully.

'No, I'm not. But there is something I've not told you.'

'What is it?'

'It's to do with the war. Something I'm involved in. I'm not supposed to talk about it.'

'Don't then, if it will get you into trouble.'

'It won't. I know you won't say anything.'

'You don't have to be a hero. I like you very much exactly as you are.'

'Listen. Don't say anything, Josie, please. Just listen. I'm not an infantry officer; I'm not even in the army. I've never been to Norfolk. I'm a chemical engineer so I know about explosives.'

'I don't want to hear any more, Peter. Please, stop now.'

'I want you to know. A couple of weeks ago I was parachuted into occupied France to blow up a railway bridge.'

'My God,' she whispered. 'You shouldn't be telling me this.'

'I was sent here to be out of the way. I imagine most of the officers the landlady thinks come to see tanks are here for the same reason.'

'I really don't want to hear any more. Stop now. Please!'

'There's not much more to tell. I may be sent me back to France soon. It didn't matter yesterday. Now I've met you it's the last thing on earth I want.'

Josie shivered and he put his arm round her. She rested her head on his shoulder. 'Let's go back,' she said softly. 'I want you to hold me close.'

'Just give me time for a quick bath,' she whispered as they reached the Bull. 'The water will probably be cold, so I shan't be long. Wait ten minutes, then come up.' She squeezed his hand and went upstairs.

He had a whisky at the bar then went upstairs. Her bedroom door was slightly ajar; he pushed it open and stepped inside. There was total darkness; he felt on the wall for the light switch and clicked it on. The curtains were drawn, but the bed cover was undisturbed. She must still be in the bath, he thought, turning to go and find her. At the door he was suddenly aware of the total emptiness of the room. He wrenched open both doors of the heavy oak wardrobe: the shelves were bare, on the rail the wire hangers hung empty. He stood helpless and unbelieving then stumbled down the passage to the bathroom. It was dark and empty, cold and unused.

'Josie! Where are you? Please, where?' he called. But there was only silence.

He walked slowly back to the room and sat on her bed, lost and alone. He had no idea how long he was there. Eventually he got up and walked in a daze down the back stairs to the car park and saw by the light of the moon that her motorbike had gone. Perhaps, he thought illogically, if he went back to her room, and stood where she had stood, he would understand what had happened. He went back upstairs. After a minute, alone in the dark, the idea came to him that she may have received an urgent call to do with her work and had to leave at short notice. A crisis in the egg supply industry? His lip curled involuntarily as his mind filled with self-disgust at his own stupidity.

Hope flickered for another instant. Perhaps someone in her family, her mother perhaps, had taken ill, and she had rushed home to be with her. But that too was nonsense. She would have come down to the bar, asked him to go with her. And anyway, how could she have received such a call? The only phone in the pub was on the bar counter and it had not rung while he was there and she was supposed to be in the bath. The landlady would have told him if there had been a message left for her. Slowly his mind accepted the only possible explanation: he faced a hard, terrible truth. Josie had got what she wanted from him. Instead of going for a bath, she had crept down the back stairs with her things and pushed the motorbike down the alley beside the pub. She must have started it on the freewheel, releasing the clutch when she was on the hill and out of earshot. She had disappeared like a thief in the night, probably laughing at how easy it had been to fool him into talking about his real job.

He walked slowly downstairs to the bar and asked the landlady for a large whisky. She hesitated for a moment but on seeing the dazed look on his face seemed to realize it was no ordinary request. As she handed him the glass, the phone suddenly began ringing, a jarring disturbing noise. She picked it up.

'Black Bull speaking. Captain Farquhar? Yes, he's here. Hold on.' There was a strange look on her face as she handed him the phone. 'It's for you.'

'Hello. Farquhar here,' he said, hoping desperately it was Josie calling to give an obvious explanation. In five seconds everything would be clear....

'Farquhar!' Colonel Fraser's voice was crisp and brutal. 'You stupid bloody idiot. There's a train from Wylam in twenty-five minutes. It connects at Newcastle for London. Be on it. You'll be met.'

The line went dead and Farquhar handed the telephone back to the landlady. She had hovered close by and must have heard what the colonel had barked.

'I have to leave at once,' he heard himself say. 'Please have my bill ready. The young lady left earlier.'

'She came to the kitchen to pay me when you were here in the bar. She left no message. I thought the two of you must have had a row.'

He shook his head. 'No, not a row. She had to leave suddenly.'

He gulped the last of his whisky and went upstairs to pack.

As he stepped off the train at Kings Cross, two red-capped military policemen seized his arms and frogmarched him along the platform. They steered him wordlessly through an arch to an army staff car parked in a corner of a goods yard. One of the men opened a rear door and thrust him roughly inside. Colonel Fraser sat in the front seat, staring ahead. He did not turn round.

'You're a bastard, Farquhar,' he said evenly. 'You wanted to rut that woman so you made yourself out to be some sort of sodding hero. Your big mouth has already cost lives. There was a message from France this morning. The Gestapo took Pierre and his daughter and shot them both on the farm dung heap last night. I hope you're proud of yourself. Last night you told the girl you weren't in the army. Well, you bloody well are now. I've had your exemption torn up. From this minute you're an infantry private and I shall personally see that's what you stay if this war lasts fifty bloody years. And, when it's over there's not a university in the land that will touch you with a bargepole. Get out of my car before I vomit.'

In the goods yard one of the policemen took his officer's cap while the other stripped him of his jacket. Bare headed and in shirtsleeves, he was marched across to a three-ton army lorry standing with its engine running. Farquhar climbed over the tailgate into the dark interior and the lorry roared out of the station into the early morning traffic. There were no seats and he stood clutching the metal frames supporting the canvas cover.

The Royal Norfolk captain's uniform, a few days' relaxation at the Black Bull, Josie looking for eggs – they had just been stage props, all part of the colonel's pantomime, a farce aimed at trapping him. Josie had let him fall in love with her; an easy task as she didn't have to try. Her job had been to see if he talked about France. He couldn't bring himself to hate her; he wondered if she had felt love for him. She had warned him not to go on. He had opened his heart to her; perhaps as she was on the verge of telling him the truth, that she had been sent to trick him....He stood swaying, staring out of the back of the lorry at the retreating view of Euston Road, wondering where he was being taken.

Chapter Ten

A gusty October wind threw rain against the windows and ripped leaves from the trees in the square outside. Moody and restless, Magda moved from room to room, adjusting a curtain here, an ornament there. She did not allow her thoughts to dwell on the past; the misery of the present filled her mind. On a table lay a scattered pile of magazines sent by Blanche in the faint hope of brightening her morbid thoughts. Slumped in an armchair she picked up a recent copy of *Verve*, the Parisian arts and literature magazine, well known for its bold covers and the quality of its artistic critiques. She was flipping through the pages when she found herself staring at a painting by Pierre Bonnard of a villa in Estoril in Portugal. She leapt to her feet and ran to Carol's study.

'Darling!' she yelled as she flung the door open and rushed to his side waving the magazine. 'Look what I've found! It's meant for us. A lovely house in a neutral country, far from Paris and the horrid Germans. Darling, please, please, phone someone to buy it for us. No matter what it costs! This instant. Please, darling....'

Carol ordered his solicitors to act immediately. A private detective was dispatched to Estoril to identify and investigate the villa and ten days later his report was on Carol's desk. It included a dozen black and white photographs surreptitiously taken of external views of the house, its gracious gardens and sweeping lawns. The most exciting news of all was contained in the report's final paragraph. The detective had discovered the present owner, an elderly countess, was infirm and about to move into a nursing home. The villa was therefore likely to come onto the market in the near future. Great interest was expected among those with the means to purchase this wonderful property. Magda was delirious with excitement. At her insistence Carol instructed his solicitors to place an open offer for the villa as soon as its sale was announced. Two weeks of agonizing waiting passed before news was received that the son of the countess had been granted full legal powers to handle his mother's affairs. He was demanding an outrageous price for the house. Despite Magda's pleading,

Carol, ever cautious where money was involved, refused to be rushed. Through his solicitors he extracted a promise from the selling agent that a sale would not be agreed until he was offered the final option to buy. This eminently suitable situation was short-lived when it transpired the agent had given the same undertaking to at least two other potential purchasers.

'You must take the matter to court, darling,' Magda insisted. 'You are a king and cannot be made a fool of in this way.'

Since the villa was in Portugal the case was heard in Lisbon. The judge, after listening to two days of argument, ruled that in fairness to all parties the villa should be sold in open auction rather than by private treaty.

Magda was outraged. 'You, a noble king, bidding against people in trade! The whole affair is preposterous! That fool of a judge must have been drunk. You must appeal.'

Carol was weary of the whole business but due to Magda's persistence had become firmly mired in it. He consulted an international lawyer who studied the case papers and came to the conclusion that the ruling did not carry the force of law. In his learned opinion, which came at a very high price, the judge's decision had been merely a recommendation. Its intention was to bring the parties to negotiation, a practice common in Portuguese courts.

'Negotiation, my arse!' Magda snorted when Carol showed her the lawyer's letter. The worry over the villa had caused her to lose her appetite and she was again thin and gaunt. Carol, much concerned, took decisive action. Without telling her he found a stockbroker who specialized in the international property market and instructed him to discover the cost of closing the deal immediately without involving other potential bidders. The avaricious son was discreetly approached. The price he demanded was four times the highest valuation yet placed on the property. Resigned to the inevitable, Carol instructed his Zurich bank to place the money in a separate account, payable to the owner only when the contract was signed and delivered.

Three weeks later the deeds were delivered to Quai Voltaire. Carol ordered an enormous bouquet of flowers brought directly to his study. He buried the deeds in the blooms and called for Magda. She tore open the bulky envelope and gave a shriek of delight at the contents. Carol pointed to the covering letter from his solicitor confirming that she was the legal owner of the villa. No one could deprive her of it after his death.

A chartered aeroplane, its flight authorized by the German authorities, flew Carol and Magda from Paris to Lisbon. A week later they moved into the villa in Estoril. The town, formerly an obscure fishing village, had become the home of several fabulously rich deposed families, including King Umberto II of Italy and the Count of Paris. It was noted for its graceful avenues of palms, numerous spectacular golf courses, and an internationally famous casino. The villa, like several others in Estoril, was sumptuous, surrounded by sweeping lawns and beautiful sheltered gardens overlooking the Atlantic. The climate was Mediterranean with blissful summers and gentle winters. Life, Magda decided, could not be more idyllic than this.

Chapter Eleven

Grigor found life on board the *Milos* surprisingly comfortable. The crew were friendly and the food well cooked. He rarely visited his cabin below the bridge; it was merely a rusty box with a porthole. The trunk and his suitcase were securely stowed in the single locked cupboard. One of the crew rigged a shady tarpaulin for him and he spent every day in an armchair on the fore-hatch enjoying the soft Aegean breeze and reading through a pile of tattered American detective novels from the saloon bookcase. At night he slept on a mattress on deck beside the off-duty watch.

Shortly before sunset of the fifth day out from Canakkale, under a spectacular peach and mauve evening sky, a German U-boat rose like a monstrous grey shark out of the depths close by the *Milos*. Water was still streaming from her ballast tanks when figures appeared on the conning tower. A large swastika ensign was hoisted and a sailor could be seen fitting a heavy machine gun to the tower casing. A long burst of red tracer shells arched like fireworks across the bow of the *Milos*. The crew shouted in alarm; from the bridge came the jangle of a bell when the master rang down to the engine room for full astern to bring the ship to a stop. She lay wallowing in a gently heaving sea as a rubber dinghy was launched off the deck of the U-boat. Four men clambered down into it and began rowing across to her. A rope ladder was dropped and three German sailors, each brandishing a Schmeisser machine gun, followed by a lieutenant gripping a heavy pistol, scrambled on board. The officer, blond, blue-eyed and baby-faced, exuded a distinct air of menace. He fired two shots in the air for no obvious reason and looked contemptuously round the deck. 'Does anyone here speak German?' he demanded.

Grigor stepped forward. 'I do, sir,' he said, speaking in a rough Hamburg accent.

'Are you the master?'

'No, sir. That's him up there in the wheelhouse.'

'Everyone is to muster on deck,' the lieutenant ordered. 'You will stay at my side and translate as necessary. Try any tricks and I'll shoot you in the guts and have you thrown over the side to feed the sharks. Understand?'

'I understand, sir.'

The master came down from the bridge and Grigor translated the officer's orders into Arabic. The crew lined up against the port rail.

'No one is to speak or attempt to leave the deck,' the lieutenant barked. 'Anyone who does so will be instantly shot.'

Grigor repeated the order to the crew adding, 'The leprous son of a pig means it, lads. Go along with what he says for now.'

'Open the holds,' the lieutenant snapped. 'I want to see what you are carrying.'

The German sailors stood over them with guns cocked as the deck hands removed the hatch covers to reveal the cargo.

'What's in those?' the officer snarled, waving his pistol at the barrels.

'Turkish figs for Cyprus, sir.'

'Open them up and strew the contents across the deck. They may be concealing arms.'

You stupid Nazi bastard, Grigor thought. *The crown jewels of Romania are under your big German snout and you are worrying about figs.*

'I want to see the manifest. And the log.'

Grigor led the way to the bridge where the master laid out the ship's books. They were written in his scrawled hand, intelligible only to a native-born Turkish seaman. The lieutenant nevertheless pursed his lips and made a pretence of studying them.

'Where is the radio?' he demanded.

'On the bulkhead, sir,' Grigor replied.

The lieutenant levelled his pistol and fired a shot into the set which disintegrated in a shower of sparks. He walked out onto the open end of the bridge and emptied the remainder of the magazine at the ship's only boat, shattering the keel.

'You are now without radio or lifeboat,' he sneered. 'If I find anything illegal in the cargo, or if anyone causes trouble, I shall return to the U-boat and order this rust bucket to be torpedoed. She will sink in minutes and none of you will ever be seen or heard of again.'

'May I speak, sir?' Grigor asked.

'Shut your mouth.'

'The matter is urgent, sir.'

'One more word and I'll blow your head off. You will return with me to the U-boat. Your German is too good for a foreign sailor. You are a spy. My captain will wish to question you before your execution.'

In the dying minutes of daylight, as the crew of the *Milos* began re-packing the figs, the dinghy with five men in her was rowed back to the U-boat. The crew hauled them onto the narrow slatted deck where the lieutenant jabbed his pistol into Grigor's ribs and ordered him to climb the conning tower ladder. On the bridge the U-boat captain, cap perched on the back of his head and a heavy pair of binoculars slung round his neck, glared at Grigor.

'Why have you brought this flotsam on board my boat?' he asked the lieutenant.

'He speaks very good German, sir. I suspect he is a spy.'

'He is correct,' Grigor said coldly, abandoning the Hamburg accent he had used on the *Milos* and addressing the captain directly in perfect German.

'I attempted to inform your lieutenant of the fact but he told me to shut my mouth or I would be shot. I would not travel on a pigboat like the *Milos* for the good of my health, or for the pleasure of the company of her rabble crew.'

He clicked his heels and gave a slight bow. 'I am Colonel Werner Bergholz of the Abwehr, Captain.'

He chose the Abwehr, the German Intelligence organization, as his employer since their operatives rarely went to sea. His function and motives would likely be a mystery to a naval mind, rendering interrogation difficult. The captain stared hard at him before switching his gaze to the lieutenant who stood gaping open-mouthed at his side.

'Take him below,' he ordered. Grigor noted his tone was less harsh and carried an air of curiosity. 'I shall interview him in the control room.'

The hatch cover at the rear of the conning tower was hinged open. The lieutenant led the way down a vertical steel ladder with Grigor following and the captain close behind. The control room was brightly lit and crammed with a tightly packed array of pipes, tubes and trunking. There was a confusion of heavy cables and coloured wiring, and a multitude of valves, gauges, indicator dials and controls. Like the trunk of a shining steel tree, the periscope rose from the floor into the dark recesses of the conning tower above. There was a constant roar from the ventilation system; a distant rumble and vibration underfoot reached the compartment from the diesel engines idly revolving at the stern to charge the batteries. Despite the draught sweeping through the boat, a sickly aromatic cocktail of oil fumes, unwashed human odours and rotting food pervaded the air.

'Take the bridge,' the captain snapped to the lieutenant who squeezed past wordlessly and disappeared back up the ladder.

'Chief!'

'*Kaleun!*' came the reply, the naval abbreviation of *Kapitänleutnant*. The steel door leading aft was clipped open; the chief engineer, unshaven and wearing oil-stained overalls, appeared in the opening.

'I am not to be disturbed whilst I interview this prisoner. Clear the forward accommodation and keep everyone out of earshot.'

'*Jawohl, Kaleun!*'

The chief hurried forward; his voice could be heard rousing the men from their bunks in the bow. Half a dozen scuttled past naked, clutching towels and bits of clothing to themselves. While this activity was in progress Grigor took the opportunity to study the captain. He was far removed from the smart Aryan figure depicted on propaganda posters as the war-winning U-boat commander. Squat and dark haired with piggy features, his head was set on a tremendously thick neck and broad shoulders. He looked more like a Dortmund street fighter than a naval officer. This is not a man to be trifled with, Grigor decided.

'So, you are a spy, Colonel Bergholz,' the commander said quietly when the last man had disappeared through the hatch.

'That is so, Captain,' Grigor replied. 'I am on a secret mission approved by Grand Admiral Doenitz.'

The mention of the Commander-in-Chief of the German submarine service failed to impress the captain in the way Grigor had hoped. Instead of showing deference, he smiled. Grigor realized he had made a serious error. Doenitz was known to have a strong paternal interest in his U-boat crews and was on first-name terms with each of his commanders.

'Indeed. One of my Uncle Karl's spies,' the captain said, smiling. 'And what proof do you have of the truth of this claim?'

'One does not carry identification when working undercover, Captain.'

'I am aware of that, naturally. But you must have a means of confirming who you are. For instance, how do you communicate with base?' The crooked smile remained on his face.

'A device built into the radio of the *Milos* enabled me to transmit reports to Berlin on a discreet wavelength,' Grigor replied, snatching a reply out of nowhere. 'Your lieutenant destroyed it, seriously compromising my operation.'

'What is, or was, its purpose?'

'I cannot disclose details, Captain.'

'I am the commander of a U-boat on active service, Colonel Bergholz. My integrity is beyond doubt. If you are what you claim to be there is no possible reason for you to withhold information from me. Not when your life depends upon it. I assure you it does.'

'Very well, Captain. I accept your word. The Führer sees the war in the Mediterranean as pivotal to victory, in the east as well as the west. Our Italian allies are fighting the British in Egypt. The Greeks oppose us and must be crushed. I have been sent to investigate British defences on Crete with a view to our invasion of the island in the near future. Once it is captured we shall dominate the eastern Mediterranean.' He hesitated, as if unsure how to proceed. 'You may shoot me if you wish, Captain. It is a professional risk I am prepared to face on behalf of my country. However, I must bring to your attention a matter of greater importance to Germany than my life.'

'Go on.'

'The *Milos* is a Turkish vessel, registered in Istanbul. As you are aware Turkey has so far remained neutral in the present war. The Führer is keen that she should join us in our struggle. You found the *Milos* in international waters and were justified under the rules of war in stopping her and investigating if she was carrying cargo useful to your enemy. But, as your over-zealous lieutenant soon discovered, the *Milos* is carrying nothing but barrels of figs for the civilian population of Crete. She ought to have been allowed to proceed without further hindrance. Instead your officer chose to destroy her radio and wreck the ship's only lifeboat. These actions imperil the lives of the crew and safety of the vessel. It is a situation unlikely to endear Germany to the Turks. In addition, my mission has been seriously compromised. The lieutenant may have to justify his conduct at a court martial.'

'You talk like a sea lawyer, Colonel Bergholz. No doubt you have a solution in mind.'

'Allow me to go free, Captain. When the *Milos* docks in Crete I shall visit the Italian consulate and make use of the facilities we operate from their premises. I shall report to headquarters in Berlin that the severing of wireless contact arose from an electrical fault. I will, if you agree, say that your U-boat stopped and searched the ship and that your radio officer did his utmost to carry out a repair but was unable to do so for the lack of a vital part. I will see that a new radio and lifeboat are provided for the ship and with luck this unfortunate incident will be quickly forgotten. German relations with Turkey will remain on their present friendly footing.'

Am I talking too much, being too glib for my own good? It's as well night has fallen; the boat's been on the surface with the conning tower hatch open for almost half an hour. If it had been daylight a British aircraft could have seen her and attacked.

'Do you wish me to continue, Captain?' he asked.

'Please do, Colonel. You tell an intriguing tale.'

'If you kill me, my reports of observed shipping movements will cease. Aircraft will be sent out from our Italian bases to search for the *Milos*. My superiors in Berlin will wonder if my mission has been uncovered, or the ship sunk, or if I have been taken for questioning. I am expected in Crete. If the *Milos* arrives without me, the Italian consulate will immediately inform Berlin. The master will report details of the incident to the owners and the news will not be favourably received by the Turks.'

Grigor felt he had recovered from his earlier mistake. His growing confidence was boosted by the recollection of the success that had followed the lies he had told Günter. The captain looked hard at him; Grigor looked steadily back. The wait seemed interminable.

'You may return to your ship, Colonel,' the captain said at last. 'I find it difficult to believe you are a genuine spy. But your assessment of the political reaction to the unfortunate zeal of my officer is quite correct. As you rightly say, it will not endear the Turkish government to our cause. I could torpedo the *Milos* and she would sink without trace. But I am a professional sailor and have no wish to destroy ships that are not harming my country, or kill honest seamen who are not active participants in the war.'

'Thank you, Captain. Perhaps when ultimate victory is ours we shall meet again under happier circumstances. Until then may I wish you good luck, and safe harbours.'

The dinghy took Grigor back on the *Milos* where the crew greeted him with a cheer and the master warmly embraced him. He turned to the rail; the U-boat was just visible in the darkness, sliding under the sea in a swirl of turbulent foam. He allowed himself a long sigh of relief, knowing how fortunate he had been. Had the lieutenant carried out a proper search the crowns would have been found and his lies to the commander would have been of no avail. As an afterthought he wondered if it was just possible that Hitler was contemplating an invasion of Crete.

Ten days later, after delivering the figs to Heraklion and picking up a cargo of tobacco leaves, the *Milos* sailed into the port of Alexandria. When the harbour master came on board, Grigor arranged and paid for the delivery of a new radio and lifeboat. The master and crew stood in a line on the deck to wish him goodbye. They regarded him as their hero since, by means unknown to them, he had persuaded the U-boat commander to spare their ship. The master, seeing no reason to disclose to her owners that he had carried a fare-paying passenger on the voyage from Turkey, had not entered Grigor's name in the log. It was a helpful omission. When he stepped ashore, his final link with Turkey was broken. *The Gestapo will never find me now*, he thought.

Passengers rarely disembarked at the commercial docks so there were no customs procedures at the exit. Grigor found a flat trolley outside one of the sheds and wheeled his trunk and suitcase through the open gates. A taxi took him to the main railway station. After a two-hour train journey across the desert, he arrived in Cairo.

For half an hour Grigor stood watching the left luggage store at Cairo central station. It appeared well organized and efficiently run. Baggage receipts passed to and fro smoothly and luggage was efficiently wheeled into, or retrieved from, a cavernous storeroom behind the long, well-staffed counter. He signalled to a porter who carried his trunk to the desk. The clerk stuck a numbered label on top and handed Grigor the corresponding receipt. The trunk was wheeled away and Grigor walked out of the station carrying only his suitcase.

It is an Arab maxim that Alexandria belongs to the Mediterranean whilst Cairo is owned by Egypt. The city lay sweltering in the pitiless oven-hot heat of the sun. Traffic was at a standstill and the streets choked with people. On the crowded pavements bazaar owners pressed their wares; beggars scarred by leprosy cried for alms, plucking at the robes of passers-by. Agile children twisted and turned through the throng, selling water and trinkets. Urged on by the sticks and harsh shouts of their drivers, heavily laden camels and donkeys pulled carts piled high with goods, forcing their way through the mass of humanity and traffic. The horns of buses, lorries and cars blew ceaselessly in a hideous cacophony. The stench of the east, a compound of animal and vegetable marinating in cloying heat, hung in the foul exhausted air. At the taxi rank under the station portico, Grigor asked a driver to take him to a good quality hotel. The man shook his head.

'That will be difficult, *effendi*,' he warned. 'Due to the war Cairo is as full as a pomegranate ready to burst. There are few rooms to be had. It would be better for you to become Bedouin and go to live in a tent in the desert.'

'I have important business here,' Grigor snapped, speaking the Arabic of an educated upper-class Egyptian. 'I need somewhere to meet my clients.'

The driver sucked in his breath through his brown-stained teeth. 'I understand, *effendi*. The best hotel in Cairo is Shepheards but you will not get a room there these days. I will take you to the Damietta. It is expensive but comfortable. Before the war it was popular with elderly English ladies seeking young men. The manager may have a spare room although he will charge the maximum rate.'

It took over an hour to reach the relative calm of the Damietta, a graceful old building overlooking the tree-lined Nile. Groves of shady palms overhanging the quietly flowing river brought much-needed relief from the heat. At the reception desk Grigor enquired if there was a vacant room. The suave manager, with a pencil-line moustache and hair like black patent leather, demanded to see his papers. Grigor presented the permit Magda had obtained from the Turkish ambassador.

The manager merely glanced at it and shook his head. 'That is not acceptable,' he said dismissively. 'It is not an official document. Cairo is far from Istanbul and I speak not only in terms of distance. You Ottomans are detested here having ruled cruelly over us for three centuries. We Egyptians have long memories. If you require proof, go and look at our pyramids.'

Grigor ignored the insult. 'I have business in Cairo, sir,' he explained patiently. 'And I am no Turk. My father was a wealthy Lebanese merchant and my mother an Arabian princess.'

The manager shrugged then paused as he crafted words to embellish his fleeting moment of triumph. 'Even if your royal mother were the Queen Cleopatra herself, we would be unable to accommodate her without notice,' he replied dryly. 'A reservation is essential. The Damietta is not an establishment that caters for casual travellers. I regret I cannot help you.' His tone indicated his sorrow was merely fleeting.

'My business is very important,' Grigor insisted.

The manager gave an indifferent smile and hunched his shoulders, spreading his hands outwards in a gesture of helplessness. Recognizing the international signal, Grigor took out his wallet and wordlessly extracted three one hundred dollar notes. He laid them on the counter. The manager slid the hotel register over them with practised ease.

'Do please forgive me, sir,' he exclaimed, suddenly deferential as he deftly removed the notes and slipped them into his trouser pocket. 'A thousand apologies! I have just remembered. A small room on the top floor was vacated only this morning. It is available for the next three nights. Although not of our usual superior quality, you may find it acceptable in this present emergency.'

Grigor smiled his relief. 'You are most accommodating,' he said. 'I will take it. Thank you.'

*

The room was tiny. There was barely enough space for the single bed and a small chest of drawers. It was immediately below the eaves and very hot. A small barred window facing a blank stone wall across a narrow gap completed the impression of a prison cell. Grigor stripped and lay naked on the bed, bathed in sweat. *I must find somewhere better than this. Shepheards is where I'd like to be but the taxi driver said it was impossible. Well, I'll see. I'm glad I've not got the trunk. I couldn't have hauled that about with me.*

He drifted off to sleep, waking an hour later. The corridor outside his room led to a dingy bathroom. Ignoring the cockroaches scuttling across the tiled floor he showered, changed and went down to the lounge for a drink before dinner.

The following morning after breakfast he handed in his key at reception. The manager was absent and Grigor told the clerk on duty he would be out for the remainder of the day but would return for dinner.

'May I suggest you turn left when you leave, sir?' the man murmured respectfully. He spoke with an educated accent and was clearly trying to be helpful. 'There are very beautiful views across the Nile in that direction. Also you will find the best hotels in Cairo there. You may be lucky and find one with a cancellation to suit you.'

Grigor nodded his appreciation. On leaving the hotel he took the route the clerk had recommended. The views across the river were spectacular. Laden *feluccas*, each with the traditional forward raking mast and broad lateen sail, glided effortlessly past. It was a sight far removed from the traffic bedlam in the city streets less than a mile away. Grigor, his mood elated, strolled contentedly along the riverside path. In the distance the Shepheards Hotel sign was clearly visible above the rooftops. Internationally renowned for comfort and opulence, in keeping with its distinguished reputation the prices charged were notoriously high, deterring all but the wealthiest patrons. To Grigor this was a distinct advantage since he had ample money and anticipated no difficulty in securing a room to his taste. On turning a corner the hotel stood in front of him. But he stopped short when he saw the wooden barricades and tall sandbagged enclosures surrounding it. Armed soldiers stood on guard and others patrolled the street outside.

'You, 'op it,' a voice snapped behind him as he stood staring. 'No civvies allowed 'ere. Orficers only. Find somewhere else to flog your dirty postcards.'

Grigor turned. A British soldier, in khaki shorts and jacket, was gripping a rifle with a bayonet attached. Below his steel helmet his glowering face was badly scorched by the sun.

'I'm sorry, Officer,' Grigor said, giving a friendly smile.

'Orficer?' the soldier snapped. 'Don't come that bullshit wi' me. I'm a soddin' private. Now be orf, afore I stick this bayonet up yer arse.'

'I'm sorry,' Grigor repeated, still smiling. He had understood little of the soldier's strange dialect but his tone and accompanying gestures left little doubt as to his meaning.

'I have an appointment with Captain Murphy,' he said, giving the name of a character in one of the novels he had read on the *Milos*. 'I was told I'd find him here, at Shepheards Hotel.'

'It ain't a 'otel no more. It's the orficers' fuckin' mess an' army HQ. Got any papers?'

'I left them in my hotel for safekeeping. I brought this document for Captain Murphy. It explains why I wish to see him.'

He held out the Turkish travel permit written in Ottoman script. The soldier examined it, frowning and obviously puzzled.

'What's this?' he asked. 'Fuckin' Chinese? Who are you lookin' for? Murphy, was it? Bloody Irish, I suppose. Never 'eard of him. What lot's he with? Hey, Sarge!' he called over his shoulder. 'Come and see what you make o' this geyser.'

The sergeant sauntered over and wasted no time in coming to a decision. 'Lock the bugger up. And see this paper gets to the major *pronto*. Let him decide what to do with Alfonso here.'

'Sir, I protest!' Grigor exclaimed. 'The document is signed by His Excellency the Turkish ambassador to Romania. It asks that I be afforded every assistance. You are treating me as if I were a common criminal. My mother was an Arabian princess, my father a wealthy Lebanese merchant.'

'Oh yeah? And I'm the Duke o' soddin' Buccleugh.'

'My name is Grigor. I am an Arab businessman.'

'You look like a bloody Itie to me. I reckon you're one of old Musso's spies. *Comprendo Italiano*? Lock the bastard up, Jim.'

'Forward march,' Jim snapped. 'An' no funny business or I'll spill your guts all over this nice clean pavement.'

They walked through a sandbagged enclosure and into what had been the ornate lobby of Shepheards. Fragments of the hotel's colonial splendour still lingered. Crystal chandeliers hung from the high ceilings and vast murals of Pharaonic themes, faded and dusty, adorned the walls,

'Turn left down that passage,' the soldier ordered, 'An' 'alt at the desk.'

The duty corporal looked up on their approach.

'One for the jug, corp,' Jim announced. 'I caught him sniffin' around outside. Sarge Elliot thinks he's an Itie spy. Speaks English nearly as good as me. Any char goin'?'

'Name and address?' the corporal demanded.

'My name is Grigor. I am staying at the Damietta Hotel.'

The corporal wrote it down. 'Now turn out your pockets. The lot. On the desk, here in front of me.'

He whistled when he saw the thick wallet of notes.

'Not stuck for a few bob then, Mr Grigor,' he remarked. 'Pay well, the Ities, do they? Give me your belt and shoelaces. We can't have you stringing yourself up in your cell. I'd have to write a report.'

The room, or cell according to the corporal, reflected the great superiority of Shepheards over the Damietta. It was spacious and furnished with a large bed, writing desk and chair. There was a tiled bathroom *en suite* with a toilet, washbasin and shower. Grigor lay on the bed trying not to worry about the crowns in the station left-luggage room. It was two hours before the corporal returned. 'Major Howard wants to see you, Alfonso. On your feet. Follow me.'

'Will you return my belt and laces, please,' Grigor asked. He had found it most undignified to clutch his waistband to keep his trousers from falling down whilst shuffling along in unlaced shoes.

'It's standing orders for anyone in custody. Sorry.'

The major's office was on the top floor of the hotel. The wide windows looked over the city rooftops, baking like biscuits in the strong afternoon sun. Major Howard was a stocky, sharp-eyed man with Intelligence Corps shoulder flashes. Grigor's Turkish travel permit lay on the desk in front of him.

'Sit down, please,' he said with cold politeness. 'You gave your name only as Grigor. Who are you? Where are you from?'

'I am Lebanese, sir. I have lived in various parts of Europe, including London, since graduating from Beirut University. My Arabic name is Eban Albaba. Whilst living in Romania I adopted the Russian name of Grigor Grigorovanovich. I became known simply as Grigor.'

The major held up the permit and stared across the desk. 'This is the document you showed to the soldiers who arrested you. A Turkish-speaking officer on my staff has examined it. It is handwritten on Embassy notepaper and apparently signed by His Excellency the Turkish ambassador to Romania. It says: "*All assistance is to be afforded to the bearer who is authorized to travel throughout Turkey without hindrance on confidential government business.*" May I ask how you came by it?'

It was a question Grigor had expected and he gave a considered reply. 'Until recently I held a position in the royal palace in Bucharest as one of

His Majesty's secretaries. When the threatened German invasion forced King Carol to flee, I had to do the same.'

'May I ask why?'

'The king had become unpopular and left Romania. General Antonescu and his army of fascist bullies, the so-called Iron Guard, assumed control. They were about to take reprisals against His Majesty's former supporters. As a member of his household I would have suffered greatly at their hands. I had no choice but to leave.'

'That explains why this document was useful. You have yet to explain how it came into your possession.'

Grigor felt the net closing around him. This was a highly experienced interrogator, shrewd and perceptive. He felt his mouth becoming dry and longed to lick his lips but feared it would make him appear furtive. It was vital to continue to speak in a measured rhythm to avoid giving the impression of over-rehearsed glibness. After a pause he said, 'I had hoped to escape to Turkey, Major. It was neutral and the nearest country offering temporary safety. His Excellency the Turkish ambassador was a frequent visitor to the palace and in my position as a royal secretary I got to know him well. I ventured to ask him for a travel document, explaining why I needed it. I begged him not to insert a specific name as I intended using aliases. The permit he gave me is in your hands.'

Major Howard laid down the document, pressed his fingertips together and stared across the desk. 'I cannot believe an ambassador would show such generosity to a mere secretary. This is much more than a travel permit. It is a *carte blanche* for travel anywhere in Turkey. Did you blackmail him into assisting you?'

Grigor smiled and shook his head. 'No, Major. Blackmail is not in my nature. I regarded him as a friend and he held me in some regard. Over the years I had made certain arrangements on his behalf. I looked upon these as part of my normal duties, not in expectation of reward. Nevertheless His Excellency proved generous in his appreciation.'

'Clearly. What was the nature of these arrangements?'

Grigor hesitated, giving an impression of a reluctance to explain, and took the opportunity to clear his throat.

'You will understand that, as a high-ranking diplomat and strict Muslim, His Excellency was obliged to observe certain rigid conventions. He was however cursed – some would say blessed – by a strong libido despite his advancing years. From time to time he would point out to me a particular lady at court whom he desired sexually. On his behalf I would then negotiate a liaison between them and arrange discreet accommodation in the palace for their rendezvous. For obvious reasons the lady could not visit him at the Embassy or his home. He was a generous man and most courteous. Once a woman had spent an afternoon with him he made no further demands on her.'

'In other words, you were his pimp?'

Grigor sensed the major was trying to anger him. He shook his head and smiled. 'In Romanian court circles such arrangements are, or I should say were, not unusual, Major. Morals in Bucharest high society were much less restrictive than those in force at your Buckingham Palace, for instance. It was public knowledge that the king himself was a great lover of women. His Excellency the ambassador, as befitted his position and circumstances, conducted his affairs with due diplomacy.'

'Very well. Let us proceed with this wonderful tale. King Carol had fled. You were in possession of a permit allowing you complete freedom to travel in Turkey. How did you get there? By magic carpet?'

The blatant scepticism was clearly intended to goad Grigor further. He again smiled and shook his head. 'I had hoped to take the daily ferry from Constanta to Istanbul but I was diverted. Fortunately, and I realize this may sound somewhat far-fetched to your ears, I was able to persuade a Luftwaffe pilot to fly me from an airfield outside Bucharest to Bandirma, on the Turkish coast of the Sea of Marmora.'

'You are correct. No Luftwaffe pilot would agree to such a plan. Unless you were also supplying him with courtesans? '

'No, Major. His name was Lieutenant Günter von Schmelzburg. You may have a German staff list and could check the fact. A Wermacht general introduced me to him so my credentials appeared beyond suspicion. Over lunch I was able to convince him I was a senior Gestapo agent on a secret mission to Turkey. He was desperate to see action before the war ended and I led him to believe that, in return for flying me to Turkey, I could arrange for him to be transferred to a frontline Messerschmitt squadron in northern France. I also offered him an undercover position in the Gestapo.'

'And he was naïve enough to believe these lies?'

'He was only twenty, Major, and very gullible. I can be most persuasive.'

'So it seems.'

'He flew me to Bandirma on the Sea of Marmara in the course of what was officially an engine check flight. I sabotaged his plane so that on the return flight to Bucharest it would crash, killing him. If I had allowed him to return he would have boasted of our arrangement and the Germans, realizing I had made fools of them, would be anxious to capture me. Günter would tell them he had flown me to Turkey and they would have come after me. I could not risk that.'

'How did you arrange for his plane to crash?'

'I dumped the reserve fuel when he was out of the cockpit. I calculated that after leaving me at Bandirma he would be well into his return flight before becoming aware that he had insufficient fuel to get back to base. His plane would crash in the Bulgarian mountains in darkness, killing him.'

Silence followed; Grigor wondered if the major was shocked by the callousness of the plan. It appeared he was. 'That was most ungenerous,' he said coldly, 'after all he had done for you.'

'Fortunes of war, Major. He was a Nazi and I have no regrets.'

'So you reached Bandirma. Go on.' His tone was now openly hostile.

'I caught a train from there to Canakkale. From there I travelled as a passenger in a small steamer, the *Milos*, bound for Crete then Alexandria. En route a German U-boat stopped her and I was arrested but later released. The *Milos* docked at Alexandria yesterday morning. I travelled here to Cairo by train and spent last night at the Damietta Hotel. This morning I was looking for somewhere to live permanently when your soldiers arrested me.'

The major sat looking intently across the desk; his face was a mask. After a long pause he said, 'Have you any credible evidence to substantiate this weird and wonderful tale you have just related?'

'There is the document on your desk.'

'It makes no mention of your name. It could quite easily have been written to assist someone else, perhaps a man you murdered in your attempt to escape. Where is your Romanian passport? As a member of the royal household you would surely have one?'

'I destroyed it since it would be of no use in Turkey.'

'Then how do I know you are who you claim to be? Where is the proof you were ever in Turkey?'

'The master of the *Milos* will prove I boarded at Canakkale. And confirm my arrest by the U-boat crew.'

'An Italian ship could have delivered you to Canakkale.'

'Major, all that I have told you is true,' Grigor insisted.

'Why did the U-boat captain release you? Did you tell him you were a fellow German on a spying mission en route to Cairo?'

'No. I pointed out that *Milos* was a Turkish vessel and neutral. He was not entitled to detain her or me. He agreed and returned me to the ship.'

The major sat silent, staring across desk. Grigor steeled himself to meet his eye without blinking.

'Your English is excellent,' the major said. 'Where did you learn to speak it?' His voice was quiet yet accusative.

'I read modern languages at Beirut University, Major. As I have told you, I lived in London for five years, working as a teacher. I was at the royal court in Bucharest for eight years. I am fluent in German, Italian, French and Arabic, as well as Romanian and English.'

'I see.' The major sat back in his chair, keeping his eyes on Grigor's face. 'I congratulate you on the story you have just told me. It has variety, interest, excitement.' He paused. 'And it is impossible to check. In other words, you have presented the perfect alibi. We've been to the Damietta and cleared your room. Your possessions are now in this building. They have been carefully examined and all is exactly as it should be. Your clothes were made in Bucharest and are of the best quality. There's nothing of interest in your wallet, apart from an ample supply of American dollars and Turkish lira.'

Grigor did not allow his expression to alter despite the alarming news of his room having been searched and possessions seized.

'I was on a high salary,' he said calmly. 'Some time ago I closed my account at the bank in Bucharest and converted the balance to more useful currencies in anticipation of a rapid departure. There was also a large sum of money in my office safe for which I was responsible. I took it. As an English officer and gentleman you will doubtless regard this as looting. But why should I leave it for the Germans? I have committed no crime against the British. There is no reason why you should keep me here. I demand to be released.'

The major shook his head. 'That will not be possible for some time. The fact that all appears normal arouses my suspicions. Everyone has something to hide. Your good friend the ambassador, for instance, was anxious not to allow his predilection for women at court to become known. And the Luftwaffe pilot presumably deceived his ground crew into believing he was merely taking a test flight. You carry no letters or photographs. You have no legal papers, not even a passport.' The voice became softer, in a strange way almost confidential. 'You are a self-confessed procurer of women, Grigor. You took money that was not yours, and you lied in order to reach Turkey. You betrayed and killed the man who saved your life by flying you there, excusing yourself on the grounds that he was a Nazi and therefore, if you are to be believed, your enemy. You were captured by a German U-boat and released. Despite your earnest assurances I believe you told her commander you were a spy and that is why he let you go. Here in Cairo we are in a war zone. Three hundred miles from where we are sitting at this moment my country is fighting for its life in the desert. You are a highly dangerous man whom I do not trust. You will remain in custody until I am completely satisfied you are not a spy and pose no threat.'

'What about my belt and shoelaces? The money that was taken from me when I was arrested? The luggage your men removed from my room at the Damietta?'

'All will be returned to you.'

The major lowered his head to signal the interview was at an end. The soldier took Grigor back to his cell. The door banged behind him.

Chapter Twelve

The lorry delivered Farquhar to the guardroom at the main gate of Fulwell Barracks. No one knew who he was, or what to do with him. He told the chief orderly room clerk, a dim-witted lance corporal, that he had been ordered to report there and his papers would follow. He was given an army number, put on a temporary pay roll and issued with a set of fatigues and a pair of boots. The corporal gardener gave him a rusty spade, a small bag of sand and another of seed, and ordered him to repair the vast expanse of exhausted lawn in front of the officers' mess.

In the days that followed he made no attempt to socialize. He spoke rarely, made no friends. Had he done so questions would be asked; he could not tell the truth and lacked the mental energy necessary to weave a fictitious history for himself. The corporal gardener never checked up on the lawn's progress and Farquhar guessed he had forgotten him. He joined the queue at the cookhouse at mealtimes and attended pay parade every Friday to collect his few shillings. There were spare beds in a transit hut where he slept.

Several weeks after arriving at the barracks, during which time he had done nothing except dig up a few bucketfuls of weeds, he saw the regimental sergeant major accompanied by a police constable striding towards him. He straightened up and stood to attention.

'You are Private Fucker P, Number 147999?' the RSM barked.

'Yes, sir. It's Farquhar, sir.'

'The constable wants a word with you, Fucker,' the RSM snapped. Unaccountably his voice suddenly softened. 'Sorry, lad. It's always a shock. Take your time. Come and see me afterwards.'

Mystified, Farquhar remained at attention as the RSM marched off. He turned to face the constable. 'What's this all about?' he asked.

'I'm sorry,' the policeman said, 'but we think your mother has died. Half the country's been looking for you. Her funeral was two days ago.'

*

Mrs Fox, who lived next door, had noticed the bottle of milk was still on the front step at lunchtime. She knocked but received no reply and reported the matter at the police station. Two constables broke in and found Mrs Farquhar lying dead at the foot of the stairs. A post mortem revealed she had died of a heart attack the previous day. A hunt for her son had begun at once. Mrs Fox told the detective that Peter was in America; his weekly postcards from New York stood on his mother's sideboard. But where in New York? The cards bore no address, each bore an identical message that he was fine and would be seeing her soon. Mrs Fox remembered his mother saying his going to America had 'something to do with the college'. The registrar at Leeds University soon traced his name and enquiries were made in the Faculty of Engineering. Professor Bomford proved highly evasive until, under pressure from a chief superintendent in full uniform, he confessed his reticence was due to his having signed the Official Secrets Act. He made a statement about the visit of the man from the War Office that had resulted in Farquhar being called to London to discuss their research into explosives. That was the last he had seen or heard of him.

Whitehall was contacted but it was several days before the visitor was identified. An even longer delay followed before Colonel Fraser was traced. He supplied the information that Private Farquhar was now undergoing infantry training at Fulwell Barracks. Even then the mystery was not solved immediately as no one there had heard of him and his name was not on the regimental roll call. Fortunately an orderly room clerk suddenly remembered the solitary, silent figure occasionally seen weeding the lawn outside the officers' mess and his name was found on a supplementary pay roll. By then his mother's funeral had taken place, attended only by Mrs Fox and a handful of neighbours. The RSM gave him a week's compassionate leave and arranged for him to be issued with a full uniform and travel warrant.

Mrs Fox was still in shock following the death of her dearest friend; her face was drawn and eyes red with weeping. She gave Farquhar his mother's front-door key. The familiar polished oak furniture and floral carpets were there, but no sense of his mother remained despite her having lived in the house for thirty years. He wandered through the rooms, touching the piano and looking at the photos on the mantelpiece. There was a faded snap of his parents on their wedding day in 1920 and one of himself in his new grammar-school blazer. His mother's favourite photo stood in the centre, in a silver frame. It had been taken on his graduation day when he wore a hired cap and gown. She was beside him wearing the wide brimmed hat she had borrowed for the great occasion.

Mrs Fox had sorted out what she called 'your mam's things' and taken them away. Farquhar felt empty and alone, aware there was no longer anything here for him. He thought of what could have been; how he could have brought Josie here to meet his mother.... Later in the day he called at an estate agent in the High Street and arranged for the sale of the house and its contents. Mrs Fox kindly offered to look after 'his things' for him. He bought two trunks at the auction rooms, packed his civilian clothes and a few mementos in one and his books in the other. He carried them next door and put them in Mrs Fox's spare room, 'until peace comes' as she put it.

Finally he paid a visit to the crematorium to say goodbye to his mother. He stood in the drizzling rain, holding the wreath he had brought to lay in the Garden of Remembrance. He had hoped to be alone to concentrate his thoughts but an old man on the far side began walking towards him. *Fuck off,* he thought. *Can't you see I want to be on my own?*

'Lost someone, 'ave you, son?' the man asked quietly

His tone softened Farquhar's aggression. He nodded. 'My mother. She died suddenly and the funeral was held before they could contact me.'

'That's 'ard,' the old man said. 'I know 'ow it is. I were at sea in't first war and I didn't hear mine were dead until long after she'd gone. But I never forgot her. You won't either. I'll bet on that.' They stood side by side in silence for a while. 'I come here every week to have a word wi' the wife. She's been gone a few years now. I hardly remember what she looked like. But it's done, so I'll be off. Leave you in peace. Take care o' yersel', lad.'

And he shambled off into the rain.

Two days before he was due back at Fulwell, Farquhar took a train to Wylam. He wondered if the landlady at the Black Bull would remember him and be able to tell him more about Josie. But the old lady was no longer there. Her place had been taken by an elderly man who told Farquhar she had retired and gone to live with her daughter in Blackpool. He booked a room for the night; he was the only resident. He tried the door of what had been Josie's room but it was locked. The car park where she had sat on her motorbike that morning, smiling at him before they set off for their picnic, was just the same. He walked down to the bridge and stood for a long time listening to the river surging below. He knew he would never go home again, or back to the university. Like Josie, they were in a foreign country, far beyond his reach.

On the train back to Fulwell were a hundred or more conscripts about his own age in civilian clothes. On the platform at Fulwell station a cluster of NCOs barked out orders, organizing the new arrivals into groups according to surname initial. He stood to one side at first then joined the queue for the fleet of buses waiting to take them to the barracks. They were shepherded through the main gate and formed a long straggling line outside the orderly room. Farquhar's name was added to the list by a sergeant. He was given a new number and he took the king's shilling. At the stores he was issued with a second uniform, a steel helmet and .303 Enfield rifle. As he left the stores with his arms full of kit, he came face to face with the RSM.

'Fucker!' he roared. 'It's about time you got yourself sorted out proper! I'll be keepin' my eye on you!' In a quieter, more friendly tone he added, 'Everythin' orlright at home, lad?'

'Yes, sir, thank you, sir.'

'That's good. Do your best and you'll be fine. Carry on.'

'Thank you, sir.'

His basic training as an infantryman began that same afternoon. For the next four months every day was spent in almost continuous vigorous exercise. He quickly became inured to the incessant use of foul language by the NCOs; every sentence they uttered contained crudities, frequently inserted between syllables. Soon Farquhar was swearing and blaspheming like everyone else. Occasionally he worried that on leave he may let slip an oath in front of his mother; then he would remember she was dead and it would never happen.

He was a member of a thirty-man squad. There were daily sessions in the gym under the eyes of a sadistic PT sergeant instructor, a ju-jitsu expert proud to be known as the Black Bastard. An exhausting hour of strenuous exercise was followed by a session of 'milling', a punishing activity intended to increase aggression in the timid. Pairs of recruits were ordered to don boxing gloves and climb into the ring for two one-minute rounds refereed by the Bastard. Failure to show enough enthusiasm, 'not putting on a good show' in the Bastard's words, incurred his wrath. He then pulled on a pair of gloves himself and proceeded to batter first one then the other of the combatants in order to encourage a more belligerent spirit in the remainder. Farquhar had no experience of boxing but, to avoid a close encounter with the Bastard's fists, when the bell rang he charged across the ring with a snarl and rained wild blows on his opponent, forcing him to his knees, overwhelmed with surprise rather than the effect of the punches. The Bastard heartily approved and demanded similar action from the remainder of the squad.

A trio of bloody-minded corporals, no longer capable of normal speech as their world lay solely within the confines of the parade ground, super-vised hours of marching and drill movements with the rifle. A much-feared element of training was the twice-weekly timed charge by the squad along the regimental battle course. A half-mile stretch of thick glutinous mud, it was blocked by horrendous obstacles that had to be climbed, crossed or crawled under whilst wearing full kit, including a tin hat and carrying a rifle loaded with live rounds. Recruits failing to complete the course within the specified time were made to repeat it the following day, and the day after if necessary. Repeated failure resulted in the infliction of a penalty known as 'back-squadding' when the offender joined the latest band of recruits and started training once more from the beginning. Forced marches, of increasing length, were made several times a week, regardless of the weather. Entire days were spent out on windswept firing ranges, often in pouring rain, with repeated practice on rifle, Bren gun and three-inch mortar.

After sixteen exhausting weeks, the surviving members of the squad were deemed sufficiently trained to be ready for active service. There was an impressive passing-out parade with the regimental band playing rousing marches and a Gilbert and Sullivan selection. The following day each man was allocated a job in the barracks pending posting to one of the regiment's four battalions. Their long-term future was uncertain. The possibility of a German invasion remained; if that happened they would be fighting on home soil. A fifth battalion was being formed which, it was rumoured, was to be sent to Burma to fight the Japs. Latrine gossip included tales of drums of yellow camouflage paint being delivered to the stores, suggesting that at least one battalion and its vehicles were bound for the desert to join the Eighth Army, currently facing Rommel's Afrika Korps in North Africa.

Throughout his training Farquhar made no mention of his university education or brief experience as a saboteur. On the form he was given to assess his potential he had scrawled 'nothing' in reply to an enquiry as to his educational qualifications and 'labourer' when asked his civilian occupation. He was put to work in the cookhouse on one of the least desirable tasks in the army. The cooking and serving of three meals a day for 2000 men produced hundreds of greasy baking trays and tins. Farquhar's job was to scrape off the residual scraps and scrub the utensils in water that was never more than tepid. In the sinks at which he stood for hours, rings of jaundicely iridescent malodorous fat accumulated on the surface of the water; a thick rime of grey grease formed around the edges. Queasiness was his constant companion. He grew to hate the cookhouse with an intensity greater than anything he had previously experienced.

Miraculously, on breakfast duty one morning, as he shovelled a greasy fried egg into every mess tin thrust in front of him, he overheard a soldier who worked in the stores telling his mate he was being posted home to Scotland on compassionate grounds as his father was seriously ill. As soon as he had washed his quota of slimy tins, Farquhar slipped off to the barrack room where he changed out of fatigues into his best uniform. Calling briefly at the kitchen, he rushed across to the stores to offer himself as a replacement. Sergeant Phipps was in charge of the regimental stores. A long-serving regular soldier, he was a survivor of the Battle of the Somme in the First World War. Farquhar introduced himself and said he had heard of the vacancy and was keen to work with him. The sergeant lolled back in a chair with his feet up on a table, smoking (an activity strictly forbidden in the stores) and drinking the tea Farquhar had brought from the kitchen. It was proper army cooks' tea, brewed from the best quality brand of leaves reserved for the officers' mess. The steaming pint mug had been laced with six heaped spoonfuls of sugar and a large dollop of sweetened condensed milk. Alongside, on a sheet of greaseproof paper, lay a thickly buttered slice of rich fruitcake.

'So, you want to be a storeman,' the sergeant said. He prodded his wire-rimmed spectacles further up his prominent bony nose and stared hard at him. 'Got any sort of experience?'

'In civvy street I worked for a furniture removals firm, Sarge.'

'What about nicking?'

Farquhar shook his head. 'I wasn't into that. None of the lads were. We took a pride in our work. "Safe and secure" was the firm's motto and we stuck to it like glue.'

The sergeant smiled momentarily, exposing badly stained equine teeth protruding from receding gums. He nodded sagely. 'Yer,' he said. 'Nicking's a mug's game in a job like this.'

'I can imagine,' Farquhar agreed earnestly.

'Trustworthy and honest is what I am. An' that's what I look for in any lad what works for me.'

'I promise that's what you'll get, Sarge.'

Phipps repositioned his spectacles and eyed him thoughtfully. 'You've got a posh name, lad. Fuckwar. I like that. And you seem a bright sort. Went to college, did you? Know a bit about clerking?'

'Yes, Sergeant. It's Farquhar.'

The sergeant pouted. 'Yer. Fuckwar, like I said. Able to keep records and that sort of stuff, can you? I'm usually too busy with other things to bother much with pen and paper. But I insist on havin' things done right. I run a tight ship if you get my meaning.'

'I'd do whatever you want, Sergeant. Anything you say. Work under your supervision or on my own. Keep the books. Anything. Just as you wish. I won't let you down.'

'The stores is a big attraction to lots of lads. I don't want to see none o' your mates hanging around here. It's strictly out of bounds.'

'Of course, Sergeant. No need to worry on that score.'

There was yet another adjustment of the spectacles and a final inquisitive look before the sergeant came to a decision.

'Orlright. I'll give you a month's trial. Then I'll decide if you're permanent. First job, go and ask Sergeant Jones for another slice of this cake. Put more butter on it this time. Do that afore you tell him you're leaving his kitchen to work in the stores for me or he might refuse. Quick about it, lad!'

The stores occupied four long wooden huts arranged like a letter H. The short structure connecting the two legs housed the office and counter over which smaller items were issued and returned. Everything in the barracks was listed in the stores register. Every item, from two-ton trucks to mess tins, was the official property of the stores and merely out on loan to those requiring them for their military duties. Only when the necessary form, designated a 108, was completed and signed by the recipient could an article be issued. When the article was returned, provided it was clean and in a similar condition to when it left the stores, it was put back in its place on the shelves. The 108 was then countersigned by the storeman and handed back to the borrower to keep as proof of return. Sergeant Phipps wasted no time in inducting Farquhar into his personal method of operating the system.

'Never give anybody his 108 back unless he asks for it,' he said. 'We've got a duty to keep the register up to the mark. If we take an item back but still have the 108 for it, it's still out on loan officially, even though it's back on our shelves. Then, if some bugger pinches one, we've got a spare ready to replace it. Nowt wrong with that, is there?'

It was not long before Farquhar realized this arrangement was not operated solely for the benefit of keeping the register up to date. The relevant 108 was rarely asked for but few returned items were put back on their allotted shelves. Instead they were piled in a locked room at the far end of the west block. Early in the morning of the fourth Sunday of every month, a covered civilian lorry arrived at the back of the stores. Under the supervision of Sergeant Phipps and with the assistance of the cheery Irish driver Paddy, Farquhar loaded the returned equipment onto the lorry, which left the barracks through rarely used gates near the store.

When Farquhar queried the likelihood of this arrangement coming to the attention of the commanding officer, Phipps shook his head. 'If nobody's bothered to ask for his 108 back after a month you can bet your boots he never will.'

'Are you certain you can you trust that Irishman?'

'Paddy? Absolutely sure! He's the salt of the earth. And he's got good contacts. Keep your trap shut about all of this. Don't go blabbing in the NAAFI of a Saturday night, d'ye hear? I'll slip you a quid or two now and then.'

It was not long before Farquhar became aware that retaining 108s was not Sergeant Phipps' only source of illegal income. The blanket store contained racks reaching from floor to ceiling. On each shelf lay ten piles of twenty dark brown or navy blue blankets, each folded with military precision and the front edge turned in a neat roll. One morning Phipps led Farquhar to the racks and told him to carry out a stock check. He set about the job, an apparently simple matter of confirming every shelf housed ten piles each of twenty blankets and multiplying 200 by the number of shelves. As he checked an upper shelf, he noticed each blanket had been folded twice. What appeared to be two blankets was in fact only one. He checked the other shelves and found they were the same. Instead of twenty blankets in a pile there were only ten. There were not 4000 blankets as shown in the register, only 2000. Sergeant Phipps nodded sagely when Farquhar pointed this out.

'Yer,' he said. 'I thought you might spot that. Robbie's to blame. He was the lad here afore you. Bloody young rogue he was.'

'What are we, er, you going to do about it, Sarge?'

'Nowt, son. Robbie didn't get to Scotland. There was a cock-up in the office and somebody else got his compassionate leave. He got sent to Burma, poor little bastard. If anybody finds out about them blankets, they're not goin' to bring him back from there for a court martial, are they?'

'I suppose not. What happened to the missing two thousand blankets?'

'Paddy took them.'

Farquhar had been working in the stores for six months when the plump orderly room runner appeared at the counter one morning.

'RSM wants to see yer, right away,' he gasped, having run all the way from the regimental office.

'He'll have to bloody well wait,' Farquhar replied tartly. 'Sarge Phipps hasn't arrived yet so I can't leave the stores.'

'It's up to you,' the runner panted. 'But the RSM said right away. If you take my advice you'll lock up and put up a sign saying you'll be back in ten minutes.'

*

He snapped to attention in front of the desk. 'Private Farquhar, 176814, sir,' he bellowed in the accepted army manner, giving his new number.

The RSM, sitting at a desk, ignored him and carried on studying the report of the previous night's football match in the local newspaper. He was tall and broad with close-cut ginger hair. The toecaps of his boots shone like black glass; brass Warrant Officer First Class badges glittered on each sleeve of his immaculate uniform. He bristled with testosterone-fuelled aggression.

'You took your time getting 'ere, Fucker,' he eventually barked without looking up from his paper.

'Sorry, sir. Had to lock up the stores first, sir. It's Farquhar, sir,' he shouted, still standing to attention.

'When I say I want yer 'ere at once, I mean at once! Understood?'

'Understood, sir.' *There must be a problem with the stores. They've found out about the missing blankets! That's why Phipps hasn't appeared this morning. He's keeping out of the way. When he does turn up he'll say he knew nothing about there being only half the number there should be. With my record I'll get the blame and end up in the glasshouse for the rest of my life....*

'Commandin' orficer wants to see yer,' the RSM snapped. 'Stand over there.'

'Yes, sir!'

'Face the wall.'

'Yes, sir!'

Suddenly the RSM's mouth was inches from his ear. ''Oo said you could stand at ease?' he screeched. 'Get to attention. And don't move.'

It was a long wait. With the wall inches from his face, Farquhar had only a sound picture of the comings and goings in the office behind him. There was not a sound from the RSM but his ominous presence could be sensed. Boots stamped in and out. There were brief staccato conversations. Metal filing-cabinet drawers were continually opened and slammed shut. Someone was laboriously typing a letter and an agonizing silence hung suspended between keystrokes. A sudden barked 'Shun!' from the RSM caused much scraping of chairs and stamping of feet followed by a combined chorus of 'Good morning, sir!' as the CO arrived. His office door closed and normal activity resumed.

Time dragged by until without warning the RSM was at Farquhar's shoulder with his pacing stick tucked under his arm. He barked a thunderous series of orders.

'Abouuuuut turn!'

'Quiiiiiiiiiiiick march!'

'Riiiiiiiiiiiiiiiight turn!'

'Layyyyyyyyft turn!

''Alt! Cap orf!'

'Private Fucker, sah!' he shouted at the colonel.

'Thank you, Sergeant Major,' the CO said quietly. 'That will be all.'

'Sah!' The RSM gave an immaculate salute, stamped his boots in an about turn and marched out.

'At ease, Farquhar,' the CO said in a friendly tone as the door banged shut. He was short and squat. With his cheery round red face and genial smile, he looked more like a benign village squire than a colonel of infantry. He sat beaming across the desk.

'All has been revealed, old man,' he said. 'The game's up.'

'If it's about the blankets, sir, I—'

The CO shook his head. 'Blankets? I don't know what you're talking about. And it's no use trying your evasive replies on me. I'm not the Gestapo!'

'Gestapo, sir? I know you're not. I meant in the stores.'

'Automatic reaction still on full alert, eh? Good man! Your commando training, of course. Big house in Scotland, was it? Hiding out on Rannoch Moor in the depths of winter?'

'I've no idea what you're talking about, sir. I'm sorry, but that's the honest truth.'

'It's all here, Farquhar.' The colonel tapped an open file lying on his desk. 'Scientist, recruited at university, parachuted into France at dead of night. The word's out. And not before time!'

Farquhar stood in shocked silence. *Somehow he's got hold of my file. Colonel Fraser's report saying I'm not to be trusted will be in there. Even if they haven't found out about the blankets, I'll still lose my job in the stores. Tonight I'll be back washing greasy tins in the cookhouse. Or on my way to Burma, like poor Robbie....*

'You're the sort of man we need to win this war, Farquhar,' the CO said quietly. 'Determined, brave, experienced. The decision not to send you back to France was, in my opinion, correct, knowing what you'd been through.'

'Sir, I—'

The CO waved his hand for silence. 'What I don't understand is why are you here? A man with your talents, still a private soldier, working as a storeman! It's ridiculous! A waste of a valuable asset! You could have worn your para wings but you've chosen not to. And I know you're not working undercover. I've checked that with Intelligence.'

'No, sir. I'm not undercover. I'm here because this is where I was sent. Colonel Fraser supervised my recruitment. He was in charge of my mission to France. His report will be in that file.'

The colonel smiled and shook his head. 'To be honest, Farquhar, there's not much in your file apart from a brief summary of your ops behind enemy lines. The War Office, I assume for security reasons, has removed everything else. But there's more than enough left to show your abilities are being wasted here.'

'Colonel Fraser's report is missing?' Farquhar was so astonished he forget to add 'sir'.

'Not a mention of it. Y'know, to me this has echoes of Lawrence of Arabia about it. TE re-enlisted, under another name, of course, in the RAF to help him forget the past. For all I know, you may be doing the same. I hope you didn't suffer in the same way he did when the Turks caught him. Ghastly business with that Bey! Ghastly! But it's your business and I won't enquire further. What I will do – indeed, what I see as my duty as your commanding officer – is to ensure the best possible use is made of your undoubted talents.'

'That's very good of you, sir.'

'Nonsense. Now, pay attention,' the CO said briskly, leaning forward. 'I've received a confidential circular asking all officers commanding battalions to look for likely candidates for security work. They mean in the commissioned ranks, of course. But because of your exceptional experience and abilities I'm putting your name forward. What d'you say?'

'Again, that's very good of you, sir. But what sort of security work would it entail?'

'It's not specified. I doubt if they'll send you back over the Channel after all you've done already. The Gestapo will have a hefty file on you. You might be put on wireless work or code breaking. I hear there's a lot of that going on. Or training agents in field craft. With your background you have the whole picture at your fingertips. That's what they'll be looking for.'

Farquhar stood silent. *Colonel Fraser swore he'd bar any prospect of my being promoted. He said he'd arrange for a report of my failure to follow me until death or demob, a sort of army Mark of Cain. For some reason the system has broken down. Why should I argue with the CO? I'll go along with this idea he's got of me as an unrecognized hero! If I ever meet a real agent he'll soon spot I'm a fraud and the truth will out. But I've never pretended to be a proper agent anyway. I wasn't trained. I might get a fair hearing at last, or a bit of sympathy. With luck I might even be discharged and get my job back at the university! If the report about me blabbing to Josie has gone astray, then perhaps the letter to the prof did too! I'd be more use to the war effort working in the lab than I am here, helping Phipps pinch blankets from the stores.*

'Very well, sir. Yes, I was sent to blow up a bridge in France. The Germans were using it to bring up supplies for the attack on Dunkirk.'

The colonel's face came alight. 'Good man!' he exclaimed. 'What happened, exactly?'

'Well, sir, it went wrong from the start. I was dropped at night, but the reception party failed to arrive. I was entirely on my own and....' *God, how glamorous it sounds, telling it like this! Like Richard Hannay in* The Thirty-Nine Steps. He described how the Lysander was shot down over Sussex and being pulled from the wreckage just before it exploded.

'Colonel Fraser decided not to send me back, sir. Instead he had me posted here under your command.' He shook his head and theatrically wiped a hand across his brow. 'I was weary of war, sir. And you have a very fine regiment. I've been happy to be a member of it.'

'You've been here more than a year and never said a word about your past,' the CO said with barely concealed admiration. 'You kept your mouth shut and buckled to! Well, just for now, carry on with your normal duties in the stores. I'll put you up for one of these new jobs in security. No doubt you'll be called for interview shortly. Dismiss.'

Farquhar did a smart about turn and marched out.

Chapter Thirteen

'I was grieved to hear of Mercedes' passing, Senor Navarro,' Magda said.

She had come to the bank to buy French francs for a coming trip to Paris. To save such a distinguished customer the indignity of waiting in a queue whilst the money was brought up from the vault, she had been courteously ushered into the manager's office.

'Thank you, Princess,' he said. 'How kind of you to mention my loss. She had a fatal heart attack only three days before we were to celebrate our silver wedding anniversary.'

'So I understand. That was most cruel,' Magda replied. 'Everyone was shocked at the terrible news.'

'I was touched to receive so many condolences. May I ask if you would care for a coffee, Princess?'

'That would be most welcome. Thank you.'

She carried her cup across to the balcony windows. The office was on the top floor and overlooked the shimmering blue water of Casais Bay.

'What a wonderful view you have from here, Senor Navarro.'

'Yes, indeed. It has played a major role in helping me come to terms with my loss. At night, when everyone has gone home, I often stand where you are now, looking out at the Atlantic and up at the stars. They bring me an inner peace that is beyond description.'

What a gentle man he is! How lovely it would be to have him as a close friend. I think he likes me!

The cashier returned with the francs. Navarro flipped through the notes, checking each was crisp and new before handing them to her. The cashier bowed and left the room.

'I very much regret this is the last service I shall be able to perform for you, Princess,' Navarro said. 'I am leaving Estoril.'

She stared at him. 'Leaving? W-when? And why?' He could not fail to hear the dismay in her voice.

'I have been promoted to Head Office in Madrid. I leave on Saturday.'

'So far away! And so soon!'

'Yes, Princess.'

They stood in silence, looking at each other.

'Perhaps, Oscar,' she said slowly, breathing his name softly, 'if I were to come this evening, I could share the view with you.'

He bowed his head. 'Of course, Princess. I wanted so much to make that very suggestion but... ' He smiled, knowing she would understand his dilemma. 'May I suggest nine o'clock? There will be a full moon tonight.'

'Nine will be perfect.'

Carol goes to bed at eight. I'll tell the servants I'm going for a drive as it's such a fine evening

She parked her open SS Jaguar in the square as the town hall clock was striking and walked to the darkened entrance of the bank. Oscar was waiting for her. She took his arm and they crossed the empty vestibule in silence. In the lift they turned to each other and gently kissed.

'I've fallen in love with you, Magda,' he whispered.

She smiled but made no reply. *How many men have said that to me? Forty? Sixty? More, perhaps.*

The bay was a shining pool of silver. They undressed without haste, laying their clothes neatly on the floor in separate piles. Naked, they kissed. Magda slid to her knees and began worshipping him.

Chapter Fourteen

Grigor lay on his bed, thinking over the interview with the major. *On the whole, I did quite well. I stuck more or less with the truth, making no attempt to gloss over my misdeeds. Admitting I was one of the king's secretaries accounted for me knowing the Turkish ambassador and at the same time explained what I did all day. There was no need to mention Magda. It was a shock to hear they've been to the Damietta and cleared my room. They can't have found the receipt. If they had he'd have questioned me about it....*

It was five days before he was sent for again.

'Get up, Alfonso.' The corporal was shaking his shoulder; the glare of the ceiling light was blinding. 'Get dressed. The major wants to see you.'

'What time is it?'

'0430 hours. Get a move on.'

The major was sitting at his desk. Apart from a table lamp at his elbow, the remainder of the office was in darkness.

'Sit down, Grigor,' he said in a friendly tone. 'I trust we're looking after you properly. Any complaints?'

'My room is comfortable, thank you, Major. But the food is poor. I dined much better in the servants' hall in the palace in Bucharest.'

'I'll pass your criticism on to the sergeant cook. He'll be distressed to hear you are not enjoying comparable fare.'

'I also wish to protest against my continuing incarceration. Have you uncovered any offence for which I can be charged?'

'You are detained under military law. You will be held until I am fully satisfied you pose no threat.'

'Can I lodge an appeal? Am I not entitled to visits from the International Red Cross?'

'The answer to both questions is no. An appeal is not permitted. The Red Cross is concerned only with the conditions under which you are being detained, not the reasons for it. You are a suspected spy. That gives me sufficient cause to lock you up. You say you are comfortable and have no serious complaints regarding your treatment. That satisfies the requirements of the Red Cross.'

'Why have you sent for me?'

'For two reasons. First, a three-engined German aircraft has been seen in a hangar at Istanbul airport.'

Grigor stared in amazement. 'Then Günter survived!'

'I did not say it was his aeroplane.'

'Can you name any other German aircraft with three engines, Major? I think not. He must have discovered his reserve tank was empty and diverted in time! I'm glad he survived. What will happen to him?'

'If it is him, he is no doubt being held for questioning. The Gestapo will be keen to get him back and find out what he was up to so far from base. I imagine your friend the Turkish ambassador in Bucharest will be under strong pressure to have him released. Life will be uncomfortable for Günter whatever happens. Turkish prisons are notorious for brutality, and the Gestapo won't be gentle if they lay hands on him.'

'I hope he survives, whoever has him. But surely this is good news for me, is it not, Major? You now have no cause to detain me.'

'This development changes nothing. However, I said there were two reasons why I sent for you. Informing you of the German plane at Istanbul was one. The second is that I have been authorized to offer you a position as interpreter.'

'Interpreter?' Grigor gasped. 'Major, this is indeed a surprise! A British *volte-face*! From suspected spy to trusted employee in the space of a few sentences! In what languages are you seeking my assistance?'

'Mainly translating from German into English to begin with.'

'You cannot expect me to work from a prison cell.'

'No. You will be allocated an office on the top floor and sleep in an adjoining room. You will take orders from no one but me. You will speak to no one but me. You will not leave the building without my express permission. Anything you need to perform your duties will be brought to you. You will take your meals in the Officers' Club dining room. You are not permitted in the bar and will not be served alcohol.'

'Thank you, Major. Your rules are stringent and wholly unnecessary. But I accept your offer and the conditions. You can trust me to do whatever I can to assist your country win the war.'

Later that morning the major spent an hour explaining what was required of him. Each day he would be given copies of documents containing transcripts of intercepted enemy wireless transmissions. In their original form they would have been sent in a military code which, unknown to the enemy, the British had succeeded in breaking. Although the major made no mention of the fact, Grigor guessed the close restrictions placed on him were to prevent him warning the Germans their radio traffic was no longer secret. His task was to translate the deciphered messages from German into English. A multilingual officer who had moved elsewhere had previously carried out the work.

Grigor enjoyed his new freedom. After a month the major gave him permission to take an early-morning stroll along the Nile embankment. At that hour the air was delightfully fresh and cool and there were few people about. He felt at home in Cairo. He had a sense of belonging to the city and wondered if some inherited memory had been stirred. He remembered Magda claiming to have some such ancestral trait; he had dismissed it as nonsense. Perhaps he had been wrong.

He suspected the major was having him followed although he never saw anyone tailing him. He took care never to be absent from the hotel more than an hour. He spoke to no one and varied his route daily. On occasions he strolled past the entrance to the Damietta Hotel but never gave it a glance. On his return to Shepheards he immediately went up to his office and began work on translating the messages intercepted and decoded overnight. Throughout the rest of the day a constant stream of later transmissions was brought to him. He worked hard to impress the major, taking care to consult a variety of dictionaries and military handbooks in both languages to ensure accuracy. The signals often contained strange words in army slang and numerous acronyms with which he became familiar. On occasions when the context was ambiguous or the meaning otherwise in doubt, he offered a choice of wordings from which the most appropriate could be selected by whoever received his transcript. As the weeks went by the signals he was given had increasingly higher security classifications. Although the major made no mention of this – he remained as cool and detached as ever – Grigor guessed he was relying on him more and more.

The work continued to fascinate. Daily situation reports gave a word picture of the bitter struggle in progress far to the west. He was soon able to recognize the writing styles of different German officers. Their transmissions fell into place like successive episodes in a serialized story. He began adding footnotes to his translations, suggesting possible developments. The major called him in and informed him he was exceeding his authorization.

'You are not employed to anticipate the enemy's plans and add notes to official documents,' he said curtly. 'However, since you appear to derive enjoyment from doing so, I have no objection to you putting your ideas on a separate piece of paper, for my eyes only. Your views are unfettered by the constraints of a military mind and I enjoy a laugh now and again.'

Three months passed before Grigor was confident he was no longer being followed. He was now permitted to take a stroll in the afternoon as well as in the morning and in the course of one of these he paused at the entrance to the Damietta Hotel. He pointedly hesitated, as if deciding whether or not to enter. Catching sight of him, a liveried porter stepped forward and invitingly held the door open. Grigor squared his shoulders, mounted the front steps and entered. The oily manager who had greeted him on his first visit was at the reception desk and instantly recognized him.

'Mr Grigor!' he exclaimed. 'Welcome back, sir! How very nice to see you again!'

'Good afternoon. How pleasant that you should remember me.'

'It is always delightful to greet a former guest. How can I be of help to you today?'

'I have been staying with a friend since I left the Damietta. He must go to Alexandria on urgent business this evening. Naturally he would not be happy for me to spend a night in the house alone with his beautiful wife. He has not said as much, and I suspect the lady herself would raise no objection but, for the sake of their harmony, it is better that I sleep elsewhere tonight.'

The manager nodded in an understanding manner.

'I was wondering if my former room is available, by any chance?' Grigor continued. 'I would deem it a great favour if you could accommodate me for a single night once again.'

The manager carefully adjusted his tie, covered his mouth and politely coughed. 'I trust your business venture in Cairo has gone well?'

'Extremely well, thank you. As you may remember I came to you with the intention of staying for only a few days. Thanks to the war I have been fortunate enough to secure two large contracts. It looks as if I shall be here for some time.'

'And your difficulty with the military authorities? I trust that was quickly resolved?'

'How kind of you to ask! Yes, it was merely a matter of checking certain credentials with my company in Switzerland.'

'I am relieved to hear it was nothing worse. I regret I was unable to prevent the military authorities removing your luggage. And they refused to settle your account for the hospitality you enjoyed with us.'

'I was unaware of their discourtesy although I am sure it was merely an oversight. Please accept my sincere apologies.' Grigor pulled out his wallet and allowed the manager to see that it bulged with notes. 'I shall rectify the matter at once.'

The manager pursed his lips; Grigor sensed he was deciding how best to maximize his personal benefit from this unexpected opportunity. From the wall he took down a chart, liberally marked in various colours, and laid it on the counter. 'This is our room plan, Mr Grigor,' he explained helpfully. 'As you can see, we are heavily booked tonight and well into the future. However, bear with me one moment whilst I see how I can help you.'

He leaned over the chart, muttering to himself and stabbing his finger here and there. At intervals he shook his head and groaned aloud, making it theatrically plain his heartfelt disappointment as various solutions were considered then rejected as impractical.

'I am sorry, Mr Grigor,' he finally admitted. 'It distresses me to turn you away but alas we have nothing suitable. At the Damietta we take immense pleasure in obliging guests who have previously enjoyed our hospitality.'

'Surely you must have something?' Grigor pleaded. 'Circumstances render my situation most difficult as I have explained.'

The manager wagged his head. 'Sadly, there is nothing. Apart, that is, from our bridal suite on the second floor which has unexpectedly become vacant. I received news only an hour ago that the prospective groom was shot in the groin by his intended. He is in hospital, and not expected to recover. She is reported to have fled to Memphis with his much younger brother. But of course the bridal suite would be of no interest to you as a single gentleman. And it is the only vacancy we have available tonight.'

'What is the price of the suite, may I ask?'

'Two thousand two hundred and fifty dollars per night, excluding extras. Plus the two hundred and eight-five dollars you owe for your one-night occupation of the bijou room on the fourth floor plus dinner and breakfast.'

The manager took him upstairs to inspect the bridal suite. It was sumptuous, and extremely vulgar. The lounge had tall glass doors opening onto a wide balcony overlooking the Nile. Many of the items of furniture were faithful copies of pieces found in the tomb of Tutankhamun and looked most uncomfortable. The bedroom boasted voluptuous luxury, reminding Grigor of an expensive brothel he had visited in Vienna. There were wide mirrors on each wall and another on the ceiling above the circular bed. In the bathroom a colourful mosaic of the Sphinx at dawn covered an entire wall. The floor tiles depicted stylized slaves toiling on the construction of the Great Pyramid at Giza as the Pharaoh and his vast entourage looked on.

The manager, an ingratiating smile fixed on his face, followed him from room to room. 'Of course, Mr Grigor,' he murmured on completion of the tour, 'there is no need for you to occupy this wonderful accommodation alone. We are very cosmopolitan here at the Damietta. I can arrange for a most delightful young lady to help you enjoy these amenities to their fullest possible extent. I have a folio of tasteful photographs you may peruse at your leisure. Every shape, nationality and colour is represented. Or of course, should you prefer something a little more unusual....'

Grigor left the hotel and walked back to Shepheards. He spent the remainder of the afternoon compiling a summary of the week's translations and took it along to the major.

'Would you have any objection to my attending midnight prayers at the mosque, sir?' he asked. 'It is the anniversary of my father's death and it is our family's custom to pray for him every night for the following month. It will be early morning when I return. I shall of course report for duty as normal.'

'I had no idea you took religion so seriously, Grigor.'

'I attend prayers on special occasions, Major. Like many sinners, I find it strangely comforting.'

He dined at the Damietta. Afterwards, in the bridal suite, he lay on the bed, with a bottle of whisky on the side table, and read until after eleven. He got up, opened the door a fraction and listened; the hotel was quiet. He stepped into the corridor and walked to the stairs. There was a sudden crash from a lower floor as the lift doors closed; the motor whined noisily. Grigor moved quickly out of sight; the lift stopped at the floor below and he heard the murmur of voices. The door crashed again and the lift began its descent to the foyer. He walked up the remaining flights to the top floor. The corridor was in darkness. He had seen on the chart in reception that the attic room he had occupied on his previous visit was vacant; naturally the manager had failed to mention the fact with the prospect of letting the bridal suite looming.

The door stood open; the room itself was in pitch darkness. Grigor pulled open the top drawer of the chest of drawers and felt inside. His fingertips found the slim folded edge of the receipt he had tucked into a narrow gap where the frame met the top. The search carried out by the major's men had not been quite thorough enough. He slipped the receipt into his jacket pocket and returned to the bridal suite. He showered, slipped on his dressing gown and lay on the bed.

The girl tapped lightly on his door at twelve precisely, as arranged. Tall and stunningly beautiful, she walked with elegant grace; her face had the high cheekbones of classic depictions of Queen Nefertiti. The photograph in the manager's portfolio had shown her reclining on a chaise longue wearing nothing but stockings and suspenders and an academic mortarboard. The accompanying notes, included for the benefit of potential clients, stated she was a professor of economics at Cairo University. They exchanged few words as she went through her routine with professional skill. Precisely two hours later she went to the bathroom, showered, returned to the bedroom and dressed. Solemnly she picked up the roll of notes Grigor had placed on the dressing table and with a casual wave strolled out of the suite.

Grigor lay in bed reflecting on the interlude. *When will I learn whores are worthless? She could have been cutting my hair or giving me a manicure for all the interest or enthusiasm she showed. No one can ever replace Magda! Lovemaking to her was always an event, a moment to cherish. She made no secret of having other lovers when the need arose. The minister who forged her a travel permit, for instance, or that old Turkish ambassador who provided mine. Occasionally she would take a fancy to someone and not rest until she had bedded him. She was always honest enough to tell me. Where is she now? Still with Carol probably. What lies ahead for us both? The coming month is crucial....*

He left the Damietta soon afterwards and took a taxi to the central station. At the left-luggage counter he handed in the receipt he had retrieved from the chest of drawers and collected the trunk. A porter wheeled it out to the waiting taxi. He ordered the driver to take him to an address in the jewellery quarter famed for high-class workmanship.

Grigor had observed the night orderly officer at Shepheards changed every four days. It was therefore by design that he returned from the mosque a month later on a night when the corporal who had first arrested him was on duty at the reception desk. Behind the counter an assortment of his cronies clustered round a radio tuned to the Forces Programme of the BBC. Seeing Grigor walking past, the corporal hurried across to him.

'Good evenin', Alfonso. Been for a stroll, have we?'

'Good evening, Corporal,' Grigor replied genially. He theatrically cupped a hand to his ear. 'Ah! The delightful Miss Vera Lynn if I'm not mistaken. And singing "We'll Meet Again"! How very appropriate!'

'Fancy you knowing that, er ... sir!' the corporal spluttered. His surprise was evident and genuine. 'I heard you was working upstairs for Major Howard. Enjoying it, are you?'

'Very much, Corporal. I'm most grateful to you for arresting me.'

'That's all right, sir, no offence meant, I was just doing my job. I'm glad it turned out all right for you.' He glanced around rather furtively and dropped his voice. 'Er, I let a few of the lads what's on duty listen to my radio when it's quiet, sir. There's no harm in it but best not mention it to the major, eh?'

'I quite understand, Corporal. I have his permission to attend the mosque to say midnight prayers for my late father. That's where I have been. I have no wish to spoil your men's entertainment.'

'That's very good of you, sir. It keeps them in touch with home. Some of them haven't seen Blighty in three years! I have to ask what you've got in the suitcase. It's routine orders.'

'Just prayer books I've borrowed from the mosque.'

'I'll get one of the lads to carry it up to your room for you. One good turn deserves another, right?'

'Thank you, Corporal. That is most kind of you. Good night!'

'Good night, Mr Alfonso, sir.'

Chapter Fifteen

Sergeant Phipps was saddened by Farquhar's departure. 'You gave my stores a bit o' class, lad,' he said sorrowfully, pressing a five-pound note into his hand as a farewell present. 'You've got a posh name, an' nice manners. You're willin'. An' you kept your mouth shut. Where d'you say you're goin'?'

'Army Staff Training College, Sarge.'

'Where's it at? You told me but I've forgotten.'

'Rodmel Manor.'

'Never 'eard of it.'

'It's in Sussex.'

'Still never 'eard of it. Don't say owt about them missin' blankets.'

'What missing blankets is that, Sarge?'

'Good lad.'

He travelled by train to Lewes. His orders instructed him to enquire at the station for directions and a porter told him it was a two-mile hike to Rodmel Manor. As soon as he set off, kitbag on his shoulder, he had a distinct feeling of *déjà vu* but it was not until the spiralled brick chimneys came into view over the crest of a smooth green hill that he recognized his destination. It came as a severe shock. This was the Tudor mansion where Colonel Fraser had talked to him after his discharge from hospital following the Lysander crash. The ATS girl with the attractive bum had driven him here but hadn't mentioned Rodmel so the name meant nothing to him until now. This was where the colonel had suggested he took a break at the Black Bull and, as a result, met Josie. She had been on his staff and may still be here....

He dropped his kitbag on the grass verge and sat on it. This was the last place he wanted to be. Ever since the night Josie slipped away from the pub he had tried to forget her but no matter how often he thrust her from his thoughts she always crept back. In Fulwell one morning he caught a glimpse of a girl on a bus who may have been her. He raced after it but it sped away from him. Fred Astair singing 'They Can't Take That Away From Me' on the radio in the store one afternoon had made his eyes burn. She continued to haunt his dreams; the thought of coming face to face with her within the next half-hour frightened him. What could he say to her? What would she say to him? The memory of what happened was still raw; it was too soon to meet again. In a few years' time, when the wound was fully healed, he may be able to face her. But not yet. Certainly not now. He had no wish to meet Colonel Fraser either. *He'll recognize me instantly. I'll get another bollocking, even be court martialled for accepting this posting under false pretences. At the very least he'll pack me off back to Fulwell and those greasy bloody tins! What will the CO think when he learns the truth about me? What will the RSM say? And Sergeant Phipps?*

'Are you bloody deaf?'

The exasperated shout broke into his consciousness. On the other side of the road stood an open jeep with its engine racing. At the wheel a sergeant sat glaring across at him.

'Going to Rodmel?' he called.

'Er, yes, Sarge.'

'Get in then. I've not got all friggin' day.'

'You must be Farquhar!' the sergeant yelled as he drove the jeep at a reckless speed along the winding lane.

'How do you know that?' Farquhar shouted back.

'I'm in Admin. I know fuckin' everything.'

'Is Colonel Fraser still at Rodmel?'

'Jock Fraser? Nope. Left for Burma a few months back. A mate of yours, was he?'

'We met a couple of times. He had a girl working for him. Josie Shirran. Is she still here?'

'Josie? Never heard of her. Good shag, was she?'

'I never found out,' Farquhar shouted, greatly relieved.

The jeep swung in between a pair of stone pillars capped by crouching serene-faced lions. A ferocious-looking military policeman, the peak of his red-topped cap resting on the bridge of his nose, recognized the sergeant and lifted the barrier. The jeep sped up a long tree-lined drive and screeched to a stop in a shower of gravel in front of the house. The sergeant led Farquhar up the wide stone steps and across a broad flagged terrace; a heavy oak door stood open and led to a reception desk in a timber-beamed hall. A second military policeman, equally ferocious-looking, led Farquhar into the front room where Colonel Fraser had enthused over the fine old English characters to be found in the village pub. Despite the sergeant's assurance he had gone to Burma, Farquhar had an uneasy sense of his presence eyeing him malevolently from one of the room's dark corners.

A captain strode purposefully into the room. He was slim, tall and very good-looking. His Intelligence Corps uniform was immaculate, the polished Sam Browne belt a perfect fit. Farquhar sensed that in civilian life he had been a successful stockbroker and had an immaculately dressed gorgeous wife ready and waiting for him every night in their large beautifully furnished home. *Lucky fucking bastard,* he thought.

'Welcome to Rodmel, Private Farquhar,' the captain said courteously. 'I'm Alan Frobisher. Please come with me.'

They crossed the entrance hall and walked up a magnificently carved, creaking staircase. With long rapid strides the captain led him along a railed gallery to a door into a panelled room with low ceiling beams. The polished Elizabethan oak floorboards sloped alarmingly; nothing was level or vertical. Small casement windows set in the thick, bulging walls overlooked tree-studded parkland stretching to the foot of the distant Downs.

The captain's desk was wide and imposing. 'Please take a seat,' he said, waving his hand elegantly.

'Thank you, sir,' Farquhar replied.

'This is not your first visit to Rodmel, Sergeant Cole tells me.'

'No, sir. I was debriefed here by Colonel Fraser last year.'

The captain flipped open a folder. 'There's no mention of that in your file,' he said. 'In fact, there's not much here at all. A note on your suitability for the operation, and confirmation that you completed a parachute course prior to being sent to France. No details of your mission or its outcome. However, I've received a strong recommendation from your CO, who thinks very highly of you. Tell me why he should do so.'

This is like being cross-examined in the dock at the Old Bailey. He must have been a barrister, not a stockbroker. Perhaps a KC! He's a smooth bugger; I'll have to watch my step.

'I honestly don't know, sir,' Farquhar replied. 'I've been with the regiment a year but I'd not spoken to the CO until he called me in last week. He had a file that said I'd been in occupied France. It was probably the one you have there. He thought I may be the sort of man you were looking for.'

'Before you met Colonel Fraser, what were you doing?'

'I was a graduate chemical engineer, carrying out research for a PhD at Leeds University. My final year BSc thesis was on industrial explosives. I had no idea the dean was interested in the subject but after reading my thesis he offered me a job as a post-grad research assistant in his lab. Under his supervision I was developing an improved form of pliable explosive.'

The captain held up his hand. 'Before you continue, tell me more about that,' he said politely.

'Yes, sir. Explosives work by sending out a shock wave through the material in which they are buried. A pliable explosive is a mixture of gelignite and an inert additive which can be moulded round the target. Unfortunately the additives used at present slow down the velocity of the shock wave, reducing the effect of the charge. We were trying to minimize that effect.'

'Had you made progress?'

'Yes. We'd solved the major problem and had a working compound called PBF, from our initials. The prof was Philip Brasher and I was the F. A man from the War Office came to see our work and seemed impressed.'

The captain made a note on a pad. 'I see. Please continue.'

'I was called to a meeting in London where I met Colonel Fraser. I was expecting to be questioned about PBF but he told me I was being sent to northern France to blow up a railway bridge. It would slow down the German advance towards the coast. I was to use standard dynamite, not PBF. He told me it had been classified secret so its use was being restricted in case the Germans got hold of a sample.'

The captain made another note on his pad.

'I did a three-day parachute course at Ringway,' Farquhar went on, 'and a few nights later was dropped in France. The Resistance man waiting for me, Pierre, had been wrongly briefed and took me to a bridge that wasn't the assigned target. However it seemed a suitable alternative so I blew it. Pierre killed a German guard with his bare hands whilst I was setting the charges. I hid in a derelict cottage for ten days before word came for me to return to England by Lysander. It picked me up OK but was shot down by home defence gunfire as we crossed the coast not far from here. Luckily I was pulled out of the wreckage before the plane exploded. I got away with nothing but a bit of concussion. The pilot bailed out too low and was killed. After discharge from hospital Colonel Fraser gave me a final debriefing here.'

The captain pursed his lips and stared across the desk.

'What you have just told me could have come straight from the pages of *Boy's Own Paper*,' he said, his dark eyes fixed on Farquhar's face. 'But I can see why your CO was impressed. He won't have many private soldiers in his ranks with your background. Do you speak French?'

Farquhar shook his head. 'Just what I recall from grammar school.'

'Hmmm. Odd that you should have been sent to France in that case.'

'Colonel Fraser said there was no one else available to do the job. He said the Resistance man waiting for me would speak English but Pierre didn't speak a word. And I couldn't understand his French.'

'You'd had no training in sabotage?'

'No, sir. I told the colonel I was just a chemical engineer, not a demolition expert. But he insisted there was no difference. He told me that as I'd signed the Official Secrets Act I had to follow his orders. Or be shot by firing squad.'

'That's Jock Fraser for you,' the captain said with a smile. 'Up guards and at 'em. So how did you end up in the infantry? You'd done a good job, despite a lack of training. You'd shown initiative, blown a bridge that wasn't your specified target. What went wrong?'

He bloody well knows what went wrong. A barrister never asks a question unless he already knows the answer. Fraser would write a report on me and even if it's not in my file there'll be a copy here at Rodmel. And this bastard's read it! But why bother to interview me? Perhaps he's giving me a chance to redeem myself. I'll tell him the truth and see what he makes of it.

He gave an audible sigh and shrugged. 'The colonel sent me to a country pub for a few days' rest after the plane crash,' he said, spreading his hands in a gesture of frankness. 'There was a girl, Josie Shirran, also staying there. She told me she worked for the Ministry of Food, something to do with eggs and the black market. We became close, nothing improper, just very close. I told her I'd been to France and blown up a railway bridge. I said that I may be going back, but after meeting her it was the last thing I wanted to do. Which was true. She tried to stop me telling her all this but I insisted that she listen. We went back to the pub. She told me she was going for a bath but slipped away. She must have been working for the colonel and phoned him from a call box, telling him I'd blabbed about having been in France. He rang the pub and ordered me back to London. At Kings Cross next morning he tore me to pieces. I was stripped of my uniform, driven in the back of a lorry to Fulwell and dumped at the barracks. That's how I came to be in the infantry.'

The captain sat drumming his fingers on the desk, staring at him. After a long silence he said quietly, 'It was no more than you deserved. No doubt you had been warned to keep your mouth shut.'

'Yes, sir,' Farquhar said miserably. He paused, not wanting to sound over-eager to excuse himself. 'I don't blame Josie; she was just doing the job she'd been sent to do. And did it very well. To be honest, and I feel foolish telling you this, I'd fallen in love with her. Desperately so. At first sight, the way it's supposed to happen. I'd never met anyone like her in the whole of my life. Or since. She told me her brother had been badly wounded at Dunkirk. I felt humiliated since my cover story was that I was in a cushy office job in Norfolk.'

The captain sat silent for a long time; when he spoke his voice was scathing. 'What you really mean is that you thought you'd stand a better chance of getting into her knickers if she thought you were a hero.'

'It wasn't like that, sir,' Farquhar protested. 'That's what Colonel Fraser said. But he was wrong too. I loved her. The most important thing in the world at that moment was for her to know that. I wanted her to understand how much I cared. Telling her the truth was part of it.'

'When your CO said he was recommending you for security work, what did you think?'

Farquhar said nothing; he sat with his head bowed.

'I want to know your thoughts at that moment,' the captain went on remorselessly. 'Were you too ashamed to tell him you'd let Colonel Fraser down? Or was it a second chance to impress Josie? Tell me what you felt.'

I'm being bloody vivisected. I've told this bastard my deepest secrets yet he's probing me as if I was a rat pinned to a board in a biology practical.

He jumped to his feet. The chair toppled backwards and he kicked it skidding across the room. Bending forward, he pressed his fists on the edge of the desk and glared at the captain's face.

'Fuck you,' he snarled; the words shot out like a cobra spitting venom. 'I'd have shoved my hand in the fire if she'd asked. Colonel Jock Fucking Fraser's orders meant nothing to me!'

The captain showed no emotion.

'I'd do the same thing again,' Farquhar said quietly. 'Again. And again. And again.'

'Pick up your chair and sit down,' the captain ordered.

'Don't patronize me, sir,' Farquhar said. 'I've taken enough bullshit over this. Just do what you have to do.'

'Sit down, please, Private Farquhar.'

He picked up the chair, set it in front of the desk and sat on it. He met the captain's eye with a steady gaze.

'You underestimate me,' Frobisher said evenly. 'We all have a breaking point. I wanted to find yours.'

'You must have read the report,' Farquhar said dully. 'You knew all about her already. And about me.'

The captain shook his head. 'No. But I guessed there was a Josie, or someone like her, behind it all. It could just as easily have been a man; that's not unknown. I knew Colonel Fraser wouldn't have dumped you without reason. On the other hand, you'd not been trained to keep your mouth shut. You were, as you say, "just" an engineer. I understand why you told the girl about France.'

Farquhar remembered the colonel telling him the Germans had shot Pierre and Elise on a dung heap. 'Fraser was an unfeeling arrogant bastard,' he said.

The captain looked steadily at him. 'He's dead,' he said quietly. 'The ship taking him to Burma was torpedoed off Java. He was badly wounded but survived eighteen days in a leaking lifeboat before reaching the coast. Two of the men with him escaped and lived to tell the tale. Colonel Fraser and the rest of the wounded were bayoneted on the beach by Japanese soldiers.'

Perhaps this is another lie, like the one Fraser told me about Pierre and Elise. Something to make me feel rotten. But the expression on the captain's face showed it was true.

'I'm sorry,' Farquhar muttered. 'I mean it.'

The captain nodded but said nothing. A long silence followed.

'What happens now?' Farquhar asked wearily. 'Another ride in the back of a lorry to Fulwell Barracks?'

Frobisher shook his head. 'No. Things have changed a lot in the past year. There's an outfit called the Special Operations Executive, SOE for short. Its job is to organize sabotage in German occupied countries.'

'The colonel mentioned it. He was going to offer me a job after I came back from Wylam. Josie changed his mind.'

'Anyone sent over to France in future will be properly trained. They'll be multilingual and technically highly competent in all departments. The days of the enthusiastic amateur agent are over.'

'I was never all that enthusiastic. I went under protest.'

'You are a graduate with a substantial knowledge of explosives. You are articulate, as you have just proved' – the captain gave a wry smile – 'and you carried out a successful operation in occupied France despite a lack of training. You made one foolish mistake. Luckily no harm was done. To be honest, I don't understand why Colonel Fraser subjected you to scrutiny in the way he did. He must have known SOE would never send you back to France.'

'Thank you, sir.'

'That in no way excuses what you did. But the incident is in the past. It has taught you an invaluable lesson, however painful.'

'Yes, sir. And I apologize for my outburst.'

'That too is in the past. Let's turn to the future. SOE are planning to send a large number of agents into Europe between now and the invasion, whenever it comes. They'll organize and carry out the blowing up of roads, railways, bridges, telegraph lines and storage facilities. They'll need specialist training, and some of it will be carried out here, at Rodmel. I want you to be one of their instructors. That may have been what Colonel Fraser had in mind for you. What you teach the agents about explosives could shorten the war by months. It's not glamorous work but it's vitally important.'

The sudden change in fortune made Farquhar's head spin. *A chance to work here, at Rodmel Manor! As a teacher! Of secret agents in wartime! What would Mother have thought! And Josie! What happened at Wylam doesn't matter any more....*

'I won't let you down, sir.' It was all he could think of to say.

'The lives of the trainees will depend on the knowledge and skills you pass on to them,' Frobisher said. 'I wouldn't have wasted my time on you if I'd thought there was the remotest chance of you making a second mistake. From this moment you're a second lieutenant in the Royal Engineers. Let me be the first congratulate you!'

Farquhar was disappointed to discover he was not to live in the manor house where accommodation was limited and reserved for senior officers. A group of wooden buildings had been built in woods half a mile away and he was allocated a room there. Some of the huts were to serve as dormitories and classrooms for the trainee agents; the first group was expected in six weeks.

He wrote to Mrs Fox, his mother's old neighbour, asking her to arrange for the railway van to collect the trunk containing his books and send it to him COD by train to Lewes station. He needed them to plan his lectures; until they arrived he was at a loose end. Luckily the weather was dry and sunny and he was able to explore Rodmel's ancient woods and take long walks alone across the Downs.

He often thought of Josie. He was sure she had had genuine feelings for him and must have known how he felt about her. Did she ever think of him? She would be married by now, probably had children. But were there perhaps moments when something reminded her of him? He hoped so. She had worked at Rodmel but nothing of her lingered in its ancient rooms and timbered galleries. Whenever he walked up the Elizabethan staircase his hand gripped the oak banister rail, worn as smooth as silk after 400 years. He imagined her doing the exactly same. The moment was fleeting but the memory always real.

Chapter Sixteen

In the rocky wastes of the Libyan desert a German army driver took the right-hand track at an unmarked fork. Had he turned left that morning, all would have been well. Instead, a few miles further on his armoured car ran into an ambush laid by a British army desert patrol group operating far behind the front line. The driver stopped the car and got out with his hands raised. On the back seat a high-ranking German officer, on his way to a divisional meeting chaired by Rommel, sat white-faced and clutching his briefcase. It contained a thick sheaf of unencoded documents marked 'Highly Secret'. The following day they arrived on Grigor's desk.

He read through them several times, wrote out a translation and placed it in a confidential file cover together with the original pages. Clipping a red 'Urgent: For Immediate Attention' label on the front of the file, he took it along the corridor and handed it to Major Howard's clerk. Back in his own office he stood at the window looking down at the traffic crawling along the street below. 'All good things must come to an end' was an English saying he knew well. And unfortunately today it had proved all too correct.

The easy unhurried life of the past five months was over. The German documents he had just translated contained nothing new; they were a comprehensive summary of the current situation of the war in North Africa. But they brought the realization that he had become too immersed in the minutiae of the campaign. For months he had dealt with reports on the movement of supply convoys, the transfer of tank squadrons from the rear to front-line positions, the withdrawal of exhausted infantry regiments and their replacement by others. He had never stood back to look at the full picture; perhaps that was what the major had meant when he told him he lacked a military mind. The papers had been the latest German interpretation of their strategic position in North Africa. And the inescapable conclusions it made shocked him.

The capture of Tobruk had long been essential to the success of the Germans in their advance on Cairo and the Suez Canal. The Afrika Korps led by Field Marshal Rommel surrounded the city. The present front line now lay far to the east. The supplies and reinforcements – men, fuel, armour, ammunition and equipment – necessary for the continuation of the victorious German advance had to be shipped across the Mediterranean from Italy. The nearest available North African port at which they could be unloaded was Benghazi from where they had to be transported to the front line along 300 miles of rocky desert road. Throughout this journey they were subjected to low-level bombing attack by RAF Hurricane aircraft carrying armour-piercing 'tank-busting' bombs. This tenuous chain of supply could not be extended. No further German advance was possible until the harbour at Tobruk, 200 miles closer to Cairo than Benghazi, was in their hands.

A valiant force of Australian and British troops continued their stubborn defence of the encircled city. Badly wounded men capable of firing a rifle were carried on stretchers to frontline positions to carry on the fight. Even Rommel, the German commander, praised their fortitude and gallantry. But they were in a hopeless situation. A convoy of ships bringing American tanks for the relief of Tobruk had been at sea for several weeks. Their route lay round the Cape of Good Hope but due to the presence of U-boats in the Atlantic they were forced to steer a course as far west as the coast of Brazil. They could not now arrive at Suez in time to relieve Tobruk. The latest German Panzers, superior in all respects to the British tanks, were moving up for a final attack to crush all resistance. Once the port was taken the British would have no alternative but to fall back to El Alamein, the next defensive position to the east along the coast. Beyond that lay Alexandria, the final obstacle to the advance on Cairo, a mere hundred miles further on. When that city was captured the glittering prize of the Suez Canal would fall to the Germans. British links with the Indian Empire and their colonial territories in the Far East not yet captured by the Japanese would be severed. The roads leading to the vast oil fields of Iraq and Persia would lie open. All resistance to German forces would end and Churchill, despite his bold promise never to surrender, would be forced to concede victory.

Standing by the window, Grigor recognized the fateful truth in the newly captured documents. He sighed, locked the filing cabinet and dropped the keys in the desk drawer. Glancing up at the ceiling for the last time, he walked down the stairs and out of Shepheards. He was burdened with the guilt of betrayal. *I'm repaying the trust the major placed in me by deserting when he needs me more than ever. Perhaps he'll be disciplined for allowing me access to highly classified material, or for lifting restrictions on my movements. But I have no choice. It would be useless to try to persuade him to let me go. He'd refuse to accept the British no longer have a hope of stopping Rommel. When the Germans arrive they will find my name in the files; my connection with Günter will be remembered and I'll be hunted down. There'll be no prisoner of war status for me. The Gestapo will take their revenge for being made to look the fools they are. Sorry, Major Howard. Perhaps after the war we'll meet and I'll be able to make you understand why I had to go.*

To hide his trail he walked over a mile from Shepheards before taking a taxi to the central railway station where he bought a first-class single ticket to Alexandria with the money the major had returned to him. The express took three hours to complete the 200-mile journey to Cairo. Outside the central station Grigor got into the rear seat of the first taxi in the queue by the pavement and told the driver to take him to the harbour.

The man shook his head. '*Effendi* cannot have been in Alexandria for some time,' he replied with a sad smile. 'Entry to the docks is now strictly forbidden. Only British ships are allowed to use the port. Even the fishermen cannot go out except in small boats without engines, and are not allowed to pass the bar. The only way a man can leave Alexandria by sea these days is to swim.'

'You are correct, my friend,' Grigor replied. 'It is some years since I was last in Alexandria. My home is in Cairo and I was hoping regulations would be easier here. Yesterday I received news that my old mother is dying in Cyprus. I am her only son, and must get to see her before she passes into the loving arms of Allah. Can you help me? Surely there are ferries operating? Or perhaps you know of someone with a boat who would take me to Cyprus?'

Again the man shook his head. 'I am sorry, *effendi*. There are no ferries, and all motorboats have been impounded. This war, which is not of our making, has ruined everything.'

'So there's no way I can attend my poor mother's funeral?'

'None, *effendi*. Unless you swim, or grow wings and fly there.'

'I am determined to reach Cyprus. Tell me, what is your name?'

'I am Omar, *effendi*.'

'Very well, Omar. I would like you to become my assistant for a few days until I can find a way of getting to Cyprus. Do as I say and I will pay you well. Do you agree?'

Omar sat silent for a few moments. Grigor could see his eyes staring at him through the taxi's rear-view mirror. '*Effendi*, is your mother truly dying in Cyprus?' he asked quietly.

Grigor shook his head. 'No, Omar,' he admitted. 'I am happy to say she went to Paradise some years ago.'

'I guessed that was the case. I do not wish to get into trouble. Are you wanted by the police?'

'Not the police but by the British. And the Germans, when they arrive. I speak both languages fluently so my services will be in great demand. But I am a man of peace, and have no wish to serve either side in their war on our sacred soil. That is why I must leave.'

'Spoken like a true Egyptian, *effendi*! Yes, I will do as you ask. I know Alexandria well and have many trustworthy friends. If there is a way for you to reach Cyprus, I will find it.'

'Excellent. First of all, take me to a hotel somewhere near the harbour where I can stay.'

The Hotel Internationales had a room available. The cost was grossly inflated and did not include meals but Grigor was pleased to take it. The room was on an upper floor at the rear of the building. From a window in the corridor outside there was a distant view of the tops of the harbour cranes but tall warehouses obstructed any sight of the ships in port. Grigor nursed a faint hope of finding the *Milos* again. The crew would still remember him as the man who had persuaded a U-boat commander to let them go unharmed. They would welcome him back on board to sail with them wherever they were bound. Perhaps the master would even take him to an out-of-the-way island on which he could settle until the war was over.

When Omar arrived at the hotel the following morning, Grigor told him to drive to the commercial docks. 'It is impossible, *effendi*,' he said. 'All roads around the harbour are closed. If I drive you there you will see.'

'Then take me as close as we can get.'

They had not travelled far when two large concrete fortifications came into view. They were heavily sandbagged with a heavy steel gate barring the central gap. Omar immediately stopped the car.

'We can go no further, *effendi*. Every vehicle entering or leaving the docks must stop at this roadblock. Drivers have to produce their documents for examination. Only when the guards are fully satisfied is the gate opened and the vehicle waved through. If you do not have proper papers you may be arrested for trying to enter illegally.'

A soldier on the roof of one of the buildings was already looking at the taxi through binoculars. In Cairo Major Howard would by now know he was absent and an alert for his arrest issued. Grigor could not risk questioning and told Omar to turn round and drive off.

The following morning he took a novel from the lounge bookcase. In the hotel garden he sat on a shady bench below a softly rustling palm; a gentle breeze from the sea tempered the searing heat. *How wonderful it must be to live here, to walk in this ancient city with history in every stone! Two and a half thousand years ago a stonemason idly chiselled on a slab that by the light of the moon reflected from the marble walls of Alexandria a tailor could see to thread his needle without need of a lamp.... Magda would not be happy here. She had no concept of history, no eye for real beauty. A contemplative life was far beyond her imagining. Her pleasures lay in the transient attractions of Paris, the vacuous social round and the constant fawning of sycophantic men.*

The news Omar brought him that evening was disappointing. He had made numerous enquiries but none of the people he had spoken to was able to help. He had used some of his precious store of petrol to drive along the coast to see his uncle who had a modern boat and before the war had made a good living catching squid for the best hotels. But even he could not help. With no fuel available, he had hauled his boat out of the water and it would remain on stocks on the beach until the war was over.

Grigor read the national newspapers avidly each morning. Although subject to strict censorship by the British, an official bulletin admitted the German Afrika Korps had launched a new attack on the Tobruk enclave. In an aside that had escaped the blue pencil, a brief editorial stated the defenders could not hold out for more than a few days. Egyptians were warned to brace themselves for the tide of battle sweeping along the coast; the citizens of Alexandria and Cairo could expect fighting in their streets within the month.

'I must get into the docks,' Grigor told Omar when he appeared the next afternoon to report another fruitless search. 'That is the only place where I will find a seagoing ship. I shall try to stow away on a vessel about to sail.'

Omar shook his head. '*Effendi* has seen how every road leading to the harbour is closed except to military vehicles.'

'I must escape, Omar.'

'Be patient, *effendi*. Allah will provide.'

Grigor remembered this prophecy two mornings later when he stopped to scan the large message board in the hotel foyer. A fresh warning had been posted asking guests to ensure the blackout curtains in their rooms were properly drawn at night in case of air raids. To make space on the board for this important notice, an earlier instruction had been moved to a different position and Grigor now read it for the first time:

The management regrets our famous roof garden is closed until further notice. We apologize to our guests for the loss of this facility on the orders of the British military authorities.

Why, Grigor wondered, should the army demand the closure of a roof garden? There had to be a sound reason and it was something he must investigate without delay. After lunch, with the hotel wrapped in the drowsy afternoon silence, he walked up five flights to the top landing. A painted sign, 'To The Roof Garden', with a pointing finger drawn alongside, was still fixed to the wall of a spiral staircase. A heavy metal grille secured in place by two padlocks barred access to the stairs.

'This is Ali, *effendi*,' Omar announced next morning. With a flourish he presented an unprepossessing little man with only one eye. He was respectably dressed in clean baggy trousers and a checked cotton shirt. Squinting at Grigor, he smiled and bowed.

'Yesterday you asked me to find you a locksmith,' Omar continued. 'Ali is the finest in Alexandria, if not the whole of Egypt. He can be trusted with your life. The explosion in which he lost his eye also rendered him deaf and dumb. He cannot read or write. Many banks and the best jewellers constantly employ him. The police ask him to open locks that defeat the efforts of their best officers. He never indicates the nature of the tasks he performs. Secrecy and discretion are his watchwords. His charges reflect his amazing abilities.'

'Provided he does what I require of him he will be well paid.'

Ali studied the lower padlock on the grille blocking the roof garden staircase. From his pocket he produced a well-used leather wallet, flipped it open and selected a hooked metal probe which he carefully inserted in the keyhole. A look of total concentration settled on his face as he manipulated the tool with practised ease. There was a soft click and the padlock sprang open in his hand. He nodded at Omar, who promptly knelt on the adjacent step. Ali scrambled onto his back and stood to reach the top padlock. It took him less time to open it than the first. He pulled the grille open on its hinges and the three of them walked to the top of the staircase. The wooden door giving access to the roof was fitted with an old-fashioned mortice lock which Ali opened in seconds. He grasped the knob and the door swung open, allowing a shaft of brilliant sunlight to enter the staircase.

'Ali's fee is two hundred dollars,' Omar said when they returned to the landing. The top door had been closed and the grille and padlocks replaced. Grigor thought the charge reasonable; he had been expecting to be asked for much more.

'Per lock, *effendi*,' Omar added. Grigor guessed this included his personal fee for finding Ali and making the introduction. 'Ali will take one of them to his workshop and make a key to fit both. The cost will be an additional two hundred dollars.'

'What about the door to the roof?' Grigor enquired.

'That will have to be left unlocked,' Omar replied. 'To make a key for such an old heavy lock he would have to remove it to his workshop. It is not worth the trouble. Wedge the door shut each time you leave and no one will know it has been opened.'

Omar returned later in the afternoon with the promised key. Grigor checked that it opened both padlocks smoothly before paying him. When he left, Grigor returned to the top landing and mounted the staircase. He opened the locks then pulled the grille shut behind him and continued to the top door. Ali had left it closed but unlocked and Grigor stepped out onto what had been the hotel's roof garden. It had a neglected air with weeds sprouting from cracks in the paved surface; sand and windblown refuse lay piled against the surrounding parapet walls. In the centre, stacked in a disorderly heap, were the chairs, tables and folded parasols formerly used by guests.

In the hotel's photographic shop that morning Grigor had bought a pair of binoculars. Crouching behind the parapet wall, he began a study of the complex of docks visible over the tops of the warehouses that hitherto had hidden them from view. Warships, tankers, cargo vessels, liners converted for use as troopships, barges, even a flotilla of submarines moored alongside their supply ship, were clearly in sight. The nearest vessel was less than a mile from him. It was obvious why the military authorities had ordered the closing of the roof: an enemy agent positioned here could obtain details of immense strategic value.

Grigor felt a surge of excitement. Apart from Royal Naval ships there were merchant vessels that would be crewed by civilian seamen. Some of these would fall sick, others wounded by enemy action and many would desert on reaching port. There would be a constant need for replacements. During his days on board the *Milos* he had watched the crew at work and was confident he could pass himself off as an experienced sailor. Not as an officer, perhaps, but as a deck hand or cook. Allah, as Omar prophesied, had indeed provided.

He could not stay on the roof for long; he could be spotted by someone on lookout in the harbour. He returned to the stairs, closed the top door and replaced the locks on the grille before returning to his room. His first visit had been much more useful than he had imagined possible. He lay on the bed planning how to talk his way onto a ship.

On his visit to the roof after lunch the following day he was surprised how the picture had altered overnight. Five of the ships he had seen the previous day had gone from their berths; two had sailed and three had changed their moorings, presumably to make room for others to discharge cargoes. He swung the glasses in an arc, sweeping across the harbour and out to sea. A large passenger ship, a former Cunarder from her chunky lines, was moving slowly into the bay. She was white overall apart from a red cross on her side, extending from near the waterline up to her promenade deck. A second large cross was painted on an upper deck, clearly visible to aircraft. There could be no doubt as to her identity. She was a hospital ship, arriving to rescue soldiers wounded in the battle for Tobruk.

Omar arrived the following morning, despondent at once again having to report his failure to find a boat.

'Never mind that,' Grigor said sharply. 'Take me to a shop that sells equipment for doctors. I require a stethoscope.'

'There is no such shop, *effendi*. But I know a way to obtain the article.'

'And what way is that, Omar?'

'Go to a hospital and steal one.'

It was late afternoon when Omar parked his taxi in a narrow street surrounded by slums. The hospital lay on the opposite side of the adjoining main road. Its buildings were single storey and ramshackle. The walls originally painted green had faded to the yellow colour of rotting cabbages. The roof was patched with flattened kerosene cans.

There were patients everywhere. Many had bandaged limbs and heads, some hobbled on homemade crutches whilst others stood in silent groups or lay on rough litters on the verandas. Many lay stretched out on the bare earth. A long winding queue of new arrivals, which never seemed to move, stretched from the road up to the main entrance.

Grigor stared in dismay through the windscreen of the taxi. 'How do all these sick people get treated?' he asked Omar.

'Very slowly, *effendi*. They are *fellaheen*. They have nothing, and they expect nothing. The hospital is free for them but they must wait their turn. Perhaps for days, since there are so few doctors.'

'Is there nowhere else I can obtain a stethoscope?' Grigor asked. 'I am ashamed to steal from such a place.'

'*Effendi* is too kind-hearted. What difference will the loss make to the *fellaheen*? All they look for is death.'

'My conscience still tells me to take from them is very wrong. There must be other hospitals.'

'For the wealthy, yes. That is why there are so few doctors here. They prefer to be well paid for treating the rich in their private clinics. But such places are guarded and I do not know how you would enter. You say you require this instrument urgently. This is the easiest place in Cairo to obtain it.'

'I am ashamed, but my life depends upon it. Wait for me here.'

Grigor crossed the road, strode past the queue and pushed through the crowd into the gloom of the main building. The air was filled with the stink of humanity, a gut-wrenching cocktail of sweat and vomit, urine and excrement. Great bouts of sputum-loaded coughing punctuated the wailing of sick children; the agonized screams and shrieks of the sick and injured mingled with the terminal groans of the dying. The blind stumbled over the leprous, the insane grappled with each other in bizarre wrestling matches. Dense clouds of fat black flies buzzed and swarmed overhead.

Attempts were being made to bring order out of chaos. A few harassed men, hard-faced and dressed in khaki drill uniforms, seized those at the front of the crowd and hustled them to long tables behind which sat the grim-faced medical staff. There was no time for a physical examination. A doctor shouted a few questions, scribbled a note on a pad and handed it to the wretched patient who was pushed by a porter into another queue stretching into the murky corridors of the hospital beyond.

What new horrors await them there? Grigor wondered. *Another interminable wait before an exhausted so-called specialist spends less than a minute dealing with their case? If they're lucky they may be handed a few pills, or a bottle of linctus, to relieve a possibly life-threatening condition. For some there'll be surgery carried out in a butcher-shop operating theatre with no sterility and a minimum of anesthetic....*

He thought of the useless crowns hidden in the hotel. If he were to donate them to this hospital, what a difference it could make! The million dollars they brought would attract doctors, nurses and specialists. New facilities and equipment could be provided, the latest drugs bought....

But even as the idea blossomed in his mind he realized its futility. The money would disappear like sand before the desert wind. Corrupt officials and politicians would pocket it, not a cent would be spent to alleviate the misery of the *fellaheen*. He squared his shoulders and slammed the door on thoughts of philanthropy. He was here to save himself, not dream of fantasies to save the already doomed. A door in the wall behind the seated doctors had a sign:

Strictly Private: Medical Staff Only

Grigor sidled along behind them, murmuring apologies to those whose chairs he accidentally bumped. The room was lit by a single bare light bulb. In the centre, lounging in chairs set around a circular table, were five men. They looked up at him, unsurprised but curious.

'It's hectic out there,' he said cheerfully as he closed the door.

'It's the cholera season,' one of the men grunted. 'What do you expect?'

'Are you on the beta rota?' another asked. 'I've not seen you before.'

'I'm on secondment,' Grigor replied smoothly. 'I've just come from the faculty in Cairo.'

'Ah! An academic! That should raise the tone of the place.'

'Are you a lecturer?' enquired an elderly man with grey hair.

'Yes. In psychiatry.' It was the first specialty that came to mind.

'You've come to the right place, then. We're all batty here!' the youngest of the group piped up.

'After a month of seeing nothing but shit and chancres anyone'd be off their trolley,' grunted another.

'You must know old Prof Alweeri,' one of the doctors said cheerfully. 'Does he still grope his women patients?'

'Not in the cholera season,' Grigor said, which drew a laugh.

'What's your name?' enquired the older man. 'I'm Dr Hassan.' He pointed across the table. 'Meet doctors Mohammed One and Mohammed Two. That's Dr Ali and on the end is Dr Masood.'

'I am Dr Eban Albaba. I'm very pleased to meet you all.'

There was a murmur of acknowledgement; Dr Hassan pulled out a chair.

'Take a seat. Would you like some tea?'

It was twenty minutes before they stood up. From their comments Grigor gathered they were about to exchange places with the team at present on duty at the table outside.

'I must go and find the boss,' he said. He had no idea to whom he was referring but he needed an excuse not to accompany them.

'We'll be seeing you again soon,' Dr Hassan said. 'We're a friendly lot; brothers in adversity you might say. It's depressing work, but you'll become hardened to it. And it doesn't last for ever!'

'Teaching will never feel so good after you've been here a week!' Dr Mohammed One (*or is he Two?* Grigor wondered) said with a sad smile.

As they filed out, the uproar from the crowd outside filled the room for a few moments until the door closed behind them. Grigor moved quickly, knowing it would not be long before the other team returned for their break. One of the walls was lined with narrow wooden lockers. The doors of the first six he opened were empty but in the next a white coat hung from the hook, and in the top pocket was a stethoscope. He slipped on the coat. In the far corner of the room was a second door, presumably leading into a hospital corridor. As he stepped across to it he heard the sound of voices as the first of the relieved team entered. He hurriedly left the room, pausing only to close the door quietly behind him.

The corridor was dark and packed with queuing patients. To his right was the reception area. Dare he risk leaving the hospital by the same route he had used to get in? He would have to push his way through the crowd, past the curious gaze of the porters. The doctors he had been speaking to may glimpse him, from behind admittedly, assume he had lost his way and call out to him. It was an agonizing decision but he put his head down, hunched his shoulders and barged into the melee, waving the stethoscope and demanding to be let through. It was several minutes before he managed to reach the main entrance and force his way outside.

Night was falling and the cool evening air struck his face. He felt dirty and contaminated. There was no sense of achievement, no thrill at having secured his objective. All he wanted was a hot bath, a change of clothes and a bottle of whisky to help blot out the memory of the horrors he had seen.

Chapter Seventeen

Blazoned across the front page of every Alexandrian newspaper the following day was the fall of Tobruk to the Germans. The victorious Afrika Korps, previously forced to rely on supplies brought by trucks driven along the hazardous 300-mile stretch of desert road, would soon receive whatever they needed through the newly captured port. The British were retreating east to the coastal town of El Alamein; the German advance on Alexandria was expected within days. Grigor, sitting in the hotel lounge, enjoyed a surge of self-satisfaction. The assessment set out in the captured documents had been accurate, justifying his decision to leave Cairo. The wounded men evacuated from Tobruk before it fell would be on their way to the hospital ship so he had to move quickly. He made his way to the top floor. Loitering on the stairs until there was a quiet moment, he moved up to the grille, opened it and slipped the padlocks into his pocket before pulling the grille shut behind him.

On the roof he scanned the docks through the binoculars. The Cunarder was in a dock on the south side of the harbour. Alongside her a line of ambulances and troop-carrying vehicles extended back almost to the dock gates. He rapidly descended the stairs, replaced the padlocks and returned to his room. He packed his suitcase, went down to reception and checked out.

He was waiting outside the hotel when Omar arrived.

'Take me to the road on the south side of the docks,' he ordered.

'We will not get far, *effendi*. As you saw last time we will be turned back long before we reach the harbour.'

'Not today, Omar. Doctor Grigor is taking up his new duties.'

In the taxi he put on the white coat stolen from the hospital the previous day. At the roadblock a mile from the port an armed soldier held up his hand. Grigor wound down the taxi window and gave him a friendly smile.

'Good morning, Officer,' he said.

'Where the fuck d'ye think you're going?' the soldier demanded.

'I am a surgeon. I've come to help in the treatment of the wounded embarking on the hospital ship that arrived yesterday afternoon.' He held up the stethoscope as a badge of his profession.

'Oh yeah,' the soldier replied suspiciously. 'First I've heard of civvies helping us. We've got our own medics.'

'I used to work at Guy's Hospital in London.'

The famous institution came to mind as he spoke. He hoped it would impress the soldier but he gave no sign that it did.

'Show me your papers,' he snapped.

It was the awkward moment Grigor had been expecting. Major Howard had kept his Turkish travel permit so the only document he possessed was his military pass to Shepheards in Cairo describing him as a translator. He held it out and the soldier snatched it from him.

'I meant proper papers,' he snapped after peering at the pass. 'Where's the signed order saying I can let you through?'

'I work for British Intelligence in Cairo. The pass you are holding allows me to enter any army-controlled premises.'

'You said you were a doctor, not a fuckin' spy.'

Although the man spoke aggressively there was a note of doubt in his voice and Grigor pressed home this apparent advantage.

'It's possible to be both, Officer,' he said quietly. 'You really must let me through. I assure you I have the highest priority.'

As he spoke there was a series of loud blasts on a hooter. Glancing in the rear-view mirror, Grigor saw an army ambulance had pulled up behind and more vehicles were following. The driver of the ambulance hooted again and leaned out of his cab.

'Get a fuckin' move on there!' he yelled. 'I've got a poor sod what's bleedin' to fuckin' death in the back here.'

Grigor flung the taxi door open, jumped out and snatched the pass from the startled soldier's hand. 'I must attend to him!' he shouted. 'Let my driver turn round and go back. He can wait for me at the hospital.'

Turning to Omar, he said rapidly in Arabic, 'Go back now! Keep the money and get rid of my suitcase! Forgot you ever saw me! Goodbye!'

He slammed the taxi door shut and, waving his stethoscope, ran back to the ambulance. 'Drive on as quick as you can,' he snapped at the driver. 'I'll see to the patients.'

He wrenched open the rear door and climbed inside. The ambulance was packed with men. Its four stretchers were each occupied by two patients lying side by side, their limbs bound with blood-soaked dressings. Ten others, all heavily bandaged but capable of sitting, squatted on the outer frames of the two lower stretchers. In the central aisle, huddled at their feet, lay a man with a medical orderly bending over him.

'This is the man who is bleeding heavily?' Grigor asked assertively. 'Where is his wound? Let me examine him, please.'

The orderly stood up. 'Shrapnel in the belly, sir. His guts are hanging out. He's asleep now.'

'You have administered morphine?'

'Overdosed him, sir, to be honest. He wouldn't stop screaming for his mother. He was upsetting the rest of the lads.'

'You acted correctly. Nothing else can be done for him until he reaches theatre. Show me who else is in a serious condition.'

The ambulance had canvas sides with ventilators but no windows, making it impossible to see outside. At times the vehicle raced along with the engine roaring and the body pitching and rolling as the tyres bumped over an uneven road surface. Without warning the brakes would be slammed on; everyone was thrown forward and progress was reduced to a crawl. The driver blew his horn repeatedly and his voice could be heard demanding to be let through whatever obstacle lay in his path. His extreme language was apparently effective since none of the hold-ups lasted long.

Grigor made a pretence of examining each patient although in fact he did little more than read their notes. He asked each man how he was feeling and made slight adjustments to some wound dressings. He placed his hand on the brows of others and made a pretence of taking a few pulses. He was touched by the mumbled words of gratitude he received in return for such meaningless gestures. Each man seemed to believe he had performed a heroic medical action on his behalf. Eventually after much starting and stopping interspersed with weaving and grinding along in low gear, the ambulance jerked to a stop, the rear doors were pulled open and sunlight flooded in. Grigor jumped out and looked around. He was standing on the quay; towering above him was the vast white hull of the hospital ship. An RAMC captain stepped forward. 'What have you brought?' he asked sharply.

'Good afternoon, Captain,' Grigor replied. He had memorized the notes pinned to each man's shirt. 'One mortally wounded, shrapnel in the abdomen. Sixteen head and limb injuries, five probable amputees, and two with minor trauma but severely shellshocked.'

The captain nodded and turned to the sergeant beside him.

'Get them on board,' he snapped. 'Gut case to theatre, prioritize the rest.'

He swivelled back to Grigor. 'And you are...?' he asked.

'Doctor Grigor Grigorovanovich, Captain. Medical Intelligence.'

'Medical Intelligence? What the fucking hell's that?'

Grigor smiled. 'If you have not heard of us then our security is as good as we hoped. We are a specialized branch investigating enemy developments in battlefield medicine. I am a German speaker and was employed as a translator at army headquarters in Shepheards Hotel.'

'And what particular enemy development are you hoping to investigate here, Doctor?' The contempt in the captain's voice was plain. 'I suggest doing something to end the fighting would serve a damned sight better purpose.'

'I could not agree more, Captain. Our work was important, but the war has reached a critical stage as you are doubtless aware. I therefore felt as a surgeon I would be of more use in my original trade, as it were, than peering through keyholes to see what the Germans were up to. I therefore applied for a frontline post and was told to report to this ship.'

'What is your experience?'

'I qualified in medicine at the University of Beirut. I became a surgeon at Cairo General, and took my fellowship in orthopaedics at Guy's in London six years ago. I was also a consultant at Ormond Street Children's Hospital.'

He was surprised how easily he lied. Fear was said to lend wings to the terrified; perhaps lying came readily to the desperate.

The captain nodded cautiously. 'Very impressive,' he said. 'And what, may I ask, are your intentions now?'

'I am at your disposal.'

The captain stood silent. Grigor guessed what he was thinking. *Is this man genuine, or trying to escape the fighting? There's no time to have him investigated. If he is a surgeon we could do with an extra pair of hands on board. The only other alternative is to send him back but since he speaks German he could slip across the line and offer them his services instead. They're probably as desperate for sawbones as we are....*

Once again the army came to Grigor's rescue. The sergeant returned.

'Next ambulance waiting, sir,' he reported to the captain. 'Three dead, eight serious. Two thoracic and one with no legs.'

The captain nodded. 'It appears blood and gore aplenty await you, Doctor Grigovanovitch,' he said without warmth. 'Go on board and find Colonel Postlethwaite. He's head of surgery and will find plenty for you to do. We'll speak again later.'

'Thank you, Captain. I shall look forward to that.'

An assortment of gangways and ramps sloped up from the quay to large open doors in the ship's side. The walking wounded, including men on crutches, were being marshalled into line to mount the first of the gangways. Those unable to walk waited in a long winding queue of wheelchairs waiting to be pushed by orderlies up a broad ramp. The most seriously injured were carried on board on stretchers. Grigor, still wearing the stolen white coat, strode to the foot of the gangplank being used by the walking wounded.

'Excuse me!' he called, waving the stethoscope. 'I'm a doctor! Let me through! I'm needed in the operating theatre!'

'Fackin' bladdy orficers,' an Australian voice behind him shouted. 'Always at the fackin' frant when we're fackin' retreatin'.'

'Can't wite ter get at the feckin' gin,' a Cockney voice piped.

'Aa bet 'ees's go' a wee bitty crumpet waitin' for 'im,' yelled a Scot.

Inside the doorway at the top of the gangway an RAMC sergeant was directing the wounded traffic.

'I'm a doctor,' Grigor said sharply. 'I've orders to report to Colonel Postlethwaite.'

'Down that passage, sir. You'll find the colonel in the theatre amidships, two decks down. Just follow the signs.'

Grigor set off down the passage although he had no intention of seeking out the colonel. *My role as a surgeon has come to an end,* he thought. *I'm leaving the stage before reaching the theatre.* Amused at his own wit, he tried out the pun in Arabic but the subtlety was lost in translation. He walked purposefully on. Doors lined the passage on both sides and he wondered what lay behind them but it was too risky to take a peek at that moment. He had to find a new identity until the ship sailed. Once at sea it would be unfortunate if he was discovered to be a fraud but with several thousand wounded on board the ship would not return to port to land him. He would be locked in a cell until the destination port was reached.

He found an empty toilet block. In a cubicle he took off the white coat, stuffed the stethoscope into one of the pockets and shoved the bundle out of a porthole into the harbour. He tore his Shepheards' pass into small pieces and flushed them down the toilet. No trace of his former identity now existed; he was ready for a new life, whatever it may be. He stepped out into the passage. A few yards away an unattended trolley stood stacked with medical records. Glancing about to check no one was watching, he picked up three of the files. Close by a stairway descended to the deck below and he hurried down. Pausing at the bottom to tuck the files more comfortably under one arm, he assumed a purposeful look and strode on. *I'm wearing a suit and a tie and look like a civilian official*

entrusted on board with confidential papers so I can walk about all day,
looking as though I know where I'm going. No one will ask what I'm
doing....

His plan worked well for a couple of hours. He stepped out purposefully, frowning as if burdened by heavy responsibilities. The ship was a
complicated maze through which he strode from one end to the other and
back. He climbed and descended numerous staircases and walked lengthy
corridors, becoming familiar with the general arrangement on board.
Bulkheads had been removed to provide spaces for twenty or more beds set
out Nightingale fashion along each side. The infectious disease wards were
on the upper decks to take advantage of the sun and fresh air; the four
operating theatres and associated surgical wards lay low in the hull where
the ship's movement at sea was least. A loud tannoy chimed every couple
of minutes; its irritating three-note signal was invariably followed by
instructions for someone to report somewhere without delay. Grigor
listened carefully to each announcement in case one of them referred to
himself. The captain he had spoken to on the quay may have checked to
confirm he had followed instructions and contacted Colonel Postlethwaite.

At five o'clock the tannoy suddenly gave a new signal, seven successive
notes struck in a musical sequence. A metallic voice said: '*First sitting for*
dinner for medical and nursing personnel.' Three army nurses, dressed in
khaki drill shirts and skirts and chattering loudly, came round a corner.
Grigor slipped the files on top of a cupboard in the corridor and followed
them. They joined a stream of uniformed men and women heading for a
lower deck. The smell of food increased then a pair of swing doors opened
into an area the full width of the ship. Evening sunlight streamed through
portholes on either side revealing incongruous traces of the glories of what
had been the ship's main saloon. Crystal pendants hung from the ceiling
and a line of marble-faced pillars stood along the centre of the room. At
the forward end was a wide stage on which the ship's orchestra, seated
among potted palms, had once played Strauss and Lehar as passengers
dined in evening dress.

Gone were the attentive waiters and the acres of starched white tablecloths, the silver cutlery, thick carpets and elegant chairs. In their place was
a lino-covered floor and rows of scrubbed wooden benches and forms. A
counter at which weary army cooks stood ladling out stew for the evening
meal replaced the buffet sideboards.

With sudden dismay Grigor realized that he had come to the Other
Ranks dining room. Everyone was in military or nursing uniform and
eating out of metal mess tins they had brought with them. He was
completely out of place, without utensils of any sort. His white suit was

sweat-stained and badly crumpled. If he presented himself at the counter the military police would be called and he would be arrested and taken ashore for questioning. He walked wearily to a vacant bench at one of the wooden tables and sat looking casually around as if waiting for someone. *What can I do? It's rotten luck to have got this far then fail for the lack of a couple of mess tins.*

'Cheer up, mate.'

The voice came from behind. He quickly turned; on the other side of the table sat three soldiers staring at him.

'Good evening, gentlemen,' he said. 'That dinner smells good!'

'Where's yours?'

The speaker was a ginger-haired lance corporal. His pale skin, ill suited to exposure to a tropical sun, was scorched scarlet and his face showed signs of flourishing acne.

'It's coming,' Grigor replied vaguely. He waved his arm at the long queue along the counter.

'There's no waiters here, y'know. This ain't the Adelphi,' a small soldier wearing thick glasses said.

'Adelphi?' Grigor queried.

'Big hotel in Liverpool, mate. Where the knobs go to eat.'

'And in Aintree week,' the soldier next to him put in, 'it's full of cocky wee shites less than five feet high.'

'Pardon?'

'Bloody jockeys. Up for the Grand National.'

Grigor stared at them, totally bemused. It was as if they were speaking in an ancient unrecorded tongue. A half-remembered quotation drifted into his mind: *'In the hands of such weak men doth my salvation lie.'* English? Marlowe? Shakespeare maybe. But which play? His thoughts were dragged back to the present when the first soldier spoke again.

'You all right, boyo?' he asked gently.

Grigor shook his head. 'Since you kindly ask, no, I'm not.'

'We thought you looked lost, didn't we, lads? Out of place somehow.'

All three sat gripping knives and forks in their fists and stared as they waited for an explanation of his plight.

'I'm in a bit of a state,' he added lamely.

'Here. Have some of this.' The lance corporal pushed his mess tin across the table and held out a spoon. 'Get that down and tell us what's bothering you.'

The smell reminded Grigor it was ten hours since he had breakfast in the hotel. The men watched him bolt the stew, saying nothing until he had finished.

'I'm Ginger,' the lance corporal said. 'I'm in charge of these idle sods.'
He nodded to his left. 'This is Tom. And the little fat bugger with the specs
is Taffy. What's your handle? What sort of trouble are you in? We might
be able to help.'

'I've lost my memory,' Grigor said; the lie came just a second before he
spoke. He braced himself in readiness for weaving a new web of deceit.
The three men sat waiting to hear more.

'I don't know my name,' he went on, 'or where I came from. Or what
I'm doing here. I've no papers and my pockets are empty. My mind's a
blank.'

'Jesus,' Taffy said. 'You are in a bloody state, right enough.'

'I remember travelling in a car. It was very hot.' Grigor spoke in a dull
detached voice as if talking to himself. 'Suddenly there was gunfire.
Perhaps from an aeroplane.' He paused to add dramatic effect. 'Yes, yes,
there was an aeroplane. I remember now. It flew over very low. It had
black crosses on the wings....'

'A Jerry bastard then,' Tom said. 'Probably a Messerschmitt 109,' he
added knowledgeably.

'Were you on your own?' Ginger asked.

'Yes. No. Yes. There was a driver ... he fell out of the door ... covered
in blood. I remember thinking ... he must be dead....'

They sat enthralled, waiting for the next instalment. Grigor seized the
chance to make up more lies.

'What then?' Taffy demanded. 'Did the Jerry come back?'

'I don't know. I've no idea what happened after that. An hour ago I
found myself up on deck, leaning against a rail, watching wounded
soldiers being brought on board. It was like a door opening in my head.
As if I'd just woken from a long sleep. I didn't know where I was. But
when I saw them bringing injured men up the gangplank I guessed I was
on a hospital ship. They were in uniform so I must be in a war zone. I
had no idea where.' He wiped a non-existent tear on the cuff of his
jacket.

'You're right about being in the middle of a war,' Taffy said. 'That's
bloody Egypt out there.'

'Egypt?' Grigor gasped. 'I've never been here in my life!'

'Well, you are now. Sand and camels, King Farouk and belly dancers.
The whole fuckin' show.'

'But how could I have got here?'

'Where do you think you should be?' Tom asked.

'I don't know. But Egypt seems wrong.'

'What I can't figure out,' Ginger said, clearly puzzled, 'is how, if you've

forgotten everything else, you still know how to talk. I mean, you understand what I'm saying to you, right?'

'He must have had a bump on the head,' Taffy said. 'It happened to a
bloke in Swansea. It was in the paper. He fell down the stairs an' when he
woke up he didn't recognize his own missus.'

'I bet she was an ugly old cow from Cardiff an' he was just pretendin','
Tom said with a snigger.

'Look,' Ginger said sternly. 'It's no good sittin' here talkin' rubbish
about some daft Welsh bastard. We've got to help this poor bugger.'

'Like how?'

'I don't know. Get a doctor to give him a jab or summat.'

'No, please, not a doctor,' Grigor said quickly; becoming involved with
medics would be far too risky. 'I'm sure I'll be all right in a day or two.
Until then, if you can get me some army clothes instead of this suit, I can
pretend to be a soldier. Like you three.'

Ginger looked hard at him. 'We can get hold of a set of fatigues for you,
no trouble. And boots. And a set of mess tins and a hammock. But you'll
need a place to sling it. And a job of some sort in case some nosey sod asks
what the fuck you're up to.'

'Trouble is,' Tom said, 'an' don't take this the wrong way, mate. No
offence meant an' all that, but you don't look like one of us. You're
different, older and, well, sort of posh. Nobody'd believe you're a
squaddie.'

He looked embarrassed but Grigor guessed he had merely said what the
others were thinking.

'Then there's the roll calls,' Taffy pointed out, giving support to Tom's
doubts. 'You'll have to go on them but you don't know the proper drill.
You'd be spotted as different straight off.'

'No he won't. His name's not on the roll so it'll not be called out.'

'Oh yer, I'd forgotten that.'

'I don't want to get you into any trouble,' Grigor said anxiously.
Melting into the background was going to be more complicated than he
had imagined.

Ginger shook his head. 'Don't worry about that,' he assured him. 'We're
all from Liverpool,' he said. 'Even Taffy. He had just enough sense left to
do a runner across the border from bloody Wales. We're a bolshy lot. We
don't like officers, or NCOs. We run rings round them all day long.'

'Ginger's an NCO, being a lance corporal,' Tom explained, 'but being a
Scouse, it doesn't count.'

The other two nodded and grinned. 'We run this ship,' Taffy said, 'not
the bloody captain. What we say goes.'

'What jobs do you all do?' Grigor asked.

'We're GDOs,' Tom said proudly. 'General Duties Orderlies. Best job in the fuckin' army.'

'Everybody thinks we work for somebody else,' Ginger explained. 'If we're told to do summat today we say we can't do it till tomorrow cos we're busy with summat we got told to do yesterday. Then tomorrow if somebody tells us to do summat else we say we can't cos we're busy doing what we promised somebody yesterday we'd do what they wanted today.'

'But we tell them we can do it tomorrow,' Tom added helpfully.

'An' so it goes on till Friday and we have the weekend off,' Taffy added. 'Then by Monday every bugger's forgotten what they asked us to do last week and it starts all over again.'

'It sounds as if you have it off to a fine art,' Grigor remarked, having barely understood their explanation.

Ginger looked at him thoughtfully. 'Since you can't remember your name, what shall we call you?'

'How about Alf?' Tom suggested. 'Same name as my dad.'

'Alf is fine,' Grigor replied with a smile. He guessed it was a shortened form of Alfred and as far from his own as it was possible to get.

'Right, Alfie boy. Just get up casual like and follow us.'

The three of them shared a small two-man cabin on a lower deck close to the stern. The bare steel side of the ship, pierced by a single porthole, formed one side, curving sharply inwards from top to bottom, and from fore to aft. The two fixed bunks on either side belonged to Ginger and Tom whilst Taffy had a hammock slung between them from an overhead beam. They left Grigor – he could not think of himself as Alf – alone while they went on what Ginger called 'the scrounge'. They returned a few minutes later with a set of fatigues, a pair of boots and a khaki beret. Taffy followed carrying a rolled-up hammock.

'I hope the boots fit,' Ginger said. 'We couldn't find any mess tins, it being dinner time. We'll get some for you tomorrow.'

'You mean you've stolen these things?' Grigor gasped.

'Just borrowed them,' Tom said. 'Don't worry. The blokes we've pinched them off'll go and nick somebody else's. That's how the army works. Nobody minds.'

Taffy tied the ends of the hammock to the beam next to his and showed Grigor how to clamber in and out without falling onto the deck. He was aware of how fortunate he had been to meet the trio. He had a suspicion that, of the three, only Ginger was unconvinced of the truth of his lost memory tale. It was vital therefore not to say anything likely to damage their still-fragile friendship. It was sheer bad luck that he made an almost fatal error the first evening.

Even with the porthole and door both hooked wide open and the forced ventilation system roaring at full blast, the cabin remained unbearably hot. The situation was worsened by four of them now crowding into a space designed only for two. Because of the ever-present danger from scroungers, they could not all go up on deck together leaving the cabin empty. The solution was to work to a rota, with one pair going up on deck for a half-hour spell, then the other two. It was agreed that Ginger and Tom should form one pair, Taffy and Grigor the other. Blackout regulations were strictly enforced on board to prevent Luftwaffe bomber pilots identifying the precise location of the docks. Each porthole and every doorway opening onto a deck was fitted with a heavy curtain kept closely drawn. Smoking on deck at night was prohibited in case enemy aircrews caught sight of the flares from matches.

Grigor and Taffy's last spell of the night on deck came to an end. There was just time before 'Lights Out' sounded over the loudspeakers for Ginger and Tom to go up for a final breath of air. As Grigor reached the top of the ladder he said casually to Taffy, 'I'll use the heads before we go back down.'

The Welshman made no comment at the time but when they got back to the cabin he said quietly, 'Alf calls the bog "the heads", like us. He must have been to sea before.'

'Heads' was the expression for 'toilet' used by seafarers the world over. Grigor had become familiar with the term and had used it himself numerous times on the *Milos*. Ginger spun round and glared at him.

'Did you say that?' he demanded aggressively.

Grigor was shocked at having made such an elementary mistake. He gulped and said, 'Yes. I wanted to pee and just said it. I've no idea where it came from. The words just entered my head.'

'You must've been a sailor like Taffy says,' Ginger said suspiciously. 'Nobody else calls the bogs "heads". You never told us that.'

'I might have been at sea at before,' Grigor agreed lamely. 'The ship sometimes seems strangely familiar.'

'Come on, Tom, let's go on deck. You come with us an' all, Taffy,' Ginger said sharply. Turning to Grigor, he snapped, 'You mind the shop.'

They left the cabin in silence. *They're going to decide what to do with me*, Grigor thought. *Why did I say something stupid like that when everything was going so well? Should I make a run for it while I have the chance? Go ashore and hide until I find another ship? But I'll never be as lucky as I was this afternoon, meeting these three. And if I do run they'll take it as proof I'd been lying. After all, they may decide I've been to sea before and it was a genuine flash of recollection. There's no harm in that. I'll stay and hope that's how it works out.*

He undressed and climbed into his hammock, which was more comfortable than he had expected. He drifted off to sleep before Ginger and his mates came back to the cabin.

The hammock's comfort was merely an initial delusion since it gave no spinal support. When Grigor woke in the morning his back ached painfully. Tom was already up, pulling on his shorts. Without looking at Grigor, he announced, 'I'm gasping for a smoke. I'm going up top.'

Smoking was forbidden at all times below but allowed on deck during hours of daylight except for those on duty. Ginger ignored Grigor until he had got into his fatigues and picked up his towel and washbag. He came across to the hammock and stood looking him straight in the eye.

'Me and the lads have decided we'll take your word, Alf,' he said. 'About you mentioning "heads", I mean. I hope you've not been tellin' us fuckin' lies.'

'I haven't, Ginger, honestly. I don't know what made me say it.'

Ginger stared at him from close range; his pale eyes were hard and cold. 'All right. We've agreed to say nowt more about it. Get up now. You can borrow my razor when I get back.'

Taffy was still asleep in the adjoining hammock. Grigor slid to the floor and got dressed then sat on the edge of Ginger's bunk waiting for him to return. When he did Tom was with him and Grigor guessed they'd come to a decision.

'Tom and me reckon it would best for you to stay in the cabin during the day while we're out. We'll have to lock you in in case some bugger sees you. One of us will come back now and again to let you go to the heads. We'll bring your meals so you won't have to show yourself in the mess hall. At night you can go up top with one of us for a breath of air. OK?'

It's far from OK. They don't trust me any more and they're locking me in for their own protection, not mine. But I've got no choice but to agree.

He forced himself to smile. 'That's fine, Ginger. Thanks for going to such trouble for me. Being alone will give me time to think about things. Perhaps I'll remember how I came to be here in the first place.'

'That's what we hope,' Ginger said, not very convincingly.

As the morning wore on, the heat in the locked cabin became intense. The ventilation ducts roared continuously without effect. Not a breath of breeze entered the open porthole. Through it came the usual bustle of quayside activity. Lorries rumbled past, a harbour crane trundled endlessly to and fro, and there was the intermittent whine of a heavy winch. Grigor lay naked on the upper bunk; time seemed to have stopped. He tried to concentrate on the problems facing him but as quickly as they came to mind they slipped from his mental grasp like phantom eels. He craved a book. He needed something deep and intellectual to seize his imagination and distract him from this wretched state. A literary work casting new light on old beliefs and ideas. Or an imaginative political thriller ...

He sat upright, unable to believe his eyes. A shed on the quay had just slid past the porthole! *My God! We're sailing!* Until now the ship had been nothing but a depressing depository for the sick; badly ventilated and filled with the stench of disinfectant. But not for much longer. She was moving out to sea where there was clean air and a cooling breeze! He thrust his head out of the porthole. A powerful tug was towing the ship stern first out of the dock. The crews of the last ambulances to arrive stood in a line along the quay, waving and calling farewell messages. *They must know this is one of the last ships to leave. In a few days' time the Germans will be here and they'll all be taken prisoner, caged behind barbed wire out in the desert perhaps for years.* He stretched an arm out of the porthole and waved to them, aware of how very lucky he was.

When Tom came at lunchtime he had brought a bottle of water and a mess tin containing a single slice of tinned corned beef and two dry biscuits.

'I'm sorry, Alf,' he said, sounding as if he meant it, 'but that's all there is. They don't give us much when the ship leaves port in case it's wasted. Lots of the blokes get seasick. But there'll be a good dinner tonight for them that can keep it down.'

'Where are we going?' Grigor enquired. 'I asked Ginger yesterday but he didn't know.'

'Nobody does, not even the captain yet they reckon. Not till he gets a coded message. The Med's a big place. Last time we left Alex with a load of wounded we went first to Malta then on to Gib. Might do the same this time. Or mebbes Cyprus. I don't take much notice of the news so the Jerries might have captured it by now. There's nowt we can do about it any road. Enjoy your bully and biscuits. I'll come back in a bit and let you go to the heads.'

'Can you find me a book, Tom?' Grigor asked. 'I'm going mad lying here on my own with nothing to do or read.'

'A book? I think I saw some in the officers' mess. I'm going there later to pick up tablecloths for the laundry. I'll see what I can do.'

As he left, the ship gave a gentle pitch, the first of the voyage.

That evening there was a carnival atmosphere on board. The ship was in her true element, independent of the shore, and the medical and nursing staff were freed from the demands imposed by the constant arrival of ambulances and their grim contents. The debilitating heat of Egypt had been left behind; sixty miles from land the evening air was refreshingly sweet. The sea was calm; only those highly prone to seasickness were still losing the contents of their stomachs over the side. No one knew the ship's first intended port of call but it was not a matter of concern. The wounded were ultimately bound for Blighty. With luck the ship may even take them there instead of transferring them to another vessel or unloading them at Gibraltar.

In the cabin the four of them held a private party. Alcohol was forbidden on board except at the officers' dinner table but the problem had been easily solved. On his afternoon visit to the mess to collect the used tablecloths, Tom had taken advantage of the catering sergeant's momentary absence to pick up two bottles of port and one of sherry, and a tin of shortbread biscuits, from the collection of provisions on the sideboard. He had buried them in the laundry bag, separating the bottles by the tablecloths to prevent them clinking. He had also snatched three paperbacks for Grigor from the bookcase.

They sat on the edges of the two bunks, munching shortbreads and passing the bottles to each other to take a sip. Grigor's indiscretion of the previous night seemed to have been forgotten so to avoid the risk of making another he merely wet his lips when a bottle reached him. His companions had no reservations and their faces became flushed as the unaccustomed drink began to take effect. Timeworn jokes were resurrected, the strange habits of some of their former mates were discussed in detail and favourite scrounges of the past lovingly recalled.

They clamoured for a 'turn from Alf' so he obliged by singing a comic song in Romanian. When he finished there was unanimous agreement that his performance was a good sign his lost memory was beginning to return. When the alcohol and shortbreads were finished they took the risk of locking the cabin door and they trooped up on deck. The blackout regulations strictly enforced in Alexandria no longer applied. Under an international Red Cross agreement, hospital ships at sea during wartime sailed with all lights ablaze with the crosses on their hulls and topsides well illuminated. It was impossible for a vessel or aircraft to mistake their identity; vessels carrying wounded were as safe at sea as they were during peacetime.

Taffy and Tom joined a group of mates on the lower promenade deck. Tom had drunk more than the others and began boasting how easy it had been to steal the three bottles from the officers' mess. It was dangerous talk, putting them all at risk of arrest by the military police on board. Grigor noticed Ginger on his own, leaning against the rail, smoking and gazing out to sea. He went across to him.

'Tom's talking a bit too much, Ginger,' he murmured. 'I hate having to tell you but he could get us into trouble. It might be best if one of you took him back to the cabin. I'd do it, but he'd probably object to that.'

Ginger nodded. 'Stupid bastard,' he said, wearily. 'He's like a kid. Can't take a drink without letting the bloody world know about it. I'll see to him.'

'Thanks, Ginger. I thought it best to tell you.'

Ginger looked hard at him with a strange look on his face.

'You're OK, Alf,' he said, after a pause. 'I don't know what your fuckin' game is, but you're OK. Keep out of the way till I get Tom off the deck. Why don't you go up top? You'll like it better there than down here.'

He turned away. Grigor climbed the steps to the next deck. At the top a notice said: 'Strictly Out Of Bounds To Other Ranks.' He ignored it and walked to the rail, keeping in the shadows beyond the lights from the lounge. The swimming pool, a favourite spot during the ship's peacetime cruises, had long since been emptied and boarded over. During the day shady awnings were rigged and bed-fast patients were brought up from the lower decks to take advantage of the daylight and sea air. At sunset they were taken back to their wards and tables and chairs arranged on the open deck. For the rest of the evening officers were able to enjoy the company of the ship's off-duty nurses and ATS and WAAF personnel, regardless of rank. It was a privilege much enjoyed by the girls, who were outnumbered by the men by twenty or more to one. The tables were crowded. An officer wearing dark glasses, he had probably been blinded, sat at a grand piano near the stern playing an Ivor Novello medley.

Grigor stood in the semi-darkness listening to the music. *I'm relieved Ginger's come round. It's good to be on a friendly footing with them again. I wish I knew where we're going. It can't be Gibraltar. It's 2000 miles away at the far end of the Med. German convoys would be crossing our track on their way from Italy to Tobruk now they've taken it. Their escorts would stop us and we'd be taken into Naples. The patients would be delivered to hospital, the rest of us locked up as prisoners of war. But the Italians are easy-going, despite Mussolini. They have none of that idiotic Master Race arrogance. They have good food, superb wine and glorious women. My God! I could do with one now, this very minute! I'll tell them I'm a conscientious objector and stowed away on a hospital ship to escape the war. As a civilian I'll be eligible for internment. Peace can't be more than a few months away ...*

The torpedo struck with a silent orange flash, far brighter than the ship's lights. A thunderous explosion followed, shaking the life out of her. Immediately the stern rose and Grigor's feet slipped on the suddenly steepening deck. He locked an arm round a stanchion as an avalanche of tables, chairs and tumbling men and women swept past him. The grand piano slid down the deck like a huge boulder dislodged on a mountainside, smashing into the screaming mass of bodies thrown against the bulkhead. A deafening blast of escaping steam came from the funnels. The ship lurched to starboard and the deck tilted even steeper. The deck lamps shone a cold brilliant light on the wrecked piano and the tangle of bodies it had crushed. A pitiful few struggled to free themselves, screaming and cursing, waving arms....

Grigor clung to the stanchion watching impassively. *I can't shift a grand piano or drag any of you to safety. There are thousands in a worse state than you on board. Legless, armless, blind, guts hanging out. You're all going to die, dragged down with the ship as she goes under. It's not my fault. Blame that blue-eyed baby-faced bastard of a lieutenant in the U-boat that stopped the* Milos. *He must have had the watch....*

He looked over the side. The sea was already scattered with the specks of red lifejacket lamps that had switched on automatically on contact with seawater. There were no lifeboats in sight; the steep angle of the ship was probably preventing them being launched. In any case there would not be sufficient to take the 4000 or more on board. Not that they would be needed, he reasoned. Only a few of the injured could be brought up from below in time. What chance had a stretcher case of reaching a lifeboat anyway? At this very moment in the pitch darkness of the lower decks there would be doctors and nurses preparing to stay with their patients as the waters rose about them. What had become of Ginger and Tom? They must have gone below only minutes before the torpedo struck....

Clutching the rail, he began dragging himself up the slope towards the stern. He reached a crate fastened to the rails and wrenched open the top. It was packed with lifejackets; he fastened one round himself. There was a rope ladder in the crate, rolled in a bundle and held by a strap. He grabbed it, slid the hooks over the bottom rail and dropped the ladder overboard. It snaked down the ship's side towards the sea. She was moving restlessly as the final moments of her buoyancy approached. Water must still be pouring through the gash torn by the torpedo. She wouldn't last much longer. He looked back to where the remains of the piano lay against the bulkhead. Its lid pointed towards the sky, shaped uncannily like the stern of a ship poised to sink. Cries for help still came from the injured. He was about to climb the rail but stopped and reached into the crate. Pulling out the remaining lifejackets, he threw them onto the deck one by one. They slid down the slope coming to rest against the debris. If the ship rolled as she sank the piano may shift and release some of those it had trapped. The time saved in searching for a lifejacket could make the difference between surviving and being dragged down with the ship.

He could do nothing more. Turning his back on the screams, he climbed the rail and swung his leg over, groping with his foot for the rope ladder. He clambered down the ship's side. Rivets and the edges of the hull plates scraped his skin through his shirt and trousers. Twenty feet above the water the hull curved inwards and the ladder hung free, swinging like a pendulum. He looked down; a life raft lay heaving on the swell 200 yards away. He let go of the rope and fell backwards into the sea.

The water was much colder than he had expected. It closed over his head and several frightening seconds passed before he managed to kick himself to the surface, spluttering and gasping. He swam to the raft and pushed his way between the men hanging onto the rope lifelines looped along the sides. 'I'm a doctor,' he called up, gulping for air. 'Let me on board.'

'Just what we need,' a voice said. 'You'll be a bloody sight more use to us than a padre.'

Hands came down to grasp his arms and haul him to onto the raft.

Chapter Eighteen

Returning from a long walk over the Downs one morning, Farquhar found a note pinned to the door to his room asking him to report to Captain Frobisher without delay. His heart sank. Everything had gone so well in recent weeks, too well in fact; he had found it difficult to believe it could last so perhaps his fears were about to materialize. *Perhaps the colonel's report has turned up and Frobisher is sending me back to Fulwell....*

'Take a seat, Lieutenant,' the captain said. They had maintained the courteous formality formed at their first meeting.

'Thank you, sir. You wished to see me?'

'Yes, I have a job for you before your new students arrive.'

A job! A bloody job instead of the sack! Farquhar was exultant. The captain sat looking steadily at him as if rehearsing what to say.

'Despite the German occupation of Europe,' he began enigmatically, 'a surprising number of people still manage to reach this country. They cross the Channel, or more dangerously the North Sea, in anything from a canoe to a stolen fishing boat. Most are fervently anti-German, anxious to do their bit for our victory. The attitude of others is sometimes less clear and at times highly dubious. Some of the latter are sent to us for interview. In the past year we've uncloaked several spies and two raving lunatics. Tomorrow a decidedly suspicious character is arriving. He was on that ambulance ship that was torpedoed in the Med. He was rescued from a raft loaded with dead and wounded; he had been posing as a doctor. A destroyer took him to Gibraltar where he continued the pretence of being a medic. He was flown to England with a load of seriously wounded. He admitted he had lied to get to England, but insisted he was anti-German. He's spent a month in custody undergoing interrogation in what's known as the London Cage. A certain Lieutenant-Colonel Scotland who has a reputation for achieving solid results runs it. Most of his guests are eventually persuaded by some means or other to tell the truth about their past. Unusually, this man has stuck doggedly to his original story throughout.

It may be true or merely a well-rehearsed cover. Despite his resilience, Colonel Scotland is convinced he is hiding something. Our job is to find out if that's the case and, if so, discover what it is.'

The captain flipped open a file. 'His English is excellent; he also speaks Arabic and several European languages. He's cultured, educated and most charming. He worked for British Intelligence in Cairo for a spell. After a spell in the London Cage a friendly approach in the relaxed surroundings of Rodmel may persuade him to reveal whatever he's so far kept to himself. Study his file before you meet him. When you do, chat informally by encouraging him to talk about his experiences. Wear your parachute wings to let him see you've been around a bit. Press him on anything he says that is odd or unusual. There'll be a hidden microphone in the room. I'll be listening and your conversations will be taken down verbatim in shorthand. We'll go over every word he says to discover if he's let anything slip. His name is Grigorovanovich although he prefers to be called Grigor. I would too, if I had a handle like that.'

Farquhar spent the rest of the day and evening going over the file. It contained a report from a Major John Howard, an Intelligence Officer in Cairo. He summarized the description given by 'Grigor' of his flight from Romania to Turkey and the voyage from Canakkale to Alexandria in the *Milos,* including the episode with the U-boat. His arrest in Cairo, and his translation of German wireless intercepts, which Howard described as 'first rate', were described in full. His disappearance had come as a complete surprise to the major as there had been no prior indication of his intention to desert. He was amazed when told Grigor had reached England.

There was a note from Surgeon-Commander Rowan Armstrong, RNR, medical officer of *Hotspur,* the destroyer that had picked up Grigor among other survivors from the life raft. Commander Armstrong had been astonished to learn the man who had worked so diligently with him in the ship's sickbay had no medical or nursing qualifications.

A report from Squadron Leader Tom Wright, Airport Medical Officer at Northolt, described the arrival from Gibraltar of 'Dr' Grigorovanovich on board an RAF Wellington with thirty wounded personnel and his arrest by the military police following his voluntary disclosure of a false identity.

A report from Lt-Col Scotland, Commandant of the London Cage, (officially known as the Combined Services Detailed Interrogation Centre with an address in Kensington Gardens) stated, 'I am of the opinion this prisoner knows more than he is prepared to admit. He should not be released without further questioning. I would be prepared to re-admit him to this centre in six months' time for further examination.'

Next morning, after a Royal Signals sergeant had tested the microphone hidden somewhat unconvincingly in an inkstand on the desk, Farquhar settled down to await the arrival of the man about whom he had read so much. He was escorted to the room by two military policemen who saluted then left.

'Welcome to Rodmel, Mr Grigorovanovich. I am Lieutenant Farquhar. Please take a seat.'

'Good morning, Lieutenant. Thank you. But please call me Grigor. It will shorten our conversation considerably.'

They studied each other in silence. Despite Frobisher's description and his close reading of the file, Farquhar was unprepared for the charismatic appeal of the man sitting opposite. The rigours he had endured in past weeks had left no visible mark; he was urbane and totally at ease. Dark and slim with a well-chiselled face and firm jaw, he could have been a merchant banker or a high-court judge.

'I trust you found your room comfortable?' Farquhar asked.

'Thank you. I slept well.'

'No complaints?'

'Every prisoner has complaints, Lieutenant. For instance, why am I about to be subjected to yet another round of questioning? I have already told all I know numerous times.'

Farquhar nodded. 'You are a remarkable man. Everyone you meet wants to hear of your experiences first hand!'

'You will have read my file. Why must I repeat what you already know?'

'I want to help you, Grigor. You could be useful to us. You are fluent in German and other languages. You have worked for British Intelligence. Major Howard's report from Cairo is full of praise for you. He was most surprised to discover you had reached England. You will be relieved to hear he has called off the intensive search for you!'

Farquhar had expected a smile but Grigor was staring at him like a fox inspecting a trap. 'Major Howard?' he asked in a surprised voice. 'Is he not in a prisoner of war camp in Egypt?'

'No. Do you think he should be?'

'Has Cairo not yet fallen to the Germans?'

'No, Grigor. It remains in British hands. As does Alexandria. Tobruk has been recaptured. The Germans are on the run in North Africa. Has no one told you about the battle of El Alamein?'

As Grigor shook his head in disbelief, Farquhar felt a surge of excitement.

This man of mystery, this suave, articulate prisoner, is lost for words!

No one at Gibraltar told him of Montgomery's victory. And it's not information the Cage would divulge to a suspected spy. But if he's on our side as he claims, why should the news of a German defeat shake him so badly?

'You seem surprised, Grigor,' he said loftily. 'Like many before you, you appear to have underestimated we British. Your friends Hitler and Rommel were not infallible after all!'

'Underestimated, Lieutenant? Never! Friends? You insult me! Infallible? Certainly not!'

'Then why did you show such great surprise at the news of our victory at El Alamein?'

'Because the odds were so much against it! In Cairo I translated a secret German report which stated their victory in North Africa was imminent. Tobruk was about to fall, the Afrika Korps were confident of being in Cairo within the month. On reading their assessment I was forced to agree. It was then I deserted my post with Major Howard, reluctantly since I held him in the greatest respect. But I did not dare risk capture by the Gestapo. The major's report will have explained my reasons. But the Germans never reached Cairo! I could have continued to work as interpreter. I might have drowned when the hospital ship sank. That is why I am so shocked at your news.'

Farquhar nodded. 'Hitler has been defeated in North Africa. Soon we will invade France across the Channel and Italy from the Mediterranean. The Russians will sweep in from the east. The Third Reich is doomed.'

'Excellent!' Captain Frobisher said when Grigor had been returned to his secure room with a sentry permanently posted at the door. 'First round to us! Let's keep the advantage. Did you get any sort of feeling about him? That he's hiding something, as Colonel Scotland at the Cage thought?'

'He was desperately keen to reach England. Over-anxious perhaps. He claims he was terrified the Germans would catch him. But surely he could have found a place in Cairo to hide? Instead he boarded a ship that was torpedoed! He must have known the risk. And to make sure he got here, he didn't reveal his true identity until he arrived at Northolt.'

'We'll give him a couple of days to think it over.'

At the second interview Farquhar adopted a more brisk, official attitude. He gestured at the file lying open on the desk in front of him. 'In a statement made by one of the men on the life raft, he says you called out you were a doctor. That was why you were pulled to safety whilst others were left to drown. Is that true?'

Grigor shrugged. 'I was not to blame for the shortage of life rafts,

Lieutenant. I had arrived at Alexandria docks in an ambulance filled with seriously injured men having been accepted by them as a doctor. Their medical orderly was pleased to answer my questions. Although I was what you may regard as being under false colours, I believe I did a great deal of good simply by talking to the wounded. I admit claiming to be a doctor in order to get onto the life raft. Like everyone else, I had no wish to die. But even had I been medically qualified I would have been of no practical use. The raft was overcrowded. There were no medical supplies and the dead lay with the dying. Yet the psychological effect of believing there was a doctor on board did much to raise the men's spirits. Of that I'm certain. I spoke calmly to them, giving reassurance and hope. I was neither dismayed nor disgusted by their appalling injuries, unlike some who showed horror at the sight of such carnage. When we were rescued I was welcomed as a colleague by the medical officer and his staff on board the warship *Hotspur*. Later I was similarly accepted in the hospital at Gibraltar. I accompanied a doctor and six nurses on the flight back to England. My competence was never questioned although I took care not to display my ignorance. It was only when the wounded were safely unloaded at Northolt that I admitted to a military policeman that I was not a qualified doctor. I was taken to the London Cage where, as I have told you, I was most cruelly treated. But it is pointless to complain about that.'

'I can report your comments to the proper quarters.'

'I would rather you expended your energy in securing my release. I am willing to work for British Intelligence again. I admit that in Cairo I let Major Howard down but only because I dared not risk capture by the Germans.'

'Because you had persuaded one of their pilots to fly you to Turkey?'

'Yes. And made them look fools. They'll never forget that. The Gestapo would have shown me no mercy for pretending to be one of them.'

'You are an accomplished liar, Grigor. You lied your way from Alexandria to England! How do I know you are not lying now?'

'Because I no longer have reason to lie, Lieutenant. I have reached England. Since leaving Bucharest that has been my aim. I'm a determined man and usually achieve my goals.'

'Major Howard's report makes no mention of you wishing to come to England,' Farquhar said, rather lamely. It was becoming clear Grigor was too clever, too glib, to allow himself to be trapped by straightforward questioning.

Grigor smiled. 'I would have been foolish to let him know that. Had I done so to prevent my escape he would have withdrawn the few privileges I had been granted. At that time I saw no means of reaching England from Cairo. However, I assure you that was always my intention. Had I stayed a little longer, and become aware of the British victory in the desert, I would have remained there until the war ended. Then I would have come here.'

Farquhar nodded wearily. 'Like everyone who has talked to you, I consider you a most remarkable man. Your journey from Romania is a fascinating tale.'

Grigor bowed his head in acknowledgement.

'But there is something missing. You have not been totally frank with me. I know that, and so do you. Telling only half a story is the same as lying.'

With a pang Farquhar remembered saying the same to Josie, and her reply. '*I like you very much, just the way you are,*' she had whispered.

'Where is the microphone, Lieutenant?' Grigor suddenly asked. His tone was innocent, as if he was simply asking the time of day.

'Microphone?' echoed Farquhar.

'The microphone,' Grigor repeated, now smiling. 'I cannot see it, or feel it under the edge of the desk, so it must be at your side. Or perhaps it is in the ink stand which I assume is false since it contains no ink.'

Farquhar said nothing; he merely gave a narrow-lipped smile. Grigor had completely reversed their roles. The fox was now the hunter. 'Surely you don't think I am so gullible as to believe our conversations have not been recorded?' he asked.

'If so, they can have evoked little interest,' Farquhar replied. 'You have told me nothing we did not already know. Until we are satisfied you are telling the whole truth, you will be remain in custody. I urge you to consider that.'

A week passed before Farquhar received a message that Grigor had asked to see him. When he was seated, Grigor waved his hand at the window. 'It's a beautiful English summer morning, Lieutenant. Would it be possible for us to take a walk together outside?'

'May I ask which county we are in?' he asked a few minutes later as they strolled under the trees. A hundred yards away two armed military policemen were keeping pace with them.

'This is Sussex,' Farquhar replied.

'Ah! Sussex! Where the best cricketers are born! Then those green hills must be the world-famous Downs!'

'That is so.'

'I have often wondered why are they called Downs and not Ups.'

'"Downs" originates from "dun", an old English word meaning "hill".'
'I see.'

They walked on in silence. 'Is that why you asked that we take a walk?' Farquhar asked eventually. 'To see the Downs, and to enquire why they are not called the Ups?'

'No, Lieutenant. I am considering disclosing something I have kept to myself for a long time. I have no wish to broadcast it through your hidden microphone to people I have not met. That is why I suggested we take this walk. Now I am pondering the best way to tell you.'

'Then take your time.'

'I must also consider the price to charge for the information."

'You are hardly in a position to bargain, Grigor.'

'That depends on how much you want to know what I know. May I ask you a question?'

They stopped and turned to face each other. 'Of course.'

'Have you heard of Magda Lupescu?'

'No.'

'Then I suggest you find someone who has!'

'Why?'

'Because I was her lover. And I would like to know where she is now.'

'It must have been a long time ago.'

'It was. But I need to know. Find her, and I'll tell you why.'

'Magda Lupescu?' Captain Frobisher was incredulous when Farquhar repeated Grigor's question.

'Yes, sir. I told him I'd never heard of her. He seemed surprised at my ignorance.'

'So am I! Your knowledge of modern European history is sadly lacking, Lieutenant. She was a famous courtesan in the thirties, a beautiful busty redhead. There was a portrait of her in the National Gallery before they took it down and stored it with the rest of the masterpieces in an old tube station when the bombing started.'

'They didn't teach things like that at grammar school, sir.'

'You never know when a bit of culture will come in handy. She was the mistress of the future King Carol of Romania. It caused such a scandal he was forced to abdicate his succession and move to Paris with her. It sounds like the Duke of Windsor and Mrs Simpson although they've been cast out into the wilderness for good. Not so Carol. When his father died he returned from France, his abdication was rescinded and they made him king. Magda rejoined him in the palace and they carried on as before. God only knows where she is now! How does he expect us to trace her?'

'I've no idea. We left it at that. I don't understand why he couldn't tell me all this in the interview room. Why insist on us going for a walk?'

'He'd rumbled the microphone. Perhaps he was scared of saying more than he intended. When I heard him invite you into the woods I wondered if he had wicked designs on you.'

'I'd have told him I was engaged to my commanding officer, sir.'

'You're not my type, Lieutenant. And now you tell me Magda was his lady friend, my suspicions of his intentions were plainly absurd.'

A week later Frobisher sent for Farquhar. 'Magda Lupescu and King Carol are living in a villa in Estoril in Portugal,' he announced.

When Farquhar told Grigor the news, he smiled. 'I am most grateful to you, Lieutenant. Portugal is still neutral, I assume? And therefore it is possible to communicate with the king?'

'It may be difficult.'

'But not impossible. Put this question to him.' Grigor paused, adding further to Farquhar's already mounting tension. 'Where are the crown jewels of Romania?'

Sweden had looked after British interests in Portugal since the war began. One morning early in 1944 the Swedish consul in Lisbon received telegraphed instructions from Stockholm to visit ex-king Carol of Romania, now living in Estoril. He was to seek confirmation from His Majesty that the Romanian crown jewels remained in his possession. The British government had made the request. No reason had been given for their enquiry.

An appointment was arranged by telephone and a few days later the consul was driven in his official Rolls-Royce along the twenty-five kilometres of winding coastal road to Estoril. He enjoyed lunch with King Carol and Madame Lupescu in their lovely villa overlooking the Atlantic. Visitors were rare and the couple's pleasure at their cultured guest's presence was obvious. All three spoke excellent French and the conversation sparkled.

Later, as they sat under umbrellas on the terrace, the consul delicately broached the subject of his visit: did the Romanian crown jewels remain in His Majesty's possession? There was an immediate change in the tenor of the hitherto enjoyable afternoon. The king became imperious, demanding to know on whose authority the consul had made such an outrageous enquiry. Madame Lupescu left the two men and began walking to and fro along the terrace in an agitated manner. She clutched a handkerchief and seemed deeply shocked. The consul was concerned at the obvious distress he had caused his hosts. He explained, in most deferential terms, that the enquiry had come from the British government and he was merely an intermediary acting on London's behalf. The king demanded to know the reason for their enquiry. The consul stated none had been given, but diplomatically added that he was certain Mr Winston Churchill, the British prime minister, would have the best interests of His Majesty at heart.

It was some time before Magda had sufficiently composed herself to return to sit by the king. Taking her hand, the king replied curtly that, so far as he was aware, his crown and that of his son, Prince Michael, together with Queen Helen's diamond tiara, were locked in a secure safe in the palace in Bucharest. That was where he had left them, in their rightful home. He had every intention of returning to Romania immediately hostilities ended in order to resume his rightful position as the country's monarch.

The consul thanked His Majesty for his gracious co-operation and apologized for any painful memories he had evoked. He left the villa and was driven back to Lisbon where he wrote a report on the statement made by the king and mentioning the great anxiety shown by Madame Lupescu. His report was encoded and transmitted in a telegram to London.

Chapter Nineteen

The information was relayed to Rodmel and Frobisher handed a copy of the consul's report to Farquhar.

'Read this. Take our friend Grigor for another walk in the woods. Tell him the crowns are in the palace in Bucharest unless the Germans have found them. I'll be very interested in his reaction.'

'How did Whitehall find out?' Farquhar asked.

'I've not the slightest idea,' the captain replied truthfully.

'He laughed, sir,' Farquhar said when he returned from the walk.

'The devil he did! Does he know better?'

'He claims to. He described the jewels precisely as in the consul's report. Two crowns, one the king's, the other Prince Michael's, the heir presumptive. And a diamond tiara belonging to Queen Helen. He claims Magda helped him pinch them from the palace after the king bunked off to Paris, and that they're worth a fortune. "A king's ransom," he said. I think that's what he's hoping to collect in return for telling what we want to know.'

'So Colonel Scotland at the Cage was right. He was keeping a secret!' Frobisher exclaimed.

'Yes. Grigor says when Magda left Bucharest by train to re-join Carol in Paris, he set off by car with the crowns packed in a leather trunk. Initially he was hoping to reach Turkey, as he said in his original statement to Major Howard. But he was forced to change his plans and travelled by sea to Alexandria then to Cairo by train.'

'What happened to the trunk with the crowns?'

'He hid it somewhere on his travels.'

'Will he tell us where if we let him go?'

'I suspect he's looking for a lot more than just his freedom. He's still thinking how much to charge for the information.'

Frobisher's report reached Prime Minister Churchill, who found time to write a private note to Anthony Eden, his Secretary of State for Foreign

Affairs: '*The crown jewels of Romania are to be recovered by whatever means available and regardless of cost. They are to be returned promptly to ex-King Carol in Portugal. We must do all we can to maintain good relations with him since Stalin views Romania as a possible jumping-off point for post-war conquests further west.*'

'We'll see Grigor together this time and hear his terms,' Frobisher said. 'I'll play the baddie. You be the soft-hearted type, trying to defend him.'

'The crown jewels of Romania are at a location known only to myself,' Grigor said. 'I am prepared to reveal it on payment of one million United States dollars and a passage to America with a guarantee of permanent residence there. I agree to remain in custody until the jewels are recovered. If they are not found, I will be owed nothing and shall remain in your custody until the war ends. My terms, gentlemen, are non-negotiable.'

He sat back, folded his arms and waited for a response.

Farquhar cleared his throat. 'Thank you, Grigor. You have set out your demands succinctly and clearly. We shall of course have to consider them carefully before reaching a conclusion. This situation is, so far as I am aware, unprecedented.'

'His Majesty's government is not in the habit of bargaining with thieves,' Frobisher growled.

Grigor smiled. 'I am not a thief, Captain. Rather, I am a liberator! In removing the jewels from the palace I prevented the Germans seizing them. I have guarded them with my life ever since, taking great personal risks, and suffering much abuse in British hands. The price I am requesting merely reflects a reasonable recompense for all that I have suffered.'

'You are a rogue, Grigor, through and through! A rogue and a liar. If it were left to me, I'd have no truck with you!'

'Wisely, the matter has not been left with you, Captain Frobisher. Since you are prepared to listen to my terms, despite your opinion of me, I suspect your government, perhaps Mr Winston Churchill himself, has taken a more enlightened view.'

Grigor smiled, stood and bowed. Two military policemen escorted him from the room. As the door closed, Frobisher gave a frosty smile.

'I think our friend has disclosed more than he intended,' he said quietly.

'I heard nothing new,' Farquhar exclaimed. 'Only his conditions for telling us where he hid the damned things! There were no clues as to where that is!'

'For a million dollars he is prepared to tell us,' Frobisher countered. 'No jewels, no dollars. Think on that for a moment. Wherever they are, he knows we will be able to retrieve them. Otherwise he won't get paid. To figure that out we must consider where he has been.'

Frobisher began counting on his fingers. 'Bucharest. Turkey. The *Milos*. Crete. Alexandria. Cairo. The hospital ship. The lifeboat. Gibraltar. London. Ten places! Yet he is confident we can recover them. From where? Not Romania or Turkey certainly. The Germans occupy the former, the latter remains neutral and we have no means of access. It's unlikely we could ever trace the *Milos*; she may well have been sunk. She called briefly at Crete but he would not have taken the risk of being seen lugging a trunk ashore and returning without it. If he had it with him on the hospital ship it went down with her. That also rules out the lifeboat and Gib. The trunk is therefore in Egypt. Either Alexandria or Cairo, to be exact!'

'I can't argue with that,' Farquhar agreed. 'But which? His statement to Major Howard covers his arrival in Alex on the *Milos*. He immediately took a train to Cairo, spent the night at the Damietta and was arrested outside Shepheards next morning. Howard had his room at the Damietta searched but the only luggage mentioned in the report is a suitcase. There was no trunk.'

'Agreed. But put yourself in his shoes. You disembark from the *Milos* at Alex. The trunk is an encumbrance so you are anxious to hide it. But to make a clean break in your trail you need to get away from Alex fast. So you jump on the first train to Cairo. You spend the first night at the Damietta and are arrested outside Shepheards the following morning. Your room is searched but there is no trunk. Why? Because you hid it somewhere between the docks at Alex and the hotel in Cairo! More precisely, if my theory that you made a quick departure from Alex is correct, between Cairo railway station and the Damietta. It seems reasonable to assume you will want the trunk available in case another sudden departure is necessary. So where is it?'

Farquhar pursed his lips. 'Left-luggage store at the station?'

'In Cairo? The city of thieves!' Frobisher smiled and shook his head. 'Never in a hundred years! It's got to be in the hotel. Howard's men searched his room, and only a suitcase was found. But what were they looking for? No one knew anything about a trunk. He hid it somewhere, under the floor, in the roof, somewhere. We've got to demolish the Damietta, brick by brick if necessary. It's the only way to find the trunk.'

Farquhar sat a full minute collecting his thoughts. 'All that you say is feasible. But you assume he hid the trunk. He speaks Arabic and could have numerous connections in Egypt. Family, friends, diplomatic acquaintances from the past whom he could trust? There are two crowns plus a diamond tiara to hide. He may have decided to dump the trunk and hide each piece separately. The discovery of one would not mean the loss of all three.'

'That would make our job well-nigh impossible,' Frobisher admitted. 'But to do that he'd need three secure hiding places or trustworthy accomplices. They are those who would doubt there are that many honest men in the whole of Egypt, let alone Cairo. And to get the money from us, all three pieces must be retrieved. From three different places, or trustees? Or a mixture of both? After all this time? Not a chance. They're in the Damietta, mark my words.'

'He worked for Major Howard in Shepheards. And he lived there. Could he have smuggled the trunk in and hid it somewhere in the building?'

Frobisher shook his head. 'Impossible. I was in Cairo last year and stayed at Shepheards. There's only one entrance and it's guarded round the clock by armed men and the military police. A fly couldn't get in without being seen. Everyone entering or leaving is logged and rigorously searched. It's the Eighth Army's military headquarters, for God's sake. A fortress, as you'd expect. He couldn't have got a matchbox through, let alone a trunk of jewels. I'll ask for a check to be made but I can't imagine it bringing us any nearer a solution.'

'It would seem,' Farquhar said, 'if the trunk isn't found at the Damietta after we tear it down, Grigor is bound for the Land of the Free.'

In Cairo the manager of the Damietta became so violent that he had to be remanded in custody whilst his hotel was systematically demolished. Nothing was found. At the same time security arrangements at Shepheards were closely examined. Grigor's daily walks had been fully logged, as had his late-night visits over an entire month to attend the mosque to offer prayers for his late father. The duty orderly officers had signed each entry night and morning. The possibility of Grigor having smuggled the trunk into military headquarters was considered 'so unlikely it cannot be considered feasible'.

A meeting at Rodmel was chaired by a senior civil servant from the Colonial Office, Sir Gordon Briscoe. Grigor's file and the reports of the various enquiries made in connection with the search for the trunk were discussed at length. It was concluded all that could be done to trace the jewels had been done. Sir Gordon reaffirmed the order of the prime minister to recover the crowns regardless of cost. Grigor was the only person aware of their location so there was no alternative but to accept his terms.

The following week saw much activity in Whitehall. The Bank of England was instructed to credit one million US dollars to an account in the name of Grigor Grigorovanovich at the New York branch of Credit Suisse. The bank issued confirmation that only the account holder, on presentation of proof of identity, could access the account. Anthony Eden and Herbert Morrison, the British foreign minister and home secretary respectively, confirmed in writing the guarantee of a passage across the Atlantic; a copy was lodged with the High Court. The United States Embassy in London issued a visa and written permission for Grigor to reside permanently in America provided he committed no criminal offence. To fulfil his part of the agreement, Grigor dictated the following statement:

I make the following declaration of my own free will in the presence of Captain Alan Frobisher and Lieutenant Peter Farquhar at Rodmel Manor in the County of Sussex, England, on April 30 1944. Whilst in Cairo in 1942 I worked for Major John Howard of British Intelligence. The office I occupied was on the top floor of Shepheards Hotel. In the ceiling above my desk was a hatch leading into the roof space. There are seven brick-built ventilation shafts passing up through the space and the tiles above. The suitcase containing the Romanian crown jewels is in the narrow gap between the eaves and the central shaft. If the trunk is not found, I agree to being interned for the remainder of the war.

This description was encoded and telegraphed to British Military Headquarters in Cairo, still housed in Shepheards. A major and six sergeants of the Royal Military Police were marshalled on the top floor of the building, which had been cleared of all other personnel. Major Howard was no longer serving in Egypt but the office Grigor had occupied for two years was easily located. It was the only room on the top floor with a hatch in the ceiling; all other means of access to the loft were situated in corridors and in public view.

Below the uninsulated roof the daytime temperature could exceed 140 degrees Fahrenheit so no search of the space was possible until well after dark. The sergeants stripped down to their underpants and the hatch was prised upwards. The blast of heat that greeted them was like the opening of a furnace door. The sergeants, armed with powerful torches, followed the directions sent from London. The suitcase was quickly located. Having lain in blistering heat immediately below the roof for so long, the leather had completely dried out and crumbled to dust when handled. The crowns and tiara lay in the remains of their wrappings, the diamonds glittering brilliantly in the light of the torches. What was left of the suitcase was lifted onto a canvas sheet and it was lowered, like a rotting corpse, in rope slings through the hatch into the office below. The jewels were carefully wrapped and placed in a new wooden crate. An armoured car, protected by heavily armed Royal Marines, raced across the desert from Cairo to Alexandria that night. The crate was unloaded and put in the strong room of a British destroyer which sailed immediately for Gibraltar. From there it was flown in an unmarked de Havilland Mosquito to neutral Lisbon.

Grigor was taken to Southampton; Frobisher and Farquhar accompanied him. The *Queen Mary* in her wartime role as a troopship was due to sail that afternoon and the three men lunched together at the Grand Hotel before departure.

'May I ask a question, Captain Frobisher?'

'Certainly, Grigor!'

'Where are the crowns and tiara now?'

'They have been returned to King Carol in Portugal.'

'Is Madame Lupescu still with him?

'I believe so.'

Grigor gave a strange smile.

Wearing the uniform of an American army major, Grigor was allocated a cabin in the ship's sick quarters and forbidden to leave it for the duration of the voyage. A guard was placed on the door and his meals were brought to him. Scotland Yard unofficially tipped off the FBI regarding the impending arrival of a master criminal on the *Queen Mary*. When she arrived off New York, a posse of agents travelled out on the pilot cutter and boarded her as she approached land. After she docked at Pier 90, Grigor was followed down the gangway by a selection of New York's finest. But somehow, in the milling crowds thronging the quayside to welcome home the 3000 GIs on board the *Queen*, he gave them the slip and was never traced.

Ten days after the dramatic discovery in Shepheards, the Swedish consul was again driven from Lisbon to Estoril. Beside him on the rear seat of the Rolls lay a new leather trunk containing the crowns and the tiara nestling in separate compartments. A short informal ceremony was held at the villa to mark the return of the crown jewels to His Majesty. He became distraught on seeing them again. Fortunately Magda was on hand to comfort him.

His Majesty's initial excitement was soon replaced by a depressing sadness. The crowns had revived images of past glories, reigniting his fervent belief in the future restoration of the Romanian monarchy with himself as King and Prince Michael as his successor. It was a pitiful hope and, for Magda, happily impossible. Two months later, when his euphoria had faded, she ordered the servants to carry the trunk up to the attic. They were, of course, quite unaware of its contents.

Chapter Twenty

Magda owned the villa in Estoril; her name was on the title deeds. And in Carol's will a clause provided her on his death with a generous allowance for the remainder of her days. But this was, in her opinion, both inadequate and demeaning. Was she merely a skivvy, to be thrown a pittance after a lifetime of service? Had she not remained devoted to him for over twenty years? Surely she deserved the whole of his estate, not a miserable pension. His wealth had survived the war, slumbering safely in various Swiss and Swedish banks and accruing large sums in interest.

She tried on numerous occasions to make Carol see the justice of her case without success. He retained a strong sense of imperial duty, stubbornly clinging to a hope of restoration of the Romanian monarchy. He had been bitterly disappointed when Hitler refused to grant it. The Russians had replaced the Germans as the occupying power of his beloved country and under communism there was not the faintest chance of him returning to the throne. But he remained convinced that eventually a combined Europe, probably led by the British, would rise against the Bolsheviks (as he still called them) and bring their rotten regime crashing down. His restoration would quickly follow. On his death, Prince Michael would succeed him and it was therefore he who must inherit the family wealth to enable him to carry out his royal duties. This was Carol's mantra and he would not be persuaded otherwise, however much Magda pleaded.

Events alter circumstances. In the spring of 1946 Carol, now fifty years of age, suffered a mild stroke. Magda summoned his solicitor and instructed him to prepare the papers necessary to award her power of attorney. This would give her day-to-day control over His Majesty's finances should his condition worsen and he became incapable of managing them himself. To her great consternation the solicitor informed her the king had already entrusted that power to him. The man had had the impudence to suggest that when Carol passed away she should sell the villa and move to a more modest property. Or worse, spend the rest of her days in a hotel. Magda ordered him to leave her house and never return.

In the weeks of brooding following this meeting, Magda conceived a cunning plan. She had always loved intrigue and now derived much pleasure in solving the problems her embryonic scheme presented. If she was not to receive a substantial inheritance, why should she not sell the jewels to compensate for its loss? Since his stroke Carol's memory had become very poor. In the days immediately following their return, the crowns had been a daily topic of conversation between them, particularly the mystery of how they had come to be in British hands. But discussions on the subject eventually dried up and they had not once been mentioned in the months leading up to Carol's stroke. Magda was convinced he had forgotten their existence.

When they were planning the theft in 1940, Grigor had assured her the crowns were worth at least one million American dollars. Now, with the world about to enter a second year of peace, they would be worth substantially more. Magda remembered the name of the jeweller in Amsterdam to whom Grigor had intended selling the jewels after the war. His name was Eshkol, the same as that of her very first love. He was the little boy who had sat next to her at school and often held her hand. Bless him, she thought. Where is he now? Dead, most probably. He had looked very Jewish even then so he couldn't have survived. Had he remembered her at the end, perhaps? She hoped so. He was called Jacob, but what was the first name of Grigor's friend? Try as she might she could not recall it. Finally she wrote letter, in French on villa notepaper, addressing the envelope simply to Mr Eshkol, Diamond Centre, Amsterdam:

Dear Mr Eshkol,
A mutual friend has recommended you as a man to trust. If you can be of professional service to me please write and let me know.
Yours sincerely, Magda Lupescu

She waited anxiously for three weeks until his reply arrived:

Dear Madame Lupescu
Thank you for your letter. You do not mention the name of our mutual friend and I shall be interested to discover who it is. I lost many of my family and friends during the war so it will be a pleasure to receive news of someone who has survived. I myself returned to Amsterdam after spending four years in a concentration camp in Poland. I presume you have articles for sale and will be travelling to

*Amsterdam by air to obtain my valuation. If you advise me by
telegram of the day and time of your arrival I shall meet you at the
airport and handle the formalities on your behalf.*
    Yours sincerely, Reuben Eshkol

Magda was ecstatic. Her letter had reached him, he was still in business
and his reply was all she had hoped for. Reuben! Of course. That was the
name Grigor had given her. She read the letter through again. He would
even get the trunk through customs for her. Another problem solved. She
was sure everything would go as smoothly as she had planned.

Later that morning she telephoned Lisbon airport and made enquiries
about a flight to Amsterdam. Yet again the news was good. There was a
regular weekly service to Paris, leaving at ten every Tuesday morning. The
journey took six hours, including a refuelling stop at Madrid where lunch
could be taken. From Le Bourget there were frequent connecting flights to
Amsterdam.

On her next trip to Lisbon Magda bought a cabin trunk at the flea
market. It was one of the best German makes with a key and strong
working lock. It had a well-travelled look and was adorned with the labels
of various pre-war shipping companies. It was exactly what she had hoped
to find, a piece of good-quality, carefully used luggage, precisely what a
respectable, middle-aged lady would take when travelling to spend a
holiday with friends. A van brought the trunk to the villa the following
day. Magda gave the driver a little extra to carry it up the three flights of
stairs to the attic. Carol was in the library immersed in his beloved books
on central European witchcraft and remained blissfully unaware of the
extra activity in the villa.

The following Sunday morning the house fell quiet after the servants
had gone to church. Carol's stroke made it difficult for him to climb stairs;
he would never venture alone up to the attic so Magda was safe from
interruption. The wooden crate in which the jewels had been delivered had
lain in a locked cupboard ever since it was moved there under her supervision. Now she took the key from its hiding place and opened the door.
She lifted the lid of the crate and took out the three crowns. She packed
them carefully in the cabin trunk bought at the flea market the previous
week.

'I must go shopping in Paris, darling!' she announced excitedly to Carol at
breakfast next morning. 'All the big shops will be fully stocked again and
I need so many things! Will you come with me? Please say you will.'

'Do you mind too much if I don't, darling?'

It was the reply she had expected. Since his stroke the poor dear was reluctant to leave the villa for even half a day.

'Oh! That's disappointing. But I'll only be gone a couple of days. I'll stay at the Montmartre. Do you remember the times we had there in the old days? I'll see Blanche and some of the girls for lunch. And hear all the gossip!'

'Don't let them keep you from me for too long!'

'Of course not! Would I do such a thing?'

'How will you travel? By car? Or train?'

'Car or train?' She gave a merry laugh. 'Darling, either would take weeks! Everyone travels by air these days!'

'By air? In an aeroplane?' queried Carol.

'Of course, darling! How else?'

Later that day the chauffeur drove her into Lisbon. At the bank she withdrew a thousand French francs from her private account; she would need to go shopping in Paris to back up her alibi. The post office was next door to the bank and she sent a telegram to Mr Eshkol advising him to expect her in Amsterdam the following afternoon.

Next morning the chauffeur brought the trunk down from the attic and put it in the car's luggage compartment. One of the servants carried Magda's two suitcases and placed them alongside it. In her cream suit and feathered blue hat she was at the peak of Lisbon fashion and positively glowed with health and happiness. There had been a fleeting moment of passion with Carol that morning and now she was about to fly to Paris. With luck an encounter with someone new and exciting may await! Life could not be more perfect. Carol came out onto the terrace to see her off.

'Goodbye, darling,' he called. 'Have a good journey!'

'I will, my dearest. Remember to take your medicine!'

They waved to each other and she blew him a kiss through the rear window as the car pulled away.

The aeroplane was a passenger version of the Ford Tri-Motor known in America as the Tin Goose. It was twenty years old, noisy and slow, and took over three hours to complete the flight to Madrid. Magda, tired and irritated, went by taxi to a nearby hotel where she only picked at the cheap lunch provided by the airline. The afternoon dragged slowly by; the under-powered plane creaked and groaned as it laboured to cross the Pyrenees. A headwind added to the journey time causing the consumption of extra petrol so an unscheduled landing had to be made at Bordeaux to refuel. It was almost six before the plane banked over a leafy Paris bathed in evening sunlight and slanted down onto the main runway at Le Bourget.

Long accustomed to a life that ran as if on rails, Magda had assumed she would immediately step from the Lisbon plane onto a KLM flight for the final leg of her journey to Amsterdam. It came as a considerable shock to discover the last plane of the day had left forty minutes before her arrival. The next would not leave until ten in the morning. She stood alone in the baggage area of the airport building; her fellow passengers were already queuing at the passport and customs counters. The long flight from Lisbon in such cramped conditions had exhausted her and she struggled to think what to do. Her expensive cream suit was creased and she desperately needed a hot bath followed by several drinks and a decent meal before bed.

But she could not leave the airport. Customs would require her to open the trunk and the crowns would be discovered. Awkward questions would follow and Carol would inevitably become involved. How could she possibly explain the situation to him? She had expected to transfer immediately to the connecting plane and be met by Mr Eshkol at Schipol airport. But since that was now impossible she had to find a hotel for the night here in Paris. She saw a gendarme walking towards her and had a moment's panic.

'May I be of assistance to you, madame?' he enquired.

He was dark and handsome with a strong, resolute face. He looked steadily at her.

'Oh, thank you! I am sure you can.' She took a deep breath and gabbled a reply. 'I have arrived from Lisbon too late for the aeroplane to Amsterdam. I shall have to spend the night here in Paris. It's such a nuisance! My suitcases contain everything I need. The trunk has only spare clothing and gifts for friends. Is there somewhere I can leave it here at the airport until morning?'

The gendarme smiled. 'You've had a long journey, madame,' he replied courteously. 'I'm sorry you missed your flight. But you can leave your trunk in my office. It will be quite safe, I assure you. Let me show you the way.'

'Thank you, Officer. You are most kind.'

He brought a porter's trolley and loaded the trunk and her suitcases on it. She walked beside him down a corridor. He unlocked a door, opened it and stood aside to let her enter. She suddenly remembered Heinrich doing precisely the same thing, long ago.... Happily this was a real police office; clean, brightly lit, with official posters on the walls. The gendarme lifted a flap in the counter and they walked down a short passage. He unlocked another door and pulled the trolley inside; Magda followed him and suddenly stopped in amazement. The tiny room contained a single bed and a small table; there was a single window, high in the wall, protected by metal bars.

'This is the lock-up!' the gendarme announced, smiling when he saw the look of surprise on her face. 'From time to time a passenger gives trouble and has to be taken into temporary custody. Your trunk will be as safe here as if it were lodged in the Bastille. It cannot escape!'

Magda laughed. 'I cannot thank you enough, Officer!' she exclaimed. 'I shall sleep soundly tonight, knowing it is so secure!'

'If you care to wait in the front office for a few minutes I shall conduct you to the taxi rank.'

'Thank you once again!'

When he emerged he had changed out of uniform into a smart grey suit with a white shirt and blue tie. The astonishment on her face must have been evident as he grinned and said, 'My shift finished over an hour ago but I have to remain on duty until the last international flight arrives. For once the wait was worthwhile. Otherwise I would have missed the pleasure of assisting you.'

'And your suit!' she enquired with a laugh. 'Is that in my honour?'

He smiled. 'No, the uniform is part of my job. I don't wear it off-duty.'

'You've made my return to Paris most pleasant,' she told him.

'But you are bound for Amsterdam, madame!'

'Yes. I have business to attend to there. But I intend doing some shopping here on my way back to Lisbon. I lived in Paris for some years.'

'Ah! That explains your charming accent! Let me have your passport and I shall see you through control and customs.'

Magda stifled a gasp; she had forgotten she would be required to show her Portuguese passport before leaving the airport. The gendarme would discover her name but there was nothing she could do about that. She took the passport from her handbag and handed it to him. She watched as he walked across to the desk and spoke to the elderly uniformed clerk. They held a short discussion and the clerk stared across at her before stamping her passport. When the gendarme returned he smiled as he handed it back to her.

'You are Madame Lupescu!' he exclaimed. 'I have heard a lot about you!'

She gave a weak smile. 'Indeed? I have not been here for some years.'

'Nevertheless Paris still remembers you. By all accounts you have been away from us far too long.'

What on earth did that clerk say to him? 'You are too kind,' she replied.

'May I also say your famous beauty has been much understated.'

'You say that, seeing me like this.' Magda gasped theatrically. 'After six hours packed in a terrible little aeroplane. With my suit crumpled and make-up totally wrecked. I cannot believe you are being serious.'

'I assure you I am. Never more so in the whole of my life.'

'I think you must say that to every lady in distress.'

The customs officer waved her through when he saw she was being escorted by a gendarme. There was one taxi standing at the rank. The driver loaded her suitcases as she took her seat.

'Where will you stay, madame?' the gendarme enquired.

'I'd not expected to have to spend the night so I don't have a reservation. In the past I always stayed at the Montmartre.'

He shook his head. 'I regret that is being rebuilt and will not reopen until late next year.'

'Is there anywhere not too far away that you can recommend?'

He pursed his lips in thought. 'I have lived in Paris all my life so I have never needed to stay in a hotel. The bar of the Fertel Etoile is very pleasant although I have not spent a night there.'

'Is your wife expecting you home?' Magda enquired. 'If not, let me buy you dinner. It's the least I can do in return for all your kindness!'

His face registered genuine surprise. 'Dinner, madame? I shall be most honoured! And no, I'm not married. My cat and I share a flat. I leave a window ajar for him. We both come and go as we please and ask no questions.'

Hotel Fertel Etoile stood in a dignified tree-lined street facing a park. Magda asked for an en suite room.

'We only have a double available tonight, madame,' the receptionist told her.

'That is acceptable. It's only for one night. I arrived too late for the aeroplane to Amsterdam this afternoon.'

'Please sign the register, madame. Do you have luggage?'

'Two suitcases. In the taxi.'

'The porter will bring them in.'

'I've already done so,' the gendarme said, turning to Magda with a smile. 'And I've paid the taxi.'

They took the lift to the top floor. The room was comfortably furnished; tall glass doors opened onto a balcony overlooking the park.

'I need a drink, then a long soak in the bath,' Magda announced.

'I'll call room service for you whilst you unpack.'

'Order me a martini, please.' She smiled at him. 'You know I'm Magda,' she said. 'And you are...?'

'Paul,' he said. 'Paul Gueret.'

They shook hands and laughed. Paul left, leaving her to bathe and change. She rang room service and asked to have a dress ironed. The waiter arrived with the martini Paul had ordered for her and she asked for another to be delivered in ten minutes. She ran the bath, tipped in a generous amount of her perfumed salts and slid into the foaming scented water. She lay sipping the martini, wallowing in the warmth. The weariness of the journey and the worries it had brought slid away. She drifted dreamily, contemplating the prospect of dining with a handsome young stranger. Stepping out of the bath, she dried and slipped on a dressing gown. In the corridor her second martini stood on a silver tray. Beside it her freshly ironed dress hung on a stand.

Heads turned and there were gasps of appreciation as she entered the cocktail bar. She guessed news of her arrival had spread and her entrance had been eagerly awaited. A minimum of expensive jewellery glittered against the simple white dress. Her hair, restored every week to its original glorious copper colour, was piled high; her face was serene and smiling. She glided across the floor to where Paul was waiting for her. In the elegant surroundings he looked more handsome than ever. There were murmurs of approval around the room as he took her hand and kissed it. Magda was thrilled; at last she was back in Paris!

They talked softly across the candlelit table as they dined. Coffee and liqueurs were served in the lounge overlooking the park where coloured lanterns hung in the trees. Afterwards Paul walked her to the room. At her door she laid a hand on his shoulder. 'I want to make love to you,' she said. 'But not now. I'm too tired.'

'Then we shall sleep in each other's arms.'

'And nothing more?'

He shook his head. 'Not until you are rested.'

It was four in the morning when she woke and turned towards him. His strong arms folded around her.

Dawn was breaking when Paul slipped out of bed and began dressing. She was only half awake but remembered him saying at dinner his shift began at the airport at seven. Sleep returned and she was unaware of him leaving the suite. Later, fully awake, she stretched her legs luxuriously, experiencing the almost forgotten sensation of being a totally satisfied woman. Paul's lovemaking had exceeded her wildest dreams. She would appoint him to the household as her secretary; Carol would never suspect he was her live-in lover, as Grigor had been. Sadly, with a busy day ahead there was no time to meditate further on this thrilling prospect. She laid out a smart green suit for her meeting with Mr Eshkol. A crisp white blouse, delicately embroidered, expensive stockings and a new pair of hand-made Italian shoes completed her wardrobe. Soon after eight she showered and dressed; room service brought coffee and a warm croissant. Down in reception she paid her bill and ordered a taxi to take her and the two suit-cases to the airport.

She had expected Paul to be at the main entrance to greet her but there was no sign of him. *How tiresome,* she thought. *Surely his duties can't be all that important!* A porter came forward, loaded her suitcases onto his barrow and wheeled them into the airport building.

'I have a trunk to collect from the gendarmerie,' she told him.

The door was locked and there was no sign of Paul.

'Where is the gendarme?' Magda demanded. 'My trunk is locked in the cell. I must have it. My plane leaves for Amsterdam in less than an hour!'

The porter gave a Gallic shrug. 'Who knows where he is, madame? He does not report his movements to me. Perhaps his girlfriend insisted on him staying at home with her today.'

She gave him an icy stare and tried the door again. It was undoubtedly locked. 'What can I do?' she wailed.

The porter shrugged again and extended a hand, palm uppermost.

Magda fished in her handbag for a ten-franc note and thrust it at him. 'There'll be another for you, if and when I get my trunk,' she snapped.

'What does it look like?' the man asked, rather cheekily.

'Brown leather. With coloured labels and two straps.'

The man pursed his lips and held out his hand again. 'Is that it?' he asked languidly, taking the second note and nodding. Her trunk stood on end in a dark corner of the short passage. Magda gave a whoop of delight and dashed to it. She checked the lock and lid for signs of forced entry; they appeared intact. *Paul must have been called away on urgent police business. Unaware of its precious contents, he had brought it from the cell and left it out for me. How thoughtful of him! It was the best he could do and he has taken care to keep it out of public view.* Her relief was so great she gave the porter another ten francs despite his insolence.

At the KLM desk she bought a return ticket to Amsterdam. The trunk and her suitcases were labelled and wheeled away for loading onto the aeroplane. She bought a copy of *Le Monde* and went to the ladies' waiting room where several passengers were already seated. A short time later one of the pilots entered. After collecting the tickets he announced the plane for Amsterdam would depart in ten minutes and asked everyone to walk out to it.

To Magda's intense dismay Paul had still not appeared. *He knows I am leaving at ten. How very inconsiderate of him. And after last night! What does he think I am? A common tart?* She walked, elegant and unhurried, to the aeroplane, forcing herself not to give a backward glance. She fervently hoped Paul was watching and would see how unconcerned she was at his non-appearance.

The aeroplane was a wartime C-47, more commonly known as a Dakota, converted to civilian use. Compared to the flight from Lisbon, the journey to Amsterdam was smooth, and took only two hours.

Chapter Twenty-One

Farquhar was unmarried. With no dependants or responsibilities warranting early demobilization, he was not released from the army until 1947. Keen to resume his academic career, he rented a small flat in Leeds close to the university where his research post had been kept open for him.

He was saddened to hear that Professor Brasher, his former Head of Department, had retired the previous year and died soon afterwards. To his dismay, work on pliable explosives had been abandoned. The equipment, together with his copious notes and research results, had been bundled into cardboard boxes and dumped in the bottom of a cleaner's cupboard. The newly appointed professor, in Farquhar's view an upstart who had avoided call-up and showed animosity towards those who had served during the war, gave him a chilly reception. He made it clear that under his direction the department was heading in a new and more stimulating direction. Future research was to be focused on the development of coal derivatives, a subject about which Farquhar knew little and cared less. All hope of him acquiring a PhD had gone.

It was not his only regret. He soon became aware that the university was no longer the place he had once known and enjoyed immensely. Unattractive concrete buildings were being planned alongside the century-old red brick and stone edifices of his student days. An unwelcome culture was eroding long-held standards. Academic gowns were no longer required to be worn in class, students were permitted to address lecturers by their first names, and one of the young professors wore sandals without socks. Few lecturers bothered with a tie; rumpled cords and creased jumpers were the usual garb. Farquhar, who invariably wore a suit and well-polished shoes, was an anachronism. He hated the changes to informality but was helpless to prevent their spread.

He bought a second-hand red 1937 Morris 10 Tourer with a folding canvas top and began spending his weekends exploring rural Yorkshire, staying at farms offering bed and breakfast accommodation. Back in

Leeds, as each Monday dawned, he was already yearning for Friday when the department closed at lunchtime for the weekend, leaving him free to drive north to the glorious empty lanes winding through the dales. One Saturday, whilst staying at a dairy farm in Swaledale, he picked up the latest copy of Farmer's Weekly to read over breakfast. An advertisement seeking a research chemist to work on the development of animal foodstuffs caught his eye. Instead of his planned excursion he spent the remainder of the weekend in wellington boots and overalls, helping the farmer with the mucking-out, milking and feeding of his herd of pedigree shorthorn cattle. In the laboratory on Monday morning he typed a reply to the advert giving brief details of his true qualifications and an exaggerated account of his intimate knowledge of livestock management based on the experience gathered during the two previous days. He claimed familiarity with French dairy operations having spent a night in the barn on Pierre's farm. He ended his application by stating a career in animal foodstuff research had been his longstanding ambition.

The following weekend he returned to the farm and again worked for two full days without pay although the farmer's wife did not charge him for bed and meals. It was years since he had felt so happy. Memories of days spent at Rodmel, walking in the shade of its ancient oaks with rooks soaring overhead, came sweeping back. They had nothing to do with farming but his mind was made up. No more towns, it's the rural life for me from now on. Exactly where animal feed research fitted into the picture he was as yet unsure but it seemed a step in the right direction.

In anticipation of a reply to his application he delayed leaving home for the university each morning until the post had been delivered. This also helped shorten the tedium of another day analyzing samples of coal dust. He received little mail other than bills so when a white envelope dropped through the letterbox one morning he snatched it up. To his intense disappointment it was not the expected reply from the animal feed company inviting him for interview. His name and address were handwritten and it felt like an early birthday card. He threw it unopened on the table in disgust and went to work.

That evening, at the end of yet another depressing day in the lab, he went straight to the pub, got mildly drunk and returned home with a supper of fish and chips. The white envelope lay beside him and he tore it open to find an invitation from Captain Alan and Mary Frobisher to the wedding of their only daughter, Mary Phoebe Elspeth, to Dr James Conroy-Phillips. He had met neither of them, nor did he wish to do so. Written across the bottom in Frobisher's familiar hand was: '*I shall require your full support. Fail me at your peril. That's an order!!*'

Farquhar groaned. *A damned wedding! Why can't they be sensible and just bugger off to Gretna Green? Leave me to get on with mucking out the cows! I'll have to go, of course. Frobisher'll be hurt if I don't. And I can't upset him, not after all he did for me. I'll have to find them a damned present....*

The wedding in Manningtree in Essex was to be held a week the following Saturday. He skipped work on the preceding Friday and drove as far as Cambridge in the Morris. He spent the night at a pub and left early next morning to complete the journey. The sun was shining and he drove with the car top folded flat, adding further joy to the glorious country run. He was the first guest at the church and chose a gloomy pew at the back. Beside him, wrapped in brown paper, lay the reading lamp and cumbersome shade he had bought that morning in a high street furniture shop. *I'll skip the reception and drive straight back to Keld. I'll be there in time for evening milking. I wonder if old Daisy has calved yet?*

The ceremony seemed endless and was followed by an inordinate wait before the bride and groom emerged from the vestry and the organist began the 'Wedding March'. The happy couple came down the aisle, nodding and smiling left and right at the standing congregation. Fortunately the church door was on the opposite side to Farquhar's pew and they turned left before drawing level, sparing him their looks of curiosity. They were followed by the best man and five bridesmaids then the Frobisher and Conroy-Phillips families and their friends. In the final group was Josie ...

Josie! He stared at her, his heart thumping. It was her, without a doubt. In a yellow dress and a wide-brimmed hat perched on top of her dark hair. The way she walked, and held her head, were unmistakable ... They Can't Take That Away From Me ... the memory of Fred Astaire's voice on Sergeant Phipps's radio in the stores at Fulwell long ago came rushing back. Josie was chatting to an elderly lady and did not glance in his direction.

Frobisher planned this, the bastard. His note on the bottom of the invitation, about needing me to support him, was to make sure I'd be here. He must have traced Josie through army records. It's the sort of thing he'd enjoy doing. He can't have told her I'd be coming or she'd be looking around for me. And she must be single otherwise he wouldn't have invited her....

Abandoning the reading lamp for the vicar to deliver, he made his way outside. The guests had dispersed in chattering groups on the grassed area in front of the doors and he sidled behind them, peering about. Over the tops of the mossy gravestones he saw her, twenty yards away, watching the two families being herded into line by the photographer.

Give me my Josie and when she shall die, take her and cut her out in little stars and she shall make the face of heaven so fine all the world will be in love with night.... He edged closer and was almost within touching distance when she seemed to sense his presence and turned her head. They stared at each other, both equally unbelieving. The next moment they were in each other's arms, oblivious to all else.

At the back of the church was a wooden seat below an ancient spreading yew. They sat holding hands, looking at each other. *What can I say? After seven years? What if....* 'Would you still have come if you'd known he'd invited me?' he blurted out; the sentence formed as he spoke.

'Yes,' she replied, without hesitation.

'You've never been out of mind.'

'Nor have you, from mine.'

'Will you marry me?'

'Yes.'

'Not like this, though. Let's run away to Gretna Green.'

'I don't think Mother would approve.'

'I'll talk her round.'

'You can try.'

There was so much they both wanted to say. Where to begin? Did it matter? Farquhar could only gaze at her. She rubbed her thumb across the back of his hand.

'Did you marry someone else?' she asked.

He shook his head. 'I thought about it. But you kept getting in the way. I have a girlfriend, though. She's called Daisy.'

'Daisy?'

'Yes. She lives on the farm where I work at weekends. She's had five sets of twins.'

'Were you the father of them all?'

'No, but I love her very much. She's due to calve again today.'

'That's a relief.'

'How about you?'

She smiled and shook her head. 'The nearest I came to matrimony was getting engaged. I was never sure if it would work out but it seemed the thing to do at the time. He was nice; I remember thinking you and he would have got on well. He was killed in Normandy on D-Day.'

'I'm sorry.'

'You were always in my head. That's what worried me.'

'I know what you mean.'

'I wanted to explain. About the Black Bull,' she said.

'That doesn't matter any more.'

'It does to me. And it will later on. If we don't talk about it now it will always be a barrier between us.'

'All right, if that's what you want.'

'What did you do that night? After I vanished?'

'I was nearly out of mind. I couldn't understand what had happened. Then the phone rang in the bar. It was the colonel and he ordered me back to London. He knew I'd told you about France. He was waiting at Kings Cross. My uniform jacket was ripped off and I was driven to Fulwell Infantry Barracks and conscripted as a private. Fraser thought it a suitable punishment for me boasting to you about being a hero. He didn't know that losing you was far worse. Or that it would last so long. It only ended when I saw you coming down the aisle this morning. Meeting you again has always been my favourite dream.'

'Talking about it will draw a final line under it. For both of us. There are things you don't know.'

'If you feel it's important, I'll listen.'

'I'll start at the beginning. After secretarial college my first job was as a junior typist at Scotland Yard. I did quite well and after a while was moved to a section dealing with classified material about the black market. I lived with my parents and travelled to work on a two-stroke motorbike. When the war came I joined the ATS. After basic training, learning to march and salute and all that silly stuff I was put back behind a desk again. At Rodmel.'

She looked along at him. 'That's the boring bit. I'd been there a couple of months when Colonel Fraser sent for me. He asked if I'd like to do a job for him "up north". He'd seen me riding my motorbike and knew from my file I'd worked at the Yard. He said these talents would be useful for what he had in mind for me.'

'It must have come as a shock?'

'I was intrigued rather than shocked. I was twenty-four and nothing interesting had ever happened to me. At last I was being offered a chance to do something different. He said, "I want you to book into a country pub for a few days. Take your motorcycle clothing; there'll be a bike waiting for you at the station. If anyone asks tell them you work for the Ministry of Food and visit farms, checking where their eggs go. They should be sold to the Ministry but a lot find their way onto the black market. Make that your cover story. Go out each morning pretending to tour the local farms but hole up somewhere comfortable until it's time to go back for your evening meal. Afterwards sit around in the bar or the lounge, reading perhaps, having a drink. Keep your eyes and ears open, observe what's going on. I can't say any more at the moment. Sit tight until you get further orders from me."'

'You played your part well. You certainly took me in.'

'I just did what I was told. I took a train to Newcastle and then another to Wylam where the porter was expecting me. The ex-army bike was on the platform. I changed into my jodhpurs in the Ladies' Room, tied my case on the pillion and rode to the pub. I spent the night there, and rode out to the Roman wall the following day. When I walked into the dining room that night there you were.'

'Before you say any more, I've never blamed you for what happened. You were asked to do a job and did it supremely well.'

'I had no idea you were the reason for me being there. It wasn't until later, when we were standing on the bridge and you began telling me about France, I realized why I had been sent. It was to spy on you!' Her voice broke. 'I felt a rotten bitch! I tried to stop you talking about it but you insisted. I was falling in love, for the first time in my life. And I sensed you felt the same. But what a mess we were in. If I told the colonel you'd talked about France you'd be punished and would want nothing more to do with me. But if I told him you'd insisted you were just a pay and rations officer as you'd said, I'd be lying. And letting myself down as well as the colonel.'

She fished in her handbag for a hanky and dried her eyes. Farquhar reached out and stroked her hair.

'God, this is awful,' she said. 'I can't believe you don't hate me ...'

'Not then, or since. I knew you'd not done it deliberately. Go on.'

'I told you I wanted you to hold me very close. Do you remember?'

'Yes. I've gone over every word you spoke, countless times.'

'I thought if we went to bed and made love it would make it easier to explain things to you. We could decide what I should tell the colonel. I even wondered at the time if he was thinking of using me as an agent, and had sent you to test my reliability!'

'I'd have told you, when we were sitting by Hadrian's Wall.'

'But then I had no idea what I was supposed to be doing. The colonel had told me to hole up somewhere during the day and taking you there gave me a perfect alibi.'

'He picked the wrong one to be a spy. You're the smart one and would have done a much better job than me.'

'I doubt it. When we got back to the pub I left you at the bottom of the stairs and went for a bath. I said the water would be cold so I'd not be long.'

'Only seven years,' Farquhar said, giving a wry smile.

'If only I'd known that then! When I reached the landing I got the fright of my life when the landlady stepped out of the gloom. You'll remember how spooky she was, dressed in black. She was icy with me. "You have to leave now, Josie," she said. She held out my suitcase. "I've packed your things. Colonel Fraser phoned whilst you were out. You're to go back to London tonight. Leave the motorbike here. There's a car waiting outside to take you to Newcastle station."'

Farquhar stared at her in amazement. 'The old landlady?' he gasped. 'She said the colonel had phoned, ordering you back to London?'

'Yes, just like that. She was part of the colonel's plot. She must have phoned the colonel and told him we had gone off together. A policeman appeared beside her out of the darkness. "Best do as the landlady says, miss," he said. "I'll take you down to the car." I said you were waiting for me in the bar and I must see you before I left. But he moved round, barring my way, and took my suitcase. "This way, miss," he said, and pointed to the back stairs leading down to the car park.'

'But how did the colonel know I'd told you about France?'

'I'll come to that in a moment. The car's engine was running with two men sitting in the front. As soon as the policeman and I got in the back it roared off. At the Newcastle central station a woman was waiting with tickets for a first-class compartment, all to ourselves. She was pleasant enough, Deborah she was called. We didn't talk much, I was too upset. A waiter kept bringing us coffee. Deborah came with me to the toilet as if I was a dangerous convict. You may have been on the same train. There was a car waiting at Kings Cross and I was whisked to Rodmel for breakfast. An ATS captain met me. '"Clear your desk," she snapped. "You've been posted." I asked where and she said, "Bletchley Park in Buckinghamshire. You'll feel more at home there. They're all brainy types." I had to leave my motorbike at Rodmel. For all I know it's still there. I didn't see the colonel again. I was driven to Bletchley that afternoon and was there for the rest of the war.'

'If you didn't phone the colonel, how did he know I'd blabbed to you?' Farquhar asked.

'When he accused you of telling me about France, did you deny it?'

'No.'

'That told him you'd talked. He didn't need me to tell him.'

'I should have worked that out. I feel a fool,' he said.

'Don't. We were both amateurs, swimming with sharks. It was a neat operation. Neither of us was of further interest to them. You'd condemned yourself so they turned you into cannon fodder. I was just a stupid little tart. Some day I'll tell you what went on at Bletchley.'

'Is that where you met the man you were going to marry?'

'Yes. He was a lieutenant in the Royal Signals. I told him about Wylam. He explained how they'd trapped you. He knew a lot about stuff like that.'

They sat in silence for a while. *She doesn't know the colonel was bayoneted to death. I'll tell her some time, but not today.* They kissed for a long time then walked hand in hand round to the front of the church. It was deserted; the wedding party had long since left for the reception.

'It's too late to join them, I suppose,' Josie said, her mock disappointment very evident.

'I'm afraid so. But I've got something to make up for it.'

'What is it? I hate secrets.'

'You'll see.'

When they reached the Morris, she gave a delighted shriek.

'Is this yours?' she exclaimed.

'Yes. Do you like it?'

'I adore it! Even more than my old bike!'

He opened the door and she slid behind the wheel. 'I'll let you drive, when we're married,' he said. 'But not before.'

'Have you heard of The Swan at Laverham?' she asked. 'It's in Suffolk, not too far from here.'

He shook his head. 'What about it?'

'It's superb! One of the bedrooms has a four-poster!'

'Ah, well! Drive us there at once!' Farquhar ordered.

They were married a month later in the church in Askham village where Josie was a schoolteacher and lived with her widowed mother. At the start of their two-week honeymoon in Kenya, the BOAC Empire flying boat took off at dawn from Southampton Water. Breakfast was served over the Channel; they had lunch above the Italian Alps. Dinner was taken while the plane refuelled at Alexandria. They flew south over Egypt and at midnight touched down on the Nile at Khartoum between a mile of parallel lines of red lights reflected in the black water. A second dawn was breaking as the long descent began towards the old colonial town of Kisumu. Farquhar was fastening his seat belt when a hostess made an announcement:

'Good morning, ladies and gentlemen. In a few minutes we will be landing on Lake Victoria. On behalf of Captain Günter von Schmelzburg and the rest of the crew, may I thank you for flying with BOAC and hope ...'

Farquhar looked along at Josie. 'Schmelzburg?' he queried. 'That's a name I've heard before. Does it mean anything to you?'

She shook her head. 'Perhaps it's one of your German girlfriends you've not thought of in a while.'

'Called Günter? Captain of a flying boat? Hardly. I wouldn't forget that. Nope. I've a feeling he had something to do with Grigor.'

'Will the memory of that man never leave you?' she asked.

'So long as I have you, I don't care.'

She leaned over and tickled his ear with her tongue.

Josie's uncle was the manager of a large country estate in the Lake District and was looking for an assistant to take over when he retired. There were 12,000 acres of woodland and three upland farms carrying large herds of sheep. A vast moor offered rough shooting to wealthy clients and for those who preferred trout fishing a well-stocked stream ran through the estate. An attractive house went with the job. And, by a wonderful coincidence, the local primary school had recently advertised for a new head teacher. Life, Mr and Mrs Farquhar agreed, could not be sweeter.

Chapter Twenty-Two

Magda waited in the main arrivals building at Schipol airport, hoping her elegant dress sense and the cabin trunk at her side would identify her to Mr Eshkol. Her assumption was proved correct when a large shambling man came towards her. Dressed entirely in black with a Homburg hat set squarely on his head, he had a bushy grey beard and deep-set sad Jewish eyes.

'Madame Lupescu?' he enquired, speaking French with a heavy Dutch accent.

Magda held out her hand. 'Mr Eshkol! I'm delighted to meet you.'

He nodded, ignoring her hand. 'I have an arrangement with customs,' he said coldly. 'As a registered diamond dealer I am permitted to examine items in a private room before they officially enter Holland. If we do not agree on a sale you will be free to return to Paris without having your luggage examined further. If you give me your passport I will deal with the formalities.'

He returned a few minutes later. Wordlessly he loaded her luggage onto a barrow and wheeled it to a room behind the customs counter. The windows were heavily curtained; a table was covered with a green baize cloth.

'Please be seated, madame,' he murmured. 'Your letter informed me a mutual friend recommended me to you. Can you tell me his name?'

'Grigor Grigorovanovich.'

Mr Eshkol smiled for the first time; his shaggy eyebrows shot up. 'My old friend Grigor!' he exclaimed. 'How is he? Where is he?'

'I do not know. It is some years since we last met.'

Mr Eshkol looked disappointed and merely nodded. 'Madame Lupescu.'

He spoke her name in a soft, puzzled voice, as if trying to recall where he had heard it before. He fixed his sad eyes on her face. 'Were you not at one time the consort of King Carol of Romania?'

'Yes. And I remain so.'

'You reside with His Majesty in Portugal?'

'Yes.'

'Is he in good health?'

'He has had a stroke and is very frail.'

'I am sorry. That must be hard for you.'

'It is. We are not wealthy and medical expenses are heavy.'

'Is that why you have come to see me?'

'His Majesty wishes to dispose of certain items to meet mounting costs.'

'The items are in this trunk?'

'Yes. Here is the key.'

Mr Eshkol knelt on the floor in front of the trunk, unlocked the lid and took out the three padded bundles. He unwrapped them and put the two crowns and tiara carefully on the table. Drawing up a chair, he switched on a powerful table lamp. With an eyeglass fixed to his spectacles, he spent several minutes examining each item. He sat back and looked at her.

'You have His Majesty's written authority to sell these pieces of regalia, Madame Lupescu?' he asked quietly.

'Not his written authority, that is unnecessary. He is unwell, as I told you. He trusts me to handle our financial affairs.'

'How much does His Majesty anticipate these items are worth?'

'Two million American dollars.' *It's twice the price Grigor said they'd fetch seven years ago. They must be worth at least double now....*

After a long pause Mr Eshkol said, 'His Majesty will be disappointed.'

'We were recently advised of their value by an expert,' Magda lied.

'The expert was mistaken. The stones in the crowns are not diamonds, Madame Lupescu. They are crystals.'

'Crystals?' Magda gasped. She swayed in her chair, fearing she was about to faint. Vomit welled into her mouth and she snatched a handkerchief from her handbag just in time. She managed to swallow and croak, 'Crystals? That is impossible, Mr Eshkol. You must be mistaken!'

He shook his head. 'There is no mistake, madame. Jeweller's marks on the headbands show the crowns were made in Paris in 1835. More recent marks show that four years ago they were taken to Egypt where the diamonds were removed and their settings altered to accommodate the crystals. The workmanship is superb and carried out in Cairo by a craftsman whose work I instantly recognized. The emeralds and rubies in the headbands and buttresses were left untouched. They are semi-precious and of limited value. I presume after removal the diamonds were sold separately. They would bring a considerable sum, possibly in excess of one million US dollars. Substituting them with crystals would deceive the unwary so the crowns themselves could then be sold on the pretence of being in their original condition. Do you know who was responsible for this deceit, madame?'

Magda, too stunned to speak, shook her head. *It could only have been Grigor. There's no one else....*

'Do you wish me to continue?' Mr Eshkol enquired.

'Yes.'

'The tiara is the only item of value in the collection. It too was made in Paris, in 1912. The diamonds are genuine and of good, although not the highest, quality. They are in their original platinum settings.' He paused and looked steadily at her. 'In the absence of the king's written authority, there is additional risk. Taking everything into account, I offer you twenty thousand American dollars for the three pieces.'

Magda stared in disbelief. 'Twenty thousand? That is an insult, Mr Eshkol. They are the royal crowns of the King and Prince of Romania. And that is the tiara of Her Majesty Queen Helen!'

'Those facts are not in dispute, Madame Lupescu. But they do not add a centime to their value. In their present state none of the pieces can be sold on the open market. Their provenance would be investigated giving rise to legal enquiries. The matter would then become common knowledge and result in great embarrassment to His Majesty. To dispose of them, each item will have to be broken up. The platinum has some value but the market is at present awash with Nazi gold. As for the stones, the tiara diamonds are suitable for medium-priced jewellery but the market for rubies and emeralds is weak. The price I have offered is generous, I assure you.'

'Grigor stole the jewels from the palace in Bucharest,' Magda sobbed. 'At the beginning of the war. He abandoned me to make my way to rejoin the king in Paris. He must have reached Egypt and had the diamonds replaced.'

Mr Eshkol nodded but made no comment. The silence was broken only by Magda's quiet sobbing. Eventually he asked softly, 'May I enquire how the crowns came to be returned to King Carol?'

Magda dabbed her eyes. 'The Swedish consul in Lisbon brought them to us. The British had something to do with it but we weren't told the whole story. They must have bought them from Grigor thinking they were genuine and handed them back to the king in order to retain his favour after the war. What am I to do, Mr Eshkol? What can I tell His Majesty? It will break his heart!'

'I am sorry. You will not receive a better offer than mine. I strongly advise you to accept.'

'I cannot. Your offer is outrageous!'

'If you wish to consider the matter overnight I know a comfortable hotel where you can stay. You may leave the items with me for safe-keeping until you decide.'

'Only twenty thousand dollars?' she pleaded. 'Nothing more? Like you, I am Jewish and fled the Germans. We have both lost so much. You mentioned a hotel, Mr Eshkol? Perhaps...?'

She re-crossed her long silk-clad legs slowly and suggestively. If Eshkol noticed the implied invitation, he ignored it. Instead he delivered a further shock. 'Did you declare the items to customs on leaving Portugal?' he asked.

'No.'

'Then they will be regarded as new imports and subject to examination when you re-enter the country. You will be required to pay a substantial amount of import tax on them.'

'That is ridiculous!' Magda exclaimed. 'Tax would have been paid when the Swedish consul in Lisbon took delivery of them!'

Mr Eshkol shook his head. 'I fear not. They almost certainly arrived in Portugal via the British diplomatic bag and were exempt from customs duty.'

Magda said nothing. A final door had been closed against her.

'It could place His Majesty in a difficult position. Particularly if he is unaware the jewels have left Portugal,' Mr Eshkol murmured remorsefully. The significance of his warning was plain.

'Did you know this when you made your miserable offer?' Magda demanded.

'No, madame. Your mention of the Swedish consul alerted me to the situation. Had I been aware, my offer would have been even less.'

There was nothing more she could say or do; she slowly nodded.

'With great reluctance, Mr Eshkol, I am forced to accept your terms.'

He drove her to his bank where he drew a letter of credit in her name for twenty thousand US dollars. She presented it at the foreign exchange counter and arranged for the money to be converted and transferred to her personal account in Lisbon. Mr Eshkol drove her back to the airport. Not a word passed between them during the journey. He carried her suitcases from his office to the waiting room then went to enquire the time of the next flight to Paris. He returned with the news that an aeroplane would leave in two hours. He wished her a safe journey. She made no reply as he walked away.

Sitting alone in the waiting room Magda's thoughts were only of Grigor. *A master stroke! How typical of him! He must have planned it from the very beginning, when we first discussed the theft. That was the reason for his insistence that he should be the one to take the crowns when we separated. By selling first the diamonds, then the crowns, he has made himself rich. He said repeatedly that he loved me more than life itself, that he would never abandon me. Yet the moment I opened the safe my usefulness to him was over. But I won't let him get away with it. Somehow, some day, I'll have my revenge. Then he'll curse the day he was born....*

From his office window in Schipol airport's main building, Reuben Eshkol watched Magda walk out to the Paris-bound Dakota. He waited until she was mounting the steps then picked up the telephone and booked a call to a number in Buenos Aires. Ten minutes later, as the plane lifted off the runway, he was connected.

'Ja?' The voice was guttural.

'Eshkol,' he said quietly. A Germanic voice still induced a chill of fear. 'Romania. Two crowns and a diamond tiara. They will make a fine addition to your collection.'

'Condition?'

'Some substitution but only to an expert.'

'Price?'

'One hundred thousand US.'

There was a pause, not too long. 'My man will collect.'

It was not until the aircraft crossed the French border, a moment marked by the serving of a complimentary glass of surprisingly good Beaujolais, that Magda rallied. After the disappointment of the morning and the realization of how she had been deceived, she could not face the final leg back to Lisbon.

I'll spend tonight at the Hotel Etoile. Paul will be waiting, anxious to explain why he didn't appear this morning. He'll be desperate to make amends. Or maybe I'll meet someone else, even more handsome and charming....

The Dakota slip-slopped onto the runway and rolled up to the terminal building. As Magda reached the exit and was about to descend the steps, one of the pilots stepped in front of her.

'You are travelling on to Lisbon, Madame Lupescu?' he enquired.

'Yes,' she snapped. 'Do you have any objection?'

'On the contrary, I have some good news for you. If you wish you may return to your seat. As soon as this aeroplane has been refuelled it will fly directly to Lisbon, arriving in a little over two hours!'

Her mood changed immediately. 'How wonderful!' she declared. 'I'm longing to rejoin my husband. And I shall be delighted to avoid another journey in that dreadful little machine that brought me here!'

The pilot gave her a strange look but made no comment.

At the villa Carol was standing on the terrace at precisely the same spot from which he had waved her off the previous day. It was as though he had not moved since she left. She ran up the steps with her arms held wide to embrace him. She was dismayed at how fragile he felt. How could he have lost so much weight? His ribs felt like hoops. In the excitement of planning to take the jewels to Amsterdam, she had failed to notice how thin he had become. Paul's muscular frame suddenly came to mind; how strong he had been! Carol took her hand and they went indoors.

In the library they kissed, something he would never do in front of the servants. Stepping back he held both her hands and looked into her eyes. She hoped they did not show her concern at the worrying change in him.

'You look well, darling! ' she said brightly. 'Have they being feeding you properly in my absence?'

'Don't move, my sweet,' he ordered, ignoring her question. 'There's something very important I wish to say.'

He picked up a cushion from a nearby chair and dropped it on the floor. He tried to bend his right knee but staggered and pathetically fell on all fours at her feet. Magda quickly knelt in front of him.

'What is it, my darling?' she asked anxiously. 'What is it you wish to say to me?' She held out both hands and he seized them.

'Marry me, my darling,' he pleaded. His voice was breaking. 'Marry me, and promise you'll never leave me again.'

'Of course, my dearest love. I am yours for ever.'

Both kneeling, they fondly kissed.

As she was dressing for dinner, her maid told her the small aeroplane in which she had flown to Paris had crashed in the Pyrenees during its return flight to Lisbon. All on board had died. On hearing the news on the radio Carol had become distraught and confused, mistakenly thinking she was one of the victims. It had taken much effort from his doctor and members of the household to assure him she was alive and well. Nevertheless he had continued to weep and refused to eat, fearing he would not see her again.

The marriage ceremony took place two weeks later. Short and dignified, it avoided all religious connotations. Carol was greatly improved; he had already put on weight and his voice was stronger. The British ambassador, the Swedish consul and the Portuguese foreign minister all attended, together with a dozen close friends. Blanche, accompanied by a much younger and devastatingly handsome ski instructor, arrived from Paris by chartered plane. It was a lovely occasion, held in a beautiful setting above the sparkling blue Atlantic. The wonderful buffet, champagne toasts and cutting of the cake were followed by one final surprise. In the library, assisted by the foreign minister, Carol formally bestowed on his bride the title of Princess Elena. Some of the guests thought, although none openly commented on the fact, the choice was a curious one. Elena was the Greek form of Helen, the name of Carol's first wife, who now lived in Switzerland with their son Prince Michael. Carol had been divorced from her for many years.

Magda was thrilled to receive the honour. Her role as loyal consort for the past quarter of a century had at last received due recognition. Although not of royal blood, as a princess and his wife she now held a strong claim on Carol's estate.

Chapter Twenty-Three

Carol was diagnosed with abdominal cancer in 1949. Magda flew with him in a privately chartered aeroplane to Paris where he underwent radical surgery in a private clinic under the care of a leading oncologist. All appeared well and after three months' convalescence in the Austrian resort of Bad Gastein, he was able to go home to Estoril. Sadly the cancer returned two years later and in 1953 he died at the age of fifty-eight.

There followed a long legal wrangle over Magda's right to inherit Carol's vast fortune despite the precise wording in his will that it was his wish that she, as his widow, should do so. Magda had no desire to become publicly involved in the dispute and appointed an internationally renowned legal team to act on her behalf. The Russians had occupied Romania at the end of the war and continued to do so. They claimed Carol's wealth 'belonged to the people' who, they declared, were strongly opposed to it passing to the 'fascist puppet Magda Lupescu'. A special court in Lisbon was set up to examine the case. It was decided that as Carol was domiciled in Portugal, and had died there in exile, he could no longer be deemed 'royal' in the normal interpretation of the word. His fortune was therefore his to dispense however he chose. Probate was granted and Magda became wealthy beyond her wildest dreams.

At fifty-six she remained physically very attractive. Observing an informal mourning, she lived quietly in Estoril for more than a year before beginning a series of modest improvements to the villa and its extensive gardens. Supervising much of the work herself, in consultation with architects and designers, she made final decisions on colour schemes, new furniture and fabrics. She selected plants and flowering shrubs for the newly made borders and west-facing slopes. The terrace was levelled and re-laid with the old much-loved stone paving slabs. Modern appliances replaced the ageing fittings in the three bathrooms and the central heating system was completely renewed. The kitchen was refurbished with new cupboards and marble work surfaces. An indoor heated swimming pool, the first in Portugal, was installed in a new annexe and Magda swam twenty lengths every morning as part of her fitness and beauty regime.

Although her libido was as strong as ever she took care to guard her reputation. Numerous men, including the husbands of some of her closest friends, confident that such an attractive widow would welcome their romantic attentions, received short thrift when they attempted to put theory to the test.

On shopping trips away from home, however, or when on holiday abroad, an encounter with a man with the right appeal occasionally resulted in a brief romance. During cruises to South Africa and Australia she enjoyed several temporary lovers. On visits to Paris, if accompanied, she and her consort stayed at one of the elegant but discreet hotels with which the city abounded. Otherwise she was entertained in great style by Blanche, who now lived in a beautiful penthouse overlooking the Champs-Élysées.

Magda had long since decided Mr Eshkol's offer of twenty thousand dollars for the crowns and tiara had, after all, been reasonable. As a Jew the poor man must have suffered terribly under the Nazis and on that account alone she was able to excuse him a great deal. Of greater value to her had been his revelation of Grigor's deceit. There was no forgiveness in her heart for her former lover. He had stolen her share of the crowns and then at least doubled its value for himself. Because of him she had suffered gross humiliation at Amsterdam on being told of the substitution of the diamonds. That she was now wealthy did not excuse Grigor of the grievous hurt he had caused her. They had arranged to meet in New York after the war ended to share the proceeds of their joint crime. It had been impossible for her to travel to America due to Carol's poor state of health, whom she had promised never to leave alone again. But why had Grigor not got in touch with her when the war ended ten years ago? It would not have been a difficult task to trace the whereabouts of a former European monarch. Perhaps he (Grigor) had died. Or was it possible he still waited for her on the first day of the month at the foot of the Statue of Liberty? *'I'll wait as long as it takes,'* he had sworn. *'You'll only need to come once.'* What greater proof could there be of his love for her? He may have invested the fortune from the crowns and become extremely rich. But even if he had nothing, and had waited for her, she would gladly share every-thing she possessed with him. She reached a momentous decision. She would go to New York and discover the truth.

*

The most famous ship plying the Atlantic in 1963 was the Cunard liner *Queen Mary*. After noble service as a troopship during the war she had undergone the most expensive refit in maritime history and been restored to her former glory. Studying the cruise brochure for the coming year, Magda discovered the ship's itinerary included a round trip from Southampton to New York with a three-night stopover that included Wednesday 1 May. If Grigor was continuing to keep his promise, he would be at the Statue. She telephoned the head office of Cunard in London and booked a first-class suite.

After an extended shopping trip to Paris she returned to Estoril with two trunks packed with fashionable new clothes. A week later she flew to London, spent the night at the Dorchester Hotel and travelled to Southampton by boat train the following morning.

The glossy brochures had failed to prepare her for the size and magnificence of the *Queen Mary*. Her suite on the top deck was the epitome of elegance and comfort, even to a princess. The thought of a long-awaited reunion with Grigor filled her thoughts and the excitement was enhanced by a strong sense of his presence. Her ancestral trait was at fever pitch. There was no doubt in her mind that he had been on this ship. Perhaps he was on board for this voyage! The information folder in her suite included a list of her fellow passengers; disappointingly his name was not among them. The aura of his presence was so strong she suspected he was travelling *in cognito* and they may come face to face on deck. But there was never a sign of him.

The weather during the crossing was perfect and the ship docked in New York on a glorious Tuesday afternoon. First-class passengers were given the option of staying in a luxury hotel in Manhattan whilst the ship was in harbour during the stopover. Magda elected to remain on board. Her suite offered all that she could ask for in comfort and service. And she had the freedom to visit, on a day of her own choosing, the Statue of Liberty.

The brochure insisted no visit to New York was complete without a trip to the world's most famous structure. It entailed a trip by ferry from Battery Park in Lower Manhattan to the island in the Hudson River on which the statue stands. The sun was shining as she walked up the steps on Wednesday morning, awestruck by the majesty of the figure towering above her. She stood on the esplanade recalling the days when she had imagined meeting Grigor here, at this very spot. Memories of her daydream swept into her mind; the running towards each other with open arms, that first passionate embrace after so long. It seemed so real it was impossible for the moment not to become reality....

But there was nothing of Grigor at the statue; her sense of his presence failed to register as it had on the ship. He had travelled in the *Queen Mary*, but had not come here. Probably he never intended to. Standing in the shadow of the statue the last whisper of the love she had once held for him evaporated. And at that moment Grigor's fate was sealed.

She wanted proof for herself that she had kept the rendezvous even if he had not. She took out her new camera. As she raised the viewfinder to her eye, a female American voice behind her said, 'Like me to take a shot of you standing in front of her, honey?'

It was the lady from the ship who occupied a suite further along the deck from hers. They exchanged smiles in passing but had not previously spoken.

'That's most kind of you,' Magda replied. 'This is my first visit and I need proof for friends back home that I was really here!'

'I'm not in New York often now,' the lady said with a sad smile. 'But when I am, I always come here. My husband and I met right here for the first time. Exactly where you're standing!'

Magda handed her the camera and turned her head to the best side for the photograph. They lunched together in the restaurant close to the statue.

'I'm Winfred,' the lady said. 'Friends call me Winnie, which I don't care for all that much. It's what horses do, in America anyway. But I guess I'm used to it. I'm a widow. Don't be fooled by the accent. I'm almost British. I've lived in London for the past thirty years. Right through the war and all that terrible bombing. My late husband ran Pinkertons' London bureau.'

'Pinkertons?' Magda echoed, never having heard the name previously.

'You know, the famous detective agency?'

'Oh yes, of course! How interesting!'

'Not any more. Originally, back in the last century, they were part of the real old West, hunting down outlaws and gunslingers. Like in the movies. Really bad guys like Butch Cassidy and Sundance, and The Hole in the Wall Gang. You've heard of them? Yeah, most folk have. But in the thirties the FBI began spreading its wings under Hoover and eventually got to take over the big criminal investigations. Like Al Capone and the mobs. Poor old Pinkertons just faded into the sunset. They kept John on until the war was over since they were short of operatives. He was one of the last of their real agents, travelling all over the world, tracking down mobsters.'

They returned to the ship together and agreed to meet for dinner in the famous Veranda Grill, an exclusive *à la carte* restaurant on the Sun Deck renowned for its fabulous night-time views over Manhattan. They both wore expensive gowns and were two of the most glamorous widows on board.

'Now, you've gotta tell me lots about yourself, Magda,' Winifred said, sipping a champagne cocktail. 'A well-travelled, highly attractive girl like you sure must have had a real exciting life. I can't wait to hear all about it.'

It was a question she had been expecting but care was needed. Winifred may seem a featherbrain but her late husband was well travelled in Europe. It was possible he may have heard of Carol, even of herself, and had mentioned their names. Not wanting to give anything away, she shrugged her shoulders.

'There's not a lot to tell, Winfred. My husband and I are, or once were, Romanians. He was highly placed in the government when the war began. The Germans were about to invade and we were forced to flee Bucharest. We lived in Paris for some time during the occupation. Later we moved to Estoril in Portugal. He died there three years ago and I am still trying to adjust.'

It's the truth, almost. I'm glad I appear in the passenger list as plain Magda Lupescu to avoid attracting attention. If by chance Winifred discovers my real identity she'll assume I didn't mention I was a princess and married to a real king – surely every American woman's idea of heaven – due to natural modesty and not a deliberate attempt to deceive.

Later, over coffee and liqueurs, Magda said, 'Tell me more about your husband's Pinkerton adventures. He must have led a very exciting life!'

'He was very secretive,' Winifred replied. 'He didn't talk much about what he got up to. I know he often went armed and worked in Paris with Interpol. He often spoke of writing a book about his experiences but never got round to it.'

'Did he always get his man? Like the Canadian Mounties claim to?'

Winifred smiled and shook her head. 'Most times, but not always. He often said, "Winnie, there's some darned smart criminals out there!"'

Chapter Twenty-Four

Returning to Estoril, Magda had the satisfaction of knowing her trip to New York had served its purpose. Had she not gone for the rest of her life she would have been haunted by the thought of Grigor having remained true to her. But her visit destroyed all such speculation; he had never visited the rendezvous. He had deceived and deserted her and for that he must die. She told no one her intention, not even Blanche. It was something she would carry out alone.

Finding him was obviously the first step. Precisely how this was could be done had puzzled her until she met Winifred in New York. For the first time she heard about Pinkertons and their record of hunting down criminals. They were no longer the world force they had once been but there would be modern equivalents. She would find an international detective agency that specialized in personal investigations. Grigor was more cunning than a fox and would be just as difficult to trap. *There are some darned clever criminals out there,* Winifred's husband had said. But there would be firms in Europe who employed people as clever, even cleverer, than Grigor. And they would start with a major advantage. He would never imagine after all this time she was determined to find him.

She flew to Paris and booked into a quiet hotel under the name of Marie Dublanc. There was a wide choice of detective agencies in the classified advertisements in the newspapers and telephone directory, some established long before the war. Chevron's elegant but discreet display was one of them, claiming to have international connections throughout Europe and the Middle East, two areas in which Grigor may have taken refuge. Magda phoned the firm to make an appointment in her assumed name. She was informed that one of their principals, Mme Madeleine Duchamp, would see her three days hence at two in the afternoon.

Chevron's sumptuous offices were on the fourth floor of a busy street near the centre of Paris. Madeleine, tall and elegant in a black and white suit, was waiting for her at reception. They walked to her office and sat in large comfortable chairs facing each other. After an introductory exchange, in which Madeleine suggested they use each other's forenames, the interview began.

'How can Chevron be of assistance to you, Marie?' she asked.

'I wish to find a former acquaintance of my late husband.'

'Do you have any idea of where he may be?'

'No. I last saw him in Bucharest in 1940.'

'That was twenty-three years ago! Millions died during the war. Do you have proof that he is still alive?'

'No. But if you are certain he is dead it will suffice.'

'What was his date of birth?'

'1895.'

Madeleine arched her eyebrows in astonishment. 'You wish to find a man aged sixty-eight whom you have not seen for twenty-four years?'

'Yes. There is some evidence he may have been in Egypt in about 1942.'

'What is this evidence?'

Mr Eshkol had said that was where and when the crowns had been altered but she had no intention of bringing them into the investigation. 'A friend told my husband he had seen him there,' she replied.

'That is hearsay, not evidence, Marie.'

'I chose your firm since you have connections in the Middle East.'

'That is so. But it covers a vast area, with a population of millions.'

'I realize that. Nevertheless, I would like him found.'

'It will cost a considerable sum of money.'

'I have ample funds.'

'We are unable to guarantee success.'

'All the same, I wish you to carry out a search. If, after six months, you have not found him, I shall abandon my quest.'

'Do you wish this person to know that you are seeking him?'

'Under no circumstances must he discover that.'

'Very well. We will take every precaution, but once again, no guarantee can be given. We will wish to keep in contact with you. Clarification may be necessary on certain points. Hopefully, at some stage, we shall require you to identify the person you are seeking. Not face to face, but from a photograph perhaps, or other positive evidence. If he can be found, Chevron will find him.'

'I would like you to begin as soon as possible.'

'In that case we must agree terms. Our standard charge, which includes normal expenses, is six thousand American dollars per month. Payment is to be made monthly, in advance. If the man you seek is found, or if his death is proved, there will be an additional charge amounting to fifty per cent of the total. If you agree, I shall have the papers drawn up for you to sign within the hour.'

'I agree,' Magda said without hesitation.

Madeleine rang for a secretary and instructed her to draw up a standard contract for signature. Turning to Magda she said, 'The investigation starts from this moment. I require as much information as you can provide. Let us begin with the man's full name and those of his parents.'

'He is Grigor Grigorovanovich, born in Beirut in 1895 . His father was a wealthy Lebanese businessman and his mother an Arabian princess. I have seen documentation proving this. Their names were ...'

The questions flowed for twenty minutes. Madeleine noted Magda's confident replies in a thick pad. When they were finished she laid down her gold fountain pen, closed the pad and pushed it aside. She linked her fingers together and, making a bridge with her elbows on the desk, rested her chin on it. She fixed her new client with a steady gaze.

'You wish Chevron to find this man for you, Magda. In order for us to do that there must be a genuine and honest relationship between us.'

'I understand that, Madeleine.'

'You showed no surprise a moment ago when I called you "Magda".'

'No ... er ... no. That is my name.'

'When you made this appointment you said you were Marie Dublanc.'

'It is a name I often use when travelling.'

'But you are in fact Magda Lupescu?'

Magda contained her surprise. 'Yes, I am,' she replied coolly.

'Or would you prefer me to call you Princess Elena?'

Now she sat rigid, shocked into silence.

'You are the widow of King Carol of Romania and reside in Estoril?'

'Yes.'

'And Mr Grigorovanovich, whom you seek, was at one time the king's private secretary?

'Yes.'

'And also your secret lover?'

'Yes.' Magda was stunned. 'How do you know all this about me?' she mumbled, ashamed to meet Madeleine's stare. 'I keep my private life to myself. I am shocked that you know so much.'

'I assure you your details will remain completely confidential. We select our clients with great care and check their credentials very carefully before acceptance. That is why you waited three days for this appointment. You lived in Paris with King Carol when he was exiled before the war and for two years during it before moving to Estoril where you married in 1948.

He died in 1953. The information is in the public records. Chevron has access to sources throughout the world.'

'So it appears. I have to assume there are no secrets?'

'Very little of a personal nature ever passes unmarked. That is why my agency is so successful. If you wish to retain a secret, do not speak of it.'

Magda bowed her head. *The fact that Grigor was my lover could only have come from Blanche. In her circle of Parisian friends there must be someone with a Chevron connection who has been asking about me. Pillow talk, perhaps. Maybe female. Madeleine herself perhaps! I'm glad I did not tell Blanche about stealing the crowns. Chevron may know a lot about me, but not everything.*

'Forgive me, Madeleine,' she said after a long silence. 'But my sins are omissions. The information I gave you on Grigor is full and true.'

Madeleine nodded. 'You are not alone. It is rare that we have a client who is totally honest with us at the beginning. Is there any other aspect of this case we should know about?'

The crowns! Tell her about the crowns! She'll find out sooner or later! Better tell her now! The warning voice screamed in her head.

She shook her head. 'No, Madeleine. You know everything.'

A month later Magda returned to Paris and again saw Madeleine.

'I regret as yet there is nothing to report,' she said. 'Our operatives have begun their investigations but normally it is at least three months before anything of interest emerges. I shall call you when I have news.'

It was during the fifth month of the contract that Magda received a curt phone call at the villa. The female voice simply said, 'Madeleine wishes to see you.' Seconds later came the drone of the dialling tone. She took the first plane to Paris next morning and was given an afternoon appointment.

'Does the name "Damietta" mean anything to you?' Madeleine asked when they were seated.

Magda shook her head. 'Is it a woman?' she enquired.

'No, it was the name of a Cairo hotel, now demolished. Before the war it had a reputation as a haunt of gigolos looking for lonely English ladies on holiday. Or vice versa. It was razed to the ground by the British army in 1944. Its books, including the register, are now in the central library in Cairo. They show a Mr Grigor, birthplace Beirut, stayed at the hotel on two occasions for a single night, several months apart, in 1942. That may be when your husband's friend saw him. On the second visit he was the sole occupant of the hotel's honeymoon suite. He may be our man. He gave his year and place of birth exactly as you stated.'

'Why are the hotel's books in the library? Are they of historic interest?'

'They once had legal significance. The hotel was the subject of a compensation claim by the owner after the war. The British army demolished the building without justification and the books formed part of the evidence. When the case was settled, at enormous expense in favour of the Egyptian litigant, he presented them to the museum as war souvenirs.'

'I am glad the hearsay I reported to you was accurate.'

'We are continuing to work on the assumption that it was "our" Grigor who stayed at the Damietta. Instead of looking for a needle in haystack, as the English would say, all we have to do now is the equivalent of finding one particular fly in Notre Dame cathedral.'

Magda returned to Paris shortly before the six months of the contract expired. It seemed she had gambled and lost. The hope that had flared on the discovery of Grigor's name in the Damietta register had not produced a breakthrough in the investigation.

'Sadly, nothing more has been uncovered,' Madeleine told her.

Magda nodded; Grigor had escaped her wrath. Surprisingly, she felt a lightening in her breast, perhaps relief that she would not, after all, have to commit murder.

'Nothing more, that is, until now!' Madeleine added triumphantly. From a desk drawer she took out a large black and white photograph.

'Is this him?' she asked.

Magda's hands trembled as she took the frame. The man was looking sideways at the camera, his elbows resting on the ornate metal railing of a balcony overlooking the sea. His dark hair was streaked with grey, his face rounder than she remembered but his facial expression was unmistakable.

Suddenly the room was spinning and she swayed in the chair. Madeleine's voice became muffled, distant ...

'Magda ... Magda ...' An arm folded round her shoulder and a glass was pressed against her lips. The brandy slid warmly across her tongue.

'Are you all right? Would you like to lie on the sofa?'

She shook her head and dabbed her face with a handkerchief.

'No, no. Thank you, Madeleine. I'll be fine in a moment. What a shock!'

'It was foolish of me. And very unprofessional. But I couldn't resist it. When I said there was no news the disappointment on your face was so profound.'

'There's no other way I'd have preferred to hear you've found him!'

'It is Grigor? Are you are absolutely sure?'

Magda looked at the photograph again. His face was half in profile.

And as well as greying, his hair had receded a little. But there was no mistaking that quizzical expression. She nodded firmly.

'There's no doubt that is the man I know as Grigor Grigorovanovich.'

'It was taken only five days ago in Alexandria,' Madeleine said. 'It was sent to me via airmail by our agent. I received it less than an hour ago.'

'I thought your people were searching Cairo for him!'

'We were. But Alexandria is a much superior city. The agent had guessed the reason Grigor stayed at the Damietta in Cairo for two single nights was because he was merely visiting, rather than living there. No one lives in Cairo unless they have to, it's so vile. Our agent guessed that as a man of means he would live in Alex, so he began a search for him there.'

'A wise move, it seems.'

'Yes! And he had a stroke of luck. Whilst searching records in the public library in Alex, he noticed a local newspaper lying on the next desk. He picked it up and on the front page was this photograph with Grigor's name. He had been on the balcony of his flat when he saw a yacht in difficulties and phoned the harbour authorities. A high government official was on board and when he reached the shore demanded to know who had saved his life. Grigor had given his telephone number so it was easy to trace him. His name and this photograph were in the paper the following day.'

'He would enjoy that!' Magda burbled, almost too thrilled to speak. 'He loved to make himself out to be a hero. Surviving air crashes, and car racing. That sort of thing. A big man. And a big liar!'

'There was no address given,' Madeleine continued, 'but our man soon found him. He lives in apartment eight on the top floor of an expensive block of flats with balconies facing the sea. He must be wealthy; the address is in one of the best areas of Alexandria, overlooking the bay. There are commissionaires at the entrance in the afternoons and evenings but not the mornings. It's an arrangement for the convenience of tradesmen making deliveries, and servants going shopping.'

'This is marvellous news, Madeleine. Finding him was only a dream but you've made it come true! Thank you from the bottom of my heart.'

Madeleine came to the hotel the following morning with copies of the agent's report. She also brought a detailed invoice that Magda paid with a cheque drawn on her Paris account. They went out for lunch at a Left Bank restaurant. Madeleine was more relaxed and companiable than Magda had known her, unsurprisingly perhaps with a final payment cheque to Chevron of twenty-four thousand dollars in her handbag. She laid a hand on Magda's arm.

'I've not been able to fathom the attraction, darling,' she said. 'He looks very fetching and is probably as randy as a *bouc*. But there are millions of men like that. What's he got that's worth so much to you? I'd love to know!'

'My pride,' Magda said simply. 'He humiliated me in front of a man who had survived four years in a concentration camp in Poland.'

Pointedly she said 'man', not 'Jew', but Madeleine would understand.

'And you are seeking revenge?'

'Yes.'

'Can Chevron help?'

'Vengeance is mine, Madeleine. But I would be grateful if you would move the agent who traced him. He reads too many newspapers.'

'There is a case in Hong Kong that will keep him busy for a year.'

'That will be long enough. And sufficiently far away. Thank you.'

'Are you in a hurry to return to Estoril?' Madeleine asked over coffee. 'Why don't we spend a few days together and get to know each other much better? I have a nice big flat, and some lovely friends. I'll throw an exclusive party. Ladies only, of course!'

'I'd love to, Madeleine.' She wondered if Blanche would be there.

A quarter the size of the *Queen Mary*, in Magda's opinion the new French ship provided far superior cruising. The sheer size of the *QM* had been overpowering and the multitude of passengers thronging the on-board shops, dress salons and beauty parlours was more suited to a city centre than a ship. By contrast on *La Reine* there were just enough people to make life interesting. Magda's first-class cabin, one of only twelve, was roomy and very comfortable. A swimming pool, exclusive to passengers with cabins on A deck, was only a short distance from her door. The orchestra comprised a mere dozen players but was excellent and a wonderful pianist playing unforgettable melodies in the cocktail bar before dinner enlivened the early evenings.

The voyage to America in the *Queen Mary* had been tedious once the excitement of leaving Southampton and sailing down the Channel had passed. Out of sight of land only the occasional passing ship had provided relief from the monotony of the empty ocean. On *La Reine* it was very different. Magda had joined the ship at Gibraltar and thereafter land remained almost constantly in view. There was interest even at night when the horizon glowed with the lights of coastal towns. The ship stopped at places she had heard of but never visited, and she was able to spend time exploring Genoa and Naples. On the evening the ship entered the surging Strait of Messina, between the toe of Italy and Sicily, the sky was a delicate orange from the glow of Stromboli's volcano. Piraeus, the ancient port of Athens, was the last stop before Africa.

Alexandria, the most eastern point of the voyage, was reached on the morning of the tenth day of the cruise. The ship dropped anchor in the bay. After breakfast passengers were ferried ashore in a tender to a pier where a line of air-conditioned coaches stood waiting to take them on a tour of the sights of one of the world's most ancient cities. Lunch was served at an outrageously expensive restaurant and the day ended with a visit to a market selling Egyptian *objets d'art*, souvenirs and tourist bric-a-brac. It had been a tiring day and Magda was pleased to return to the ship, take a long hot bath and go to bed for an hour before dressing for dinner. There was dancing on deck afterwards and the orchestra played a selection from her favourite Broadway musical, *My Fair Lady*.

At breakfast the following morning the loudspeakers reminded passengers that the ship would sail at two in the afternoon. The tender was available for those wishing to go ashore but its final trip back to the ship would be at noon. Regretfully anyone not on board by then would be left behind. Only a handful of passengers collected at the top of the gangway where a steward noted their names and repeated the warning to be back in plenty of time. The tender came alongside and the group stepped on board. Magda, in cotton trousers, red top and her hair tucked in a scarf, and carrying a leather shoulder bag, avoided the other passengers clustered in the bow. She stood at the stern, taking pictures of the receding *La Reine* at anchor. When the pier was reached she was one of the first ashore and hurried across to the taxi rank. She told a driver to take her to Maamoura Hotel car park. She had studied a tourist map of the city and it was a five-minute walk from there to the apartment block where, according to Chevron's agent, Grigor lived.

She recognized the building at once from a photograph in the report. At the top of the front entrance steps the door was, as expected, unmanned. As she crossed the elegant vestibule the lift doors slid silently open and a tall slim man in a dark suit stepped out and walked past her without a glance. Her ancestral powers told her Grigor was close at hand. The lift took her rapidly to the top floor; the door to apartment eight was directly opposite. She removed her headscarf and with her gloved hand felt in the shoulder bag for the German pistol from Carol's collection of wartime memorabilia. Her fingers closed round the butt; she eased off the safety catch with her thumb.

She rang the bell. There was an agonizing wait before the door silently opened and Grigor, stouter than she remembered, stood looking at her with a quizzical expression. *Wait until he knows for certain it's you.* It was two, perhaps three, seconds before his expression registered his recognition. The familiar easy smile spread across his face, his eyes crinkled at the corners as they always did when he was being assertive. He held out his arms to her.

'Magda, darling ...'

The silencer made a muffled *pop* and the bullet smashed into his chest, catapulting him backwards into the apartment. His body, in a crimson dressing gown, slumped in a crumpled heap; satisfyingly bright red blood flowed into a rapidly widening pool on the carpet.

Magda did not move. In the bag her hand still firmly gripped the pistol. But no one came to investigate; Grigor had been alone in the apartment. Perhaps the man she had seen leaving the lift was his manservant. She reached out a gloved hand and drew the door shut. The lock clicked. The tiny exit hole in the end of her bag made by the bullet was unnoticeable.

The vestibule was still empty; she walked unhurriedly down the steps and back to the taxi. *There are more than a thousand murders in Alexandria every year. All wealthy men have enemies so Grigor's death will attract little attention. No doubt his manservant will be the principal suspect.*

She was back on board the ship by eleven.

La Reine was an island of brilliant lights as she slid through the warm soft darkness of the Mediterranean bound for Grand Harbour in Malta. Dressed for dinner in an elegant blue ankle-length gown and high heels, Magda carefully negotiated the two flights of external stairs down to the deserted promenade deck and walked to the rail at the stern. She slipped the bag from her shoulder and held it by the strap. Inside, beside the pistol was an unopened bottle of champagne to ensure it sank quickly. She let the bag slip from her fingers into the foaming wake.

No formal entertainment had been arranged after dinner that evening. The bar was busy; the bridge players sat at tables in the lounge, the Freemasons held a Lodge Meeting in the empty sick bay. In her cabin Magda lay back on the bed and reached up her bare arms to the young ship's officer with whom she had danced under the stars the previous night.

'I am old enough to be your mother, *ma cheri*,' she murmured.

'I adore mature ladies, madame,' he replied, smiling down at her.

After he left she buried her face in the pillow and silently wept for the only man she had ever loved. Now she was alone in the world, and always would be.